RELENTLESS

OTHER BOOKS AND BOOKS ON CASSETTE
BY CLAIR POULSON:

I'll Find You

RELENTLESS

a novel

Clair Poulson

Covenant Communications, Inc.

Covenant®

Published by Covenant Communications, Inc.
American Fork, Utah

This is a work of fiction. The characters, names, incidents, places, and dialogue are products of the author's imagination, and are not to be construed as real.

Printed in the United States of America
First Printing: January 2002

09 08 07 06 05 04 03 02 10 9 8 7 6 5 4 3 2 1

ISBN 1-57734-977-6

Library of Congress Cataloging-in-Publication Data

Poulson, Clair.
Relentless / by Clair M. Poulson.
p. cm.
ISBN 1-57734-977-6
1. Witnesses--Fiction. 2. Mormon women--Fiction. 3. Romantic suspense fiction. gsafd
I. Title

PS3566.O812 R45 2002
813'.54--dc21 2001052960

Dedication

In memory of Chief Cecil Gurr, who gave his life in the line of duty. Cecil was one of the best officers I ever had the privilege of working with. His was an example any law officer would do well to follow.

PROLOGUE

A scream turned the girl's head. Two shots rang out in rapid succession. They were close, very loud, and extremely frightening. What she saw through the small group of pines edging the little roadside park where she had eaten her lunch made the eighteen-year-old girl's legs go weak. Everything seemed to slow down as she watched. One body was already on the ground, another crumpling from the shotgun blast.

The killer must have seen her move, or else he simply sensed her presence only a couple of hundred feet from where he had just committed the most heinous act known to man. That what she had seen was murder was somehow clear to her mind. She'd seen the two victims earlier. They were unfriendly and hadn't answered when she'd spoken to them as she walked by their van. Their greasy long hair, filthy clothes, and the flowers in their hair had drawn her attention. It was like they were from another age: the sixties look. But they hadn't deserved what had just happened to them. They hadn't been hurting anyone, just eating a cold lunch.

The second body hit the ground and lay still. The gunman, a young man of maybe twenty-one or twenty-two, was looking in her direction. His shotgun was swinging toward her! Panic clutched her chest. He meant for her to be next! She had started to turn when the weapon discharged again. Pain seared her cheek. She screamed and ran, the little grove of trees providing protection from the next blast of the deadly weapon.

The man who meant to take her life shouted, his voice full of laughter. "Run girl, run!" he called after her as her legs gained strength and propelled her toward her waiting Toyota. "You can't run fast enough to get away from me!" he threatened.

He was running. His footsteps pounded in her ears. She reached her car and grabbed for the door. Her purse lay on the seat where she'd left it when she first heard the argument across the park—the one that had caused her so foolishly to have a look. She grabbed the purse and rustled desperately through it in search of her keys, praying that she would find them in time. Her fingers felt the familiar softness of her key chain and she jerked it out, jabbing the key at the ignition.

As the engine turned over and she shoved the shifting lever into drive, she saw him approaching her, running hard. Expecting at any moment to hear another shot, or worse yet, to feel it, she gunned the engine and left the park in a spray of gravel. As her spinning tires hit the pavement and propelled her onto the highway, she heard him shout, "You can't ever run far enough to get away from me!"

She was alone on a trip to meet her grandparents, just outside of Denver. The girl had been in no hurry and had chosen a meandering, but scenic route from her home in rural northeastern Utah. Her widowed mother had fussed about her—an attractive young lady—going alone, but she was an independent girl and confident of her ability to drive and take care of herself.

How she wished now for the comfort of her mother's arms!

She was speeding.

But she had to. She had seen that the killer had an old green pickup truck. Surely he would be coming after her. She was the only witness to his terrible deed. She had read books, seen movies, heard stories of things like this. Killers did not like witnesses.

His words rang in her head. "Run girl, run!" he had shouted in a voice full of hysterical laughter. And that was exactly what she was doing, as fast as her little Toyota would carry her from Pineview, Colorado. A small town in the Colorado Rockies, it had seemed like such a peaceful place as she had driven through. She had even stopped there and bought a few things to eat at the only convenience store in town. It was called the Quick Stop, and a man who looked like he was in his mid-sixties had waited on her. Sam, she had heard another customer call him. It had been busy in the little store, and he had scarcely looked at her as he rang up her purchases and handed her some change. Only as she turned to leave did he finally smile and say, "Have a nice day, young lady."

She'd smiled back. She liked the clean little store. It had been almost cozy.

Now she wanted nothing but to flee, to quickly get as far away as she could. She checked the mirror several times, and finally, after several minutes, she slowed down. The green pickup had never appeared. She hoped it never would. But she kept driving. Not for an hour or more did she even think about stopping. And then she only did so because a little warning light came on in her dash, cautioning that her gasoline tank was nearly empty.

As the gas pumped into her starving tank in another town, not as small, not as scenic, but a reasonable distance from Pineview, she tried to think rationally about her situation. The man with the shotgun had meant to kill her. Of that there was no doubt. She, a good girl, a Mormon girl who *usually* made the right choices in her life, had been the target of his rage. But she was away now. She could report what she saw and maybe the man would be caught.

And maybe he wouldn't!

In which case, she would always be in danger. He had seen her. He had seen her car. He might even have read her license plate number. He could learn who she was. He could hunt her down. He could . . .

"Hi, looks like it's full, miss," a friendly man with a cowboy hat and boots said with a chuckle. "Hey, are you okay? What's that on your cheek?"

She had been so terrified that she hadn't even remembered the spot on her cheek where she'd felt the searing pain as the killer's shotgun had blasted at her. She touched the spot just below her eye. It burned like fire.

"Looks like you've been burned or something," he said as he stepped toward her for a closer look.

"It's nothing," she said quickly as she grabbed for the nozzle.

"Looks bad," he cautioned. "I'd get some ointment on it."

"Sure, thanks," she mumbled as he turned away.

Conscious now of the pain on her cheek, and even more conscious of how it must look, she hurriedly paid for her gas and then entered the ladies' room. Examining her face in the mirror, she began to tremble as she realized how close she'd come to death. The mark on her cheek was small and very red, but it had only burned her. It wasn't serious, although she was sure it needed something on it.

Her trembling increased as the horrible scene replayed itself in her mind. Once more, she wondered if she should report it. But she was afraid to, and even as her conscience began to bother her a bitter memory interfered. The two hippie types deserved to have their killer caught. And she could identify him. But if he was caught, and if she had to testify . . .

The memory swam through her mind, and tears stung her eyes. Several years before, in junior high, she'd been a witness to a crime. Nothing like this today, but still a crime. She'd seen a young man steal a wallet from a locker. She had done the right thing and turned him in.

And suffered the consequences.

She was taunted, had threats painted on her locker door, even had her own purse taken. Oh, it was not that serious. No one had actually hurt her, and the young man had eventually been expelled. But it had been the cause of serious reflection, and she had resolved never to interfere again.

But this wasn't the same. It was not petty theft. It was murder!

And she could be the next victim.

She broke out in a sweat as she searched her heart for a way out of this dilemma. Finally, as she leaned upon the sink in the rest room, feeling very faint, a solution came to her. She could report what she had seen, but do it without revealing her identity to the authorities. She washed her face with cold water, then left the rest room. The more she thought about her idea, the better it seemed. She could remain unknown to the killer and yet help the police in bringing that horrible man to justice.

Resolved, she went to the pay phone she had seen earlier beside the station. Still trembling, she dialed 911. When a voice came on asking the nature of her emergency, she simply said, "I need to report a murder in Pineview."

The voice on the other end of the line was all business as it answered, "There has already been one reported. What exactly do you have to tell us?"

It occurred to the young lady that she was probably being taped and that they might be able to trace where she was calling from. She had to hurry. "I saw it," she said.

"Just a moment, I'll have an officer meet you. What is your location?"

"No!" she cried in alarm. "I can't let anyone know who I am. He'll kill me if he finds out."

"Now calm down," she was instructed. "It will be easier if you talk to an officer."

"Only on the phone," she insisted. "And not on this one. Give me the number of an officer and I'll call him," she said as her brain began functioning in overdrive.

"It would be—"

"Now, or I'll hang up," she insisted.

"Don't do that. Someone will talk to you. Just hold on."

Panicked, the young woman cut the connection. As she left town, she passed a speeding patrol car. She was positive it had been heading for the pay phone she'd called from. Later, in still another town, she went to another pay phone, but this time she did not dial 911. Instead she dialed the number listed in the telephone directory for the sheriff's department. Without stating her real business, she asked for the number of an officer in Pineview, any officer. It turned out that Pineview was in a different county, but they gave her the number of the sheriff's office near there. She dialed and repeated her request.

"That would be Sergeant Mike O'Connor, but he's not available right now. There's been a murder and—"

"I know," she cut in. "I saw it happen. But I'll only talk to one person."

"Just a moment," the dispatcher said, and her call was put on hold.

She hung up again, waited five minutes and called back. "He'll take your call," the dispatcher told her this time, and she was given the number of a cell phone.

"This is Sergeant O'Connor," the phone was answered, "to whom am I speaking?"

"I can't say," she said through trembling lips. "But I saw the man who killed those two hippies."

"Who was it?" the sergeant asked quickly, as if afraid she'd hang up. She was getting a reputation it seemed.

"I don't know, but he had short brown hair and was driving an old green pickup." She then repeated the license number which she had memorized.

"Thank you, young lady," the voice on the cell phone said. "You and I need to get together. This is a serious matter, and you might be of a lot more help."

"I know how serious it is. He shot at me too," she said as desperation and fear drove her to get this over very quickly.

"Are you—" he began

"He just nicked my face. But he said he'd hunt me down."

"Okay, okay, calm down. Tell me more. What did he look like? How old was he?" the officer asked. "And what time was it?"

She answered his questions, and within five minutes she was off the phone and on her way to her grandparents' house. She'd done all she could, she told herself. Now it was up to the police. They would never know who she was, and she would never mention it again—not to anyone. She had to live with the fear, maybe for the rest of her life, but her identity in connection with what she'd seen must forever remain a secret.

And would haunt her for years to come.

Chapter 1

Five Years Later

The raucous call of a jay announced the arrival of morning to a sleepy forest. Wispy, fingerlike clouds, fringed with peach-colored light, drifted gently over stark, towering peaks—a promise of the morning sun, poised to make its colorful appearance. A small cluster of tents lay nestled beneath the tall pines, still and quiet in the crisp mountain air.

The jay bellowed another wake-up call, and a slender, dark-haired eighteen-year-old girl stirred in one of the tents. Her back ached from the hard ground to which she was not accustomed, and thoughts of a soft bed with clean pink sheets and a fluffy pillow filled her head. For a moment she lay hugging the sleeping bag, listening to the shallow, even breathing of her younger sister.

Erika sat up quietly, frowning at the peacefully sleeping ten-year-old. She could just picture her hovering in the hallway of their modest suburban home, ready to move into Erika's room the moment she left for college at summer's end. She was anxious to be on her own, but she also resented the feeling that her spoiled little sister could scarcely wait for her to leave.

Erika slipped out of the warm sleeping bag and shed her heavy pajamas, shivering as she slipped into a pair of dark-blue shorts. The T-shirt she wiggled into was tight and left a narrow ring of darkly tanned skin exposed above the top of her shorts. "I'm going to burn that blue shirt," her mother had threatened, but Erika still wore it.

Her clear brown skin was roughened with goose bumps from the cold. Reluctantly, she pulled her light-blue sweats over the shorts and shirt before tugging on a pair of thick socks and black Reeboks. Grabbing her purse, she eased out of the tent and headed for her dad's pride and joy, a new red Ford Expedition.

As she slipped the key into the ignition she thought about the scene she had caused the night before. It had been the culmination of a week of grumbling over *camp food* and the pristine environment surrounding them. Erika did not enjoy camping, and after several days of it she let her feelings be known. After an embarrassingly vocal outburst over more of her dad's fried fish, he had said, "Well, why don't you just drive down to Pineview in the morning and get yourself something. The rest of the family quite enjoys my cooking."

She hadn't given him time for a second thought on his rather hasty proposition. "Sure, I'll do that," she'd responded.

"Oh, Jim, I don't think that's such a good idea," her mother had said with a worried look. "It's over ten miles to town and the road is twisty and steep. She could have an accident."

"Mom, that's not fair. I've been driving for two and a half years. I can drive as good as you can," Erika had countered, rolling her eyes like only she could.

"Well, I'd just as soon let your dad drive. I worry about these steep canyon roads. They scare me to death. And you have practically no experience on them," her mother had said with rising anger in her voice.

Erika recognized that it was time to drive in the wedge. She was good at that. She knew how to work one parent against the other when it was to her advantage. "Dad trusts me, don't you, Dad?" she said with a smile. "I'll be just fine."

"Jim, I don't think—" her mother began again.

"Mom, Dad already said I could, didn't you, Dad?" she said sweetly.

"Yes," he agreed, clearing his throat and avoiding his wife's glaring eyes. "She'll be leaving us soon and needs to learn to handle challenges on her own. She'll be very careful, won't you, sweetheart?"

"Sure, Dad. I'll be really careful. Would any of you like me to bring you something?" she had asked slyly, enlisting the support of the younger kids.

She soon had a list of requests from everyone but her father. He wasn't about to admit that he could possibly want anything but his own open-fire cooking. Even her mother had added a request for a Hershey bar.

Not one other member of the family had yet stirred as the Expedition eased out of the campground and glided smoothly onto the canyon road. Feeling guilty for leaving before family prayer, but not wanting to give her father a chance to change his mind about her little trip, Erika pressed the accelerator and the big engine responded. She loved the feeling of the Expedition's power, but pushed on the brake with panic when the first of several miles of sharp curves appeared unexpectedly. The road was more than a little frightening, so she slowed down. The last thing she wanted was to bang up the Expedition.

The bright morning sun glared in her eyes every time the twisting road had her driving east. It had risen well above the mountains by the time she reached the small town of Pineview after twenty-five minutes of nerve-racking driving. She drove the full length of the main street, not a big feat in this high mountain village. She turned back and pulled to a stop in front of the only grocery store in town.

Closed.

She looked at her watch. It wasn't even close to seven yet. The store wouldn't be open until eight o'clock, the sign on the door informed her. She drove slowly down the street again. A small convenience store near the center of town was open. She had decided to stop there when she noticed the flashing sign of a café just a block farther on the opposite side of the street.

Impulsively, she gunned the Expedition and wheeled into the cramped parking area beside the café. Slipping the keys in her purse, she headed for the door. A little bell jangled when she shoved it open. Three men were eating breakfast at the nearest booth, and a couple more were at the counter. Their heads turned in unison, and their eyes shined with approval as she walked in. They were rough-looking country men, and she frowned at them. Selecting a booth at the far end of the room, she sat down.

Glancing at the men, who continued admiring her, she thought about Bob, the twenty-two-year-old guy she'd been dating since the first of the summer. How different he was from these men who were leering at her in their dusty baseball caps and badly worn work boots. She missed Bob—tall, athletic, and so good-looking with his short, dark-blonde hair, bright blue eyes and ready smile.

She looked around for a waitress but didn't see one. She shifted in her seat as she waited impatiently. Finally, one of the men shouted, "Hey, Penny! Better get yerself in gear and come on out here. There's a young filly come in, and she's looking kind of gant. Reckon she could use some grub."

Erika frowned, disgusted, but the men laughed heartily. A moment later the waitress appeared, wiping her hands on a greasy apron. She said to the men as she passed them, "Don't suppose none of you could give a poor workin' girl a hand. You just sit there givin' orders, sippin' coffee, and spectin' me ta get it all done."

"But you look like you need the exercise, Penny," a bewhiskered young man at the counter said as she brushed by. He warded off a blow from the sturdy waitress with his elbow, spilling coffee on the counter.

"Now look what you went and done," he complained to her retreating backside. "I suppose you expect me ta clean up the mess."

The waitress turned and threw a rag she'd pulled from the pocket of her apron and said curtly, but with a twinkle in her eye, "There you go. You know what to do." She turned to Erika and asked, "And what can I get fer you, honey?"

Erika suddenly wished she was back in camp, waiting for another plateful of *fried fish*. "I would like a menu, please," she mumbled.

"Menu? Where you from, girl?" the waitress asked, looking surprised.

"San Diego."

"San Diego! Honey, this here's a far cry from San Diego! Now, do you want breakfast or not?"

"Yes, ma'am. Do you have pancakes?" she asked, feeling totally out of place.

"Hotcakes, you mean? Sure, honey. How about a cup of coffee?"

"I don't drink coffee. Er, milk would be fine," she stammered.

"Comin' right up, honey," the cheerful waitress said, hurrying back to the kitchen.

While Erika waited, the men laughed loudly as they conversed with one another, occasionally glancing in her direction. None of them spoke to her, but from the bits of conversation that drifted her way, she knew they were talking about her.

After what seemed like an hour but was, according to her watch, not quite ten minutes, Penny arrived with a steaming stack of pancakes. As she deftly placed them in front of Erika she asked, "What you doin' way out here all by yerself, honey?"

"My family is up the canyon camping," she said, pointing north. "I got tired of Dad's cooking, so he let me come down for some real food."

Penny's hazel eyes smiled. "Well, this here's real food, so dig in."

Just then the bell jangled over the door and Penny glanced that way. "Good mornin', Mike. The law's out early today," she said brightly.

"Not that I want to be," a middle-aged deputy with receding red hair answered with a long face. "Butch Snyder escaped from prison last evening, and the sheriff asked me to have a look around. They're afraid he may come home."

Erika felt her stomach tighten at the look of fear that crossed Penny's plump face. Penny opened her mouth to speak, but one of the men at the counter spoke first. "He's not in here, Mike."

The officer smiled. "No, I didn't expect he was, but I've been up half the night. If Penny here could whip me up something to eat, maybe I'll have the energy to keep looking," he said as he straddled one of the stools at the counter.

"What'll you have, Mike?" Penny asked. The deputy's news had driven the sparkle from her eyes.

"Bacon and eggs, over easy, sourdough toast, and hash browns," he said, and Penny disappeared into the kitchen.

Erika spread some butter on her pancakes and drenched them with maple syrup. She could just hear her mother, "Erika, not so much syrup!" and grinned indulgently as she added still more.

"Who's the girl?"

Erika looked up—directly into a set of piercing green eyes. The stocky deputy was looking at her and smiled as the man next to him said, "Some filly from California. Jumped the pasture fence and come here looking fer better grass. Says her old man don't cook too good so she come to town fer real food."

Mike took a sip of scalding liquid from the cup Penny had just set in front of him, and then, still holding the steaming cup, moved over to Erika's table. As he sat down opposite her, he asked, "Mind if I join you, miss?"

Since he was already seated, she said politely, "That'll be fine."

"I'm Sergeant Mike O'Connor," he said, his piercing eyes, unblinking but friendly, locking on her face.

"My name is Erika Leighton." She paused, then added, "It's nice to meet you." She looked down at her plate. She'd never been this close to a real cop before. He made her nervous. She tried to smile.

"I don't mean to frighten you, Erika, but I think it would be best if you got back to your family right away."

She looked up. There was genuine concern on his ruddy face. She stiffened. "Why?" she asked, knowing it had to do with the escape of some guy named Butch.

"There's been a prison break down in Canyon City. One of the men who got away is from here in Pineview. He's plumb mean—a real dangerous one—and I think it would be best if people were prepared in case he shows up."

Curious and more than a little frightened, Erika asked, "What did he do to get in prison?"

The stocky, red-haired officer shifted in his seat before he answered, "Well, miss, he's a killer. Murdered a couple of folks here about five years ago. And I'm afraid he'd do it again if he got it in his head. Not someone you'd ever want to see."

Erika gasped as the deputy finished and watched him lift his steaming cup to his lips again. His eyes never left her face. She had never seen such a deep shade of green, and they seemed to peer very deeply into her soul.

His deep voice was steady when he went on. "They were both strangers in town and alone when he got them." He thought about the witness as he spoke. He never even knew her name, but like this girl, she had been alone when she came to Pineview. And what she had seen had frightened her so badly that she'd refused to reveal her identity. But her information, the description she gave and the license number, had led him to Butch Snyder. It hadn't taken long to make a case after that. "Yes," he went on, "they were alone. Never had a chance."

She was alone in town. She got the message. She shivered, and realized her pancakes suddenly tasted flat.

"Never could figure exactly why he did it," he said, sipping the coffee again. "Crazy deal. Sad."

Erika's appetite was gone. Her stomach felt like someone had poured a bottle of acid in it. She was scared and wished she'd never come to town, but her pride forced her to say, "I appreciate your letting me know about him, but I'll be okay. I just need to buy some groceries after I eat. Then I'll go back up the canyon."

"That where your folks are?"

She nodded.

"I'll feel better knowing you're with your folks, even though I really doubt Butch will come back here. I would think he'd want to go someplace where he wouldn't be recognized. I hope I didn't upset you too badly. I've got a girl at home. She's sixteen. A little younger than you, I suspect."

Erika felt the tension ebbing. She liked this man. He was so . . . well, real, she decided. "I'm eighteen," she answered.

Same age the unidentified witness had been. He had managed to get her age out of her, just not her name. "You're a right pretty girl. So's my Becky. I wouldn't want her to be out alone, no matter how remote the danger," he said and smiled.

Erika noticed the deep dimples at the corners of his mouth. Feeling somewhat reassured, she began to pick at her food. Mike asked her a few questions about California while he sipped on his coffee and waited for breakfast. She answered with growing ease.

In a few minutes, Penny arrived with the deputy's meal. "Too good ta sit with the boys?" she teased as she slipped his plate in front of him. Then, her face growing serious, she asked, "Sergeant, do you think Butch might come back? You be mighty careful. He said he'd get you someday for sendin' him to prison."

Erika tensed again. Mike's face was unruffled, amused. "Oh, Penny, quit your fussing. You're as bad as my wife. Every time I go out the door with my gun on, which is only when the sheriff tells me I have to wear it, she tells me to be careful."

"I see you got it on today," Penny said, glancing at his .357 magnum revolver.

"Yes. The sheriff told me to when he called. I can take care of myself, Penny, so don't you fret. It's Butch that better be careful. If he comes around here, which I don't think he will, but if he does, I'll get him," he said calmly.

"You be careful anyway," Penny urged as Erika was thinking about the big revolver on the deputy's belt and the confidence with which he spoke. She got the feeling that this was a man no crook would want on his trail. "Now you get busy and eat, Sergeant. I want him caught if he does come back. You may not be afraid of him, but I am."

The fear showed on Penny's face. Erika couldn't help but wonder about this Butch fellow. He must really be bad, she decided. More people came in the café. Each in turn spoke to the deputy. Some called him Sergeant, others called him Mike, but they all showed him respect and appeared confident in his ability to take care of Butch if the man made the mistake of setting foot in Pineview, Colorado. The big redhead sitting across the table from her—piercing green eyes and dimpled smile—was all business, it appeared.

Erika made it about halfway through her stack of pancakes before she was so full she gave up. She pushed her plate back and started to stand.

"You leaving?" the sergeant asked.

"Yes, I better go. Like you said, I need to get back with my family." She slipped out of the booth.

Mike had inhaled his food. He pushed the plate away and followed her to the cash register where she waited for Penny to take her money. "Breakfast is on me," he said. "You go get your groceries and get back up the canyon."

"Thanks," she mumbled and started for the door.

"Erika," Mike said, looking at his watch, "You'll have to go to the Quick Stop up the street. The grocery store won't be open for a while yet."

She thanked him again and stepped out into the fresh air. The little café had grown dim with cigarette smoke. Coming from a nonsmoking LDS family, she wasn't used to being around it, and she inhaled the clear air deeply, purging her lungs. A minute later she parked the Expedition beside the Quick Stop. It was a fairly nice, glass-front building with a single pair of sparkling gas pumps between it and the street. They looked much newer than the building.

Hers was the only car in the gravel parking space beside the store and none were at the pumps in front, so she was mildly surprised as she walked toward the door and saw that there were customers inside.

An old man was standing behind the till, facing the door. He looked like he'd been there all night from the red in his eyes and the shadow of gray whiskers on his wrinkled face.

He nodded at her as she stepped around the counter, so she smiled back as she began to gather the few things she wanted. "Good morning," a plump, pleasant woman in her early fifties said.

Erika responded with a quiet, "Hello."

A tall, slender man was filling a large thermos with coffee near the back of the room. From his cowboy boots, baseball hat, and the size of the thermos, Erika assumed he was a truck driver and absently wondered where his truck was parked.

Erika's back was to the glass door when she heard it open. She turned in time to see a dark-complexioned, good-looking man enter. She thought he must be in his mid-twenties. He needed a shave, his short, dark-brown hair was mussed, and he looked very tired. He was dressed in a bright blue western shirt and new blue jeans, and was carrying a black jacket wadded in one hand.

He walked straight to the counter, his pale green eyes taking in the room with a sweeping glance before focusing on the cashier. The old man's back was to Erika when the young man shifted the jacket in his hand and said in an icy voice, "Empty it, Sam, and no funny stuff!"

The woman down the aisle gasped. The old man didn't move. Erika's heart hammered on her rib cage and her legs turned to jelly. The old man spoke, his voice quivering. "Now, Butch, you know I ain't got much cash in here. You better just leave and I'll say ya ain't been 'round if anybody asks."

Time stood still.

Erika saw nothing but the dark-haired bandit and the old man who still stood with his back to her.

Butch!

That was the name the redheaded sergeant had mentioned. He was the—

"Just give me what you have, old man, and maybe I'll let you live," Butch said, breaking into her thoughts. "This town owes me, and I aim to collect before I move on," he said, ever so slightly waving the arm that held his jacket.

"What are you goin' ta do, Butch, if I don't give you no money—, hit me over the head with that coat?" the old man asked, his voice still shaking but angry.

"Just shut up and get it—now!" Butch shouted and shook the jacket loose, revealing a small .25-caliber, semiautomatic pistol. "You've got ten seconds, Sam, or . . ." He let the threat dangle, his voice low and dangerous. The pistol was steady.

The seconds seemed like an eternity as the old man fumbled with the cash register. Erika forced herself to look away. The truck driver was still by the coffee pot staring at the unfolding drama. He set the thermos on the counter. The friendly woman down the aisle was pale and her eyes were filled with fear.

Out the window, Erika spotted a white Dodge pickup—a big star on the door—coming down the street toward the convenience store. Butch glanced over his shoulder. He also saw the deputy's truck. He cursed, his eyes narrowing to angry slits. "You're too slow, old man!" he hissed.

A blast filled the little store and Erika watched in horror as the old cashier flew into the back counter, bounced forward, and disappeared from view as he fell with a sickening thud to the floor. A crash to Erika's right jerked her head that way. The lady had fainted. Erika feared that she would too, but somehow her feet stayed under her even though her knees were trembling so hard it made her teeth rattle. The whole terrible drama had happened so quickly that it seemed like a scene in a movie.

Butch's voice rang out as the echo of the pistol shot faded. "On the floor, both of you!"

It took a second for Erika's frozen brain to send the message to her legs that they needed to bend. The little gun was staring her in the face like a giant eye. It looked more like the barrel of a cannon.

"Miss, he means you too."

The voice came from behind her. It was the truck driver. She slowly made her way to her knees and stretched out on the floor, face down. She was surprised when she noticed groceries scattered around her; she did not remember dropping them. Tears stung her eyes, and her thoughts shifted from the mysteriously scattered items to her family. She was frightened, but more than anything, she was filled with regret. She would give anything to be with them right now.

Erika was too afraid to look up, and it seemed like hours before Butch's cold voice filled the room again. "Alright, you can all get up now," he said very calmly. "If you do as you're told, none of you will be hurt."

Erika stood and leaned against a shelf. She was shaking terribly and felt like she was going to burst into sobs. She looked beyond Butch, who was standing near the front of the store pointing his gun toward her. The red-haired deputy, Mike O'Connor, a shotgun in his arms, was leaning over the hood of his white pickup on the far side of the street.

Butch sneered. "Can you see my old friend, Mike O'Connor? He's come calling." He swung the pistol around as if he were going to shoot through the large window at the deputy. But he lowered it and said, "I guess I better not break the glass just yet. Seems like we might be here for a spell."

The truck driver spoke. "Is she okay? Do you mind if I check her?"

For the first time, Erika realized that the older lady was still on the floor. She wondered if somebody should be checking on Sam, the elderly teller, but she had the terrible feeling that it wasn't necessary.

"You two move Mrs. Smith as far back as you can get her, then the three of you stay put. I need to think for a minute. And remember: any tricks and you'll end up like Sam." He waved the gun toward the counter that encircled the escapee's victim. Erika had no desire to see in there.

Erika and the truck driver helped the woman, who had finally regained consciousness, to the back of the store where the coffee pot, a microwave oven, and a soda fountain were located. They stood nervously, not speaking as their captor paced back and forth in the center aisle, alternately glaring at them and watching armed men and cars gather across the street.

The truck driver spoke again. "Now, let me have a look at the old man. He might bleed to death."

"Probably already has," Butch said coldly. "You stay put."

Suddenly, Mike O'Connor's voice boomed into the store, projected by a loudspeaker. "Butch, this is Sergeant O'Connor. You are surrounded. There is no way for you to escape, so just drop that gun you're holding and come out."

Butch mumbled something unintelligible. Sergeant O'Connor spoke again. "Butch, I know you fired a shot in there. If someone is hurt, let us get them out."

Butch looked drained, but his face showed no sign of giving in. He said nothing, and Mrs. Smith spoke up, her voice weak and trembling. "Butch, please, let them get Sam out of here. Maybe it's not too late—"

Butch swung his head toward her, his eyes glaring. "Let him lay!" he snarled.

Then Sergeant O'Connor's voice, low and slow, came at them again. "Butch, if you're not going to come out, at least send the others. We know there are several people in there with you. Have some decency, Butch, and let them go."

To no one in particular, Butch said, "Yeah, sure, and let you shoot this place to pieces and me with it. You'd like that, wouldn't you? I'm not crazy. These people are my ticket out of here. Nobody leaves."

Sergeant O'Connor couldn't hear Butch, but Erika had no doubt that he knew what the killer was thinking. And then the ugly truth dawned on her: she was a *hostage!* How could this have happened? Violence, in her world, was only on television and in the movies. It was not a part of *real* life.

She forced herself to think rationally. She was afraid to die. She had to accept that this was really happening if she was to have any chance of surviving the mess her selfishness had gotten her into.

The truck driver brought her out of her thoughts with a jolt when he said, "I'm Ken Feldman. I'm a truck driver from Omaha, Nebraska."

"Oh, uh . . . I'm Erika Leighton. I'm, uh . . . from California," she stammered.

They both turned to the third hostage. Butch had called her Mrs. Smith. "I'm Alice Smith. I live just down the street and my grandchildren are alone there. My husband is at work. Oh, I'm so worried."

Somehow, Erika felt better just knowing who they were. Names made them real people, made her feel like she really wasn't alone. She opened her mouth to speak again, but Butch cut her off curtly. "Shut up, all of you!"

They did as he ordered, lapsing into a depressing silence. Erika found that she yearned for conversation to ease the tension, and apparently Butch did too, for only a few more minutes passed before he walked back toward them and said, "I didn't want to shoot old Sam. I just needed some money and everybody in this town owes me. He didn't need to jerk me around like that. I would have taken the money and gone if he'd just given it to me. You know me, Mrs. Smith," he went on, looking at her with a sad expression in his pale eyes, "I wouldn't have shot him if he hadn't made me do it."

"That's right, Butch," Mrs. Smith responded, her voice weak and quaking. "I'm sure you're right." She did not sound at all convinced. "But now, please, let someone try to help him."

"I never wanted to hurt anyone," Butch went on, ignoring the plea. "But people never gave me a chance, did they, Mrs. Smith?"

"I guess not, Butch," she said.

Erika could see that they knew each other. Ken thought so too, and he asked, "Are you from around here, Butch?"

Butch relaxed visibly. His pale green eyes were not darting about as rapidly as they had been. Erika felt hopeful. Butch answered the question. "I was born and raised right here in Pineview. I went to Pineview Elementary and Pineview High, didn't I, Mrs. Smith?" For the first time his lips curled into what Erika decided was a smile, but it did not contain any humor. It was an ugly smile. "She was my English teacher, and I was a good student, wasn't I?"

"Yes, you were, Butch. And you could have easily finished high school and gone on to college if you'd wanted to. Why did you drop out of school, Butch? I never did understand that." Mrs. Smith was seeming less frightened, and she spoke more easily now with Butch, even though her eyes darted constantly to the counter where Sam lay dead, or dying, on the floor.

"You knew why. Everyone knew why," he said, his face darkening again, making Erika shiver. "I got tired of the taunting. I was never as *good* as everyone else because my dad's leg was crippled and he couldn't work. I always wore old clothes and everybody thought it was funny. They always called me *Crip Snyder's kid*—wasn't even worthy of my own name!"

Mrs. Smith's face went pale. "Oh my, Butch," she gasped. "I'm . . . so sorry."

"Yeah, well this whole town is *sorry*, and I promised myself in prison that they would never forget Butch Snyder." The intensity of his voice increased and his eyes narrowed again. "And they haven't, have they?"

Mrs. Smith, becoming composed and confident, wisely steered the conversation away from Butch's troubled youth, and he relaxed a little again. Erika entertained hopeful thoughts that he might perhaps let them go before too long. She studied him as he talked. He couldn't be more than twenty-five or twenty-six she guessed. And he wasn't bad looking, just mean and angry. From his speech, she could tell that the English lessons taught by Mrs. Smith had taken.

He was shorter than Bob by at least four inches. She guessed him to be about an inch under six feet. His body was lean and muscular like Bob's. His skin was naturally dark, not tanned. And his eyes and his face were nothing like Bob's. Those pale green eyes of his were so disturbing, so full of hate and anger. And his face was hard. He frightened her.

Butch was saying, "They told me my dad died a few weeks ago. They wouldn't let me come home for the funeral. But I decided to visit his grave. That's where I was before I came here." He looked almost sad as he paused, deep in thought. "Not even a headstone . . . just a tin marker . . . I'll see that the people of this town buy him a nice one. They owe—"

He was interrupted by the shrill ringing of the telephone. Erika followed Butch's gaze. The phone was under the counter beyond the cash register. Butch just stared for a minute. The ringing persisted.

"Let me answer it," Ken offered.

"Go get it," Butch said, glaring at Ken for a moment before heading toward the front of the store. "O'Connor probably doesn't like using his loudspeaker."

Erika couldn't help but notice how Ken looked down as he stepped past where the old man had fallen. She couldn't see him there on the floor and was grateful for that. Ken grabbed the phone and carted it back toward the hostages. He looked down at the old cashier again as he worked the long cord free. Then he walked toward them with the phone ringing in his hand. As he extended it toward Butch, the young outlaw cleared a section of dusty white shelf with an angry sweep of his hand, sending cans of soup and beans rolling up the aisle. The phone continued to ring. Butch took it from Ken and slammed it down on the shelf before snatching the receiver.

"What do you want?" he demanded harshly.

Butch listened for a moment, his pale eyes narrowing again, his mouth set in a firm frown of anger. "Sure, Sergeant, go ahead and talk. I'm listening," he said curtly.

He listened, for a good minute this time. His feet shuffled nervously, and his eyes kept darting toward the front of the store and the men across the street. "Three," Butch said, his voice like a wisp of arctic air, "unless you want to count Sam."

Erika folded her arms across her chest, shivering. "We've got to stick together and wear him down," Ken whispered softly. "And we need to convince Butch to let someone get Sam . . . that is, uh, to get Sam's body out of here."

Mrs. Smith shuddered. "So he's dead," she mouthed. Ken shrugged but didn't look at either of his fellow hostages. "Oh, that's so awful. Poor Sam. But we've got to remain positive."

Butch held the receiver away from his ear for a moment before dropping it indifferently back in place.

"That was Sergeant O'Connor." His eyes bore into Erika until she was forced to look at her Reeboks. Then he said, "He thinks I should let you all go, but that would be stupid, wouldn't it?"

After an uneasy silence, Mrs. Smith said evenly, "But Butch, we can't stay here forever. Please, let them come get Sam."

"Yes, please," Ken added.

"No!" Butch shouted angrily.

Mrs. Smith's face paled, and Erika reached for her, thinking she might faint again. Erika lowered her carefully to the floor, where the older lady rested her back against the shelf, her head forward. Ken spoke to Butch, his voice calm and even. "What do you plan to do? You have something in mind, I'm sure."

"I told Sergeant O'Connor that he would have to get us a car. He's checking with Sheriff Lyght. He says it's okay with him, but he's got to locate the sheriff for permission. That's the trouble with cops, they always have to check with somebody higher up. The sheriff's not in his office or at home, but they're trying to locate him, so we'll wait right here until they do. There's plenty to eat in here, so help yourselves, but remember, no tricks." The pistol was gripped tightly in his left hand as he spoke, and Erika's eyes kept returning to it as if drawn by a magnet.

Butch moved forward an aisle, ripped open a bag of chocolate-covered cookies and began to eat. Erika glanced at her watch. It was after eight o'clock. It had been nearly a half hour since she left the café. Her folks would start to worry soon, and they were without a car in a sparsely populated campground.

Without warning, warm tears began to wash her cheeks. She dabbed at them self-consciously. A reassuring hand touched her shoulder. Ken smiled down at her and she wiped the tears with the sleeve of her blue sweatshirt. He pointed at Alice whose head was now resting on her knees. Erika sat down beside the older woman. In hushed voices they began to talk about the continuing state of unrest in the world, especially the Middle East—a topic that probably wouldn't upset their explosive captor.

Butch continued to eat cookies, keeping a constant watch on his captives, his face hard and his pale eyes like green slivers of ice. Erika had never felt so helpless or been so frightened in her life. The tears flowed again. Ken handed her a large red bandanna and it was soon soaked. She even tried to pray. She had prayed a lot in her life, but never with much intensity. She felt the need now, but wasn't up to the task. Her faith, weak at best, seemed to be failing her; she had always depended on the faith of her parents.

CHAPTER 2

Sergeant Mike O'Connor placed the phone down and rubbed a calloused hand across his worried face. His worst fears were coming true. Butch had shot old Sam. He may have killed him, but he couldn't be sure. That was a worry. If Sam happened to be alive, he was probably in desperate need of medical attention. And on top of that, Butch was threatening to shoot his three hostages if he wasn't allowed to leave town with them.

Never in twenty years of law enforcement had the forty-six-year-old lawman faced a more difficult situation. The lives of three hostages were now in his hands, and one was an innocent young woman he had sent there. He shuddered. The only murders in his town during those twenty years had been committed by Butch. Mike, with the help of an unidentified eighteen-year-old girl, had been responsible for solving those killings and sending Butch to prison for life—or so he had thought.

Leaning back in the borrowed chair of a commandeered insurance office directly across from the Quick Stop, Mike contemplated his options. He was only buying time in telling Butch the sheriff would have to okay a get-away car. Sheriff Lyght was thirty miles away rounding up more help to hit the highway to Pineview. Mike knew, and he knew the sheriff knew, that anything could happen with Butch Snyder—and at any moment.

An oil painting of a large ship on a dark-blue sea hung above the desk. Mike stared at the peaceful scene as Butch's last words—when he left him in the state prison at Canyon City—rang in his ears. "You'll regret this someday!" the young killer had threatened.

Mike hadn't worried too much the past five years since the judge had ordered two life sentences for Butch, making parole in Mike's lifetime unlikely. But all that had changed when Sheriff Lyght had called during the night with his chilling message: "Mike, Butch Snyder escaped from the pen a few hours ago. Will you go out and have a look around? And maybe you ought to have your wife and daughters go someplace for a few days."

Mention of his family's safety had chilled Mike to the bone. When Carol sleepily asked him what the phone call was about, he had explained as calmly as he could, but his words still caused her to sit bolt upright in bed. "I'll call Helen." That was her sister in Cheyenne. "She'll let us stay with her for a few days."

Carol was a woman with few faults, and indecisiveness was not one of them. In less than thirty minutes, Mike's wife and two daughters were en route to Cheyenne. In a way, he was relieved that at least he now knew where Butch was, and his family was safe—that counted for a lot.

The door opened, jarring Mike from his thoughts. Three deputies and two state troopers crowded into the office. He was grateful for the help and explained quickly what the situation was. Then he assigned them to positions around the Quick Stop and diplomatically began to remove the citizens who had first come to his aid and filled those risky positions. Most of the men left with relief on their faces. Some of the more aggressive ones hesitated, and he sent them to divert highway traffic around the edge of town. "I don't want anyone to come past but cops," he said. "When we have enough help here, then I'll have officers relieve you. But in the meantime, I'm depending on you to keep the crowds away."

Diplomacy worked, as it usually did for Mike. The men left the critical area, thanking Mike for letting them be of assistance. He asked two men to drive up the canyon and locate Erika's family. He knew how worried they would be and, even though he did not have good news, at least they could worry about something real instead of something imagined.

After the assignments were all made, Mike sat down again and contemplated the slogan that hung opposite the ship scene in the insurance office. "You, the agent, are responsible for providing the client with the best protection he can afford," it read.

With a jolt, he thought about Erika again. He was supposed to have protected her, but had sent her instead to the Quick Stop and right into Butch's hands. He tried to console himself with the knowledge that she would probably have gone there anyway, but it didn't make him feel any better. Now he could only do his best to get her out alive; and with a slam of his fist on the desk, he swore to himself that he would do it.

An hour later, Sheriff Lyght called on the radio. "I've set up a command post at the elementary school," he said. "I think it best that I not come over there where Butch might recognize me while we deal with his request for a car." The elementary school was two blocks from the Quick Stop, behind and to the east, and completely out of sight. "So hustle over and let's talk," he ordered.

After a few minutes of intense discussion at the school, Mike made a phone call from the principal's office. "Butch," he said, after the young outlaw answered with a growl, "I'm still working on finding Sheriff Lyght. You'll have to be patient until I can find him. How are the others?"

"Don't play games with me, O'Connor," Butch snarled. "If you want to see these other three alive again, you better get that car here soon."

"Who are the folks you have in there with you, Butch?" Mike asked calmly.

"It doesn't matter—now get to it!" Butch punctuated his angry order with a slam of the phone.

"He's not getting any milder," Mike said grimly as he pushed himself back from the desk. "Best be getting back over to the scene, Sheriff. I'll let you know as soon as we get the neighborhood evacuated."

"Alright, Mike. And make sure no one, and I mean *no one* who is not authorized, is allowed in the area."

"Sure thing, Sheriff," Mike said with a tired smile, running his hand through his red waves of thinning hair.

As soon as he had taken care of the sheriff's security concerns in the area of the Quick Stop, Mike returned to the school. Erika's family, tense and tearful, had been delivered there. Together, Mike and Sheriff Lyght explained what was taking place.

"We're very sorry about the danger she's in, but we're doing everything within our means to keep that fellow calm and get your daughter out of there. Now, tell us," Sheriff Lyght said, his voice full of concern, "how does your daughter handle pressure?"

"If you're asking how she'll be feeling in there now," Jim Leighton said perceptively, "I don't think she'll be hysterical, but she will be frightened, of course. She's a mature—"

Before he could go on, Mrs. Leighton interrupted angrily, her red-rimmed eyes flashing accusingly at her husband. "This never would have happened if you hadn't given her the bright idea of going to town. Sheriff," she said, turning her angry eyes toward Sheriff Lyght, "Jim has always catered to the girl's every whim. I hate to admit it, but she's rather selfish and immature. I'm not sure what she'll do."

"Thank you for your help. Everything we can learn about the folks in there with this fellow will help us determine how to most effectively deal with him," the sheriff said, expertly circumventing further conflict between the distraught parents. "Sergeant O'Connor will be going back there in a few minutes. You folks make yourselves as comfortable as you can. Some bunks have been set up in one of the classrooms for your use."

After the family had stepped out, the sheriff said, "I'd sure like to know who else is in there with Butch."

"There's a semi parked down the street, just west of the store," Mike said. "I wonder if the driver's in there."

The sheriff nodded thoughtfully. "Check the truck. See if you can find its log and registration papers. Send someone over here with them. I'll see what I can learn as soon as they're delivered. Maybe I can figure out who the driver is and learn a little about him."

"I'm sure the woman in there is from town because there are no other cars near the store," Mike said. "She must have walked from nearby."

"As soon as some more men come, I'll have a couple of them start checking the neighborhoods. I'm expecting more help shortly," Sheriff Lyght said.

Mike turned to leave, but the sheriff stopped him. "One more thing, Mike. Do you know if there's a TV or radio in the store? There'll be folks here from the press soon, and I don't want to release anything that might put the hostages in more danger if Snyder were to hear it."

"I don't remember seeing a TV, but I've heard a radio going in there quite often. I don't think Sam normally listened to it, but the gals that work there usually have it blaring."

Within a half hour the identity of the other two hostages was firmly established, and Mike was encouraged. Alice Smith was a smart, level-headed woman, and he had learned that Ken Feldman, the truck driver, was portrayed by his employer as an intelligent, dependable man.

Mike sat in the insurance office, drumming his fingers nervously on the desk. The sheriff had just called and told him to phone Butch again. He lifted the receiver and punched in the number of the Quick Stop.

"That you, O'Connor?" Butch said after just two rings.

He sounded more tense than before. Mike hesitated before plunging into the message the sheriff had told him to give Butch. He could hear Butch's nervous breaths like gusts of wind on the line. "Butch, I located the sheriff. He said to tell you that he won't even consider a car for you until you let us get Sam out of there."

For a moment, all he could hear was Butch's breathing. Then the outlaw said, "Okay, but you send in just two men, unarmed and wearing t-shirts. If they try anything stupid I'll let them have it too."

"Okay, I'll get them on their way as soon as I can."

"You've got five minutes to have him out of here," Butch snarled and the phone clicked.

Mike quickly selected two officers and sent them in wearing t-shirts and uniform pants. Both carried small boot guns just in case something went wrong. The five minute mark passed as they crossed the street. They waited while Ken, Butch's gun at his back, unlocked the door and stepped back. Then they entered cautiously.

Through a strong pair of field glasses, Mike watched as Butch covered the two men with the pistol, glancing frequently at his hostages. They stood near him at the back of the room.

In a few seconds, the officers came out with Sam's body, and carried him across the street and into the borrowed office where they laid him on the floor. Mike swore quietly in relief as he examined the grim old man. Sam was alive and wheezing. "He's not even shot!" he told the deputies. "Look here. The bullet struck this wallet in his pocket. It must be a small caliber gun or it would have passed through."

"Nearly knocked my head off when I fell, though," Sam said with a grimace. "Head hurts awful."

"Yes, I expect it does. You'll need a bunch of stitches. But you are one lucky man. How did you keep him from shooting you again?" Mike asked in amazement.

"I played possum. That truck driver in there knows I'm alive, but I whispered to him to not let Butch know. He kept my secret, bless his soul."

"We're all grateful for that, Sam. But we better get you to a hospital."

"Don't let Butch know I'm alive," Sam requested.

"Why not? You're safe now," one of the other deputies asked.

"I don't know for sure," Sam said as he struggled to sit up. "I just think he might be less likely to hurt one of the others if he thinks he killed me."

"Is the radio on in there?" Mike asked. "Sooner or later the press will learn you're okay, and they'll broadcast it."

"No, I never turn the blasted thing on. Ain't no music I can stand to listen to. Anyway, can't you tell the press I'm dead?"

"That would be up to the sheriff, but for now we'll do it your way." Mike had one of the other deputies get a blanket from his patrol car. They covered Sam from head to foot, placed him on a stretcher from an ambulance that now waited nearby, and carried him out to it. After pushing the stretcher inside, Mike instructed the driver to leave without lights or sirens and explained why.

Mike returned to the borrowed office to call the sheriff and report on Sam's condition. As he reached for the phone, it rang. Startled, he picked it up, expecting to hear the sheriff's voice. "I looked up the number, Sergeant," Butch said with a sneer. "You thought I was kidding about old Sam, didn't you? Well, I'm serious, and you'd better listen and listen good, O'Connor. I killed Sam because he was jerking me around when I asked for a little donation."

For what it was worth, the ruse had worked. Butch believed he had murdered again. The young killer went on. "Now you're the one jerking me around." Mike felt gooseflesh cover his body, as much from the tone of Butch's voice as from his threatening words. "I asked for a car, O'Connor. Get it for me and pull it right up in front of the door, driver side toward the store. Leave it running. And it better be full of gas! You got that, O'Connor?"

"I hear you, Butch. I'll call Sheriff Lyght—"

Butch interrupted with a shout so loud Mike could have heard him without the aid of the phone. "Forget Lyght! He's not here; you are. That car better be sitting out there in ten minutes, or one of my three companions will become a stiff! Now move it, man! I'm tired of waiting for you!"

The phone clicked in Mike's ear. He dialed his boss. "Things are heating up over here, Sheriff," he said the second the sheriff picked up the phone. "We got Sam out, and by a miracle he's alive and well, but now Butch has given me ten minutes to have a car in front, fueled and ready to roll."

"And if we don't?"

"He says he'll shoot one of the hostages."

"Stall him, Mike. I have a SWAT team on the way, but they won't be here for another thirty minutes. We can't let him get away with any of those people in there or he'll really be in control," the sheriff said.

From the tone of the sheriff's voice, Mike knew it would do no good to argue. His brain was churning away. "I've got it, Sheriff," he said suddenly. "Maybe we can create some kind of diversion, something to get his mind off the ultimatum he's given us."

"Or take him out with a sharpshooter," Sheriff Lyght suggested.

"I've thought of that, but if he spots a rifleman getting in position, he'll stick with those people in there like flies on roadkill."

"Get tough with him then. Try to bluff or something. Get him back on the phone. I guess I better come over." The sheriff rang off.

Mike dialed the Quick Stop. The phone rang ten or twelve times before Butch finally answered it, saying, "You're wasting time, O'Connor. You have eight minutes left."

"You don't, Butch," Mike lied, his voice as cold as an arctic wind. "We have a sharpshooter in place, and if you hang up the phone he'll shoot."

"Don't try to con me, man. I don't see anybody with a rifle."

Mike held his field glasses to his eyes. Butch was looking around at every possible angle. "Look hard, Butch, but you won't see him. You probably won't feel anything when he shoots either. He's that good. Now you listen to me, and you listen good, Butch. We've got you right where we want you now. Throw down your gun and come out or you will force us to shoot."

"You're lying, O'Connor. You better not be jerking me around. I don't like being jerked around!" Butch shouted, still searching frantically for a hidden rifleman.

Mike let him worry for a moment before saying, "I've changed my mind. I don't want you shot, Butch. I'm giving you a big break. You have one hour. When I call again, you better be ready to negotiate. Remember, one hour!"

Mike waited tensely. Butch finally started, "I . . . I—"

"One hour, Butch. You better think hard!"

There was nothing but heavy breathing on the line. Mike waited a few more seconds. He believed he had him bluffed and had, at least for now, changed the odds a little. "One hour, Butch," he said quietly and put the receiver down.

Mike's hands were clammy and perspiration was running down his face. He pulled a large bandanna from his pocket and wiped his forehead. Sheriff Lyght walked in as he stuffed the bandanna back into his hind pocket. Quickly he recited what he had just done. "I think I confused him," he concluded.

"Good work. Let's make him sweat some more," Sheriff Lyght said, picking up the phone and dialing. He waited a moment, then said, "This is Sheriff Lyght. You can cut the power now." He put the receiver down. "I don't know if it'll help, but they'll soon have no electricity over there and no air-conditioning. I'll be talking to reporters very soon, and I can't risk having Butch listen to the radio. We can turn the power back on later if we need to. It also gives us a little bargaining chip."

Mike nodded and lifted his field glasses. After a moment he said, "There, the lights are out, but it's still plenty light in there with those big windows in the front."

"Butch do anything when the power went off?" the sheriff asked.

"Not really. He looked around, but I don't think he realizes how warm it'll get in there with the sun shining through those windows like it is. The hostages are sitting down. I can't see them, but Butch is standing close to them, I'm sure. Oh, oh, he's going to sit down too. Now I can't see him."

Mike lowered the glasses. "Sheriff, do you think it would be okay if we moved the Leightons' vehicle now? I was thinking that if we could do it without Butch or the others in there knowing it would be best. We need to get it out of the way before Butch gets any ideas about using it."

"How do we do that?"

"Well, there are no windows in the back or on the side where Erika parked it, so they can't see it from inside. We could have three or four men come in from the back and they could push it as far away from the building as possible. Then they could start it up and drive away. We could create some kind of noise about then to muffle the sound of the engine."

"Good idea, Mike. Maybe a siren or . . . Hey, listen, do I hear a chopper?" the sheriff asked, moving his lanky frame to the window and peering out.

"Yeah, I think so," Mike said, straining to catch the far off *thump, thump, thump*.

"Must be a reporter from Channel 3. They said they'd be along soon. That will be perfect. Get some men ready, Mike, while I go meet the chopper and see if they'll help us. Tell the men not to start the engine until the chopper is hovering over the store."

"You've got it, Alden," Mike said, and both men hurried from the insurance office.

Mike assembled four men and gave them their assignment. "You've got to be very careful. There's a back door to the place. It comes off the storage room. So far Butch has made no move to go in there, but keep an eye on that door," he cautioned.

A couple of minutes later, the men reached the Expedition and pushed it about fifty feet from the store. Then they waited. Another minute passed before the bright red Jet Ranger lifted off from the school lawn and drifted lazily until it was hovering directly above the store. Mike watched Butch and, to his surprise, the gunman pointed the pistol toward the ceiling and pulled the trigger two or three times. Debris and dust fell to the floor.

The Expedition was pulling out of sight toward the school as the chopper banked to the left and flew gracefully away. "The tension is getting to him," Mike remarked to an officer who had just entered the office. "I sure hope he doesn't vent his emotions on the hostages. The longer they're in there together, the less likely he is to hurt them."

"What makes you say that?" the younger man asked. "I'd say just the opposite."

"There's often a bond that develops between hostages and the hostage-taker," Mike explained. "That strange phenomenon has saved a lot of lives. Of course there's a downside to it too. I've heard of hostages sympathizing with the crook, making things more difficult for the cops. Some of them actually begin to believe that they can somehow redeem their hostage-takers. That really makes it tough."

"That sounds crazy to me, Sergeant. Why would anybody try to help someone who has threatened to kill them?"

"I'm no psychologist, Deputy, but I do know it happens. From what I know of the three we have in there," Mike said, gesturing across the street, "I think it's unlikely. The girl's from a good family. Religious people, I understand. She's a bit immature, the mother says, but I think she'll be okay. The truck driver I'm confident about too. The only one that worries me at all is the woman. Alice Smith is a school teacher. If I'm not mistaken, she might have taught Butch before he dropped out of school. She's smart though, and I hope she'll think things through carefully."

The phone rang. "Good job, Sergeant," the sheriff said. "They won't be taking the Leightons' vehicle anyway. How'd they act in there when the chopper was overhead?"

"Butch came to his feet and fired a round into the ceiling. The others never got off the floor," Mike reported.

"I see," the sheriff responded thoughtfully. "Oh, I have a bit of bad news. The SWAT team I arranged for had to return to Denver. They have some kind of problem down there that just came up. They will fly up when they take care of whatever it is they have happening, if it's not too late by then," Sheriff Lyght said, sounding older than his fifty-four years.

"What do we do now?" Mike asked. "I'm not sure how much longer I can stall Butch."

"We set up our own sharpshooters, I guess, just in case he tries something. Do you have any better ideas, Mike?"

"I wish I did. What I really wish is that we could talk some sense into Butch." He was thoughtful for a minute, then he asked,

"Sheriff, the next time I talk to him is it alright with you if I try to get him to release one or two of the people in there? I'd sure like to get the women out as soon as we can. Then we'll work on getting the truck driver released."

"Sounds alright with me. Call when you're ready and be thinking where the best spot to place a couple of riflemen would be. I have some men trying to determine who're the best shots among the officers we have here. I have to go now. Those TV people are getting set up for an interview," the sheriff said wearily. "And Mike, don't be too surprised if Butch doesn't let anyone go."

"Sure, Sheriff. I'll just give it my best shot. The less hostages there are the safer it will be if we have to use sharpshooters." Mike slammed his fist down on the desk so hard a small paperweight jumped. "I was sure counting on a good SWAT team to end this thing for us."

"Me too, Mike," the sheriff said. "But we're on our own for now. They'll be here a little later. I'll be in touch in a few minutes."

Mike sat back in the chair and lifted the glasses to his eyes. To the young deputy he remarked, "Surely someone would be needing to use the rest room over there." He glanced at his watch. "It's nearly one o'clock and I don't believe any of them have been in there yet."

"Does seem like they'd need to," the deputy agreed.

"Well, I'll be a red-blooded Irishman," Mike said a few minutes later, slapping the desk with one hand. "They're all on their feet and moving toward the rest room." He paused, studying the scene through the glasses, and then he said, "I hope he doesn't try the door in the back. He probably figures we have officers there, but I've still expected him to at least crack it and have a look."

For several minutes Mike watched through the glasses, only occasionally glancing at his watch. Finally, he placed them on the desk and reached for the phone. "Wish me luck, Deputy," he said to the young officer as he punched some numbers. "We need a break in this stalemate. I don't know how much longer our luck will hold. Someone else could get hurt."

CHAPTER 3

The phone was ringing again. "Aren't you going to answer it, Butch?" Alice Smith asked when he made no move to step over to the shelf and pick up the receiver.

"Only if one of you want to hand it to me. I don't think my copper friend over there really has a sharpshooter, but just in case, I don't plan to take any more chances."

"I'll get it," Erika said as she stood and reached for the receiver. The incessant ringing was getting on her nerves. This whole ordeal was wearing on her. She didn't know how much more she could stand. She handed the receiver to Butch who had to kneel up to reach it, because the cord was stretched as far as it would go.

Butch growled into the phone. "What now, O'Connor?"

The young convict leaned sideways, not quite getting the phone to his ear. Erika could hear what Sergeant O'Connor was saying. "Butch, why don't you let one or two of your hostages go. It would be easier for you if you didn't have to watch so many all the time."

"Why would you care if it's easier for me or not? Why do you *really* think I should?" Butch asked, his voice steady but edged with anger.

"Because I'm worried about them," came the answer. "It would be easier for you too. Why don't you send the girl out first. You don't need her. In fact, send both women out, then we'll talk some more," Sergeant O'Connor urged.

Erika's heart leaped. She looked at Butch hopefully, but he was still arguing. "You just don't want as many people in here in case you miss when you try to shoot me. I'm keeping all three." Erika's heart sank.

"It'll be dark in a few hours, Butch, and we won't turn the lights back on for you. You'd be just as well off with one hostage because you wouldn't have to worry about where all three were all the time."

"Who's worrying? Maybe I'll just shoot one of them, then I'll have less problems," Butch said, his voice as calm as if he were discussing how he liked his eggs fried. Erika thought she might faint and grabbed the shelf in front of her for support.

"Now Butch, you don't work that way. You told me you only shot Sam because he jerked you around. None of the people in there have given you a hard time, have they?"

"No, but—"

"So, you see, you have no reason to harm them. Please, Butch, send the women out," Sergeant O'Connor said, his voice betraying the deep emotion he was experiencing.

"I don't know about the other two," Butch said after a moment of silence in which his face revealed uncertainty and gave Erika a renewed surge of hope. "I barely know them, but Mrs. Smith was a good teacher. She always did treat me nice when the rest of the town acted like I was dirt."

Erika almost fell to her knees as her hopes were dashed. She glanced at her companions. If either one of them was listening to the conversation, they certainly didn't betray their feelings. Both of them were staring at the floor, their faces blank. It isn't fair, she thought. If only one goes, it should be the youngest.

Her!

Butch was still wrestling with the problem, holding the phone by his side, scowling. Erika wiped her face with her sleeve. It was getting terribly hot. Mrs. Smith looked up. "Butch," she said softly, "let Erika go. She doesn't even know you. She's so young."

Erika dropped her eyes, ashamed to look at Mrs. Smith. She was such an unselfish woman. The sergeant's voice came over the line again. Butch stretched the receiver toward his ear as the officer said, "Okay, Butch, have it your way. Send Mrs. Smith out if you want to."

"No!" Erika cried.

Butch ignored her. "Okay, okay . . . she can go . . . but the other two stay," he said.

Erika felt dizzy. She was about to say something when Butch pushed her rudely out of the way and grabbed Mrs. Smith by the arm. He shoved the older lady roughly toward the front of the store. "Go on, Mrs. Smith, and get out before I change my mind," he ordered gruffly.

She looked at him, opened her mouth, and snapped it shut again when he said, "Go, and keep your mouth shut. This is your last chance."

She went. Her hand fumbled with the lock but she finally got it to turn, and a moment later she was whisked behind a car by an officer. Butch spoke into the phone. "Okay, Sergeant, now what are you going to do for me?"

"Gee, Butch, I don't know. I can't believe you really let her go. That's great. Thank you. I guess I do owe you something in return. I tell you what, I'll have the power turned back on in a couple of hours so it won't get so hot in there. How about Erika now? Don't you think you should send her out too?"

"Please," Erika begged, too ashamed to look at Ken.

"No!" Butch said firmly. "She stays."

"Butch," Erika said, her voice breaking. "May I at least talk to Sergeant O'Connor? I want to make sure my family's okay."

Butch stared at her, then his face softened ever so slightly. "The girl wants to talk to you, O'Connor. I'll be listening, so don't try anything cute." He shoved the phone at her.

"Sergeant O'Connor, is my family okay?" she asked as she began to sob.

"They're safe, Erika. I sent some men after them. They're worried about you of course." He could hear her sobbing and almost lost control of his own voice. Finally, he was able to say, "I'm sorry about this Erika, but Butch won't hurt you as long as you don't make him angry."

Butch grabbed the phone. "You don't know any such thing, O'Connor," he shouted and slammed the receiver down. He whirled and ordered, "Both of you sit down!"

They obeyed and sat quietly for several minutes. Erika sobbed intermittently as Butch fidgeted nervously with his little pistol.

It was getting very hot. The sun was beating unmercifully through the big windows. Ken finally spoke. "This jacket has got to go." He slipped off the bright yellow windbreaker he was wearing.

Erika, following his lead, removed the jacket portion of her sweats. Butch watched her, a new look in his eyes as he took in the T-shirt with moist brown skin exposed beneath it. She untied her black Reeboks and pulled them off, then wiggled out of the bottom half of her sweats.

"Mm," Butch said softly, admiring her long brown legs.

She was suddenly embarrassed, and began to pull the pants back on, but the anger that twisted Butch's face changed her mind. She heard her mother's voice in her memory: "Way too short!" For the first time she understood, but it was too late now.

Tugging at the shorts as if they would somehow grow longer, she pulled her bare knees to her chin and trembled. "You're really very pretty, Erika," Butch said in a voice that added new terror to her heart. "Isn't she, Ken?"

"Uh huh," the truck driver answered awkwardly, not sure what else to say and worrying about his immature cohostage. He didn't like the way Butch leered at her.

But then Butch looked away from her toward the front of the store and said, "Go lock the door, Ken. And don't even think about trying to leave. This gun may be small, but its bullets go where I want them to." He waved the pistol in Ken's face as the truck driver got slowly to his feet.

After the door was locked, another few minutes of tense silence passed, Butch's eyes straying far too frequently to Erika. She pulled herself into as tight a ball as she could, angry at herself for taking off the sweats. Suddenly, Butch addressed her. "Erika." She looked up and found herself looking directly into his pale green eyes. The intensity of his cold stare held her as he asked, "Did you drive a car here to the store?"

"Yes," she answered, unnerved by the power of his gaze. She began talking quickly, an almost involuntary response to the way her nerves were unraveling. "I left my family without a car at the campground where we were staying, but Sergeant O'Connor had one of his men bring them to town, so they're okay now. Dad probably wants the car, though. It's a new Ford Expedition, and I think he was more worried about it than me when he let me come to town alone."

Ken said, "Now Erika, you know that's not true. Oh, I'm sure he likes his Expedition, but nothing is more important to a dad than his kids. Believe me, I know. I have two of my own." For the first time, Erika sensed a fleeting betrayal of emotion in Ken's voice.

"I know," she answered quickly. "I didn't mean that like it sounded, but he does like it. He's wanted one ever since they first came out. He waxes it every Saturday." She paused, then said, "I wondered if you had kids. You look married." She wasn't sure why she said *that*. Maybe it was because she just felt the need to keep talking.

Ken chuckled. "I'm glad I look married, because my wife would be jealous if I didn't. My kids are five and nine. I'm glad they don't know where I am right now because they'd be awfully worried, and so would Susan. That's my wife. Not that you're treating us badly," he said, turning to Butch, "but they're mighty protective of me. They're really a good family."

"I never had much of a family myself," Butch said, the remembrance of distant hurts reflected in his pale eyes. "My family was in a car wreck when I was seven. Mom and my little sister were killed. I wasn't hurt at all, but Dad was, and it left him crippled and with a badly scarred face." Butch's face twisted at the painful memory. "He couldn't work after that, so we lived off welfare. Everybody always made fun of me because my dad looked funny and couldn't walk very well."

"I'm sorry, Butch," Erika said, moved by his sad story. "I guess I've never appreciated what I had very much."

"Oh, it doesn't matter anymore," he said, the hardness seeping back into his features. "I just have a few scores to settle, then it doesn't really matter what happens to me."

"Sure it matters, Butch," Ken said. Erika could see that the truck driver was also moved by Butch's tragic story. "You're very bright, and I see a good heart under that tough exterior of yours."

Butch shrugged his shoulders and Erika asked, "What did your father do without you after you left home, Butch? He must have missed you a lot."

"After I left home . . . You mean after they hauled me off and locked me up, don't you?"

"Didn't you leave before that?" she asked.

"No. I stayed and took care of him. I was twenty when I had to shoot that pair." His eyes locked on Erika's face with intensity again. "I really don't know what Dad did, but I guess he got by. He didn't write very often because his hands hurt too much, and I didn't either because I knew he was ashamed of me."

"Why was he ashamed of you?" Erika asked innocently.

"Because I killed those two people. He didn't understand why I had to do it."

"Tell us about it, Butch," Ken said.

"Do you really want to know?" he asked with a suspicious glance at Ken.

"Yes, I do."

"And so do I, Butch. Please tell us about it," Erika added. She was beginning to wonder if maybe there was more to it than Sergeant O'Connor had told her that morning in the diner. She remembered him saying that he never did figure out why Butch killed them. Maybe nobody ever asked him. She remembered Sam this morning and shuddered inwardly. It didn't add up, but . . .

Butch squinted, as if trying to remember exactly what had happened; then, after wiping the dripping sweat from his face, he said, "They were strangers. They were just passing through town. They were in here when I brought Dad that day. Dad was standing up there," he said, pointing toward the front of the cashier's stand. "He was looking at the magazines while I came back here to get what we needed.

"I didn't see them walk in, but I heard one of them say, 'Hey, old man, get your hideous face out of our way.' It was the guy that said it, but the girl laughed. Dad, he just stood there like he didn't hear them. He'd gotten that way over the years—ignoring people I mean. Well, this guy—he was long-haired and greasy looking—he just walked over to Dad and jerked the magazine out of his hand and said, 'I think I'll have this one.' The girl laughed again. She was filthy. Had on a pair of round glasses and a long dress. It came clear to her ankles. A real plain Jane, that's what she was."

Butch looked toward Erika. "Looked like a witch compared to you," he said without a trace of humor on his face.

The compliment frightened her, but she forced a smile. "Go on," she urged.

"Well, I don't think they'd seen me, or if they did, they didn't realize I was with Dad. I shouted at them and told them to leave him alone, but then the girl, she just walked over and bumped him with her shoulder, real mean-like. He fell because his legs were so bad and he'd put his cane against the counter. The guy laughed." Butch growled, his pale eyes flashing with hatred. "Can you believe that? The girl, she laughed again. Sam was right there. He should have slapped her or something, but he didn't do anything. He just watched."

"What did you do then, Butch?" Erika asked, her eyes glued to his face.

"Nothing."

"Nothing? They did that to your father and you did nothing? They had no right to do that!" Erika said indignantly. "You should have done something."

"I walked over and helped Dad stand up. I told them they shouldn't have done that, but they just laughed again. Sam, he told me to forget it. He said they were just *funning* Dad, so I put the stuff I had in my hands on the counter, handed Dad his cane, took him by the arm, and left," he said.

"That's awful, Butch. You should—" she started, but Butch wasn't finished.

"After we got home, I told Dad that I was going to go ask them to come apologize to him. He didn't want me to, but I went anyway. I found them just outside of town at the park by the highway. I was driving our old truck, and I drove right up to their van. They were in the back with the doors open—smoking pot. I told them I'd come to take them to my house to apologize to my dad. They told me to get lost, so I reached behind the seat, got my shotgun and shot them," he said calmly.

Ken had a hard time talking, but managed to stammer, "Sounds—sounds like they were real . . . uh . . . bad ones."

"They were that alright, but Sergeant O'Connor and the rest of the town didn't care."

"Even when you told them what they did to your father?" Erika asked in dismay.

"I never told them. I never told any of them anything. It wouldn't have done any good. They figured I did it and that was that. And I did, but they never would have understood. Me and Dad, we were just dirt," he said, his eyes burning with hatred. "But old Sam, he saw it all—in the store, that is." He looked directly into Erika's eyes and said, "And he never told a soul."

"Oh!" Erika gasped.

"He could have come to court, but he didn't. He just pretended it never happened. Didn't even tell anybody they'd been in this place."

Butch was apparently at the end of his story. Erika felt sorry for him in a way, and yet she couldn't imagine how he could shoot them over something like that, awful as it was. Butch kept rubbing his mouth like he was thirsty. "Want a drink?" she asked at last, just to break the awkward silence.

"Sure, a Coke," Butch said.

She got to her feet, uncomfortably conscious of his admiring eyes on her trim figure as she stepped the few feet to the cooler. She wondered what would keep him from committing other terrible crimes, and she wished she hadn't been so foolish as to remove her sweats. He frightened her in ways that stirred the bile in her stomach.

"They're still cool," she said, having a difficult time keeping her voice from betraying the fear she was experiencing. She could feel drops of sweat running down her legs and arms as she grabbed two of the Cokes. "How about you, Mr. Feldman?" she asked.

"I guess I'll have a Sprite," he said without enthusiasm.

She handed Ken the cool green bottle, then stepped past him, handed Butch a Coke and then began to sit down beside Ken. "I'm hungry," she said after a couple of sips from her bottle and stood up again. She picked up a bag of potato chips, opened it as she carried it back, sat down beside Ken again, and began munching.

She held the bag toward Ken, but he waved them away. "What about me?" Butch demanded, and she slid the bag submissively across the floor toward him. It was getting oppressively hot. Beads of moisture stood out on her skin. She reached over Ken, grabbed her sweats, and used them as a towel, rubbing her skin vigorously, but she didn't get dry. It was just too hot.

"Where did you park your dad's car?" Butch asked, watching her as she wiped at the moisture on her face.

"Outside," she said, wondering why he wanted to know. She dropped the sweats down and took another drink of her Coke.

"You have the keys?" Butch asked.

Erika gasped. She knew what was coming, and she didn't like it. She said nothing.

"The keys!" Butch demanded. "Where are they?" He waved the gun at her threateningly.

"They're . . . they're, uh, in my purse," she said.

"Get them," he ordered. "Let's go for a ride. I want to get out of here. It's too hot," he said, scrambling to his feet but keeping his head low. He stepped near Erika and offered her his hand. She hesitated, and he pointed the gun at her head. "Get up!"

Tears stung her eyes. She suddenly realized that she was in the hands of a killer and helpless to do anything about it. She had no choice but to do as he said. Slowly, she forced herself to her feet, and as soon as she was standing, Butch grabbed her roughly by the arm and shoved her in front of him, and then rose to his full height. He then looked down at Ken. "You're going too," he ordered brusquely, waving the pistol in his face.

"I'd just as soon stay," Ken said with a forced smile as he got to his feet.

Erika sensed a change in Ken. He was acting like he wasn't worried, but she knew he was. Like her, she supposed Butch's story made him wonder how much or how little it would take to provoke another act of violence.

Butch ordered Ken ahead of him. "Put your shoes on, Erika," he said. She bent over, retrieved them, and soon had them on and was tying the laces. Butch studied the scene outside while she did so, shielding himself behind Ken. "O'Connor has sharpshooters out there," he said after a minute. "I'd swear they weren't there before. We're going anyway. They won't shoot and take a chance of hurting you two, so you'll be my shields."

"Oh," Erika moaned. "Please don't, Butch," she added, her heart racing with fear.

Ken looked back at her and said, "We'll be okay, Erika." But there was little conviction in his voice and his eyes were filled with anger, something she hadn't seen in them before. She found herself hoping he didn't say something to set Butch off. But he said nothing more, just stared toward the front of the store.

Butch shoved him lightly in the back with the pistol barrel and said, "You're going first, Ken. And don't try anything stupid." Then he turned to Erika and asked, "Is the Expedition locked or unlocked?"

"I . . . I . . . I think I locked it. Dad always makes us lock it," she stammered.

Butch was deep in thought for a few seconds, then he said, "Here's what we'll do. Ken, you walk ahead of Erika. She'll have one hand on your belt. I'll be to your right and will stay low and between the two of you and the store. The gun will be in your ribs, Ken, so don't try anything."

He continued, "When we reach the front door, Ken will unlock it and push it open and we'll go out. We turn to the right. Erika, don't you let any daylight between you and him. I'll be right with you. Stop at the corner of the building and I'll look for sharpshooters out that way. If there aren't any, we'll go to Erika's car the same way, only I will be walking ahead of the two of you. Erika, don't let go of his belt."

This was sounding worse all the time. Erika began to sob uncontrollably as she said, "I won't, Butch."

"Quit bawling," he growled. "And make sure you have the keys in your hand before we leave. It will be your job to unlock the door. We'll go to the passenger side. You did pull the car in forward, didn't you?" he demanded. "I mean it, quit bawling!"

Erika fought back the sobs as the gun was waved in her face again. She couldn't believe she'd soon be in a car going who knew where with a hardened killer. She controlled the sobs but not the trembling in her legs. "What about it, girl. Did you pull in forward?" he shouted.

She nodded, tears still stinging her eyes.

Ken said softly, "You don't have to shout at her, Butch."

Butch jabbed the gun violently into Ken's ribs, causing him to double over with pain. "Don't hassle me, man," he threatened, "or I'll have one less hostage. You hear me?"

Butch had a wild look in his eyes. Ken, groaning with pain, said, "Okay, you win. I'll keep my mouth shut."

"Now," Butch continued, "when the door is open, Erika gets in first. She'll drive. Erika, you unlock the back door and I'll climb in there. I'll go backwards so I can keep my gun on you," he said, jabbing Ken again. "Then you get in beside Erika and we leave. Any questions?"

"I . . . I . . . don't think so," Erika sobbed.

"You better have it," Butch said, looking up in surprise as the lights came on and the air-conditioning started humming. "Well, can you believe this; good old Sergeant O'Connor just had the power turned on, now that we don't need it anymore."

The phone rang.

"Let's go," Butch ordered, shoving Ken forward.

"But the phone—" Ken started.

"Forget it and unlock the door," Butch hissed, again jabbing the barrel of the gun into Ken's bruised ribs.

They moved slowly toward the front of the store, the ringing phone adding tension to the already charged atmosphere. Ken easily flipped the lock, pushed the door, and they exited into the bright, early afternoon sunlight.

Butch kept low and Erika was careful to stay close behind Ken. "That's a girl," Ken whispered back at her. "Just stay calm."

She said nothing, and they moved slowly and carefully toward the corner of the building. Erika could see their reflections in the window, distorted and illusory. Across the street, Sergeant O'Connor was leaning across the hood of his truck, his big revolver in his hand. He had a half-grin on his face. She was puzzled. How could he be smiling? She was terrified.

When they reached the end of the store, Ken, who was the first to peek around it, asked, "Where's the Expedition, Erika?"

Butch cursed and Erika had a sinking feeling in the pit of her stomach. Butch peered around. "It's not there! You said you left it there, Erika!" he growled, and this time she felt the wrath of the gun barrel in her ribs, doubling her over.

When she got her breath back, she cried out, "Somebody's taken it!"

"No kidding!" Butch said with disgust. Erika was crying. "Shut up!" he ordered. Then he swore, and Erika recoiled. She wasn't used to hearing bad language. It didn't exist in her home, and her boyfriend, Bob, loathed it. "Let's get back inside. We'll just have to make them bring us a car. Unless they want one of you dead. Slowly now, back up, but don't turn around," he said, turning himself while staying well protected beside his hostages.

Erika was terrified. What if one of the cops fired a shot? She could be killed! Her fear was not only of Butch, but of the police . . . they were everywhere.

It seemed like an eternity before they were back to the door. Butch reached out and began to pull it open. In that brief moment of distraction,

Ken grabbed the gun, trying to wrench it from him. Butch let go of the door and struggled for control of his weapon. As the two wrestled for the pistol, they twisted so violently that Erika lost her grip on Ken's belt.

"Run girl, run!" Ken shouted.

She tried to, but her legs buckled beneath her. She fell, struggled to her feet, and again Ken shouted. "Now! Run Erika."

At that moment, the gun discharged. Glass shattered. Someone screamed and the world began to spin. She fell against the building. She thought she would black out.

"Inside!" she heard Butch shouting. She tried to concentrate. Where was Ken? Through a mist of tears she saw him running across the street, the gun in his hands. She felt Butch pulling her to her feet and tight against him as another shot rang out. The glass door disintegrated in front of her terrified eyes.

Butch was pulling her through the shattered door. "Cease fire!" Sergeant O'Connor was shouting. "Don't shoot; you might hit the girl!"

There were no more shots, and before she knew it, Butch had pulled her to the floor in the back aisle. He was fumbling with a pant leg. He pulled it up. Reaching into the top of his boot, he pulled out a small, shiny black revolver.

He was laughing. "They thought they had me. Well, Ken can have that gun if he wants it so badly. I've got this," he said with a smirk, waving the little Smith and Wesson .38 revolver in front of her face. "It's smaller but packs a bigger punch than that one. Just doesn't hold as many bullets, but it has enough."

He reached over the top of the counter and another shot, much more deafening than those from the gun he'd lost, echoed through the store. Erika's ears were ringing. "There, they know I have it," he said with a spiteful laugh.

Then he waved the gun in Erika's face. "Stand up!" he ordered. "See what's happening out there." He was roaring with laughter, but for Erika there was no humor in this terrible situation.

She pulled herself up on shaking legs and peered over the counter. She spotted Ken's dark head over the top of Sergeant O'Connor's police truck. Several officers were kneeling beside someone on the sidewalk. Another officer came running with a first-aid kit in his hand. A large TV camera was being set up a short distance down the sidewalk.

"Someone's hurt," she sobbed. She didn't mention the camera, afraid it might cause his anger to return.

"Is it Ken?" he asked, still chuckling.

"I . . . I think . . . it's a policeman."

"Must of hit him when I fired the pistol."

Erika couldn't believe the scene displayed before her eyes. The glass was broken out of the windshield of Sergeant O'Connor's truck, and several officers now huddled over the one that lay on the sidewalk beside the truck.

"Can you see O'Connor?" Butch asked, his laughter suddenly ceasing.

"No."

"Ha. Maybe it's him that's down. Maybe I finally evened the score."

Erika's legs wouldn't hold her up any longer and she sank to the floor—in blood! She gasped, wondering why she didn't hurt. She glanced at Butch. "You're bleeding!" she cried in relief when she saw the blood wasn't hers.

His fingers were tentatively exploring a nasty gash high in his left shoulder. "O'Connor's sharpshooters aren't so good, are they? They barely even nicked me," he said with a chuckle.

The blood pouring from his wound was making her ill. She felt like she had to throw up. She gagged. "That is not a nick," she heard herself saying.

"Well, do something," he ordered, "unless you want a bullet too!"

She choked back the vomit in her throat and tried to think and act rationally. She began by trying to roll the ruined shirt sleeve out of the way. His arm was too husky. "You'll have to tear it off," he said calmly.

She did, but with some effort. The activity made her feel better. "Put some pressure on the wound," Butch ordered. His face was pasty white. She spotted Ken's jacket and her sweats. She chose the jacket, which she pressed tightly against the bloody wound. For several minutes she held it snugly in place. Her arms throbbed.

"Check it, Erika," Butch said after a few minutes. She carefully removed the jacket and, when she did, the blood began to slowly ooze from the wound again.

"Not good enough," he growled.

"It was stopped," she reported in frustration, "but began again when I pulled the cloth away."

"You've got to put a bandage of some kind on and tie it in place," he said, his face grimaced with pain. "There's got to be a first-aid kit in here somewhere. Go look," he said. "I'll hold this jacket in place while you go see. And don't even think of trying to get away."

Erika found one in the storage room. Beside it was a door.

A door to the outside.

A door to freedom.

She looked back, hoping he hadn't followed her. Relieved, she slid the bolt back and put a bloody hand on the knob.

"Don't even think it."

She whirled. Butch was kneeling in the door, the pistol pointed unsteadily at her. "You will never get away from me! Never!"

Despair and fear overwhelmed Erika. She had tried to run when Ken shouted for her to, but she couldn't. She had tried to open the door, but Butch was there. She cried again, but Butch's cold voice dried the tears. "Bolt the door."

She did as he ordered, numbed with hopelessness.

"Now, get the first-aid kit."

She jerked it off the wall and dropped to the floor. "Get back out here," he ordered. "You're my lookout, and you can't see anything from in there."

She followed him numbly, thinking of her family crying and worrying over her. And Bob! Her handsome blonde boyfriend was probably surfing right now, his golden hair plastered to his head from the briny spray of the surf, a cheerful grin covering his face from ear to ear. What if she never saw him again? What if Butch killed her?

Impulsively, she shoved the thoughts from her mind and tried to be hopeful. She had so much to live for. She just had to survive this ordeal. She had to see Bob again. She couldn't die in this terrible place. She hated Butch, but she had to help him. And then, after she did, maybe he'd let her go, she thought hopefully—but the thought fled as quickly as it had come.

Erika dropped to her knees, opened the blue first-aid kit and began searching for large compresses. In a few minutes she had the shoulder bandaged. It wasn't great, but it would have to do.

"It feels better already," Butch said weakly, inspecting the bandage. "You'd make a good nurse."

"You look awful, Butch, but there's nothing more I can do," she told him.

"You can clean me up. Make me presentable. After all, I'm in the presence of a beautiful woman."

In the strangest way, that compliment touched her, but it did nothing to ease her tension. She crawled to the rest room that was just beyond the door with the bloody knob. She hesitated, looked at it. She thought about trying to get away one more time. But fear filled her whole body at the thought, and she simply went on, grabbed a handful of paper towels and wet them in the sink. When she left the rest room, there he was in the doorway to the storage room, his pale eyes watching her every move. "Just wanted to make sure you didn't try to leave," he said, and he waved her back into the front with the gun.

Without a word she moved with him into the aisle, and for the next few minutes she wiped the blood from him the best she could. She remembered seeing a mop in the storage room and she soon had the floor looking fairly good.

"Clean yourself up," Butch said after she'd finished.

"I'm okay," she said.

"Clean up!" he ordered more firmly.

"Okay," she agreed, not wanting to make him mad. She grabbed her sweats and looked around for her purse. It was gone.

"My purse. I need my purse, Butch," she moaned. "I must have dropped it outside."

"Forget the purse," he said curtly.

"But my comb and makeup are in my purse," she said in confusion.

"Just wash the blood off your legs and hands, Erika. It's making me sick. Move it, girl. Wash up. I'll be watching."

Butch struggled to his feet. He stood unsteadily, stooping so that just the top of his head—from his eyes up—showed over the white of the shelves, but he held the gun on her. "Hurry, before I pass out," he urged.

She started again for the rest room. She shivered a little, thinking of her sweats and wishing they were on—wishing that Butch would quit looking at her the way he was.

A shot rang out and a huge section of window shattered into a million glittering pieces, hitting the floor with a resounding crash. Butch dropped and Erika screamed. He was stunned from the bullet that had grazed the top of his head, sending a stream of blood down the side of his face and filling his ear.

She had another chance.

"Run girl, run," a voice said in her mind.

She stood. Stepped past him. Began walking gingerly through the fresh blood on the floor. *I'm going. I can do it if I keep going. It's over.* Just a few more steps and she'd finally be free of Butch and the terror he'd caused.

"Don't!"

She froze. That voice was not from inside her head. She slowly turned. Butch was no longer stunned, and his deadly weapon was pointed at her head. The look on his face was frigid and pitiless. His power over her was relentless. In despair, she sunk slowly to the floor, overcome with grief and fear.

***

"Why didn't she come?" Ken Feldman groaned. "She had another chance. Why didn't she run the first time, when I told her to?"

He was feeling guilty. He had gotten away but she hadn't. Sergeant O'Connor had explained how her legs had buckled, but it didn't help. This time Sergeant O'Connor didn't have an answer. He was sure Butch had been hit. She had started to leave, then she'd looked back, hesitated, and dropped out of sight to the floor. It didn't make sense. Butch must not have been hurt badly. Tears stung the crusty cop's eyes. Ken Feldman wiped his own.

"You better go now," Mike said. "Your family will be waiting."

***

Butch slid over to where Erika sat sobbing, her head between her knees. With his good arm, he reached around her shoulder and pulled her to him. She was repulsed but had neither the courage nor the strength to resist. "I'm sorry, Erika," the young killer said softly. "I'd let you go if I could. Don't you see that? But I need you. You're all I have. Without you they'd kill me."

She looked up and slowly turned toward him. His pale green eyes, those that usually flashed with signals of hatred, were now dulled with pain. Blood from the wound on his head was slowly seeping down his forehead into his eyebrows. Erika had never feared anything in this world as she feared this man. And yet she felt a fleeting touch of pity.

His eyes held hers. She tried to turn away, but there was a power there that she could not understand. He spoke again, his voice low and choked with pain. "I can't let you go, Erika. I need you."

She forced herself to speak. "I'm no good to you, Butch. Please. Let me go. You have your gun."

He shook his head. "I can't let you go. Not ever. That's why I'd hurt you if I had to. You can understand that, can't you?"

She finally managed to break free of his gaze. She believed him; he could and would hurt her. He was a killer. He was desperate. And she was helpless.

His voice was more harsh as he spoke again. It was like his strength was beginning to return. "Answer me. You can understand why I can't let you go, can't you?"

She nodded, signaling a desperate lie. He was satisfied. Erika was too depressed and afraid to even pray.

CHAPTER 4

Huge breakers, some six to eight feet high, pounded the southern California coastline, coaxed by a cool, stiff wind. Tall and muscular, Bob Evans surveyed the familiar scene through sea-blue eyes from the redwood deck of his parents' home. As each large wave broke and the foamy water rushed up the sandy beach, more gobs of rubbery green seaweed littered the shoreline.

Glancing upward, Bob judged the approximate time from the position of the burning sun. A grin creased the smooth tan of his face, and he ran a hand through short, wavy locks of windblown, dark-blonde hair. Stretching to his full six feet, three inches, he sauntered down the steps and across the smoothly manicured lawn to a large shed beneath a cluster of tall palm trees. He entered, then waited a moment for his eyes to adjust to the diminished light before stepping past a riding lawn mower and reaching for his surfboard.

Bob always got excited when he headed for the cool, briny water. He had grown up right here on this strip of sunny beach, and there were few who could ride a board with more grace and power than Bob Evans. He had surfed since he was a young boy.

He grinned again as he charged into the foaming water and dropped to his flat, hard belly on the board and began paddling away from the shore. His mind was on one of the prettiest girls he had met in this land of tan beauties. He first saw Erika Leighton right here on the beach several weeks ago, only days after the semester ended at school. By nature, Bob had always been shy, and it usually took coaxing from his friends to get him to ask a girl out. Instantly attracted to Erika, he had mentioned it to his friends, and they immediately set about getting him to call her up.

Bob knew a couple of the girls she was with that day. He had been in an institute class with one of them, and the other he had met at a young singles activity a few weeks earlier. Both girls were over twenty, and he had judged Erika to be the same. He was disappointed to learn that she was just barely out of high school. It took some coaxing from his buddies, but he'd finally given in and dialed her number. He'd found her to be vivacious, fun, and full of life. But at times she seemed even more immature than her eighteen years, even though she looked much older.

Bob probably wouldn't have dated Erika after that first time had it not been for their shared interest in surfing. As it turned out, they spent many hours together at the beach. He felt at ease with her on the waves, even though he never completely shed his natural shyness around her. But he had grown to be quite fond of her. He missed her companionship now, wishing she could be here to enjoy the surf with him. It was as magnificent as he'd seen all summer.

She had sent postcards and kept him up to date on what, from her point of view, was a nearly unbearable trip. He was disappointed that she was so critical of her family, but he convinced himself it was her age and that she would grow out of it.

Bob's mother didn't seem to care for Erika. "I just don't know if Erika is right for you, Bob. You have such serious goals and she is so . . . well . . . immature," she had told him. "You're twenty-two and she's barely out of high school," she had repeated several times. "Beauty is more than skin deep, son," was another of her favorite warnings.

"We're not that serious, Mom," he'd repeatedly told her. "We just both enjoy some of the same things." But he was beginning to realize that, despite her immaturity, theirs was becoming a rather deep friendship.

Bob steadied himself on the board and waited for the next wave. Erika's last card had been postmarked in a place called Pineview, Colorado. He had looked in an almanac, but couldn't find it. He decided it must be a very small place, to Erika's chagrin he was sure. He leaned forward and the powers of nature swept away his thoughts.

The next two hours he spent on and in the water. Some of his friends had joined him, and he had forgotten about Erika. Only when he finally left the cool water and shyly said, "Hi," to several girls that passed by on the beach, did he think about her again. One of his buddies asked when she would be home.

"I don't know. Soon, I hope," he said with a grin.

The TV was blaring in the family room when Bob entered a few minutes later. He stopped and was talking with his mother when his attention was attracted to it. A newsman was saying, "Pineview, Colorado, is the scene of a tense and potentially tragic hostage drama that began early this morning. Two men, including the county sheriff, have been wounded as the drama continues to unfold on an unseasonably hot afternoon in this small town high in the Colorado Rockies."

"Mom, listen to this," Bob said, motioning toward the TV. "That's the town Erika sent her last postcard from."

"Erika, Erika. Is she all you think of, Bob? She just isn't serious enough to ever be a doctor's wife. I sure wish—"

Bob waved her off with a grin and said, "She'll grow up. Life has a way of doing that to people. Anyway she's just a friend, Mom."

"Girlfriend," his mother said.

Bob chuckled. "Yeah, okay, 'girlfriend,' but it's not like we've talked about getting married or anything. Not yet, anyway." He grinned teasingly as his mother rolled her eyes.

Together, they turned their attention to the TV as footage of the scene came on the screen. The camera zeroed in on the shattered glass door of a small convenience store as the CNN newscaster continued: "The lone employee of this store, a seventy-one-year-old Pineview man, was shot at about seven-forty-five this morning. Miraculously, the bullet was stopped by a thick wallet in his shirt pocket, and he escaped with only superficial injuries. His alleged assailant was a desperate man identified by police as one of several inmates who escaped from the Colorado State Prison early last evening. Authorities believe him to be twenty-five-year-old Butch Snyder, a convicted killer who grew up right here in Pineview.

"Three other persons were in the store at the time of the shooting and were taken hostage by the gunman, who was armed with a small-caliber pistol. At this hour only one hostage remains in the store with the suspect." The screen filled with a picture of a police pickup truck with shattered windows.

"One of the hostages, a local woman, was released by Snyder. A short time later, a second hostage, an Oregon truck driver, escaped uninjured during a foiled get-away attempt by Snyder. That scuffle resulted in the single shot that wounded the county sheriff and broke out a couple of windows in his police truck. The escapee forced the other hostage, a teenage girl, back into the store after he had lost his pistol to the escaping hostage."

Bob gasped as the picture on the screen changed again, and a familiar red Ford Expedition, parked in front of a small schoolhouse, appeared. The anchorman droned on. "The gunman still has a weapon. Apparently he was carrying a second small pistol and is still holding the young woman hostage who drove to the store this morning in this California vehicle."

"Mom, that's Jim Leighton's car!" Bob cried in alarm. "Erika's in there with that guy! I've got to do something!" Bob said, his stomach turning somersaults. He felt lightheaded as an almost overwhelming fear gripped him.

"Now, son, you can't be sure—"

"Look, that's her!" he shouted as the camera showed the store and zoomed in on a girl with long, dark hair at the back of the store, only visible over the shelves from her shoulders up.

Bob focused on the anchorman's words. "Moments after this picture was taken a police sharpshooter fired a round at the gunman, who was pointing his gun at the hostage who had moved several feet away from him. He dropped, but so did the girl. It's unknown at this time what the condition of the escaped killer is, but it's assumed he is okay as the girl has not left the building. At this moment officers at the scene are planning their next move in this tense drama. We'll bring you up to date as things develop in this small Colorado town," the anchorman concluded.

Bob stood staring at the set. The anchorman reappeared and said, "Tension continues to build on the West Bank today as rebel Palestinians . . ." Bob shut the TV off and sank into a chair, his damp suit creating a dark stain on the soft tan fabric. His head sank slowly into his hands. He couldn't imagine what Erika must be going through.

"She'll be alright, son. The Lord is watching over her. You just have to have faith," his mother said reassuringly. "You know what a resilient girl she is. She'll manage to come out of it okay. The other two are free and—"

"She's scared to death!" he interrupted, coming to his feet. "I better get up there."

"Bob, what could you possibly do?" his mother asked, her eyes wide with concern. "It would take you hours to get there, and by then it will be long over with. Why son, you don't even know where that place is."

"I love you, Mom, and I appreciate your concern, but I'm going," he said, impulsively kissing her cheek and trotting across the room. He looked back at her from the doorway. "What would Dad do if you were out there?"

"He'd go," she admitted as tears misted her eyes and he disappeared from the room. "But Erika is just a friend," she whispered, realizing the girl had become much more than that to her son. "I'll call the airport and book you a flight," she shouted in motherly concession.

Within minutes he had packed what he needed and headed for his new green Grand Am in the front driveway. His mother gave him instructions on the flight to Denver she had arranged. "You can rent a car there and drive on up," she said as he climbed into the bright green sports car. "I'll let Dad know . . ." she shouted as the car screamed out of the long, curving driveway and sped up the street.

Bob drove fast, through heavy traffic, toward the airport. He had plenty of time before the plane left, but the urgency of Erika's situation pushed him hard, blinding his judgement. The Grand Am had been a present from his affluent parents after he'd returned from his mission and began his second year of college. But he'd never driven it like he was now. Erika's life was in danger, and it felt like his was coming apart.

The radio was on and he flipped from station to station, trying to find any news that might have coverage on the standoff in Colorado. He finally picked one that was about halfway through the story. He listened intently to the now familiar facts as he raced down the freeway.

He finally learned something new, and his heart picked up speed with his racing car. The voice on the radio was intense. "A SWAT team arrived at the scene and attempted to rescue the teenage hostage a short while ago. But they quickly retreated when the gunman fired one round, striking one of the SWAT officers.

"There was no injury to the SWAT officer since the bullet struck his heavy flak jacket. The officers did catch a glimpse of the hostage. She appeared to be uninjured and was sitting just a few feet from the gunman."

Bob turned the radio off, his thoughts on Erika. He had to admit that he cared a great deal for her and would be devastated if anything happened to her. His thoughts were interrupted rudely by the wailing of a siren. He glanced in the rearview mirror. It was filled with the flashing red and blue lights of a California Highway Patrol motorcycle. His eyes dropped to the speedometer. It read 85 mph! He knew he was going too fast, but eighty-five? He wondered, as he applied pressure to the brake pedal, what else could possibly go wrong.

Bob was as tight as an overinflated balloon as the officer, removing his gloves, approached the door. "You must have some kind of big emergency, buster," the trooper said gruffly. Bob's distorted face was reflected in the officer's mirrored glasses.

"Well, actually, I guess I do, sir," Bob answered tensely. "My girlfriend is being held hostage by a gunman in Colorado, and I'm trying to catch a plane to the airport so I can—"

"That's the best one I've heard in a long time," the officer interrupted with a chuckle. "I'm afraid the little gal is just going to have to enjoy the company of her captor a little longer while I write you a ticket for speeding."

Bob could see that it would do no good to argue, and his story did sound rather preposterous. He had never received a ticket before, though, and mentioned that fact to the patrolman as he fished in his wallet for his driver's license.

"I'm sure," the officer said. "Most young fellows who drive sporty new cars *never* exceed the posted speed limit," he chuckled, "which, by the way, is sixty-five here."

Bob bristled. He usually had a pretty cool head, but today was turning out to be anything but usual. "Please, just write the ticket and let me get on my way. And when you watch the news tonight and see that a girl from San Diego is being held hostage in Pineview, Colorado, please remember that I told you so. And look up my driving record if you like. I'm not one who makes it a practice to lie!" he said hotly.

The officer looked him over, pushing his glasses up on his forehead. Dark-brown eyes displayed surprise. After studying Bob's face a moment longer, he turned the license over in his hand a couple of times and said, "I'm sorry, young fellow. I didn't mean to offend you, but your story does seem a bit far-fetched, now doesn't it?"

"Yes, sir, but please hurry. Erika's in real trouble and I have a plane to catch."

The trooper gave him another doubtful glance, then handed the license back. "You just better not be pulling one on me, young man," he said.

"Thank you, Officer," Bob said gratefully. "I promise, I am telling the truth."

"Slow down," the trooper commanded with a grin as Bob pulled away.

He was more careful the rest of the way to the airport, and forty-five minutes later he was boarding a Boeing 737 bound for Denver. Later, his thoughts were jumbled as the big plane raced through the cloudless sky, high above the sweltering desert. What was he going to do when he got to Pineview if the situation wasn't resolved by then? Would Erika even be there still? He had no idea. He would just have to take things one step at a time.

He thought about Erika, and his mind became more focused. In all honesty, he had initially been attracted by her looks, but she was a good surfer and enjoyed many of the same things he did. Of course, she would be going to the University of California at Berkeley this fall; and he would begin his junior year at the San Diego campus of the University of California—studying premedicine. He would miss her, but on the other hand, maybe college would mature her. Maybe what she was going through right now was forcing her to mature *far beyond* her years.

His thoughts were increasingly disturbed. Erika was in a terribly dangerous situation. She could be killed or seriously injured. The thought tore at his heart. Why should such an innocent girl be a hostage at the mercy of an evil and desperate man? Bob wiped his sweaty brow as the cool air from the small vent above him gently blew on his tortured face.

He closed his eyes and prayed fervently for her. He knew that only God could give Erika what she needed now. And Bob pleaded that He would deliver her safely.

CHAPTER 5

Somber darkness enveloped the little town of Pineview, but the area around the Quick Stop was brightly lit. Powerful floodlights surrounded the store. It was Sheriff Lyght's intent to make it very difficult for Butch to get any rest, hoping that by wearing him down physically he might eventually relent and release his young hostage.

"Sheriff, you ought to go home and get some rest, or at least let us find you a bed here in town," Sergeant Mike O'Connor suggested. He was watching his good friend and boss grimace with pain as he shifted his lanky frame in a hard chair, trying to find the most comfortable position possible.

"You're just as tired as I am, Mike. I'll stick it out," the sheriff said wearily.

"Maybe, but I didn't get clipped by a bullet either. Are you sure the shoulder's okay?"

"Yes. It hurts a little, but the EMT said there was no serious damage. I'll survive, so quit fussing."

"Okay, have it your way, Alden. I'll be glad to have you here. You make the big money, so you really should be making the big decisions," Mike quipped with a grin.

Sheriff Lyght had been behind Sergeant O'Connor's pickup when Ken Feldman made his break, and the little .25-caliber bullet had passed through the windows of the truck before creasing his left shoulder. He had also sustained several small cuts on his face from flying glass. The sheriff had been treated by EMTs at the scene, stubbornly refusing any further aid.

Sheriff Lyght squirmed again in the unforgiving chair and said, "Mike, I sure wish I knew what that Leighton girl was thinking right now. She must be scared to death." He pulled a large handkerchief from a pocket and blew his nose, folded it carefully back up and, wincing with pain, stuffed it back where it came from. "Why don't you try another phone call to Butch. I'm sure he won't stick his head up where we can see it again unless the girl is right beside him, but maybe we can at least learn if he's had any change of heart."

"All right, I'll give it another go," Mike said, reaching for the phone.

The phone at the Quick Stop rang and rang. Sheriff Lyght finally commented, "The sound of it carrying on over there ought to annoy him before long, and then maybe he'll answer it."

It rang for another couple of minutes, but it was Erika who finally stood, brushed a long, dark lock of hair away from her face, and lifted the receiver to her ear. Her "Hello, this is Erika," sounded weak and discouraged.

"It'll be okay, Erika," Mike said gently. "We'll get you out of there."

"No you won't," she said, her voice stronger. "Butch said to tell you he'll kill me if you don't let us leave together. Please, Sergeant, get him a car. He'll let me go later if you just let us get out of here. I don't want to die."

Mike shook his head and shot the sheriff a look of concern. Ignoring her plea, he said, "Are you okay, Erika?"

"I'm not hurt, if that's what you mean." She paused and looked behind her at where, Mike supposed, Butch was sitting. "He says to tell you he's running out of patience. He says he's tired of the way you're jerking him around. He says I'll get hurt if you don't give him a car."

"I'd like to talk to him, Erika," Mike said. "Hand him the phone."

Through his binoculars he watched her turn. He listened to her over the line as she spoke to Butch. "He says to give you the phone." Mike could hear Butch in the background, but couldn't make out what he was saying. When Erika lifted the phone to her ear again, she said, "Butch said to tell you to go to . . . well, you know what he means. He says that one of your police snipers might get lucky and he's not going to give them that chance."

"Erika, tell him that we don't plan on giving him a car. It's time he lets you go and gives himself up."

"No!" she cried. "He'll kill me. Please—"

Suddenly, Erika fell out of sight, screaming, and he could hear the sound of the phone as it struck the floor and bounced. A moment later, while she was still screaming, the phone clicked. "He hung it up," Mike reported with a long face. "And he may have hurt her. Now what do we do? He just might do something to her if we don't get him a car."

The officers discussed her plight. "If we give him the car, we may never see her alive again," Sheriff Lyght worried aloud.

"And if we don't, who knows what he might do."

A young female trooper stepped into the office as they debated. Her shoulder-length, auburn hair was tied back in a severe bun. One stray lock fell across her cheek, her round face accentuated by hazel eyes, dark eyebrows, a pert nose, and small mouth. That mouth was pulled into a worried frown as she waved a greeting to the men.

"Jan, how are you?" Mike said, his face brightening a little at the sight of the young officer.

"I'm fine," she replied. "How are things over there?" she asked, pointing toward the Quick Stop.

"They could be better, Trooper," the sheriff said with a grimace. "Would you do something for us?"

"That's why I'm here. Sorry I wasn't here sooner, but I've been out of town. I just drove in a few minutes ago. When I saw all the ruckus I called in. Dispatch told me to put my uniform on and get down here and see if I could help," she said as a smile, accentuated with dazzling white teeth, replaced the frown.

"The family of the girl over there," he said, pointing across the street, "is at the motel. Would you go check on them and see if there's anything else we can do for them? They're in room eight."

"I sure will," she said cheerfully, then her face suddenly became very sober and a hand went to her cheek. It was a familiar gesture unique to Trooper Jan Hallinan. "Is it true what I heard? Is it really Butch Snyder over there?" She paused and her eyes glistened. Then she asked, "Isn't that the killer you told me about, Mike?"

"Sure is," Mike agreed.

"Why don't you fill her in before she leaves," Sheriff Lyght suggested, "while I think about our options."

Mike nodded and stepped outside. Jan followed. "Shouldn't he be in bed?" Jan asked after Mike had led her a few feet up the sidewalk from the insurance office.

"He's a tough man," Mike responded, then quickly brought Jan up to date on the situation.

"This is awful," she remarked with a shudder. "The girl's parents must be terrified."

"To say the least," Mike agreed.

"Well, I'll go talk to them," Jan said. "I just hope I can help." She turned up the street.

"Oh, yeah, and by the way, they're LDS," he informed her.

She smiled over her shoulder. "Good. Maybe that'll make this easier. Thanks for clueing me in."

Mike watched her for a moment after she started away. She walked quickly, athletically, he thought. About five-foot-six, Jan was deceptively small and pretty. She was much stronger than she looked. He wondered, as he often had, why some young man hadn't put a ring on her finger. Of course, she was LDS in a town with only a couple of LDS families. She drove thirty miles to church and did so faithfully. Everyone who knew her knew she took her religion seriously. He knew she'd dated one or two men who weren't of her faith, but never more than a few times. Someone would come along. Jan deserved the best.

Mike turned back to the office and found that the sheriff was dozing in his chair. Clearly he hadn't come to any solution. Mike sat down on the step in the front of the office and watched the brightly lit scene before him, mentally reviewing where every officer was posted. In addition to the county officers and state troopers present, a smartly dressed SWAT team had arrived and taken positions several hours earlier.

The walkie-talkie on his belt crackled and Mike grabbed it. It was the commander of the SWAT team. "I'd like to talk to you and the sheriff for a minute," he said crisply. "I have a plan that will end this prolonged standoff."

"Come on over," Mike said, hoping it was a good idea. He would certainly welcome one at this point. He was tired and worn from the stress and heat of the day, and he wasn't sure how much more delay

Butch would tolerate before doing something serious to his hostage. On the other hand, Butch wasn't stupid, and Mike was sure Butch knew that if he injured or killed Erika, it would all be over for him.

Mike never questioned the sheriff's judgement in asking for the help of a SWAT team, but he had to admit that they made him nervous. They carried more gear on their persons than he had in the box in the back of his truck. And the way they said, "Yes, sir," and snapped to attention reminded him of his years in the military. And their hotshot commander had left a negative impression on Mike from the moment of his arrival. Maybe he was just too easygoing, too much of a country cop and would never feel at home around his urban colleagues.

"Sergeant." Mike snapped out of his somber reverie as the SWAT commander joined him. "Let's go in and talk to the sheriff."

"This will be fine right here, Lieutenant Coffers," Mike said easily.

"Now you listen here, Sergeant," the commander said with emphasis on the *sergeant*.

"I'm listening," Mike said, beginning to bristle at the tone of the young commander's voice.

"This needs to be a *command level* decision." Mike's eyes drifted to the bars on the lieutenant's collar. They represented a higher rank than his chevrons, but Coffers was a guest here, and that gave Mike more authority. He could not help but resent the young officer's air of superiority. "Is he in there?" Lieutenant Coffers asked, pointing at the closed door.

"Yes, but he's finally dozed off. He was shot, you remember, and needs a little rest. That leaves me in command until he wakes up," Mike said firmly. "So tell me what you have in mind."

"Alright, *Sergeant*," he said, his face dark with suppressed anger. "I believe you have let this thing drag on much too long. We could be needed back home at any moment. Things like this are always keeping us busy. It's time to make a serious move. Now, I think we can end this thing very quickly. All we have to do is—"

"Lieutenant Coffers, I'm not so sure I want any more shooting if that's what you have in mind. We tried snipers earlier, and it didn't work, and one of your men took a bullet when you tried to move in—"

This time it was Mike who got interrupted. "He wasn't hurt. We wear protective gear, Sergeant O'Connor. We're prepared for such things. Anyway, I'm not suggesting another single-shot, police sniper attempt, although I'm sure my men could have done much better than your local man did. Nor will we try to rush him again. What I have in mind will work, believe me. After all, I am an *expert* in these things."

Mike suppressed the anger he felt at the lieutenant's criticism and cockiness, but he knew he should listen to the commander's plan. Who knew, maybe he would actually have something in mind that would end the stalemate peacefully. "All right, Coffers, let's hear it," he said, intentionally dropping the rank when he spoke to him.

The young commander's eyes flashed at the insult, but he went on quickly. "You call over there on the phone once more. When the young lady answers, we'll try to pin down where Snyder's hiding behind the shelves by watching her movements through our scopes. Then we'll open up with a heavy burst of automatic rifle fire. It'll only take seconds with her out of the way to neutralize the killer."

Mike felt his mouth pop open. He slowly lifted his lower jaw but said nothing. He was shocked by the proposal. Lieutenant Coffers, apparently interpreting his silence as approval, forged ahead. "I'll have a squad of my men positioned at both sides of the store. They'll move in and two men will remove the girl while the others secure what's left of Snyder."

Mike blinked his eyes and shook his head. "Sounds kind of cold to me, Lieutenant," he said, restoring the younger man's rank.

"Well, cold treatment for a cold con," the commander said with a smirk.

"How do we know Butch won't shoot Erika if your first rounds don't hit him, or as you say, don't *neutralize* him?" Mike asked.

"That's a chance we have to take, Sergeant, but the odds are in our favor. We'll put a lot of rounds in there in a hurry and—"

"We've played with some dangerous odds already. I want to hear something foolproof and less dangerous, Lieutenant."

"I want to talk to the sheriff," Lieutenant Coffers demanded. "I told you this needed to be a command level decision, and I'm going to have to insist now."

"Lieutenant Coffers," Mike said through a tight jaw, "I don't like your idea, and I don't think Sheriff Lyght will either."

"I'll ask him," the SWAT commander said, starting for the door.

"Not so fast," Mike countered angrily as he blocked the commander's path. "I'll fill the sheriff in when he wakes up, but not until then. Now, you go back to your men and tell them I said we will wait."

"I outrank you, Sergeant!" Lieutenant Coffers said with angry indignation. "Step aside so I can address the sheriff."

"We're not in the big city, Coffers. This is Pineview, and it is *my* town. Here a deputy sheriff outranks every lieutenant in the whole state of Colorado. Now you get out of my sight before I become unprofessional," Mike said, doubling his fists.

"I'll speak to your boss about this act of *insubordination*, Sergeant," the young lieutenant said, retreating ungracefully in the face of Mike's fierce determination. "You need a lesson in protocol."

Just then Trooper Hallinan returned. "What's going on, Mike?" she asked innocently.

"And you too, Trooper! You do not address your superiors by their given names," Lieutenant Coffers shouted at her as he stormed off. Her eyes popped in surprise.

"Just ignore him, Jan. He left his manners in the city, if he had any to leave. How did it go?"

"What?" she asked, still gaping at the cloud of fury left in the commander's wake.

"I asked—"

"Oh, I'm sorry, Mike. The girl's family is okay, all things considered. They wish it would get over with, but I told them it's best to take our time, that it's safer for her that way." She didn't mention the prayer she had with the family. That wasn't really Mike's thing. "Who does that guy think he is anyway?" she asked, pointing toward the retreating Lieutenant Coffers.

"SWAT commander. He just learned that my stripes outrank his shiny silver bars in this town and the idea kind of stuck in his craw," Mike said, cooling down as he spoke to Jan. He went on to explain Lieutenant Coffer's proposal.

"That's disgusting, Mike," she said, her bright eyes flashing. "I don't like the idea that I'm just a lowly trooper either." She chuckled and peered through the broken insurance office window. "I see the sheriff is taking a much-needed nap."

"And I wouldn't let Coffers wake him," Mike said, traces of anger still evident in his voice.

"Good for you, Mike," she said with a chuckle.

Mike respected Trooper Jan Hallinan. She had moved to Pineview nearly two years ago, following her graduation from the police academy. She was barely twenty-one when she first showed up at his door and introduced herself to him. Mike had been upset at the time. He had been happy to hear that there would be another officer in town when the State Patrol announced they were assigning a trooper to Pineview. And he was especially pleased to learn the trooper had specifically asked for the assignment here. But it had come as a shock when he discovered that the trooper who had asked to work in Pineview was a female, and that she was so young and petite. And he hadn't been overjoyed when he learned that she was a Mormon. He'd looked forward to an officer he could share the day's work with over a cup of coffee. She didn't drink it, as he'd learned the first time he offered to buy her a cup.

Pineview was about as rural as you could find, and the reality of modern police-hiring practices hadn't impacted it before. Jan had been ready for the reception, though. She ignored both the looks of distrust and negative comments in the community as well as the standoffish treatment Mike gave her. Her remedy for the negative reactions was hard, gutsy police work. In a matter of weeks she had won the hearts of the community, and few people looked at her as just a beautiful creature in a nice-fitting uniform. They came to respect her for her religious convictions, and they also accepted her totally as a no-nonsense, hardworking police officer.

Once the distrust had vanished, Mike's concern had been for her safety. "I shudder to think what will happen the first time some big drunk decides to take a poke at her," he had said one day to Sheriff Lyght.

He didn't have to wait long to find out. Jan pulled over a car containing two drunk loggers one night. Mike had heard her call the dispatcher when she made the stop and immediately headed her way. It took him ten minutes to get there, and when he arrived he was shocked to find two badly bruised drunks securely restrained in the backseat of her patrol car while Jan tied her hair into a bun again.

"Thought you might need a hand, Jan," Mike had said sheepishly as he clambered out of his truck and sized up the situation. "Looks like you have everything under control though," he had concluded.

"They thought they didn't have to go with a female officer, so they tried to jump me. I had to put them down and take them the hard way. I really don't like to have to do that," she said, her bright hazel eyes twinkling in amusement at Mike's obvious shock.

Mike recalled sticking his head in the window of the cruiser, which, as Jan explained later while wrinkling her pert nose, "I rolled down to let the stink out of my car."

Mike knew both her suspects well from bar fights in the past. "Looks like you two got yourselves in a spot of trouble," he'd observed with a chuckle.

"Nobody told us she knew karate," one of them had moaned. "She'd better be more careful next time, though," he threatened with liquored-up bravado.

"I wouldn't suggest there be a next time," Mike had warned. "I suspect that little gal may have a few more tricks up her sleeves."

"Why didn't you tell me you knew karate?" he'd asked Jan the next day as he sipped his coffee and she drank a glass of apple juice. "I've been awful worried about you, you know."

She had smiled one of her dazzling smiles and said, "Why, you never asked me, Sergeant."

"Just how good are you anyway?"

"I have a black belt. I've been studying karate since just after high school. It's something I had an interest in and finally decided to pursue. I worked hard at it. Still do." She paused, a faraway look in her eyes. "You just never know when you might need a skill like that." She paused again, looking past him, her eyes partly closed. Mike couldn't help but wonder what she was thinking about. Then she suddenly smiled at him and said, "Actually, Mike, I'm really not all that good, but I'd prefer that the local loggers and cowboys don't know it."

Following that day, Mike had accepted her without reservation. The community, in fact, respected her, and seldom did a local tough guy challenge her after that.

An officer arrived with several folding canvas cots. Mike and Jan helped him set them up in the back room of the insurance office and then Jan left. The sheriff, after Mike had briefed him on Lieutenant

Coffcr's hair-brained idea, said, "I don't like that idea any better than you do. Tell him we'll just wait it out a little longer." Then he stretched out on one of the cots with instructions to wake him up if there were any further developments.

It was only a few minutes later that Jan, her step light and jaunty, came back in. "Jan, would you watch the phone and listen to the radio for a few minutes while I go deliver a message from the sheriff to Lieutenant Coffers?" Mike asked.

"Let me go, Mike," she said with a twinkle in her eyes. "After all, I'm just a lowly trooper and not good for much but delivering messages."

"Sure, go ahead, but don't bruise him too badly if he gets smart with you," Mike joked. "Just tell him the sheriff doesn't like his idea either."

Mike sat down wearily to wait. He was more tired than he'd been in a long time. The late-night chill helped keep him awake. He glanced at the clock on the wall. It was after midnight. This thing had been dragging on for over sixteen hours. He couldn't help but wonder if Butch and his hostage were sleeping. He thought maybe a phone call about now would be in order, just to make sure Butch wasn't getting too much rest.

Mike looked in on the sheriff. He wasn't sleeping but tossed restlessly on the tiny cot, obviously in more pain that he was willing to admit. Mike told him what he wanted to do. Sheriff Lyght said, "Go ahead, Mike. It can't hurt."

Mike was just punching in the number when Jan returned. "Who are you calling?" she asked.

"Butch . . . or Erika, whoever will talk to me."

"Butch doesn't seem to be in a hurry to do anything right now, does he?"

"Maybe he has her tied up," Mike said. "He'll have to untie her before she can get to the phone if he does. I just hope he didn't hurt her when he jerked her down earlier. By the way," he asked as the phone rang steadily in his ear, "How did the lieutenant take your message?"

"Surprised me. He just nodded and said he would be glad when it was over, but if you country boys wanted to drag it on all night, he guessed he didn't care. Hey, look, Erika's picked up the phone." She was standing, looking across the street at them. She appeared unhurt.

Mike breathed a sigh of relief and waited for Erika to speak. "Hello," she said at last, sounding very tired. "Is that you again, Sergeant O'Connor?"

"It is. How are you holding up, Erika? Did he hurt you?" he asked.

"He scared me, but I'm alright, just tired is all," she said with a sleepy slur.

"How is Butch? Is he hurt?"

"A little, but he's okay, I guess. He still wants a car so—"

Mike heard Erika's terrified scream as she dropped the phone. She slapped her hands over her ears to hide the deafening staccato roar of automatic rifle fire that had suddenly erupted. "What . . . !" Mike shouted, dropping the phone and rushing to the door as splinters of wood and other debris flew into the air inside the store. Shelves disintegrated from the force of dozens of rounds of bullets.

"Cease fire," he yelled, his words swallowed up by the ear-shattering racket.

He jerked his radio from his belt. "Stop shooting!" he screamed into it. As if his command had actually been heard, the sheets of yellow flame from the SWAT team's positions stopped. Four SWAT officers emerged from the darkness behind the bright lights, running with their heads low across the street and into the riddled building.

Erika stood frozen, her hands still held tightly over her ears. She screamed again when a single shot rang out. The officers stopped abruptly at the sound, and Erika dropped behind the shattered remains of the shelves.

"Another step closer and she'll die," Butch shouted, his voice carrying clearly across the street.

Mike ran into the street shouting, "You men get out of there! You idiots! You're going to get that girl killed."

Slowly, like robots in slow motion, the four retreated. Whether they were obeying Mike's orders or Butch's didn't matter to Mike—Erika was temporarily out of danger.

Sheriff Lyght stumbled into the street beside Mike who was busy calling the four retreating officers every name for "dumb" he could think of.

"You four get that sap-headed lieutenant of yours right now," the sheriff shouted. "I want to talk to him. Move it!"

Just then Butch's pistol cracked again from within the ruins of the store and one of the officers stumbled backward. Picking himself up, he began to run, shouting to his buddies, "He's shooting again!"

The other three didn't need to be told that. They wisely dove for cover. Another shot hit Mike's truck, which was still parked in front of the insurance office. Jan, still in the office, dove behind the desk as still another bullet struck the door beside her. The cameraman, who had filmed the whole thing from his position up the street a short distance, also dove for cover.

Mike and the sheriff were on their stomachs in the middle of the street, crawling for safety. The shooting stopped. "Guess he thinks we've got the message," Mike mumbled.

"Is that officer okay?" Jan asked after the two joined her in the office. She was trembling and white, visibly shaken.

"If you're referring to that SWAT fellow who fell in the street, I'm sure he is. His body armor saved him. That's twice tonight for those guys. If it had been the sheriff or me, we'd have still been out there," Mike said angrily. "And Coffers would have been smirking."

For the next minute or so, all of Mike's redheaded Irish fury expressed itself in language he hadn't used much in years. He stomped around the office like a caged gorilla while Jan stood unmoving in the center of the room, her wide eyes glued to the carnage across the street. Sheriff Lyght said nothing, but he was seething too.

Jan continued to tremble, and her heart raced. One hand rubbed her cheek nervously. Mike finally noticed and his tirade stopped. "I'm sorry, Jan," he said. "I am so sorry. I didn't mean to offend you with such language."

She didn't react to his apology. Her eyes never flickered from what they were staring at across the street. Nor were they really seeing anything. Jan thought she was brave, and tried to be, but the shooting had unnerved her, even terrified her. And her heart was heavy for the girl across the street. And she was praying for her. She had been oblivious to Mike's tirade and obscene outburst.

"Hey, Jan, I'm sorry," Mike said again. "I didn't mean to shock you so badly."

He touched her bare arm and she finally turned her face to him. One hand covered her cheek; the other wiped at her moist eyes. "What did you say, Mike?" she asked.

"I apologized for my language. I didn't mean to offend you."

"Oh, I didn't notice," she acknowledged, and it was Mike's turn to stare.

"Are you alright, Jan?" he asked in a soft and gentle voice that he seldom used except with his own wife and daughters.

She nodded and turned to face the street once more. She shuddered visibly, but before Mike could speak again, Lieutenant Coffers came in, and Sheriff Lyght calmly asked him to take a seat. "I'd rather stand, sir," he responded stiffly.

Jan quietly left the building and joined the cameraman who was again busy filming the carnage.

"Sit down!" the sheriff roared, his face turning bright scarlet.

The lieutenant sat and Sheriff Lyght gave him a dressing down like Mike had never witnessed before. He finally wound down, saying, "I sure hope you're proud of yourself, Coffers. You nearly got some of us killed, shot up a perfectly good convenience store, scared the daylights out of an innocent hostage whose life I am responsible for, and made an already unstable killer downright furious."

"But, sir, it should have worked. I can't imagine how he could have survived the—"

"Well, I can imagine," Sheriff Lyght cut in, his eyes still boring holes into the lieutenant's face. "We're not dealing with a stupid person over there. It would have worked if you'd been in his place, I suppose, but Butch is a whole lot smarter than you'll ever be. He's about two jumps ahead of us all the time."

Lieutenant Coffers opened his mouth to speak, but Sheriff Lyght snapped, "Now take your fair-haired boys and get out of my county! And I'll thank you to never set foot in it again. We would have been better off to have never invited you up in the first place."

Lieutenant Coffers was still seated. Sheriff Lyght had not yet moved his eyes from the unfortunate man's face. "You are dismissed, Lieutenant," he said softly, then he turned to Mike who was leaning against the wall grinning. "Well, I guess we better decide what to do now," he said as calmly as a summer breeze. The lieutenant slithered out, shutting the door behind him.

A few minutes later there was a knock on the door. Mike said as he opened it, "Looks like a bullet hit the door and another the door frame."

Another SWAT officer entered, a sergeant, followed by Trooper Hallinan. The second Sheriff Lyght saw the officer he heated up again. "I just told your commander to pack you men up and get out of here. We don't need any more of what just happened!"

"But, sir," he said, "I need to say something."

"I've heard about enough for one night," the sheriff thundered.

"Sheriff," Jan said almost timidly, "we've been outside talking. Would you mind listening to him for just a minute?"

He nodded at her and then turned to the officer. "Well, spit it out. We have a situation on our hands you know."

"Yes, sir. I'm really sorry, sir. Please don't think that the rest of us are as goofy as Coffers. I tried to talk him out of that idiotic scheme of his, but he wouldn't listen to a word I said. Some of the other men tried too, but he thinks he has all the answers. He even told us that you'd given the order."

"I did no such thing!" Sheriff Lyght thundered.

"Well, anyway, we're sorry. If we can do anything—"

"You've done quite enough."

The young sergeant looked pained and turned to go. "Wait a moment," the sheriff said, the tone of his voice softening. "I guess we could still use some manpower, but Coffers has to go."

"I'm second in command, Sheriff. If you send Coffers home, you have my word that we'll do only what you ask, nothing more and nothing less."

"Thanks, Sergeant. If he's out of here in ten minutes the rest of you may stay. You be back here at one o'clock sharp and we'll discuss some strategy," the sheriff said.

After the SWAT sergeant left, Mike remarked, "The poor guy. It must be quite a strain working for a jerk like Coffers."

"When this thing is all over I'm going to call his boss and see what I can do about having the *strain* removed. I think Coffers may have just done a number on his career as a police officer," the sheriff mused.

The door burst open, bouncing off the doorstop like a football. Jim Leighton, Erika's father, rode in on the draft it created. "Sheriff," he said in a demanding, angry tone, "what is going on here? I thought your job was to get my daughter out alive! Instead, you shoot up the whole place like it's a shooting gallery, scare her half to death, and enrage that killer in there so badly he'll probably never let Erika go. I hold you personally responsible for her safety. If anything happens to my little girl I will own this whole county. I am calling my attorney first thing in the morning and will advise him of the way you're mishandling this horrible affair."

Sheriff Lyght listened as the poor man's fear and frustration poured out. When he stopped for air, the sheriff said calmly, "Mr. Leighton, I can assure you that we're doing everything we can to protect your daughter. The man responsible for that," he said, pointing at the shattered store, "has been dismissed. I am just as angry as you are over what happened. Now, would you please return to your motel room? We have work to do here and you are interfering with—"

"You aren't doing anything except trying to get her killed! You don't care about her at—"

"We do care, and we are doing our best. Now, you go call your attorney and tell him whatever you want, but whatever you do, please stay away from this area," the sheriff said as firmly but kindly as he could.

The radio came on. It was dispatch calling for Jan who had been standing quietly at the back of the room. "We have a one-car rollover about fifteen miles east of Pineview. No injuries. Would you take it?" the stern voice asked.

Jan keyed her mic and said,"Ten-four. I'm en route." She smiled at Mr. Leighton and moved past the other officers. "I'll see you men later," she said. "Sounds like the rest of the world isn't waiting around while we get this problem handled."

"Hurry back, Jan," Mike said as she headed for the door. She waved a quick good-bye, flashed him a restrained smile, and was gone.

"My daughter," Mr. Leighton started again, "is in grave danger. If you don't get her out of there immediately that crazy criminal will probably—"

"We'll do our best," Mike said, guiding him out of the insurance office.

When Mike stepped back in, Sheriff Lyght said, "Mike, this is one of those times when I wish you were the sheriff and I was the sergeant. No matter how hard a fellow tries, it's impossible to please the public. I don't blame Mr. Leighton though. What a terrible strain he must be under. We've got to figure out a way to get his daughter out of there."

The SWAT sergeant walked in before Mike could respond, but no response was expected anyway. "All right, men, let's get to it," Sheriff Lyght said, pointing to the chairs, "There has got to be a way . . ."

Chapter 6

Butch groaned. He was sitting against the wall with his revolver clutched in one hand. Erika, kneeling at his side, was changing the bandage on his injured shoulder. They were cramped in the narrow space behind a bunch of heavy pallets Butch had forced Erika to drag from the back room and stack as a shield.

The pallets had saved Butch's life when the barrage of bullets ravaged the store. They were stacked deep enough that not a single round had come through. However, on both sides of them, lead had riddled the wall and shattered the coffee pot after passing through the shelves and the groceries and goods they'd held.

"We've got to get out of here, Erika," Butch said with effort.

Erika dabbed a little alcohol on his wound then asked, "Butch, have you figured out how you're going to do it yet?" She was becoming resigned to her fate, and though still terrified, she was caring for him the best she could.

"I have an idea that I think will work, but it could put you in some danger," he said, his pale green eyes resting on her face.

Erica studied him for a moment. Butch was both a good-looking guy and the most terrifying man she'd ever met. His short dark hair, curly and thick, was matted with blood, but she had managed to clean the blood from his face. Butch needed her help. And if she didn't give it, *her* life was in danger. "That's alright, Butch. I just want out of here—I want both of us out of here. Tell me what we need to do," she said softly, trying desperately to disguise her fear.

A smile crept slowly to his face. "You're okay, you know that?" he said, taking hold of her hand and squeezing.

A strange emotion flooded through her. "I just don't want you to be hurt any worse," Erika lied, but she made no attempt to free her hand. She didn't dare do or say anything to anger him.

After a moment, he let go and reloaded his pistol. He'd crawled over to a locked bullet case at the far end of the back aisle a little earlier, broken the glass, and taken out a box of .38 ammo. His hands shook, and by the time the five bullets were crammed home, he was sweating in the cool of the store and cursing softly. And Erika was angry at her own stupidity. The gun had been empty and she hadn't realized it! Another chance to escape had passed. But then, would she have dared try? He would always be a danger to her. He had told her so several times the past few hours. And Erika believed him.

"So how do we get out of here?" she asked after he'd loaded the pistol. He explained his idea, never taking his eyes from her face as he spoke. She tried not to act too shocked at his plan, and, after he'd finished, with a voice that trembled so much she could scarcely speak, she asked, "Do you really think it will work?"

"It's my only chance. Call O'Connor," Butch ordered.

"Can't we wait until he calls again?" she asked, stalling, hoping that something less dangerous would occur to him.

"No, Erika." His eyes grew narrow and his voice low and dangerous. "Quit jerking me around. Have you forgotten old Sam already?" How could she ever forget? It could be her the next time. "Call O'Connor now! He can't call us anyway. If you'll notice, you never hung up the phone last time."

Erika turned her head and stared in dismay at the receiver dangling from the shelf. She had dropped it when the firing started. She reached for it and made the call, and a minute later, Sergeant O'Connor's deep voice came on the line.

"Hello, Erika. How are you doing over there?" he asked. "I'm sorry about all the shooting."

"Butch says we're going to leave now," she said, still struggling to control her voice. The officer's apology never even registered. She briefly described Butch's insane plan.

"That's crazy, Erika! You've got to talk him—"

"Please, Sergeant," she pleaded, her eyes filling with tears. "Don't get me killed. If you guys try to shoot Butch, he'll kill me."

"Stall, Erika. If he gets away from here with you, he might do anything."

"If we get away, maybe I'll be safe," she said weakly.

"Erika, listen to me! Butch is a dangerous man. Remember the cashier?" She didn't need reminding again. "You saw it. Butch shot him in cold blood. He's using you. Please, Erika, we'll find a way to help you. But you can't let him take you away from here. We can't let him either."

They had no idea the terror she was going through. That was clear. *They couldn't stop Butch. No one could stop Butch.* And in her mind, she believed that if she didn't do anything to anger him further, and if she helped him the best she could, that once they were away from this place and the cops, he would let her go. He wouldn't need her anymore. So she'd resolved to do whatever it took to stay alive. They hadn't been able to help her during all these hours. Now she had to depend on herself. And that was what she would do.

Butch was signaling her angrily and she quickly reacted. "I have to hang up now. We'll be coming out the door in a few minutes." Before Sergeant O'Connor could say anything more she hung up. For a moment, she looked vacantly across the ragged shelves. She was helpless. She had no control of her life and no source of help. She silently cried for Bob. She even tried to cry to her Father in Heaven, but her faith was weak. Like the officers, He had not helped her these past hours either. Why would He help her now?

"Erika, whatever O'Connor said, don't think about it," Butch said fiercely. "We're going to get ready to leave now."

She turned back to him, her vision blurred and her mind in turmoil. She simply stared at him.

"Erika." Butch's voice was low and icy—dangerous.

"All right," she said, wiping her eyes and trying to clear her mind. "I'll do whatever you say, but please don't hurt me."

Butch crawled over to the bullet case. There was a selection of knives there. He picked out a large hunting knife in a thick leather sheath. He strapped it on his belt and then, after pulling the knife from the sheath and gingerly testing the sharpened edge, said, "This ought to do."

Erika shivered. She had put her sweats back on earlier, but the night air coming through the shattered glass at the front of the store was cold, and she shook uncontrollably.

"Calm down, girl, and give me a hand here," Butch ordered. He seemed oblivious to the seeping chill or her shattered emotions.

With Erika's help, he taped the knife to his right fist. Then, kneeling side by side, they taped his arm and the knife to Erika's shoulder with the point of the blade directed toward her exposed throat. "This will work," he said with a sneer. "If they were to shoot me, the knife would cut your throat when I fell. I'll hold the gun on you too. They won't dare try anything. And neither will you."

"Butch, do we have to?" Erika asked, no longer able to mask the terror she felt. "I'll go with you, protect you, do whatever you want, but please, not this way."

"Shut up!" he ordered.

Whimpering, she helped put the rest of the bullets in Butch's pockets with some snack food they had deposited there earlier. "I wish you had pockets," he grumbled. We can't take much food with me having to carry it all."

"I'm s . . . s . . . sorry," she stammered, her heart pounding so hard it made her chest ache.

"Okay, I guess we're ready. Now, when we stand up, we've got to be together, or the knife might jerk into your neck," he said calmly. Her fright grew worse, but she had to do what he asked. She was in no position to argue.

Erika's eyes were blurred, and her legs felt like jelly. Slowly, they rose to their feet, and with the pistol pressed tightly to her back, they walked to the front of the store, stepping carefully through the clutter. After they got going, she willed her legs to hold her up, knowing that death was certain if they did not.

After shuffling through the broken glass at the front of the store, they started along the sidewalk to the east. Erika spotted Sergeant O'Connor and a couple of other officers as they watched from behind his truck. She knew other officers were watching them as well. She imagined them in every shadow and around every corner.

"Don't do this, Butch," Sergeant O'Connor called out in the crisp, midnight air. "You're making a big mistake."

"The only mistake will be if one of your hotshot cops tries to shoot me, O'Connor," he shouted back. "If I go down this knife will be stained with a pretty girl's blood, and it will be on your hands. So call off the goons, man. We're going to walk out of here." Then, in a lower voice, he said to Erika, "Keep moving, and remember, where I go, you go. If I die, so do you."

She remembered. But she could not respond to the desperate man at her side. Warm tears flooded down her cheeks and sobs racked her body. Regret stung her soul. Why did she ever come to town alone? Why didn't she listen to her parents? Other than the shuffling of their feet on the pavement, and the shrill of a low wind through the pines that lined the street, the night had become deathly still, as if mesmerized by the unfolding drama.

"Into the center of the street," Butch said, shoving her with his injured shoulder. "We can't get near any spot where they might try to jump us. There could be men behind every tree and building along here."

The hair on the back of Erika's neck stood erect. She felt a hundred eyes on her. The cold steel of the knife touched her neck when she tried to turn her head to look around, so she forced herself to look straight ahead. Although her fear of Butch was stronger than when he first took over the store, she was now experiencing an even worse fear of the men hidden in the shadows. If any of them tried anything, the knife would . . .

"You're moving too slowly, Erika, and stop shaking so much," Butch growled. "All we've got to do now is find a car."

"You mean steal one?" she gasped.

"No, I thought we'd try to *buy* one! Don't turn stupid on me, Erika."

She hadn't meant to. It was just that it was one terrible shock after another with this horrible man. They moved on in silence for a few minutes, then Butch spoke again. "There'll be cars at the motel. We'll take one and be on our way. It's only a couple of blocks."

"But how will we start it?"

"Trust me, I'll get it done," he growled.

From somewhere in the distance the silence was disturbed by the barking of a dog. Her tears had dried, and Erika thought she saw a shadow move beside a house as they passed. A moment later another moved, this time beside a large pine tree. "Butch," Erika whispered fearfully, "there are people all around us."

"Of course there are," he replied impatiently. "They're just waiting for us to make a mistake. But we won't do that, will we?"

"I'll try not to," she whimpered.

"Good, then we'll be fine. The motel is just ahead. There are several cars there. Guess we'll borrow one."

The barking dog was joined by a choir of baying hounds. A cow mooed, calling its calf to a midnight snack. An owl hooted in a nearby tree. The neon sign of the motel beckoned just a short distance ahead.

"Didn't you say your dad's Expedition was red?" Butch asked.

"Yes."

"Is that it parked beside that old van? You can just see the back end of it."

"Yeah, that could be it. My family must be staying here," she said, suddenly longing for them so badly that it made her start sobbing again.

"Hey, cut it out! We'll borrow the Expedition and be safe in no time."

"Butch, we can't take *it!* My family needs it."

"Not as badly as we do," Butch growled.

"But I don't have the keys. I dropped them in the store," she cried desperately.

Butch chuckled. "You don't give me much credit, do you, girl? I picked them up. They're in my shirt pocket. We'll just start it up and hit the road."

"Butch," Erika said, suddenly angry. "You planned on taking it all along, didn't you?"

"Kind of made sense that your folks would be staying here," he said with a smirk. "Now quit bugging me!" His voice was suddenly cold and dangerous again.

Fighting desperately with her fear and her emotions, she said, "I'm sorry, Butch. Let's go get it." She was afraid she didn't sound convincing, but she couldn't make him angry again. She kept saying things she shouldn't. She was being so terribly stupid.

"We'll go around to the driver's side. Watch for cops." They walked toward the Expedition, then Butch stopped. "Get the keys from my pocket," he said.

She carefully reached inside his jacket and found the pocket of his shirt with her fingers. As soon as the keys were safely in her quaking hand, he said, "Now, we'll step up to the car. You open the door, then we'll get the tape off and get in. I'll go first. You come in behind me. Got it?"

"What if somebody—"

"I'll have the gun on you, and you stay low. They better not . . ." he said, his voice trailing off.

Someone was standing at the end of the motel, still as a statue. "Don't think about the cops," Butch said as they stepped to the driver's side of the car. "Now, open the door."

It was locked. For a moment she fumbled with the keys but managed to unlock the door and open it. "Help me get this tape off," he whispered.

It took several minutes to get his hand free. Twice she felt the sharp knife prick her skin, and warm blood oozed down her neck. Finally, his hand pulled free, and he made her tear the rest of the tape off the knife so he could put the weapon in its sheath. He kept the gun poked in her stomach. "I'm getting in now," he whispered. "Don't try anything, Erika, or . . ."

She knew. She was beyond knowing. She was his hostage, both physically and psychologically. Moving in a trance, only vaguely aware of men closing in around her, she climbed into the Expedition after Butch, her eyes on the gun he kept continually pointed at her head. He pressed it to her temple as she straightened up behind the wheel.

"Start it and drive," he ordered.

With trembling hands, Erika inserted the key and started the engine. The thrill she'd felt when she pulled out of the campground was from another life. Only feelings of depression and gloom accompanied the even throbbing of the engine as she backed away from the motel. She was conscious of officers stumbling out of the way and of the cold steel of Butch's .38 pressing against her temple.

"Which way do I go?" she asked.

"East. To the left. And drive fast."

As she sped out of town, Butch spoke again from his position hunched over beside her. "They'll try to follow us, so I better drive now," he said.

"But you're hurt, Butch," she protested. "You can't drive."

The lights of the Expedition showed only open road ahead as Butch reached over her shoulder and slid tightly against her body. "Trade me places," he said, taking hold of the steering wheel with one hand.

The vehicle swerved wildly as she slid over his lap and he took her place. She wondered what he had done with the pistol, not that it mattered—there was no getting out now anyway. Butch drove extremely fast. Erika was tempted to ask him to slow down but feared provoking his wrath again. Instead, she fastened her seat belt and sat back in silence, hugging herself and watching the road ahead through throbbing eyes.

After a few minutes, Erika became aware of a thumping sound behind them. She looked back but could see nothing. It was soon directly overhead.

"The chopper!" Butch growled. "It must have still been in town. We've got to get away from it or we'll never get any rest. I'm really tired, you know. And my shoulder . . . it's throbbing."

They kept going, the annoying clatter of the chopper staying with them. A few miles farther and they noticed lightning penetrating the dark sky ahead. "I don't remember clouds," Butch said. "Maybe it'll storm. The chopper will probably turn back if it storms hard enough, and then we can get off the main road and lose the cops."

Butch's luck held out. In a couple of minutes they drove into a hard rainstorm, as sudden as climbing into the shower. Lightning streaked so close that the ear-splitting crash of thunder was almost simultaneous. The nerve-racking thumping of the helicopter faded and was gone.

Butch slowed down on the rain-slick pavement after the Expedition slid dangerously on a gentle curve. Erika glanced at the speedometer. It read 70 mph. They approached another curve, sharper than the last one. He touched the brakes, and as they came out of the curve, he slowed down dramatically at the sight of oscillating red and blue lights ahead.

"If that's a roadblock, we're not stopping, so hang on," Butch said through clenched teeth, ramming the accelerator to the floor. The responsive new vehicle hydroplaned dangerously as it surged to greater speeds. The lightning was providing momentary periods of near-daylight conditions. Puddles of water reflected the light of the headlights, lighting the tall pines that lined the edge of the road.

"Look, there's a wrecker up there, Butch. It's not a roadblock, just an accident," Erika said, hoping he would ease up on the suicidal speed. To her relief, he did let up on the gas, but only slowed a little, maintaining the speedometer at just under 80 mph. As they shot past the accident, a blazing sheet of lightning lit the sky like high noon. Erika gasped, barely suppressing a scream.

"What's the matter, Erika? Haven't you ever seen a wreck before?" Butch asked with a tight-jawed chuckle.

"They just . . . scare . . . me . . . that's all," she stammered, grasping for an excuse to hide the *real* reason for her shock. During the brief moment when the sky was lit, she thought she'd seen Bob sitting beside a cop in the patrol car. His eyes were wide and staring at the streaking red Expedition. In the next instant, her mind had snapped a picture of a crumpled black car being sucked up behind the wrecker.

"Must have hit that elk," Butch said, as the headlights of their car lit up the immense brown form of a dead animal lying in its gore at the side of the road. "Looks like the idiot rolled after that," he expounded.

"I wonder if he's okay," she said, her distraught mind racing out of control. The last person she would have expected to see was Bob. She began to doubt what she'd seen. It couldn't have been him. Was she losing her mind?

***

The same flash of lightning that illuminated Bob also illuminated the occupants of the red Expedition. Bob was stunned. Trooper Hallinan noticed and said, "That vehicle was going awfully fast for slick roads, wasn't it? Those crazy people could have lost control and hit us."

"Yeah," Bob responded absently. But he hadn't noticed the speed particularly. What he had seen was Erika's family's red Expedition with her inside!

Not one word about the hostage situation had passed between Bob and the officer who was investigating his frustrating accident. But sitting in her car, he could hear every word that came across the police radio. He was going nuts knowing that Erika and her kidnapper were now on their way to places unknown, and her chances of ever coming out of it alive had just become very remote.

"Are you alright, Bob?" Jan asked, suddenly concerned about the young man. He had experienced a frightening accident, but he wasn't hurt. The car didn't belong to him and, other than inconvenience at this point, there was nothing that should cause him to go into the stupor she was witnessing.

Bob slowly shook his head, then he said, "Not really."

Alarmed that maybe there was some internal injury he hadn't mentioned or maybe even hadn't recognized, or that he was going into shock, Jan said, "I better get you to a hospital."

"No! I'm okay—physically," he said

"You don't look like it," she declared.

Bob turned his head toward her. There was pain in those beautiful eyes of his, those eyes that had cast a spell on her the moment she first saw his face. For all her feigned toughness and courage, Jan had a tender heart. She didn't know what to say to him, but something was wrong, more wrong than the accident she was investigating.

"That car . . . that red Expedition, you recognized it, didn't you?" he asked as he brushed self-consciously at his moist eyes.

Jan hesitated, not sure what to say. The kidnapping was not his concern. But she had recognized the car and knew exactly who was in it. And it was not something she wanted to think about right now. Her fear for the girl in that car with Butch was intense, perhaps even unreasonable. No one knew the raging emotions Butch and his hostage were causing in Trooper Jan Hallinan. And she wanted it to stay that way. It had to stay that way.

"You did, didn't you, Trooper?" he said more forcefully. "You recognized that car?"

Jan Hallinan was a very honest person. There was no way she could openly lie to Bob. So she reluctantly said, "I'm afraid I did, but—"

"Then why aren't we going after them?" Bob shouted. "If they get clear away, he won't need her anymore, and he'll kill her!" A sob racked his body. "He is a killer, Officer. He will kill Erika! Please, let's go after them," he begged.

"I can't, not with you in here," she said as total astonishment washed over her. How did he know the girl's name? she wondered.

"Then I'll get out!" he said and began to open the door.

"No, I can't just leave you here!" Jan protested.

With the door hanging wide open, Bob looked at her again and said, "That's my girlfriend, Trooper. Somebody has got to do something. Please, go. Try if you can. Please!" he begged.

Jan's head was reeling. This was too much. She couldn't leave him here alone. But he was right; she should be pursuing.

"I could get fired," she said. "If I were a deputy, it wouldn't matter. Sheriff Lyght doesn't care who rides with his officers, but I work for the state."

"I'm getting out then. You go!" he shouted.

"No, get back in," she said, knowing that she might be risking her job. "You can come. We'll go after them." The prospect was terrifying, but it was her job and she would do it, even if she lost it later.

"Thanks, I hope they don't fire you," Bob said.

"So do I," she countered.

He was still fastening the seat belt as she spun the car around and rammed the accelerator to the floor. As soon as she was up to speed, she grabbed her mic and radioed in. "I'm pursuing a red Ford Expedition," she told the dispatcher.

Before the dispatcher could respond, Sergeant Mike O'Connor came on the air with a quick, "Don't try to take him alone, Jan. We're coming, but this storm is slowing us down. I repeat, do not try to take him alone. You'll only make matters worse."

Jan eased up on the accelerator. Mike was right of course.

"Hey, don't slow down!" Bob insisted.

She glanced at Bob, and the look on his handsome face caused her to once again press the accelerator. She spoke once more, this time talking to Sergeant Mike O'Connor. "I'll try to get the vehicle in sight," she said. "You can let me know what to do after that."

***

Butch was watching his side of the road as he continued to race east. "There's a dirt road along here somewhere that goes to the north. If we take it, we'll lose them," he reasoned.

He found the road and turned onto it, cursing as the Expedition slid almost to the edge. The road was muddy and slippery but fairly wide. He drove slower as he wound his way steeply into the mountains, and he began to talk again.

"I used to know these roads like the back of my hand," he said. "That was before they locked me up of course. I used to bring Dad up here and we tried every fishing hole for miles around. This road will eventually take us to a paved road that leads into Wyoming. It goes over a pass first and twists like a can of worms, but it's a passable road. Maybe we'll hole up in Wyoming for the day and head back into Utah tonight. That sound okay?"

Erika was beyond caring, and she said nothing.

***

"It's like they vanished into thin air," Jan told Mike as they stood beside the road twenty minutes later. She had driven until she met a trooper coming from the east. Butch and Erika had not passed him. "He's turned off somewhere."

"Yes, and it could have been any number of places. They could be anywhere in these mountains by now. We'll continue to search, but the odds are stacked against us."

"And against Erika," Jan said sadly.

"That's for sure," Mike agreed. "You better get the young fellow to town. He'll need to get some rest."

Jan nodded in agreement. She'd told Mike who Bob was, and he'd been both amazed and sympathetic. She said, "I'll leave now. I'm sorry I lost them."

"You didn't lose them, I did," Mike said disgustedly. "Butch outfoxed me all the way."

Back in her patrol car a moment later, she said to Bob. "I'll take you to Pineview. Erika's family is there."

"Yeah, I figured that," he said despondently.

She drove several miles before Bob spoke again. He said, "Hey, I've been a jerk, I know. Thanks for trying, Trooper. And thanks for letting me ride with you. I hope you don't get in trouble for this."

She smiled toward him in the dimness of the interior of the patrol car. "I'll be fine, the other officers will cover for me. And you're welcome," she answered. "I'm really sorry about all of this. You don't deserve it."

"Oh, it's not me that has troubles, it's Erika," he said. "And she doesn't deserve it."

"No, I'm sure not," Jan agreed. "Of course I've never met her, but I spoke with her family for a little bit. They seem really nice."

"They're good people," Bob agreed. "But I'm not sure they haven't spoiled Erika a little bit. She's not prepared for something like this. Of course, who would be?"

Jan was without words. Yes, who could ever be? She looked over at Bob and then back at the road. It was dry now. The storm was gone, the stars were out, and it was a beautiful night. Marred, but still beautiful.

"Are they okay?" Bob asked.

"You mean the Leightons?" Jan said turning toward him.

"Yes."

"They're upset, worried, and prayerful," she responded.

"Yes, they would be," he agreed. "They're . . . we are . . ."

"Mormons," she finished for him. "So am I."

***

Erika dreamed of sunny California, the surf running high. Bob, his tan body gleaming in the sun-drenched spray, rode a large green board ahead of her. She was floating effortlessly. It had never been so easy to surf. An enormous wave rose above him, swallowing him along with his board. She surfed on, confident that he would reappear shortly. When she spotted him, he was rising out of the midst of the wave, veiled in a briny mist, but . . . it wasn't Bob . . . it was Butch! He beckoned to her, smiling, and shouted in a strange, echoing voice, "Come to me, Erika. Bob is gone. You're mine now. Come."

Bob's voice rose from the blue depths. "Wait for me, Erika. Don't leave me here, Erika." She looked behind her as Bob rose from the sea again and bobbed about on the rough ocean surface, waving his arms at her. She turned away.

Butch's voice called again. "Erika, are you through sleeping yet?"

With a start her eyes flew open. "How long have I been asleep?" she asked, her eyes seeking the luminous clock on the dash.

"An hour or two," he said as she read the time. It was 3:30 A.M.

"Two more hours and we've got to be holed up for the day," Butch said.

She wanted to sleep more, but as she watched his bobbing head she was afraid he might doze at the wheel and kill them both. That thought caused her drowsiness to flee. She watched him intently.

She thought of the words he had spoken in her dream moments before. They weren't true. She was not his. He didn't need her now. Maybe he would let her out here, in these lonely mountains. She would be safer than in here with him.

"Butch," she said apprehensively.

"What?" he responded.

"You don't need me now. You could let me out right here. I promise I'll—"

"No!" he shouted. "You are staying with me. I'll decide when to let you go, if ever. You do want to live, don't you?"

"Yes," she said meekly.

"Then you'll do as I say. Now shut up about leaving. You got that?"

She couldn't stop the sob that came with her "Yes" this time. She really had thought he would let her go after they got away from the cops. But that sergeant had been right. She closed her eyes as tears stung them fiercely.

Shortly, they turned onto a paved road and raced northward. At a little after five they passed into Wyoming. Butch said, "We've got to find a good place to hide. I need sleep."

She couldn't argue with that.

After a while, he left the pavement and drove onto a dirt road. The storm had not been this far north, and dust billowed behind them.

"Hey, look what we've found," he said, spotting a cluster of rundown buildings a few hundred yards ahead. "Looks like an abandoned ranch," Butch added as the headlights revealed a grove of stark, dead cottonwood trees. They towered over an old multicolored house, some rundown corrals and collapsed sheds, and a large gray barn.

Butch pulled the Expedition into the barn. It was tall and spindly looking, but provided shelter. And after he'd made Erika close a pair of rickety doors that swung stiffly on their screeching hinges, it hid them quite well. You won't run off will you, Erika?" Butch asked as he collapsed on a pile of musty hay. "Remember who I am. If you ever get away, I'll track you down and make you wish you hadn't, so don't even try." He chuckled, then added ominously, "Anyway, you'd just die of thirst alone out here in this desert."

She shook her head, and the terrible events of the past day and night filled her mind. He could kill her so easily. And he would. And he was right about the desert. She couldn't go unless she took the Expedition, and he had the keys in his pockets . . . along with his revolver.

In a few minutes he was snoring softly, sound asleep. Erika wanted to sleep too, but first she crept nervously through the old barn. It was getting light outside, and peering through a large crack between twisted gray boards she could see the remains of what had once been large fields. There was nothing but a few withered, dry weeds and a little sagebrush growing there now.

Another crack offered her a clear view of the corrals. Rotting pole fences provided a resting place for several generations of tumbleweeds. Cattle hadn't filled those pens for years. What a desolate place. She was glad for the sun, which was bursting in a blaze of bright orange over the hills to the east, for in darkness this place would spawn nightmares of the worst kind.

After walking back to the musty hay, she stood watching a narrow, golden beam of light as it danced on Butch's sleeping face. He seemed so harmless lying there, but her heart twisted with fear. He had claimed her. And she was powerless to do anything about it. Her life was his to do with as he pleased, and if she tried to get away, even if she succeeded in getting away, he would find her and kill her.

She stepped toward him, but then retreated to the Expedition, opened a door, and climbed in. After a short search, she emerged with a dark-blue blanket which she spread on the rotten hay and sank slowly to the soft comfort it provided.

Never in all her eighteen years had Erika been so exhausted. She closed her eyes, ready to sink into welcome slumber when something touched her foot, bringing her to an instant sitting position. She gasped at the sight of a large rat, its long nose sniffing at her foot as if it were trying to decide how it could pack off the black Reebok it had found. Suppressing the urge to cry out, she wiggled her foot, drawing it beneath her. The rat scurried off.

She sat hugging her knees and watched nervously for more rats. Seeing none, she finally settled back onto the blanket again. Sleep refused to come as she jumped at every little sound, and the old barn was full of them. She reasoned that her fatigue was making her jumpy and tried to convince her foggy mind to ignore the creaks, groans, and whistles and go to sleep.

It almost worked. She was just drifting off when she was disturbed by a loud buzzing. It contrasted sharply with the other sounds, and her eyes popped open. With a scream that would raise the dead she leaped to her feet. Butch also came to his feet, the little .38 appearing like magic in his hand. Without a word he fired a single deafening shot, blowing the head off a large and deadly diamond-back rattlesnake that had joined them in the hay.

Shoving the pistol back in a pocket of his jacket, he dropped back onto the hay. Erika didn't even look at him for a moment. The speed and accuracy of his shooting drove her fear of him to greater heights. He knew how to use a gun.

"How did you do that?" Erika finally asked as she watched the snake writhe and twist in a morbid death struggle.

"Do what?" he asked.

"How did you shoot that snake's head off?"

"Oh, that. Practice, I guess. Dad used to be good with a gun. He taught me. I was a little surprised myself, though. I thought all the years in prison would have made me rusty. I guess I've still got the old touch. Now lie down, girl. We need some sleep."

"Not until you shoot that rat!" she pleaded, pointing at the would-be shoe thief which had stuck its narrow head around a rusty bucket and was studying them through beady black eyes.

Butch obliged her, shoved the gun back in a pocket and then growled, "Now, can we have some sleep?"

Chapter 7

"Mornin', Mike. Mornin', Sheriff. What can I get you this today?" Penny asked with a cheerful smile.

"I'll have a stack of hotcakes, two eggs over easy, and a pile of bacon," Mike said.

"The same, but cook the eggs," Sheriff Lyght quipped.

"Well, sit down boys and I'll bring you both some coffee," Penny said and grabbed the hot pot and two stained cups.

"You two ever sleep?" she asked, pouring the steaming brew.

"We grabbed what rest we could, Penny, but we've got to keep at it," Mike said with a tired smile.

"Some all-fired mad folks round here," she commented.

"Yes, I suppose so," Mike said wearily. "Seems like we never do anything right."

"Not all mad at you. They'd string Butch up if they could. All the same, I'm glad I just pour coffee and cook eggs," she said with a laugh as she swung her chunky frame toward the kitchen. "The only thing that can get me in trouble is spilling a bit a hot coffee on some ornery truck driver. I'll get your breakfast goin'." She disappeared into the back.

The two tired officers sat quietly in the corner booth sipping their hot coffee. Several other men were in the little café and it buzzed with slightly subdued conversation. The tension of the past day had taken its toll on the people of Pineview, and they were hesitant to talk too much, in the presence of the two weary lawmen, about the escaped convict and the young woman he had taken hostage.

The door opened, creating a vacuum through which blew the owner of the Quick Stop. He looked around angrily and then with great determination piled like a snowdrift in front of the officers. He spat words like ice cubes at them. "You . . . you . . . you incompetent fools!"

"Good morning, John," Mike said amiably, ignoring the frosty-breathed citizen. "Sheriff, do you know John Best? He's the owner of the Quick Stop."

Before the sheriff could answer, John released another gust of frigid air. "Quick Stop, you say! It'll be a *quick stop*, alright. Nobody will be spending much time there now. You guys really did a fine job of putting me right out of business," he sputtered.

All buzzing had ceased and every ear in the café was tuned to the conversation in the corner booth. They didn't want to miss a single word.

"Sheriff," the angry voice went on, "I voted for you in the last two elections. I thought you'd protect us taxpayers, but no, you just come into town towing your hired guns and shoot my store into tiny pieces and leave. I'll get you out of office if it's the last thing I ever do! I'll go door to door through this whole county if it takes that. I'll have plenty of time now that I don't have a store to run!"

When he stopped for a breath, Mike broke in. "John, now you just calm down. You have no right to come blustering in here, blaming Sheriff Lyght for the damage to your store without even giving him a chance to explain what—"

"Oh, you think not, huh?" John Best said, turning his icy blue eyes on Mike. "Well let me tell you something, mister hotshot deputy. I do blame him, and I blame you too! If you two poor excuses for lawmen had done your jobs, you could have had that Butch fellow taken care of a lot earlier without destroying my store. In fact, Sergeant O'Connor, you should have had him gathered up before he even got there. That's what we pay you to do."

Not so much as the tinkling of a fork on a plate came from anywhere else in the café. All was forgotten in favor of the embarrassing scene John Best was creating. Sheriff Lyght finally spoke. "I'm sorry, John. We did what we could, and it just didn't work. You do have insurance, don't you?"

"You did what you could alright! If you were just going to let him take that girl and walk away you should have done it yesterday morning and left the place intact. I cannot believe that you invited those bigheaded city boys up here and ordered them to shoot up my store like you did. I'm surprised you didn't have them shoot the girl too!"

"That's enough, John!" Mike said, his face turning scarlet as he slid from the booth and planted his feet firmly on the floor. His Irish anger was hot enough to thaw the ice John had brought in. With his eyes boring into John's, he went on, "The sheriff had nothing to do with that shooting spree. He—"

"Oh, didn't he now?" John interrupted, his voice taunting, egging Mike to let his temper take over. "Well, where in the world was he when it happened, then? I heard he gave the order and then took a nap." He stared defiantly at Mike.

"He was asleep, but he gave no such order." Mike was fighting to maintain control. "You need to know why—"

"I know enough! He was asleep on the job. Well, we taxpayers don't pay you to sleep, Sheriff!" he shouted, turning his angry gaze back on the sheriff. "We pay you to protect us. What a lazy, no good—"

"Shut up!" Mike snapped. "I didn't see you offering any advice or putting yourself in any danger. It may interest you to know that Sheriff Lyght should have been in the hospital—still should be. He got shot, if you'll remember! Now, you can just get out of here and leave us to a little breakfast."

"I'll do no such thing. I'm a taxpayer, and I pay this man's wages," he said, poking a stubby finger in the sheriff's face. "And I pay your wages too. That makes me the boss, so you'll just have to listen until I'm finished."

The sheriff pushed his way out of the booth and stood, wincing from the pain of his bullet wound. He shoved a fist into his pocket and withdrew a handful of change. He picked out a quarter and extended it to the owner of the Quick Stop. "Take this," he said.

Caught off guard, John took it and asked, "What's this for?"

"That's your share of my wages for the month, probably for the whole year. Now that you are no longer my boss, I will thank you to get out of here and leave me to enjoy my breakfast. I have had a long, hard night, and I'm rather hungry. I might suggest that you use the quarter to call your insurance agent from that pay phone out front and start getting your store put back together."

John stared at the quarter in his hand like it was going to jump up and bite his lip. One man started clapping, then everyone in the café applauded. John's ears were bright red, but he defiantly stood his ground.

Sheriff Lyght went on, "Tell your agent that I'll provide him with a complete report, and if there's anything else I can do to help you get back in business, just let me know, but don't ask unless you can be a gentleman. I really don't appreciate the way you've acted this morning."

Penny was approaching the table with two steaming plates. John, slightly embarrassed but still seething, said, "You better hope I can get the store fixed and open again soon!" He spun like a tornado and crashed into Penny, sending the hot plates and the breakfast they contained flying through the air, the food staining John's own clothes as well as Penny's. The plates hit the floor with a crash, sending splinters of glass for twenty feet up the aisle.

"John Best, what's the matter with you?" Penny shouted. "You get outta here, and don't you come back until you grow up!"

John stared at the mess with bloodshot eyes, swiped at egg yoke on his shirt, swore softly, and created another vacuum as he stormed out. "Sorry, boys," Penny said, her face crinkled into a smile, her sides jiggling with mirth. "I know it ain't funny, but that creep always did have a way a getting in people's faces and burrowing under their skin. I wish he'd just pack up and leave town!"

Mike and the Sheriff were on their knees picking up bits of broken glass. "You two get up off that floor and sit down," Penny ordered, hardly able to talk for the laughter she was enjoying. "I'll clean up this mess and get you some more food." She kept laughing right out loud, a soloist in a café-chorus of laughter. After she finally regained her composure she said, "I'd a paid for a seat to a seen that."

"I take it she doesn't care for Mr. Best," the sheriff said after she had disappeared through the door to the kitchen.

"Nobody does much. It's a wonder he's stayed in business the way he treats people. I never could figure why old Sam stayed with him. He treats his help about like he just treated us," Mike said soberly. "I wouldn't lose too much sleep about him hurting you in an election. He doesn't have a dozen friends in the whole county."

Forty-five minutes later Sheriff Lyght parked his white truck in front of the school. He moaned. "Oh, no, Mike. Looks like more trouble."

Jim Leighton was pacing up and down the crumbling sidewalk, stopping and glaring at the men as they climbed wearily out of the car. "Where's my daughter?" he demanded.

"I'm afraid we don't know, Mr. Leighton, but we have men looking all over the state and into the adjoining ones," Sheriff Lyght said calmly.

"A lot of good that'll do. Why did you let him take her out of here in the first place? You should have stopped him," the distraught father said angrily.

Still exercising remarkable patience the sheriff said, "Mr. Leighton, you're frustrated, tired, and frightened. I would be too if I was faced with your problems. I'm sorry we couldn't get her away from Butch before he left, but you have to understand, there's only so much we can do. We're dealing with a smart man—this killer she's with. Even if we'd tried something when he left with her, shot only him even, it would have killed her too because of how he'd set it up."

Mr. Leighton brushed away an errant tear, then squaring his sagging shoulders, he said, "I'm sorry, Sheriff. We're just so afraid for our daughter. We don't know what to do with ourselves. Please find her and get her back to us."

"We will continue to give it the best we have, sir. You have my word on that."

"Thank you," Mr. Leighton said softly, the anger gone, only heartache and worry left in its place. He turned and trudged away.

Mike's heart went out to him. What a burden he carried. "Come on, Mike, let's go in and get back to work," the sheriff said. "Maybe some leads have come in while we've been gone."

There were none.

Sheriff Lyght spent several minutes on the phone. Mike stared at the wall, his mind filled with worries, only half listening to the sheriff's voice. "The FBI is in on the case now, Mike," the sheriff said after hanging up. "An agent will be here to meet with us in a little while. The state patrol is also sending up some brass. Guess all we can do is take it easy for a little while. When they get here we'll give them what we have and let them help us call the shots for a while. I'm so tired I can hardly think straight."

"Sheriff," Mike said slowly, watching his friend lean back in his chair and stretch his lanky legs, "I was sort of hoping I could follow up on this case. I feel somewhat responsible for Erika. I know we're short-handed, but I'd like to be involved in the search for her. Any chance you could let me work with the federal agent assigned to the case?"

The sheriff turned his steel-gray eyes on Mike and hesitated only briefly before consenting. "Sure, Mike. You know Butch better than any other officer. I want you involved for however long it takes. I would sure like to see that man nailed, and you have the best chance of anyone of getting it done."

The door opened, stirring a gentle breeze. Mike looked up. Jan, her glowing smile in place, dark-auburn hair curling gently around her face, and wearing a pair of blue jeans and a western cut blouse was framed there. Looking over her shoulder was a tall, deeply tanned young man. It had to be the fellow from the night before, although he had never got a good look at him. "Hi, guys," she said cheerfully, looking astonishingly bright and refreshed. "Long night, wasn't it? Did you two get any sleep?"

"A little," Mike said, rubbing his eyes as if that would wipe away the evidence that it was far too little.

Jan had the ability to cheer people up by her very presence. Enthusiasm and optimism radiated from her face like rays of sunlight, brightening her way no matter how difficult things became. "You look like you never lost a wink," Mike said with a grin. "How do you do it?"

"I hate to rub it in, but I'm a bit younger than either one of you," she said easily. "Sheriff, how's the bullet wound?"

"Sore, but I'll live," Sheriff Lyght answered. "Who's the young fellow?"

"Oh, I'm sorry," she said with a deep blush that complimented her clear hazel eyes. "This is Bob Evans. He's from San Diego, California. Erika's boyfriend. He's had kind of a streak of bad luck here lately. He was in the wreck I got called to last night. An elk ran out in front of him." She smiled at Bob and said, "Lucky gal. Erika I mean." He melted under her soft gaze. "Bob, this is Sheriff Alden Lyght. You met Sergeant Mike O'Connor last night."

"It's nice to meet you, but are you okay?" the sheriff asked, immediately sympathetic toward the worried young man.

"I'm fine. After I hit the elk, I rolled the rental car I was driving. I was lucky, I guess. I never got a scratch on me," he said.

"He was being a good boy," Jan added, smiling at Bob. "He was wearing a seat belt. And the air bag helped too."

Mike, who was watching the interchange with interest, entertained an errant thought for just a moment, then he sent it on its way. He thought Jan seemed more like the kind of girl a guy like Bob would go for, more so than the less mature Erika. She wasn't movie-star gorgeous like Erika, but Jan was very attractive as well as being very capable and intelligent. But he figured it was none of his business, and he turned his attention to what Sheriff Lyght was saying.

"I'm sorry about Erika. We haven't given up though," the sheriff said, reaching for and shaking Bob's hand.

"I know. Jan told me how great you two are." Bob glanced at the trooper and smiled. "I'm sorry about Erika's father. He's really a very nice guy, but he cracks under pressure. He'll be fine and thank you both once this is all over."

"I hope so," Sheriff Lyght said, frowning. "I really don't like to have people mad at me when all I'm doing is the best I can. How much do you know about what's happened here?"

"Jan's told me most of it, I think, and I've heard a little about this Butch Snyder on the radio," Bob said. "If you don't mind, I'd like to hear the whole thing from you two men."

Sheriff Lyght nodded and said, "Certainly." For the next few minutes he and Mike gave Bob the details.

Bob's sea-blue eyes were deeply troubled by the time they'd finished. "Do you think she's cooperated with this guy a little?"

"No," Sheriff Lyght said firmly, "I wouldn't say that at all, even though it does happen sometimes in hostage cases. The victim often becomes sympathetic to the plight of the hostage-taker. In this case, Erika is totally frightened by Butch. Sheer terror can certainly cause people to act differently than they normally would."

"I can't even imagine what she's going through," Bob said, his voice cracking.

Jan watched him, thinking what a decent person he seemed to be. And then she thought of Butch. A shiver ran the full length of her body as terrible memories crept into her mind. What excruciating terror Erika must be experiencing. How could she stand it? Jan felt like crying for the girl. Her sympathy for Erika reached beyond the young hostage to Bob. How hard it must be for him to know that his girlfriend was in the hands of such a terrible and frightening man. Unconsciously, she rubbed at the small red spot on her cheek.

Bob had seen her make that gesture several times. It was endearing almost. The spot she seemed to be touching wasn't very noticeable, but it seemed to bother her. He caught her eye and winced. He saw fear there. Raw, naked fear.

"Jan?" he said. "Is something wrong?"

She shook her head, forced a smile and said, "I'm okay. I was just thinking about Erika. How awful it must be to be with B . . . with him."

Bob nodded his agreement, but he wondered what it was that *really* caused the fear he saw in her eyes. Maybe she wasn't really cut out to be a cop. But she seemed like such a good one.

Mike noticed the exchange between the two, and he also saw the look in Jan's eyes. He was puzzled. She'd always seemed so strong, so brave. He spoke up, hoping to bring her back to her old self. "Erika has likely been taken across state lines. The FBI is on the case now and have a man on the way. We'll meet and discuss how to proceed. Meantime, a massive hunt for the Leightons' Expedition is going on in several states. It'll turn up somewhere, and when it does, we'll go from there."

"I'd like to help," Bob said casually. "If there's anything I can do, I will."

"I don't mean to hurt your feelings, Bob, and I realize how difficult the waiting must be for you, but this is best left to professionals," the sheriff said apologetically.

"I know that, sir, but if anything does come up, I'll do whatever you ask."

Sheriff Lyght touched his sore shoulder lightly, then said thoughtfully, "Actually, there may be one thing. You could sit down with Sergeant O'Connor and tell him everything you can think of about Erika. We really don't know much about her; her father is a bit difficult to talk to right now, and her mother's an emotional wreck."

"Sure thing, if it will help," Bob responded, his face brightening. "Of course, I've only dated her for a few weeks, but I've come to know her pretty well in that time."

Jan cast him an interested glance. She had been instantly attracted to him, and it wasn't just his looks. He was an intelligent and caring person—as Erika must be, although she'd heard Erika referred to as immature. Not that it was any of her business. But she'd thought that Bob had dated Erika for a long time. He referred to her as his girlfriend. She wondered now just how serious he was with Erika. *Stop it!* she scolded herself. He had come all the way from California to try to help her. Obviously it was serious. She needed to get her head on straight. She just hadn't seen enough eligible young men lately she decided. She looked up and caught Mike smiling at her. She blushed and felt extremely foolish.

Mike was relieved to see the fear fade from her eyes. Bob seemed to have quite an effect on her—as he probably did on Erika.

"It will help us to know more about Erika," the sheriff told Bob. "She's almost bound to have some kind of effect on Butch at some point if she hasn't already, and the better we know her, the better we can try to predict what they might do next."

"You really are concerned that she might cooperate with him, aren't you?" Bob asked perceptively.

"We can't overlook the possibility. We don't know what kind of threats he might have made and how they might affect her," Sheriff Lyght said. "Fear is a powerful motivator."

Bob nodded and glanced at Jan. That look was back in her eyes and it alarmed him. "What's the matter, Jan?" he asked.

"I was just thinking how awful it would be for her," she said in a slightly trembling voice. "It must be terrible to be threatened by someone as dangerous as . . . as *him.*"

"Thank you, Jan," Bob said, surprising her.

"For what?" she asked.

"For caring . . . about Erika, I mean. What's happening to Erika really is important to you, isn't it?

"Of course it is, Bob," she said as that look of fear again faded from her eyes. "It's important to all of us." She waved an arm toward Sergeant O'Connor and Sheriff Lyght. "And whatever Erika does while she's with *him,* she's not to be blamed," Jan concluded forcefully. Both officers looked at her with a little surprise.

"Let's go in another room and talk while we're waiting for the federal agent and the state brass to get here," Mike suggested.

"Do you mind if I join you?" Jan asked timidly.

"Of course not, Jan. I'd appreciate any help you can give me," Mike answered quickly, always grateful for her insight. She might be young, but she was also very shrewd.

An hour later, after Mike had excused Bob to walk over to the motel, he and Jan found that three men had joined the sheriff, and they were introduced. The Colorado State Patrol lieutenant and sergeant knew Jan, but they were not her immediate supervisors, and Mike had met the FBI agent a year ago.

"Well, shall we begin?" Sheriff Lyght asked, pulling up two more chairs.

"Do you believe they've left the state?" Special Agent Harry Reed asked. Mike welcomed the opportunity to work with him again. He was a no-nonsense, experienced officer in his mid-thirties. Dark, short, and not one the ladies would call handsome, he was efficient and likeable. Through silver-rimmed glasses, he viewed the world from light-brown, wide-set eyes over the end of a bulbous purple nose.

"We've discussed that," Mike responded, "and we believe it's a good possibility." He went on to explain how broad the current search effort was.

"The vehicle has got to turn up soon," Sheriff Lyght observed. "We're checking the mountains in the area. Butch was as familiar with them as my wife is with my homely face."

Following an hour-long discussion, assignments were made to the State Patrol to have officers compile as complete a list as possible of persons Butch might seek out—old friends, former cell mates, and distant relatives. Mike volunteered to make a list of old hangouts and habits from Butch's teenage years. The FBI agent said he would begin coordinating with agents from all the surrounding states.

The sheriff yawned and glanced at his watch. "I need to step outside and greet the press," he said. "They have a few questions."

Jan and Mike followed at a discreet distance as he walked out of the school. The media representatives converged on Sheriff Lyght like a thunderstorm. Microphones were thrust in his weary face, and TV cameras were aimed with deadly accuracy. Questions came at him from every side.

He held up his arms, wincing from the pain in his wounded shoulder, and said, "One at a time, please." As soon as they had settled into a semblance of order, he said, "Thank you. Now I'll try to answer your questions."

He called on the reporter from the county's only newspaper first, then fielded questions from the others, answering them all as completely and accurately as he could. Jan leaned over to Mike and said, "I can't believe how well he handles himself. He seems to do his best thinking when he's under pressure, on his feet, and sweating."

"True, but every man has his limits. I think Alden is about there."

Mike knew the sheriff, and he was right. An arrogant reporter from a Denver radio station asked, "Isn't it true that your men fouled up badly, and that if you'd made sound decisions at the beginning this situation would have been over in the first hour?"

"It would have been over alright, and people would have been dead," the sheriff replied hotly. "We did the best we could under difficult circumstances."

"Isn't it true, Sheriff, that if you would have ordered your automatic weapons fire spree much earlier, Snyder would have been killed and—"

Sheriff Lyght interrupted, his face burning, and his steel-grey eyes boring down on the cocky newsman. "I never ordered automatic weapons fire, and the lieutenant that did was dismissed."

Undaunted, the reporter intensified his attack. "Why did you let the killer take her out of the Quick Stop? I'm told that the two of them walked side by side down the street like they were out for a midnight stroll, and that you allowed them to drive off in the Leightons' Expedition with no one even following them. That's rather poor judgement, don't you agree, Sheriff Lyght?"

"Young man, I would suggest that you get your facts together before you start shooting off your mouth. You might check with some of your colleagues here. I'm sure they can correct you on what actually took place. Now, I have work to do," he snapped and, turning on his heels, strode swiftly back to the school.

There was a flurry of activity among the press after the sheriff's departure. Several newsmen engaged in what appeared to be a very intense discussion with the haughty radio reporter. Mike smiled to himself as he signaled to Jan and turned to go inside. "Looks like the sheriff has turned that young fellow's colleagues against him."

"Sure has," Jan observed dryly. In the school a minute later, she said, "Hey, look at the sheriff's face. Something's happening. Maybe they've caught him." She sounded extremely hopeful.

The sheriff was on the phone, and his gray eyes gleamed with excitement. When he'd cradled the receiver, he said, "We've had a break. A citizen reported seeing a Ford Expedition of the correct description in Wyoming a little before dawn. He said there appeared to be two people in it. We can't be sure, but it could be them."

"We need to get up there," Mike said. "If it is them, then my guess is that they're holed up somewhere for the day trying to get some sleep."

"And maybe he's let Erika go," Jan said hopefully.

"Unlikely," Mike said. "She would have contacted someone." The hopeful look vanished from Jan's face.

The sheriff went on. "An intensive search is already underway up there. You're right though, Mike, and you'd better get cracking. I'll arrange for a chopper to take you up. You need to be ready in an hour."

"I can be ready sooner than that—say, thirty minutes—but there are a couple of problems. I'll need something to drive once I get there, and I could use some help. Special Agent Reed might be able to work with me, but I know from past experience that he gets called off assignments a lot. And two heads are always better than one. I was wondering if there was any chance that Jan might be able to get the patrol to let her help us."

The sheriff turned to Jan, whose face was as white as a sheet. "How about it, Jan, or don't you feel too well?"

She didn't feel well at all, but it was not just physical. It was also personal and private. She didn't want to go and yet, how could she ever tell them that? So she said, "I'm fine, Sheriff, and I'm sure I can get permission to work with Mike for a few days."

"Let me take care of that. I'll call your lieutenant. You have thirty minutes to be ready. Okay?"

"Sure," she agreed, her stomach turning somersaults.

"And a car?" Mike asked.

"Yes, you'll definitely need one later. And your truck is out of commission. I only have one spare. Hey, I wonder if that young fellow, Bob, would drive one up there for us," the sheriff said, rubbing his chin.

"I'll find him and send him down to see you," Jan volunteered. It was goofy, but the thought of having Bob meet them in Wyoming made her feel better about the whole assignment. Chances were good that he would want to tag along, and she knew Mike. He wasn't one to get bogged down in regulations. Somehow, the thought that the young Californian might be there was a cheerful one in an otherwise almost unbearable situation.

Five minutes later, Jan ushered Bob Evans into the school. "Would you ride down to my office with me and take one of our patrol cars up to Wyoming for Mike and Jan to use? They'll be flying up," the sheriff said as soon as he saw Bob.

"I sure will, sir. Thank you, sir. I'll be real careful—watch for elk and things like that," Bob said with a grin.

"You better," the sheriff said sternly. "This is my only spare car. I'll get you a map and show you where to go. You'll need to call my office and find out where to meet Mike and Jan later."

"That means—" Jan began.

"Your boss said to go for it."

Jan nodded and turned to leave. Bob and Mike followed. "Does this mean I can help up there?" Bob asked anxiously as soon as they were outside of the school.

"I suppose it means that you can tag along at least," Jan said hopefully, looking at Mike for reassurance. "I won't let the sergeant leave you stranded up there somewhere."

Mike nodded with a grin.

"Thanks," Bob said. "I just pray that Erika's still okay. He wouldn't really hurt an innocent girl, would he?"

He certainly would! Jan thought bitterly to herself. "I sure hope not," she said to Bob. "Hey, we'll get her back for you, Bob," she added, forcing a smile at him as he opened the door to her patrol car.

She climbed in and Bob shut the door. Mike opened the one on the passenger side. "Can you drop me off at the house and then pick me up in a few minutes?" Mike asked. "Then we'll leave your car at the school and leave your keys with the sheriff, as per your lieutenant's instructions."

"Get in," she said with a smile. "We'll see you in Wyoming," she called to Bob.

***

None of them noticed the Denver radio reporter leave the school behind them with a smirk on his face. Having entered the school after arguing with his colleagues, he had intended to talk to the sheriff again. When he got in there, however, he overheard the sheriff discussing a possible break in the case. He backed quietly away. As soon as he was clear of the school, he made a beeline for his car, anxious to get his hot scoop to the station. Somehow, he had a feeling the sheriff intended to keep this juicy bit of knowledge from the press. He grinned smugly. He was one up on the sheriff now.

Chapter 8

Erika fought the sea. The waves were huge, and she struggled to stay on her surfboard. Suddenly, a rogue wave rose from beneath her, tossing her high into the air. When she reentered the water she was sucked far beneath the surface, then spit out again. She swam frantically, trying to keep from being submerged once more, afraid that she might never breathe again. Finally in control, she swam in a circle through the frothy water, searching for her surfboard. She spotted it way off in the distance, a bright pink dot drifting out to sea.

She swam after it frantically, losing sight of it each time the ocean swelled in front of her. Then it would bob back in sight as she rose on a wave. Each time she caught sight of it, it was larger and had changed in form until it finally appeared as a large pink boat, its motor droning in ever-increasing volume. It turned until its bow was pointed toward Erika, and with a burst of speed, it bore down upon her.

The boat came so close that Erika could see Butch pressed against the glass windshield, a leering grin on his whiskered face. She awoke with a scream as the boat towered over her, the motor a deafening roar.

She sat upright, her hands clamped over her ears, perspiration drenching her blue sweats. "Shut up, Erika! It was just a low-flying plane," Butch said gruffly "They can't see in here."

Erika, fully awake now, listened to the fading sounds of the plane. "It scared me," she said lamely, afraid to admit that what really scared her was him.

He dismissed the plane and her hopes with a wave of his arm. "They don't have any idea where we are. It's probably just a coincidence. By the way, what time is it?"

"It's nearly six o'clock. We've been asleep for ten hours."

"You've been asleep for ten hours," he corrected. "I slept some, but I had to keep an eye on you too. I sleep light. Every time you moved in your sleep I woke up."

The thought of Butch watching her as she slept caused her to tremble. She hugged her knees tightly to her chest and watched him as he walked the few steps to her father's Expedition. "I noticed an ice chest in the back," he said as he stopped and turned toward her. "I could use something to eat. You probably could too."

Erika was conscious of Butch's pale green eyes traveling up and down her huddled body. His leering face added to the other kind of terror she was feeling. Killing her was not the only thing he could do to hurt her. Finally, with a grin he said, "You look good, Erika." She shuddered at the way he said it.

His eyes traveled over her one more time before he finally pulled out the ice chest. She accepted his offer of some cheese, which wasn't very cool, and ate a couple of warm apples. Butch ate ravenously. When he was done, he again looked in the Expedition. He found an unopened bag of chocolate chip cookies. They were soon half gone, although Erika ate only one.

The makeshift meal over, Butch ordered Erika to load the ice chest in the car while he went to the front and climbed in. She wondered, hopefully, if he was going to drive off and leave her here. Rattlesnakes and rats were better company than Butch Snyder.

She was disappointed when he said, "I'm going to see if I can find some news."

He inserted the key and turned the ignition to accessory. After a couple of minutes he found a station broadcasting the news. Erika drifted back to the hay and sat on her blanket. She could hear the radio, and though she feigned indifference, she listened to every word as a voice reported, "A massive air and ground search is being conducted at this hour across much of central and southern Wyoming in an attempt to find the late model, red Ford Expedition that was used by escaped Colorado killer, Butch Snyder, to whisk his teenage hostage out of Pineview, Colorado, early this morning. Sheriff Alden Lyght has refused to answer questions concerning the report, released just before noon by a Denver radio station, in which he was quoted as saying that the vehicle had been seen just before dawn this morning near Saratoga."

Butch swore and slammed his fist on the dash. "They're looking for us alright," he said. "We'll have to wait to leave until after it's dark—unless someone happens to come snooping around sooner."

Erika's chest constricted. "What'll you do if that happens, Butch?" she asked fearfully.

"We'll make a run for it," he replied. She had hoped again that he would make the run by himself. He didn't need her now.

He seemed to read her mind and came around the car with an angry set to his face. "And don't get thinking I might leave you behind. I told you, I need you girl. That hasn't changed." She said nothing, and his face softened a little, but his eyes ran the full length of her body. "Boy, wouldn't the guys in the joint be jealous if they could see me with you?"

"I'm thirsty," she said, trying to divert his attention from her. What he could do to her—alone in this barn—was more than she could bear to think about.

They drank from the red and white Coleman water cooler that Erika retrieved from the back of the Expedition. The water was lukewarm but helped quench their thirst. Butch began to prowl inside the old barn like a caged animal, occasionally peering through cracks, watching for any sign of approaching cars Erika supposed.

An hour passed. Butch asked Erika for the time again. Before she could reply, he noticed a plume of gray dust way down the old lane. "Get in the car," he ordered.

She sat alone in the car for a couple of minutes before he joined her. "Cops!" he said through gritted teeth. "They're almost here. I guess we'll have to go now."

The engine roared to life. "I'll open the barn door," Erika said, grabbing her door handle.

"Stay put," Butch ordered as he shifted into reverse.

Before she could fasten her seat belt he stomped on the gas peddle and the Expedition flew backward, showering jagged gray splinters of barn door in all directions, and continuing in a cloud of dust outside. He backed in a tight circle, suddenly slamming on the brakes, shoving the gear lever into drive, spinning the rear tires until they caught hold, and then shooting forward through the swirling dust, the engine whining noisily.

Erika, still trying in vain to buckle her seat belt, caught a glimpse of a pair of wide eyes behind the wheel of the approaching police cruiser. The officer they belonged to cranked the wheel sharply to the right and bounced off the road. Erika twisted in her seat as Butch continued to accelerate down the center of the rutted road. The police car bounced to a dust-enshrouded stop in a deep, abandoned ditch, hopelessly high centered.

He's stuck! Erika thought to herself, on the verge of tears.

"He won't be chasing me," Butch chuckled. "But he'll use his radio and call for help. We've got to get away from here fast." Butch concentrated fiercely on keeping the speeding Ford upright as he rammed it down the rough lane.

Finally, Erika succeeded in fastening her seat belt and glanced at the speedometer—85 mph! She held her breath as they approached a curve, but Butch slowed down just enough to negotiate it and jammed the accelerator to the floor as they straightened out.

Butch slowed down again as they approached the highway. A Wyoming Highway Patrol car slid to a stop, blocking the approach. Butch cursed and drove off the road, nearly overturning before he finally regained control and drove onto the highway behind the patrol car and headed south.

"Where are we going, Butch?" Erika asked, her voice shaking so badly she could hardly make herself heard.

"North," he said, slowing down and flipping a U-turn in the highway. He accelerated again and drove up the center of the road—toward the speeding patrol car that had been in hot pursuit, its siren screaming and lights flashing.

Erika watched, speechless, as the two hurtling cars drew closer together. At the last minute, the patrol car swerved to the right and off the road. Again she looked back and watched it sliding through the brush, going on its side and finally rolling gently onto its top. She was still watching as the trooper climbed out through a broken window and made wild, angry gestures in their direction.

After about five miles Butch slowed down, pulled to the side of the road, and stopped. "Get out," he said to Erika, not harshly, but firmly.

Relief flooded over her. It was frightening to be left in the middle of nowhere like this, but anything was better than being with him. She moved quickly to comply, hoping he wouldn't linger.

To her dismay, he shut off the ignition, pulled out the keys, and stepped out himself while shoving the keys in his pocket. "Look worried," he said as he pointed to a car approaching from the north.

That wasn't difficult.

Butch waved at the car frantically, and it pulled over. "Something wrong?" a mid-thirties-looking man with a red baseball cap asked.

"Yeah, I need your car," Butch said menacingly, producing the .38 and shoving it in the driver's face. "Get out, all of you."

The man's eyes nearly popped from their sockets, but sensibly, he turned to his wife and said, "Do as he says, Sue, and help the kids out."

Erika couldn't stop herself from crying. If she could just stay here with this frightened family. But it was not to be. "Get in," Butch shouted to Erika as soon as the last of the terrorized young family had stepped off the pavement where Butch was signaling for them to stand.

Butch turned the old light-blue Pontiac 6000 around and drove north again. Erika wondered about the necessity of the speed he was gaining in this unfamiliar old car as she caught a final glimpse of the stranded family bunched forlornly at the side of the road. If Butch had left the keys, she thought, they could drive off in the Expedition, but he still had them.

Butch was proud of himself. "It'll be awhile before the cops find out what we're driving. As long as someone doesn't come along with a cell phone."

He grinned indulgently. But a short time later he began to swear again as another set of flashing red and blue lights appeared on the horizon. He slowed to sixty and the patrol car sped past, its siren wailing a desperate song in the cool evening air. Butch chuckled and said, "They didn't recognize us. They'll soon know about this car though. We better switch again." Even as he spoke he was slowing down and pulling to the side of the road.

This time they deprived an ancient rancher of his equally ancient black pickup. They continued north at a much slower rate, even though Butch had the gas peddle to the floor. After a few miles Butch dug in his pocket and said, "I'm getting quite a collection here," giving Erika a glimpse of the two useless rings of keys which he then chucked out the window.

To Erika's amazement, Butch soon stopped again. "This is just too easy," he said with a laugh as they went through the now-familiar routine of changing vehicles. This time they left a young man cursing at the side of the road as they drove off in his yellow Toyota pickup.

"Gotta get off the main drag," Butch said a few minutes later as he slowed and turned onto a gravel side road that led to the west.

Several minutes, and a host of small hills, valleys, and even a few well-tended fields later, Butch pulled into a sprawling, shaded farmyard. He parked beside a shiny black Ford Ranger pickup, pretty much out of view of the road, and killed the Toyota's engine. A silver car was parked in an open garage just a few feet away. A sidewalk led through a white picket fence and up to an older, but well-maintained, white house. "Let's see if anyone's home," Butch suggested, giving Erika no hint of what was going to happen next while waving his pistol at her. "You go first."

She trudged numbly through the gate past brightly colored flowers and a neatly trimmed lawn up to the door. Butch knocked. As they waited, Erika became aware of Butch's appearance. She had been so wrapped up in their wild flight that she'd failed to notice how sick he was. Blood was seeping out of the badly saturated bandage on his shoulder. His coat, along with her sweatshirt, she remembered, were still in the barn. His face was white beneath his stubby black whiskers. She wished he would collapse right there on the gray boards of the porch floor. But he was stronger than he looked.

A small woman in her late sixties finally answered the door, pulling a faded house coat around her plump body. Her eyes grew large when she saw Butch. He spoke politely, but Erika could feel the strain in his voice. "Good evening, ma'am," he said. "Is your husband at home?"

"He's still out in the fields," she said, pointing in the direction where the sun was now hanging low over distant mountains. "Can I help you?"

"Yes, ma'am," he said, as her eyes grew wider still and glued themselves to his bloody shoulder. "Could we use your phone?"

The woman hesitated, and Butch's facade crumbled. Angrily he grabbed her by the throat and shoved her into the house. "What's the matter, lady, can't you see I'm hurt? Forget the phone lady, we need your truck. Get the keys!"

Erika was in a daze, but followed Butch as he shoved the lady toward the kitchen where, she stammered, they kept the keys. She never made it that far, because when Butch released his hold on her throat and pulled his gun, she slumped to the floor in a dead faint.

Butch kicked her in the side. "Don't pass out on me, old woman!" he screamed insanely. "Find her purse, Erika. There'll be keys in it," he ordered, waving the pistol in her face.

Erika staggered into the kitchen, feeling faint and sick to her stomach, but anxious to find the purse and keys and get away from the house before Butch did something worse than he already had to the helpless woman. The purse was on the kitchen table. She pulled out a ring of keys and returned to the living room, averting her eyes from the unconscious woman on the floor. "I found them," she called, looking around for Butch.

"Good," he answered from somewhere in the back of the house.

Erika heard the door open and spun just as an older man came through it. His face was twisted with rage. "What's going on here, young lady?" he demanded, then spotting the woman near the kitchen door, he shouted, "What have you done to my wife?"

She hadn't done anything! But before she could speak, Butch entered the room. "Don't move, mister." Butch's voice carried the unmistakable threat of harm that nailed the old farmer's dusty boots to the floor. Butch was holding his revolver in one hand and a rifle in the other. "Did you . . . shoot . . . her?" the farmer asked. His face was still twisted in anger, but there was also distinct fear in his eyes and a quiver in his voice.

"No, but I will if you don't do as I say." The man stood still as the color drained from his weathered face. "Lay down by the old woman," Butch ordered.

The old farmer shuffled across the floor and stretched out on the carpet beside her, touching her shoulder gently while looking at her face with concern and love. "Find some rope, Erika," Butch said, keeping the pistol trained at the man's head.

"I don't know where to look," she reported tearfully.

"In the barn," the old man said.

"Hurry, girl," Butch shouted, "but leave those keys with me." He was sitting down on a sofa, not looking any better, but not much worse either.

Fear for the old couple's lives was greater now than fear for her own. They reminded her of her own sweet grandparents, and that thought cut deep. Motivated by her sudden concern for them, Erika scooted out the door and around to the barn. She thought only for a second of running, but she couldn't bear the thought of Butch harming the old couple. They would be far better left tied up on the floor than anything else he might do to them. It took her what seemed like an eternity, but she finally found some rope and ran back toward the house. As she approached the porch, a shot rang out inside. Gasping, she stumbled in, expecting to see the farmer dying on the floor. She almost fainted with relief when she found that he was unharmed.

"You shot," she said blankly to Butch who was now standing at the far end of the room.

"Just reminding you who's in charge here," he said with a sneer. "You took your time."

Erika said nothing as she handed the rope to her captor. The farmer's wife groaned and started to pull herself to her knees. "Stay put, old woman," Butch ordered. She turned her head, saw his face, and slumped back down.

"Tie them up," Butch said.

"I . . . can't. I . . . don't know how," Erika stammered.

"Then figure it out," he said, aiming the pistol threateningly at the old couple. "If you don't, one of them will die." She figured it out the best she could with a numb brain, misted eyes, and trembling hands.

"I've got to get the bullets for the rifle," he said. "You wait here."

As soon as Butch had disappeared into the back, the old farmer said in a weak voice, "You're the girl who was kidnapped, aren't you?"

Erika began to sob.

"You've got to run, girl—get away while you can," he pleaded. "Take my truck."

"But he has the keys," she said.

"I have more in my pocket. Hurry. Get them and run."

Erika stepped close and knelt beside the old couple, thinking that somewhere they had grandchildren who loved them as she did her own grandparents. She tried to brush the thought aside and think of her own safety. She fumbled at the man's pocket and managed to get the keys free, but then she didn't get up. Her eyes wouldn't leave the faces of the two selfless people that somebody loved. "Go, please, while you can," the man pleaded.

"I . . . I can't," she stammered. "Not without you."

"There isn't time for us. Now go. He may not have hurt you yet, but he will."

"But if I leave," she explained slowly. "He will do something to you. I know he will."

"We're old," the farmer cried softly. "You're so young and so sweet. Forget about us. Leave now."

But Erika could not, as badly as she wanted to. She stood up, the keys dangling from her fingers.

A shot rang out and the keys literally disappeared. The strength in her legs melted away, and she slumped to the floor. She couldn't turn her head, but she knew where the shot had come from. Uncontrolled sobbing racked her body. Butch's booted foot caught her side, and she cried out in pain.

"Get up," Butch ordered in a voice that wouldn't be disobeyed.

Erika found it hard to stand, but somehow she managed. Butch grabbed her arm and spun her violently toward him. His eyes were spitting fire. "You were going to leave," he accused in low and even tones.

"No, no I wasn't," she protested weakly as she became vaguely aware that he looked different somehow. Then she realized that he was now wearing a denim jacket hiding the bloody shoulder, and a white cap concealing the wound on his head.

"Don't lie to me, Erika," Butch said, and his hand shot out, slapping her face so hard she spun, nearly losing her balance.

"Don't, please," the old farmer protested from his painful position on the floor. "I tried to get her to leave, but she wouldn't."

"And that's why she had your keys," Butch said with a wicked laugh.

Erika opened her mouth to offer her own protest, but nothing came out but a croak. The phone began to ring. Butch and Erika both stared at it dumbly on its perch beside the sofa. When it finally quit ringing, Butch raised the .38 and pulled the trigger. The telephone disintegrated in a blur of tan and silver as the sound of the shot echoed through the house.

"I don't suppose you two can get loose, but if you do, you won't be using the phone," Butch said smugly. "Now, before we go, me and my pretty hostage here will grab a bite to eat. Then you will never see us again."

Butch raided the refrigerator and began to gorge himself. Erika nibbled a little, but wasn't able to eat much. Oh how she loathed the animal in front of her. Then her thoughts turned to Bob. She missed him terribly. She'd known he was special the first time she met him, and she cared for him a lot, maybe even loved him. But now, as she contrasted Bob to the killer who sat coolly eating stolen food in a home he'd forced his way into, she knew that Bob was not only special, but the best thing that had ever happened to her.

And she might never see him again.

That dark thought drove still another twisting dagger into her heart.

After he was through eating, Butch emptied the money from the lady's purse and the man's wallet, stuffed it in his pocket and said, "I've got the keys, so I guess that's about it." Then he led Erika outside.

"God bless you, dear girl," she heard the farmer say as the door closed behind her.

Outside the sun was a blazing red ball in the western sky, turning the thin, scattered clouds to bright pink. "Pull the Toyota into the garage where the cops won't see it," he said to Erika. "We'll take their pickup."

She did as he told her, and wasn't surprised when he methodically slashed all four tires on the stolen Toyota and the couple's sedan before closing the garage door. Nothing he did could surprise her anymore. She didn't even care why he'd done it, but he told her anyway. "That's just in case you didn't tie them up very well. I don't want them to have anything to drive," he explained as they climbed into the black Ranger.

Butch drove slowly back toward the highway. "Don't ever try that again," he said, patting Erika on the knee, making her recoil. He pretended not to notice. "And don't lie to me again. I'm not stupid, girl. You were planning on leaving me."

"I was not!" she shouted in protest.

He shook a finger at her and grinned. "Oh, but you were, Erika. And next time, I may not shoot at the keys. It could have been you, you know. And don't forget that."

Butch looked terribly ill. The jacket and cap covered his injures, but he was in pain, there was no doubt about that. But despite his weakened condition, Erika didn't underestimate Butch. She knew what he could do with his gun. Her face still tingled from the slap he had delivered, and she also realized what he could do with his hands.

By the time Butch turned the black Ranger west onto Interstate 80 it was fully dark. They passed several police cars in the miles before they reached Rawlins, but none even slowed up. "Looks like we need gas," Butch said as they neared the first exit. "I'll pull off the freeway here and fill up."

They stopped at the first station past the exit. Butch got out, instructing Erika to stay put. She protested, indicating the need to visit the rest room. "All right," he relented, "but stay out of sight as much as possible."

She hurried, knowing he was watching the door. And he made no move to pay for the gas until she was back in the truck. Erika watched the blondee cashier lay her book down, take his money, give him some change, and pick the book up, instantly burying her nose in it again. When Butch was back in the truck he said, "Wow, that was close. That dumb girl didn't recognize me, but there was a wanted poster on the counter with my handsome mug smiling up at her."

Erika was beyond caring, and she didn't respond. Butch turned on the radio. "Find some music," he said as they pulled back onto the freeway. She found a rock station, but he protested immediately. "Hey, we're in Wyoming. Find a country station."

She settled on a station a moment later, not especially enjoying the music, but not daring to anger him. It wasn't long before the news came on. After national coverage about the daily comings and goings of the president and related topics, the newscaster said, "Turning to a story of local interest, escaped Colorado killer, Butch Snyder, was seen by several people earlier this evening not much over an hour's drive from Rawlins."

He went on to describe with some accuracy the series of car thefts. Then he said, "His teenage hostage appeared to be uninjured but terrified, according to witnesses. She, along with Snyder, disappeared into thin air after he stole the Toyota pickup. It's believed they must have reached Interstate 80 and headed east. It would be doubtful that Snyder would go through Rawlins with the Wyoming State Prison so close to the freeway." He chuckled, then cautioned, "If you're out there traveling tonight, be very alert, because no one knows where they are. If you're home, keep your doors locked, just to be on the safe side."

Erika grew drowsy as the truck rolled monotonously down the freeway. She leaned against the door and fell asleep. Butch continued to drive despite the intense pain in his shoulder. And the wound on his head hurt too. Sometime he would have to do something about his injuries, but for now he would keep going.

After he had turned south, off the freeway, the news came on again, but there was nothing new on the hunt for him. "Looks like I've given them the slip," Butch boasted to his sleeping hostage. "Maybe we'll try Utah for a while," he added as he drove toward Dutch John and the spectacular Flaming Gorge Dam.

CHAPTER 9

Sergeant Mike O'Connor tried to suppress a yawn. He was exhausted, and so were his two passengers, Trooper Jan Hallinan and Bob Evans. It had been a long and tiring day, and it was late.

"Let's check one more of these farm roads," he said to his two drowsy companions, "then we'll find a place to pull over and catch some shut-eye."

He turned off the highway and headed west down a washboard-roughened gravel road. He noted the odometer reading on the older Chevrolet Caprice the sheriff had sent up to Wyoming with Bob.

The first place they came to was illuminated by a bright yard light, revealing a neat, well-maintained farm yard. "Five point nine miles," Mike said, and Jan dutifully logged it down in a spiral notebook under the dim yellow dome light.

As self-appointed scribe, she kept an accurate record of all the areas they checked out as they searched for clues on the whereabouts of Butch and Erika. Several other teams of officers were doing much the same thing across most of the south-central part of the state.

Mike drove the car slowly around the circular driveway and, eyeing the dark house, said, "Nobody's staying up late here. That's strange," he continued, stopping the patrol car and climbing out, "I'd swear I heard a voice. You better stay put, Bob," he said over his shoulder to the young man in the backseat. "Jan, come with me."

"Good young man, that one," Mike said to Jan as they headed for the dark house.

She smiled, glad that it was dark as she felt her face redden. He really was a good man, a special guy in fact. "Mike, I've got this eerie feeling that something's wrong here," she said, avoiding a response to Mike's comment. "The hair's standing up on the back of my neck."

"Very professional observation," he said with a chuckle. Just then, they both heard another shout, faint but distinct.

"Now the hair's standing up on the back of my neck," Mike said soberly.

"Very professional," she quipped.

He chuckled. "I had that coming. Let's check the house."

"Something is terribly wrong here," Jan said again as they approached the front porch.

"Get behind me," Mike said, flattening himself against the wall and knocking with his left hand. He pulled his service revolver from beneath his jacket with his right one. Jan followed suit.

There was no answer, only silence. He knocked harder. Still no answer. The third time he knocked and then shouted, "Police officers. Open up."

That brought a plaintive cry for help. Mike reacted swiftly, opening the door, feeling for the light switch and scanning the room as the lights came on. He saw the old couple, but held his hand out to stop Jan. "I'll make sure there's no one else here," he said. "You check them."

A quick survey of the house assured him that only the old couple was there. He drew up short when he spotted the destroyed phone beside the sofa. He walked back to Jan. She had already finished cutting the ropes that bound the farmer and his wife, and she was kneeling beside the woman. "She's unconscious, but alive," Jan said.

The old man groaned and turned his head. "Please help my wife," he pleaded.

"I'll call an ambulance," she assured him gently. "You'll both be fine."

"You'll need to use your cell phone," Mike said soberly. "This one's shot to pieces."

Jan began to dial her cellular phone as Mike got up and went into the kitchen where he wet a dish towel and returned to the couple. He gently wiped the old lady's face. After a minute she stirred, and by the time Jan had completed the call requesting an ambulance she had regained consciousness.

The old lady gained some strength and sat up, turning her attention to her husband. He was getting weaker and complained of a pain in his side and left arm. Jan and Mike exchanged a worried glance. "What about Bob?" Jan asked a moment later as they helped the farmer onto the sofa. "He's premed."

"He's not a doctor yet. Better leave him out there until we sort things out here," Mike said sternly. "We're pushing it just letting him ride with us. If he gets hurt . . ." He let that thought dangle for a moment while he helped the farmer get more comfortable on the sofa, then he said, "We don't know if this has anything to do with Butch and Erika or not, but either way we better preserve the crime scene. We could be in trouble if we messed up any evidence for the local police."

Somehow, Jan was certain this had everything to do with Butch. And she had to force herself to be calm. It was silly, perhaps, but Bob's presence, as little as she knew about him, made her feel a little more sure of herself. There was just something about him. "I guess you're right, Mike," she finally said. "I just wondered if he could help these people."

Mike laughed. "Oh, I know how it really is, Jan. His company's a lot better than mine. After all, I'm just an old married man, but Bob's a handsome, tanned, athletic . . ."

"Stop it, Mike!" she interrupted, her face turning bright red.

Mike smiled as they turned their attention to the woman on the floor. Gently, Mike scooped her up and placed her in a plush green recliner. Jan brought some water from the kitchen and helped the man take a few sips while Mike did the same for his wife.

"The girl," the old lady said feebly after taking several swallows of water, "her name was Erika."

Both officers snapped to attention. "Were there two people here?" Mike asked.

"Yes."

"Did you hear the man's name?"

"No, I don't remember that. I fainted for a while."

"How did they leave?"

"I don't know. They came in a yellow pickup. A small one."

"It's not out there," he said. "In fact, there are no cars out there."

"No trucks either?" the lady interrupted. "Isn't our Ford Ranger there? It's black."

"Not there," Mike said to the woman. Turning to Jan he said, "There's a garage. Check it."

A moment later she came back in, her face white. "The Toyota pickup Butch stole earlier is there, so is their car, but the tires are slashed on both vehicles. I can't see the black Ranger."

"They must be in it," Mike said. He turned then to the woman. "Four-wheel drive or two?"

"Four, and it's brand new. It's Joe's pride and joy."

"Do you know the license number?" Mike asked.

"I never was good with license numbers, and we've only had the plates for a couple of weeks. I'm sorry."

"That's alright. Jan, get on the phone again," he said, looking up to discover that she was already punching numbers on her cell phone.

Turning back to the farmer's wife, he continued his questions. "What time did they leave?"

"It was still light, I think," she said.

"Officer," the old farmer said very weakly from his place on the sofa.

"Yes?" Mike said, shifting his position.

"He . . . took . . . my . . . rifle," he continued with great effort.

"Did you hear that, Jan? Butch has a rifle now," Mike repeated.

She nodded her acknowledgment as she spoke into the phone.

The old man had more to say. "She . . . saved . . . our . . . lives . . ." His voice trailed off.

"How?"

"She could have gotten away in our truck. She stayed so he wouldn't hurt us," the woman answered. "She was so brave."

Jan glanced at Mike, tears stinging her eyes. "She could have gotten away but didn't. That doesn't sound immature to me," she said.

"Perhaps she's growing up," Mike agreed. "I suppose what she's going through could do that to a person."

A siren wailed outside, and a minute later a local deputy joined them. Mike quickly explained what had happened and what he'd learned. "I think the old fellow must have suffered a mild heart attack. How long will it be before an ambulance gets here?"

"It's not far behind me," the deputy responded.

As soon as medical help arrived, Mike turned the care of the old couple over to them and said to Jan, "We better get a move on. They're several hours ahead of us now."

"But where do we go from here?" Jan asked.

"West."

"Why west?"

"Only because the radio's been saying we think he's going east."

"Okay. That's as good a reason as any," Jan agreed.

As Mike drove through the dark night toward Rawlins, Wyoming, Jan filled Bob in on the events at the farmhouse. When the deputy mentioned that Erika could have gotten away and why she didn't, Bob said triumphantly, "And my mother thinks she's immature." After that he grew very quiet though, and stayed that way for the last twenty minutes before they pulled off at the first Rawlins exit. Mike could see Bob's face reflected in the mirror whenever it was lit up by car lights. He wished he knew what he could say to make it easier on the young man.

Jan felt conflicting emotions. She was attracted to Bob, but it was all so wrong. What Erika was going through was making her a better person she concluded. If Bob didn't already love her—which she felt he didn't, although there wasn't a question he was very fond of her—he probably soon would. She hated what she was thinking and managed to make herself think of something else.

Mike and Jan kept in touch with the local authorities on their cell phones, but since the information they had passed along about the black Ranger, no further leads had developed. After gassing up later, total exhaustion made it necessary that they look for a place to rest.

They spent the night in a motel. The next morning Mike took one look at Bob and knew that he hadn't slept well. Jan noticed too and asked, "Are you alright, Bob?"

"I didn't sleep much. I'm really worried," he explained with a long face.

"We'll find her, Bob," Mike said, trying to restore some of Bob's lost confidence.

"It's not just that," he said. "I'm worried about what he'll do to her before you find her. She's changing—changing for the better. She just has to get away before something terrible happens to her. She isn't cooperating with Butch at all, is she? That took courage to do what she did, didn't it?"

Mike looked at Jan, who had become very interested in the rolling brown hills to the south. He cleared his throat. "Yes, what she did was most unselfish. She's a good girl, Bob."

"But what she did also makes it more dangerous for her, doesn't it?" Bob insisted.

"Yes, it does, I'm afraid. Now, I think we better get some breakfast."

Jan's interest in the surrounding landscape vanished as quickly as it had surfaced, and she said, "Good idea. I'm starved."

Bob talked a lot about Erika over breakfast. He was worrying more than ever now, knowing that she had risked her life for someone else. He seemed to be wondering if she would do it again. It was clear that Bob's heart ached for Erika.

Jan's heart was aching as well. She had grown way too fond of Bob in the short time she'd known him. It was immature and foolish, she knew that, but his pain caused her to suffer. As for Erika, she didn't blame Bob that his feelings for her seemed to be getting deeper. That she could endure the time she was being forced to spend with Butch was no small thing. Jan reflected to herself that she could never have done such a brave thing when she was Erika's age. The very thought of Butch made Jan tremble again. And now her heart ached more than ever for Erika.

As they left the café Mike's cell phone rang. It was Special Agent Harry Reed. He was in Colorado at the moment, but still coordinating the search. He shared with Mike more information on Butch and Erika. After checking out of their motel and loading into their car, Mike began to fill Bob and Jan in on what he'd just learned.

"Butch stole another car from in front of a house in Dutch John. That's in Utah," he said for Bob's benefit.

Bob nodded. "Near Flaming Gorge Dam, right?"

"Right. The black Ranger was found just a block or so up the street. It's only been about an hour ago that the owner discovered his car missing. They're probably headed south now through Utah. The car they stole is a white Dodge Intrepid."

"So are we headed for Utah then?" Jan asked.

"Yes. I can't think of anything else to do," he said, driving as fast as he dared toward Rock Springs, Wyoming.

In the rearview mirror a few minutes later, Mike saw that Bob was finally getting some rest. He jerked a thumb over his shoulder, and Jan looked back and smiled.

Mike wheeled off the freeway in Rock Springs. "We'll be going south from here," he said to Jan, "but let's grab a drink first."

He pulled into a 7-11 and put the old patrol car in park. There was a distinct clunking sound. "Jan," he said, "I think the transmission's going out. I hope we don't get stuck up here with car problems."

Jan agreed, her face assuming a worried expression. Bob, who had just woken up, asked, "Is something wrong?"

"I hope not," Mike said without expanding and led the way into the store.

When they came out they had drinks and assorted junk food. "At least it's not donuts," Mike joked. "Oh, I was going to get a paper and see what they're saying about Butch. I'll be right back."

When he returned a minute later, Bob was standing with his back to him, talking to Jan as she leaned against the car. Her eyes were pasted to Bob's face. Dressed in a pair of pale green slacks and a dark-green blouse, she was a sight to behold. Too bad, he thought, that someone like Bob didn't see what a truly beautiful and delightful girl she was. Of course, Bob was spoken for . . . if they could get Erika back in one piece.

"Let's go," he said, handing Jan the keys. "Your turn to drive."

"Thanks, just because you think something's wrong with the car," she said with a grin.

They piled in and she started the car, put it in reverse, and tried to back out. There was a loud pop, the car lurched backward, then it started to clang and rolled to a jerky stop.

"Mike, you shouldn't have let me drive. Now it's done for," Jan moaned, looking serious but with a humorous glint in her eyes. "We're stranded." She started to laugh.

"It's not funny, Trooper Hallinan," Mike said, starting to laugh himself. The infection spread, releasing days of pent-up tension, and even Bob began to chuckle. Jan was glad. Laughter was good medicine for pain of the heart.

"I'll call a wrecker," Mike said, wiping his eyes and reaching for his phone.

While they waited for the wrecker they discussed their options. "Harry Reed of the FBI is in Colorado, but he's headed back to Wyoming. We could wait for him and maybe he'd give us a ride until the sheriff can get another old clunker up to us, if he's even got one."

"I could check and see if we could use mine," Jan said. But then Bob couldn't ride with them, she realized, and she didn't like that idea at all. She also doubted that Agent Reed would let him in his car either. There had to be another solution that wouldn't leave Bob out. "But then, it would take forever to get it," she said, referring to her car. "We haven't got that kind of time."

"If we had the money we'd just rent one," Mike said. "I can just see Commissioner Sharp's face when the bill came in on that one." He chuckled. "If the county wasn't so poor we'd have a few better cars anyway."

"I'll rent a car," Bob said.

"What? You can't do that," Mike protested.

"You forget, Sergeant, I do have some money, and I'll do whatever it takes to help find Erika. Please."

"The sheriff might frown on that," Mike said doubtfully.

Bob grinned. "Well, I'm going to do it. You two can either walk or come with me." He paused, then said, "Well, what about it? Will you be my guests?"

"I wouldn't mind," Jan said, turning her smile on him. She meant that more than anyone could imagine, idiot that she was.

"Alright, you win, Bob. You're the host," Mike said, relenting gratefully. "I do hate to be delayed any more than we already have been."

A bright yellow wrecker pulled into the parking lot, and a greasy bear of a man climbed down from the cab. "I'm Ken," he said. "This the bucket of bolts I'm after?"

"I'm afraid so," Mike answered. "Transmission's shot."

"Want it fixed?"

"I'll have to let you know. Just take it for now."

"You're the boss," he laughed, and his ample stomach shook his black T-shirt.

"Sir, where can we rent a car?" Bob asked.

"You talking to me?" the burley wrecker driver asked, even more amused. "I'm Ken, not *sir,*" he added, and again jiggled his stomach merrily before giving Bob directions. "You'll need a ride, though. There's not room for all of you in my truck, so why don't one of you come with me and the other two can wait here."

He hooked the car, then asked, "Okay, who's coming with me?" He was looking at Jan appreciatively. "You would be my preference," he said and grinned.

"No, I'm going," Bob said sharply. "I'm the one who'll be renting a car."

"Okay, okay. Didn't mean to offend you, boy," Ken said. "Didn't know she was your girl. Get in."

"She's not," Bob said as he climbed into the wrecker.

"Well, you're missing a mighty good chance," Mike and Jan heard Ken say as he slammed his door. "She sure looks at you like she'd like to be."

Jan turned red, clenching her jaw. Mike wisely kept his mouth tightly closed.

For the next half hour, Mike and Jan wore a groove in the pavement in front of the 7-11. The sun sent its sweltering rays down on them with fury. "Here he comes," Jan said at last, wiping daintily at her warm face while Mike sopped the sweat off his forehead with a large red bandanna.

"This be okay?" Bob asked with a grin as he popped out of a shiny blue Durango.

"Looks good to me," Mike said, walking around to the passenger side. He opened the door, and Jan climbed into the backseat.

They drove to the garage and loaded their equipment and luggage from the police car into the Durango. "Mike," Jan said as they were about to leave, "look over there. Isn't that a white Intrepid?"

"Sure is. Been wrecked," he said. "Hey, didn't I say that Butch . . ."

"Sure did. You didn't say if it was new or not, but I guess we ought to check it out, just in case. That's silly though," Jan finished sheepishly.

"Maybe, but it's got Utah plates."

"It's sure hammered," Bob said as they walked over. "It's worse than the car I wrecked."

Ken strolled out of the garage. "Is there something else I can help you folks with?" He punctuated his question with a big stream of tobacco juice which hit the gravel and splattered on his greasy boots.

"When did you get this car?" Mike said, laying a hand on the crumpled roof.

"I'd just brought it in when you folks called me."

"Where—" Mike started.

"It had rolled off the highway south of Manila. Why are you interested in it? The owner lives in Dutch John. He called me and asked me to go get it. Poor guy. He'd just discovered this morning that someone had heisted it from his house. He said a friend of his spotted it and called him."

"Did he call the cops?" Mike asked.

"Sure did. They had me hook the car first and then meet an officer in Dutch John. He filled out a report there. He said he'd go to the scene later as he had another call waiting that was more urgent. After I left him I just towed it on up here."

"Do you mind if we take a look at it?"

"Help yerself. It ain't worth much now!"

Mike reached inside and found the registration papers. "This is the one Butch took, alright," he said after a brief examination. "There's blood on the seat," he added, becoming more worried. "Ken, we're looking for the guy who stole this car. Can you tell us how to get to where you picked it up?"

The color had drained from Bob's face. He jumped in the Durango and cranked up the engine while Ken gave Mike directions. "Let's go," he said impatiently, then he got out again. "Here, Sergeant, you drive. I'm too upset."

"Okay, but I need to call the sheriff's office in Manila first. Ken, do you have a phone book that includes both Dutch John and Manila, Utah?"

"Sure thing. Help yerself. Just leave a quarter on the desk," he joked.

Mike was hanging his cell phone on his belt as he trotted back to the Durango. He said, "A deputy's already trying to find the location. He'll wait there for us."

"Hurry," Bob said.

"We're doing just that," Mike answered as he climbed in, started the engine, and pulled onto the road.

Chapter 10

Thick black clouds drifted overhead, veiling the bright sun and dropping the temperature dramatically. Erika shivered and pulled her knees tight against her chest, wishing she had her sweatshirt. The scanty blue T-shirt didn't afford much protection. Butch was nearby, resting beneath a tree. He didn't seem to notice the sudden chill.

Only thirty minutes after stealing the Dodge, he had veered off the road, bounced down an embankment, and rolled. Despite exploding air bags, the wreck had reopened and enlarged the wound on his scalp, and now his thick black hair was matted with blood. He had bled quite a bit before Erika, at his insistence, finally succeeded in stopping the flow of blood.

After discovering they weren't seriously wounded in the crash, Butch had taken the guns, and they'd waited in the trees beside the road for a car to come along. After a cold hour of waiting in vain, the first strains of daylight had filtered through the trees on the mountains to the east. Butch had decided to hike into the hills and wait until dark to return to the highway, steal another car, and drive north. "We'll go to Canada," he'd informed Erika just before he lost control of the car on a tight curve.

From their vantage point on a steep, lightly timbered mountainside, Erika was watching for anyone who might happen to come along, while Butch, in severe pain from his injuries, slept in a pine-needle bed beneath the large tree he'd chosen. His pistol was in his pocket, but Erika knew how quickly he could get it out and how accurate his aim was.

Erika had dozed some, but her stomach was complaining strenuously of neglect, making her all the more miserable. They hadn't eaten since leaving the farmer's house the previous evening, and she had only eaten a few bites then.

Through the scope of the stolen hunting rifle, which Butch had forced her to hold after removing the bullets and putting them in his pocket, Erika had watched as a bright yellow wrecker appeared and towed the wrecked Intrepid away. Although she'd expected to see cops come before the wrecker did, none had appeared. It was almost noon and still no one had come. She wished they would, then in despair, wondered what good that would do. They had been powerless in helping her to this point.

"What time is it, Erika?" Butch asked in a feeble voice.

She looked at her watch. "Eleven thirty, and I'm starved and cold, Butch," she answered impatiently.

"I think it's going to rain, but we've got no choice but to wait it out," he said, attempting painfully to sit up. "Give me the rifle."

She handed it to him and he peered through the scope. "Uh, oh. A cop just stopped down there."

Even without the aid of the scope, Erika could see a car stopped alongside the road. Butch watched intently. "He's getting out," he reported. "He's snooping around." He paused, still watching through the scope. Finally, he said, "He's back in his car and just sitting there."

"Why's he doing that?" Erika asked, shivering as the wind picked up.

"He's probably waiting for someone. It's time for us to move on. They've probably got guys coming to start a search. Come on, get moving," he said, pushing himself to his feet with a grunt of pain.

He handed her the empty rifle to carry before leading the way slowly along the side of the mountain, away from the highway. After an hour they veered downhill and eventually came to a rutted dirt road. They crossed it, then rested for a while in a thicket of young pines. Erika was so weak and tired she didn't think she could go on. Watching Butch, she wondered how he'd come this far in his condition.

Why couldn't he just drop?

Thunder shook the trees and lightning cut through the air in frightening silver streaks. Rain began to fall lightly from the swollen clouds overhead. Erika thought she heard a vehicle. Butch heard it too and sat up, cupping a hand behind one ear. "A car's coming down the canyon," he said, pushing himself to his feet. "Let's hitch a ride."

Erika followed him to the edge of the trees. "Stay right here, and don't you dare move," Butch ordered, and then he stepped out of the trees and onto the road, leaving Erika—still holding the empty rifle—more or less out of sight. A moment later a light-green Bronco bounced around a curve in the road and slid to a stop in the mud as Butch waved his arms.

"Can I help you?" the driver asked, climbing out of the Bronco. He was dressed in the light-green shirt and green pants of the U.S. Forest Service. He looked concerned as he approached Butch. "You're injured," he said.

"Wrecked my car," Butch answered. "We need a ride." He signaled to Erika who stepped out of the trees.

Fear crossed the ranger's face. "Hey, you're . . ."

"It doesn't matter who I am," Butch said coldly, pulling his revolver. "You do exactly as I say and maybe I won't hurt you. Erika, get in the backseat. This guy is our chauffeur."

Erika did as instructed and Butch followed her. "Head for the highway," he said to the driver. "Make a smart move and it'll be your last."

When they approached the highway a few minutes later, Erika could see that they would come onto it very near where they had wrecked. There were several police cars there and a blue Durango.

"Get down," Butch hissed.

She did, but not before catching a glimpse of Bob coming around the back of the Durango. She was stunned. This time she knew it was him. She couldn't be wrong. But what was he doing here? Looking for her? Erika's heart throbbed with affection. He cared for her more than she'd ever imagined. He was here, looking for her! Suddenly she ached with desire. If only she could get out of this Bronco and rush into Bob's arms. Tears spilled down her face.

Butch interrupted her troubled thoughts when he shouted to the driver, "Any tricks, mister, and I'll drive—after I shoot you!"

"I'll take you wherever you want," the frightened man responded.

"Drive through Manila and keep going north," Butch instructed.

The instructions were followed, and the light-green Bronco was soon northbound in Wyoming on the road to Green River. Her heart aching, Erika numbly did as she was told and kept her head down like Butch was doing. They rode that way for several minutes. Butch peeked up occasionally, "Just to keep the driver honest," he said, insisting that Erika lie still on the floor.

Erika, not usually prone to motion sickness, was feeling ill. The smell of dirty, stale sweat along with dust from the floorboards, coupled with the dizzying swaying of the vehicle on the twisty road was making it worse by the minute. She didn't want to say anything that might set Butch off, but when it was apparent that throwing up was imminent, she said, "Butch, I'm going to be sick."

He glanced at her face and said, "You're white as a ghost." He sat up and ordered the driver to find a side road. "Fast, unless you want your car messed up," he said.

Erika sat up on the seat, knowing that a few more seconds on the floorboards would be too much. The Bronco slowed and turned onto a road that led into hills covered with junipers and sagebrush. After just a few hundred yards, Butch ordered the driver to stop.

"Hurry," Butch said as Erika shoved the seat forward, opened the door and dove out.

She was violently ill for several minutes. The rain had stopped, but her knees were soaked with brown mud from kneeling on the wet ground. Butch kept shouting at her to get back in. Her throat was burning and her eyes watering when she finally crawled back into the Bronco and it started moving.

"Back to the highway?" the driver asked.

"No, go on up this road," Butch ordered gruffly.

After they had gone about a mile from the highway, Butch said, "This is far enough. Pull off the road and into those trees," he ordered. The Bronco bounced and came to a stop. "Get out, Erika."

She did and immediately started throwing up again. Acrid yellow bile made her throat hurt terribly. After a moment she recovered enough to watch what was going on in front of the Bronco. Her chest constricted when she saw the forest ranger kneeling on the muddy ground and Butch pointing the .38 at his head. "Don't shoot him, Butch!" she screamed.

"Why not? We need his car and we don't need a loudmouth left behind."

Erika shuddered, and the terrified man said, "I won't talk." He began to sob.

"Shut up!" Butch screamed insanely. "I hate a crybaby."

"I have . . . a wife . . . and . . . and . . . three little kids," he stammered.

Butch extended his arm. A beam of sunlight broke through the clouds and reflected off the cold blue steel of the gun. Erika screamed. "Don't do it Butch," she pleaded. "He hasn't done anything to you."

"Stay out of this, Erika!"

With a burst of courage she didn't know existed, Erika approached Butch. "You don't need to kill him. Why not just tie him up and gag him." As she spoke, she was thinking of Bob, wishing she was with him, away from Butch and his madness.

Butch stood like a statue. Then he smiled a cruel smile as his pale green eyes glanced her way. "Okay, Erika. You've done it before. Tie him up, but be fast about it. I could still change my mind. Let's see what we can find to tie him up with."

Erika sighed with relief, and the tightness in her chest eased. "Erika," the ranger said, "there's some rope in the back of the Bronco."

Butch chuckled. "Helpful, aren't you?"

"Anything beats dying," he responded honestly.

It only took a minute to tie him securely to the rough trunk of a large juniper. Butch told Erika to use the man's own handkerchief to gag him, and then he stood back to inspect her work.

"That ought to hold you," he said. "You won't be a problem now. You could've been dead you know."

The man nodded an acknowledgment. "Let's go, Erika," Butch said, shoving her roughly toward the Bronco.

Tears stung Erika's eyes. Unless someone found him in time, the man could still die. Silently she prayed that somehow, someone would find him. She was sick with worry, again for someone other than herself, as she dragged herself back into the Bronco, wondering where Butch would take her now and what other horrors she would be subjected to.

They were back on the highway, driving north again, when Butch said, "I hurt awful bad. We've got to find someplace to clean up, eat, and get some rest." He glanced at her, then concluded, "You could use some cleaning up too. You aren't as pretty when you're dirty."

Erika didn't respond. The last thing she wanted was to look good for Butch. So she just leaned back in her seat and fell asleep, dreaming of the man she did want to look good for, dreaming of Bob

Evans. When she woke up they were on a dirt road. A large farmhouse loomed just ahead. "We'll borrow this house to get cleaned up and eat," Butch said as he turned off the road and into the yard.

There was a blue car parked in an old frame garage about thirty feet from the house. The house was in better repair than the garage, and was surrounded by a green lawn in need of a trim. A net-wire fence surrounded the yard with a white picket gate between the garage and house. Erika could see a fairly new barn, made of peeled logs, with a high loft window facing the house from across the yard. Behind it and to its right was a maze of sturdy plank corrals. Large elm and weeping willow trees shaded the house from the sun—now heavily favoring the western sky.

"Where are we?" Erika asked as he stopped the Forest Service Bronco beside the garage. "Have I been asleep long?"

"Yes, and we're beyond Green River. I'm not sure exactly where we are. We've been on back roads for quite a while."

Butch ordered her to lead the way up to the house. She prayed that he wouldn't hurt anyone here. Every time they came in contact with other people, lives were endangered. Slowly they approached the house, stepped up on a long, deep porch with pillars supporting the roof, and stood facing the door. Butch knocked. A fly buzzed in Erika's ear as the door opened. She brushed it away as the woman, a slender, pleasant brunette in her late twenties said, "Can I help you?"

She was looking them over, a mixture of astonishment and apprehension etched clearly on her smooth round face.

"Yes, ma'am," Butch said politely. "We need something to eat and would like to clean up."

"I'm sorry, but . . ." Her voice broke as fear twisted her pleasant features.

She tried to shut the door, but Butch's size eleven boot stopped it. "We're hungry and dirty," Butch said, pushing her aside and stepping into the house. "The old man at home?"

"No, he's at . . ." She stopped, apparently realizing her error. After a moment of indecision, she said, "He'll be here any minute now."

"You better be lying," Butch growled, pulling his pistol. "If he comes home before we're finished here, it won't be healthy for him. Where's your phone?"

"It's right in here," the lady said with a trembling voice as she led him into the kitchen. "You may use it, but please don't hurt us," she begged. "You may have whatever you need."

Butch shot his second phone in as many days.

The woman screamed as gray plastic showered the kitchen. "My baby's in there!"

"In where?"Butch asked calmly.

"In there," she wailed, pointing at the wall where the remnants of the shattered phone hung. "That's the bedroom in there."

Erika's heart sank. But Butch coldly said, "Go get your kid."

The lady wasted no time and came out carrying a little boy and crying. "Please, mister, take what you want and go."

"Fix us something to eat while my girl here takes a shower. You don't mind if she uses your bathroom, do you?" His voice was calm as he spoke, but Erika could see the pain in his eyes, and once more she wished he would just keel over and let this nightmare end. But Butch was proving to be too tough for that.

"Whatever you need, sir. It's okay," she said.

She put the little child in his high chair and he immediately began to howl. "Feed the kid, lady, before I lose my temper. You don't want me to lose my temper, do you?" Butch asked, his voice rising.

"No, sir," she said, hastily handing the little guy a cookie. That did the trick and Butch's hard features softened a little as the wailing ceased.

Erika stood in the middle of the kitchen, not sure what to do. Butch solved that. "Erika, go shower. And don't try to leave or anything or I'll hurt this kid," he said, pointing his pistol at the child.

Erika left in search of the bathroom, praying that Butch wouldn't hurt the woman or the child while she was showering. She turned on the water and returned to the kitchen. "I need some clean clothes," she said to Butch. "Maybe we can buy some from her."

Butch exploded. "We don't buy anything!" He glared at the housewife and back at Erika. "You two are about the same size. She should have something that'll fit. Is it okay if she helps herself?" he asked the housewife who was busy pulling food from the refrigerator. The angry tone of his voice left no room for a negative answer.

"Yes of course," she said, her eyes drifting to the little pistol he held loosely in his hand. "What would you like to eat?"

"We missed breakfast," he growled. "Fix some bacon and eggs, toast, milk, the works."

Erika left in search of clean clothing. She felt terrible raiding the lady's closet, but she didn't have a choice. After finding something that would work, right down to underwear and socks, Erika showered. She shampooed her hair three times and scrubbed her whole body twice with soap and a washcloth. Feeling clean at last, she stepped out of the shower. She jumped when Butch hammered on the bathroom door and shouted, "Hurry, Erika. Our breakfast is ready."

"Just a minute," she said and frantically dried herself and got dressed. There was something else she wanted to do before leaving the privacy of this bathroom.

Erika dropped to her knees beside the tub and prayed. She prayed like she'd never prayed in her life. The few prayers she had offered since the ordeal began were sincere, but short and somewhat shallow. But when she prayed now, she felt like she couldn't stop. She told the Lord of the terrible plight she was in and asked Him to help her. "Please don't let him kill me," she pleaded silently. "And please don't let him hurt anyone else. And help Bob to understand what I'm going through and not to give up on me."

She was beginning to feel a measure of peace when Butch interrupted, pounding loudly on the door again. "Get out of there!" he shouted.

She hurriedly closed her prayer, more angry than ever at the man who held her hostage. She got to her feet, resolving to pray again when she could, and joined Butch in the kitchen. He looked up, anger in his pale eyes, but it faded quickly. He gave out a low whistle and said, "Wow, babe! You look great."

She shuddered. She didn't get cleaned up so he could call her "*babe.*" She did it out of fear for her life! But the clothes were an amazing fit, and despite the fact that they weren't her style, she probably did look pretty good in the tight-fitting pair of stone-washed blue jeans and the red, western-cut blouse. And her long dark hair felt clean as it fell softly around her tan face and across her shoulders. Always one who took pride in how she looked, she wished for the first time in her life that she could be homely and plain for a little while—unattractive to the loathsome man who sat leering at her.

They ate bacon, eggs, and toast until they couldn't hold any more. Pushing back his plate, Butch said, "My turn to clean up." He shoved his pistol in his pocket, and looking with cold eyes at the slender housewife, he said, "The baby's coming with me."

"Oh, no, please don't," she begged.

"I wouldn't want you two getting chummy or anything while I'm in there," he said. "Erika has yet to earn my trust."

"Please," the woman begged.

Butch reached for the toddler. "I won't hurt him if neither of you attempt to leave this room. And I mean *this* room. I suppose you might have guns in the house, lady. Don't even think about trying to get them."

The woman looked at Erika for support. "Please, Butch," Erika implored.

He slammed his fist against the wall. "I'm calling the shots here!" he reminded them both. "Tell her what I can do if I have to," he said with a sneer, and then, the screaming baby in his arms, he entered the bathroom. Erika offered a silent prayer.

"I . . . I'm sorry," she said as the woman wiped her tears.

"*You're* sorry?" the woman said in amazement. "This isn't your fault. I'm so terribly sorry for what he's doing to you. If only there was something I could do."

"He is a terrible man," Erika said. "We can't take any chances. He *will* do what he threatens. I'm so scared," she added, her bottom lip starting to tremble.

The good lady slipped an arm around Erika's shoulders, and the two of them shared a long cry together. Finally, Erika said, "Let me help you with something. The time will go faster if we're busy."

"Well, there are the dishes."

"Good, I'll get to clearing up," Erika volunteered.

Side by side, the two women worked for the next few minutes. A bond had formed between them. Each felt for the other's plight. They worked silently, the heartrending sound of the baby's crying from the bathroom never letting up. Butch finally returned wearing a pair of blue jeans that were only slightly too large and carrying a flowered, blue western shirt, a bottle of rubbing alcohol, and his pistol. Erika gasped when she saw him.

The wound on his shoulder was full of yellow pus and the flesh for inches around it was a dark, angry red. The woman noticed too. "That looks pretty nasty," she told Butch. "I'm a nurse. I'll tend to it as soon as I get my little boy and calm him."

To Erika's surprise, Butch did not object. He just fingered the pistol and sat down, looking dreadfully dangerous. The woman calmed her little son and placed the boy back in his high chair. She was trembling and weeping again. But as she began to treat Butch's wounds, the trembling ceased, and she worked calmly and professionally. "You must see a doctor," she said as she helped him into the shirt, easing the sleeve over the neat bandage she'd made. "You have a severe infection. I can tell by the color of your skin that you don't feel well either. You'll feel worse as more of the infection gets into your bloodstream. It's slowly poisoning you."

"Don't you have something you can give me?" Butch asked.

"I have some penicillin tablets. They'll help, but you need a doctor. I don't think you realize how bad that wound on your shoulder is. The one on your head is not as serious, but it also needs a little—"

"Thanks for the advice," he interrupted sarcastically. "Where are the pills?"

She reached high into a cupboard near the kitchen sink and retrieved a blue plastic bottle. "Take two now and one about every four or five hours," she instructed as she filled a glass with water and handed it to him.

"That wound on your head could use some stitches," she said, and before he could protest, she went on, "but if you don't mind my cutting some hair out of the way, I could tape it closed for you."

"Do it," he growled.

She went into another room. Butch followed. Erika picked up the little boy and was singing to him in a soft but clear soprano voice when they returned. "Put the kid down!" Butch ordered brusquely.

Erika did as she was told then dropped her eyes, fighting back fresh tears. When the wound was taped, the housewife handed Butch one of her husband's blue caps in place of the soiled one he had been wearing before his shower. When he put it on, it concealed the injury nicely. "Erika," he said, standing up, "find a suitcase and pack yourself some more clothes. Get me a change too while you're at it. And get some deodorant, toothpaste—you know, that kind of stuff."

The woman raised no protest, but set about caring for her child. Erika had soon gathered what they needed, taking only enough things to keep Butch from having another of his dangerous temper tantrums. "This should do," she said upon returning to the living room where Butch was waiting while the housewife rocked her child.

At that moment, the door opened and a stocky, deeply tanned man, slightly taller than Butch and several years older, walked in. His dark-blue eyes swept the scene in his living room as he said in a deep, demanding voice, "What's going on here?"

"These people needed some help, Bill," his wife said, her eyes pleading for him not to rile Butch.

"Looks like my shirt you're wearing, and . . ." his voice trailed off as Butch raised the gleaming .38 and instant understanding filled his intelligent eyes. He spoke again. "Looks like you've given them what they need, Sandy. I suppose they plan to go now."

"Your keys," Butch said, rising to his feet and holding out his empty hand.

"What?" Bill asked, clearly puzzled.

"Your keys. We need to borrow your truck."

Understanding dawned again. He reached in his pockets and pulled out a small key ring. "One's for the truck and the other one fits the Honda."

"Now, you two sit on the floor—I'm going to have to tie you up. Find some rope, Erika," Butch ordered, "and don't try anything stupid."

"In the truck," Bill said calmly, although his face was clouded with anger.

Butch followed her to the door and watched the couple on the floor as well as Erika as she ran out, found the rope, and returned to the house. Butch placed the pistol in a back pocket of his jeans, the grip in sight. He began to tie the pair together. The baby was wailing again.

Erika wanted to run, but she feared what he would do to the couple and their baby if she tried to. She silently prayed again and stood still, wringing her hands while watching helplessly.

The pitch of the little boy's screams rose, and she finally stepped over and picked him up from his position on the floor. The little one calmed down almost instantly as Erika hummed softly and rocked him in her arms.

Butch looked up and glowered, but he said nothing until the couple were secured. Then he stood, pulled the pistol from his pocket and said, "Drop the baby beside them and let's go."

She gently placed the child against his mother's knee, tried to smile at the woman she now felt was her friend, and then headed for the door ahead of Butch, stopping beside the kitchen door to pick up the suitcase.

Butch slit the tires on the Forest Service Bronco and Bill's Honda. Then, as Erika threw the suitcase in the back of the truck, he retrieved his rifle and bullets from the Bronco and climbed in the newly stolen truck. As Butch pulled onto the road and turned west, Erika noticed a school bus approaching from the east. She didn't think much about it. Butch either didn't see it, or didn't figure it was important as he gunned the truck, leaving the farmyard in a cloud of gray dust.

"Well," he said, smirking, "looks like we're off again. And I think we've given old Sergeant O'Connor and company the slip."

"Company" included Bob. What would Butch think if he knew about Bob? Worse yet, what would he *do?* She feared that she knew, and it made her sick at heart. She couldn't let Butch do anything to Bob. She had to protect Bob, no matter what it took. Even though Butch didn't trust her, Erika was fairly sure that he wouldn't hurt her as long as she did exactly what he told her to. The safest thing for her, and for Bob, was to go along with him. As much as she hated to, for the time being it was her only choice.

As they rode, her thoughts shifted to the young family Butch had left tied in their living room. Would they be alright? Or would the baby crawl off somewhere and get hurt while the parents were helpless to prevent it? She remembered the old couple that had been left in such similar circumstances, and hoped they were both okay. And she wondered about the man they had left tied to a tree in the forest so many hours ago. Her heart ached for each of them. Suddenly, and surprisingly, her own plight didn't seem quite so terrible as it had. Silently, she again tried to pray, not for herself, but for those others left behind. And she wept for them, especially for the little boy she had so lovingly held, sang to, and calmed.

***

Bill Grossman comforted his wife. "You did right, Sandy," he said. "As usual, your cool head prevailed. That guy is dangerous. It's worth losing the truck to have them gone."

He couldn't see her eyes, as they were tied with their backs to each other, but he could imagine the fear they held, and it made the anger swell in him. He'd grown to deeply love this woman he'd met seven years ago. At the time he was a heavy equipment operator in his mid-twenties and she a newly graduated nurse working in a hospital in Cheyenne. He'd been brought into the emergency room with a broken finger, and he believed love had been instant and lasting when their eyes first met in that antiseptic room.

They had married within two months and moved to the old farm near Green River following his parents' death in an auto accident two years later. He farmed for a living now, only working occasional construction jobs to supplement their income. They were content and happy. Bill loved Sandy intensely, and if anything ever happened to her . . .

His thoughts were interrupted as the front door opened and their six-year-old son, Stevie, burst through like a miniature tornado. As usual, his mind was on the refrigerator, and he stampeded through the living room so fast on the trail to food that he didn't see his parents and baby brother in the far end of the room.

"Mom!" he called. "I'm hungry."

"In the living room, Stevie," she answered.

Bill's anger faded away, and he chuckled at his son who stormed back into the living room as quickly as he'd blown through it. His eyes popped and he skidded to a stop when he saw his parents.

"Hey, whatcha doing?" he asked, a puzzled but unalarmed expression on his cherubic face.

"Come get my pocket knife out, Stevie, and cut us loose," Bill said seriously.

The little boy did as instructed, sawing away vigorously on the tough hemp at the point least likely to hurt either of his parents. "How come you're tied up?" he asked cheerfully as he worked.

"How was your first day at school?" Sandy countered.

"Fine. Mrs. James is really nice. She had treats for us," he said.

"Oh, what were they?" Bill asked, following his wife's lead and steering Stevie still further from his question.

"Cookies," he said. "Got it," he announced in the next breath.

Bill quickly pulled his hands free and finished cutting the ropes on their legs and around their stomachs while Sandy grilled Stevie on his day. "I'll call the cops," Bill said when he had finished and started for the kitchen.

"It doesn't work. Butch . . ." Sandy called after him.

"What happened to the phone?" Bill thundered as he reappeared.

"I was just trying to tell you. Butch shot it."

"Oh, no—the cell phone is in the truck, and they took it," he revealed as he looked out the window. "Give me your keys. I'm going after help," Bill said urgently.

"Not without us, you're not," Sandy protested. "That Butch is mean, and he could come back."

"You're right. Get the kids and let's go. I'm going to get a gun, just in case," he said, taking the steps two at a time to the second floor where he kept his guns locked safely in a gun cabinet.

He strapped on his Smith and Wesson .357 magnum revolver. He had bought it before he met Sandy and used to practice a lot with it when he was away on road construction jobs. He was quite a good shot.

"Come on," he said as he reentered the living room. As they approached the garage, he moaned at seeing the flat tires. "I wonder . . ." he started to say as he turned toward the Bronco. "Guess not," he said, seeing the flat tires there too. "Probably no keys anyway."

"Now what do we do?" Sandy asked, tears welling up in her eyes.

"I guess we'll take the tractor," he said, leading the way to the big barn. He threw open the solid wooden doors and helped his family up into the cab of his big green John Deere. He started the powerful diesel engine and backed out of the barn. Stevie, not understanding what was happening, grinned happily.

It took several minutes to reach the nearest neighbors who lived west about two miles. He swung the John Deere into Frank and Millie Kramer's yard and stopped in a cloud of boiling dust. He looked at his watch while he waited for the dust to settle. He didn't want to fill the cab with it when he opened the door. "Almost five," he mumbled.

Millie Kramer, a plump little woman of about sixty-five, came trotting from the house, wiping her hands on a dish towel. She met Bill as he dropped to the ground from the high cab. Her already puzzled eyes grew wider when she saw the long silver pistol on his side. "What in the world . . ." she began, looking thoroughly shocked.

"I need to use your phone, Millie," he bellowed over the throb of the diesel engine in a tone that caught her by surprise.

"Come on in," she said, her short legs pumping furiously to keep stride with his long gait. "Is yours out of order?"

"It's been shot."

Her chubby little chin dropped and she stared at him, speechless, as he dialed the phone. She gasped and sank into an overstuffed chair as Bill explained on the phone about Butch and Erika. "My, oh my. My, oh my," she murmured over and over again.

"Oh you poor souls," she said when he hung up the phone. She scurried outside to console Sandy. "This is just horrible! Something has got to be done about people like that," she scolded, huffing around like a bantam rooster.

"Not them. Just him," Sandy said. "She's a victim too. I'm so worried about her. She's such a nice girl."

"They'll set up roadblocks and send an officer out to get a report from us," Bill said soothingly as he boosted his family back into the tractor. "Millie, do you have a gun in the house?"

"I surely do, and I know how to use it if I have to," she said. "Frank will be home soon anyway. We'll be careful. You kids are welcome to stay here until the police come if you'd like," she shouted as Bill climbed into the tractor's cab.

"No, we'll run home. We'll be alright now," he shouted down at her.

"Would you like Frank and me to come over when he gets here?" she asked.

"No, that won't be necessary. Lock your doors, Millie," he instructed and pulled the door shut, getting madder by the minute. "If I could get my hands on that guy, I'd . . ." he mumbled as he put the tractor in gear.

By the time a deputy arrived, Bill had his chores done and was waiting in the house with Sandy and the children. "We've got planes in the air and have officers searching every road for miles around. We should have them trapped in the area," the young, fair-haired deputy said confidently after looking briefly through the house. "We'll have them soon. How long after they left your place did you call?"

"Couldn't have been over fifteen minutes," Bill decided.

"Good. They're trapped then. We'll get that scumbag killer," the deputy said, pulling out his notebook.

Chapter 11

"I thought I was dead," Paul Dixon said dramatically to his wife Susan, who listened sympathetically to his distressing story. "That guy, Butch, he pointed his gun at me and all I could see was the barrel. It was big as a cannon! I expected it to go off any minute. I was praying like I never prayed before. He would have killed me if it hadn't been for that girl, Erika. She's the one that was taken hostage in Colorado by that crazy man. Good girl, that one, and she's got courage. She saved my life. I'm one lucky man," he concluded.

That was an understatement.

Paul hadn't been tied to the tree for much over thirty minutes when Tom Shroude came down the road. Tom had fought with his wife that morning and had gone for a long drive to cool off and think things over. He'd picked the little-used, out-of-the-way road merely by chance, or, as Susan later said, "Because God wanted him to."

His old green truck slid as Tom slammed on the brakes and shoved it into reverse. He'd caught a glimpse of color in the trees that looked out of place and wanted a closer look. To his surprise, one of the local forest employees, Paul Dixon, was tied to a big juniper.

Tom had jumped out of the truck and charged up through the trees and untied Paul. As he sped back to Manila, Paul's terrifying tale unfolded. The two men made a beeline for the sheriff's office to report the abduction. "The officers are all out looking for a man that escaped from—" a middle-aged secretary had started to say.

"We know," Paul had interrupted impatiently. "They can quit searching out there. The guy they're looking for took my Bronco!"

Radio contact was made, but they were told it would take some time for the men to arrive since a lot of them were searching the mountains on foot. "We'll go meet them then," Tom volunteered quickly.

When the old green truck rattled up to the scene of Butch's earlier crash, Jan and Bob were talking to Mike, anxiously awaiting the arrival of the man who claimed to have been abducted by Butch. For the second time, Paul related his story. He'd thanked Bob when he discovered that Erika was his girlfriend. "I owe my life to that girl," he'd told Bob with moist eyes. "He could have easily killed her too. For a minute I thought he was going to."

"We've got to get Butch before something happens to her," Mike had assured them. He was impressed by the man's story. But it also caused him to worry more. Butch lived on a short fuse, and he was afraid Erika could easily get herself killed if something like this happened again. He chose not to mention his concerns to Bob. The young man had enough worries already.

And indeed, Bob Evans was worried. He was scared to death for Erika. He felt all bottled up inside. He had to say something to someone or he'd explode. Just then, Jan walked over and laid a hand on his arm and said, "Quite a girl, isn't she?"

"Jan, she was so close by. She was in the Bronco. We shouldn't have let it get away."

"Hey, Bob, the worst thing we could have done was try to stop them. Butch would have done something terrible if we had," Jan said as she looked into those grief-stricken eyes. She wished she could take him in her arms and comfort him, but of course, that could never be.

"Jan, I'd gladly take her place," he said suddenly. "I don't know how much more of this she can stand."

"Hey, she's getting pretty strong it seems to me," Jan said. "I can't believe the courage she's shown."

For a moment Bob gazed at Jan, deep in thought. If Erika was as strong as Jan, he thought to himself, he would be a little less worried. He'd never met anyone quite like her. He spoke his feelings, saying, "If you were in her place, I'd worry less. You're so strong."

Jan managed a grin and said, "Yeah, but you don't love me. It's her you love. Of course you'd worry less."

Bob's eyes dropped as he said, "Truthfully, Jan, I really do like her a lot. I've never enjoyed anyone the way I enjoy her, and . . . well, who knows what'll happen. But as much as I like her, I can't say I love her. Not in the way you mean it."

He looked back into the young officer's eyes, and this time she had to look away. She was so afraid of betraying the attraction she felt for him. They'd spent many hours talking, getting to know each other as they searched for Butch and Erika. She could tell by his modesty that he wasn't one to brag, but as they'd talked she'd learned of his priorities in life—of the time and honest care he freely gave people, and especially how much he had admired and loved those he served on his mission. And they had discussed why he was training to be a doctor; he genuinely cared about people, and wanted to help relieve the pain and suffering they felt. Jan had also noticed how he treated others as they followed Butch's trail, and she'd concluded that he wanted to help anyone he could. She was impressed that he cared so much about making a difference in the lives of others. And he'd been so interested and sympathetic as she told him of the police academy and how difficult it had been competing with the young men there, and especially of the taunting and humiliation that she'd been forced to endure.

Yes, she was attracted to him, for he was such an unselfish, giving person. She felt guilty as he went on. "Maybe someday I will come to love her. She's changing. She's growing. I just pray it doesn't get her killed." He paused and Jan's eyes again made contact. "I meant it, Jan. I'd worry less if it were you because you're so able to take care of yourself. But don't take that wrong. I'd be sick if anything like what's happening to Erika ever happened to you. You're great."

"And you don't know me," she said, and as she spoke that same look he'd seen in her eyes before, appeared. It couldn't be fear, and yet it looked like it. She was silent for a moment and again broke contact with his steady gaze. Finally, she said, "I'm afraid, Bob. Believe me, I could never do what she's done."

She might have said more, but Bob, despite that mysterious look in her eyes, wasn't believing her. She seemed so solid, so brave, so full of faith. She was strong in more ways than any girl he'd ever known. But before either one could say anything, Mike called out, "Let's get moving. We haven't time to waste."

They loaded up in Bob's rental car and once again headed for Wyoming. Bob was quiet and withdrawn as he drove the rented Durango toward Green River. Mike was worried that he might slip into a depression and become a burden to Jan and himself as they searched for Butch and Erika. Mike tried in vain to draw him into conversation several times, but Bob didn't want to talk. Mike couldn't blame him.

Jan had also become withdrawn. She sat silently in the backseat, alone and morose. She struggled with thoughts of her own: terrifying, bitter memories best forgotten, and the frustrations of a heart that had been drawn to a guy she could never allow herself to fall in love with. Her place in his life was to somehow save the girl he came all the way from California for, a girl he . . . *liked* an awful lot.

But didn't love. Not yet anyway.

Jan tried to think of something else, but it was hard. She noticed that Sergeant O'Connor had fallen asleep. She tried to do the same, but later, as they approached Green River and Mike woke up, she hadn't slept a wink.

The day was fading fast when Mike, Jan and Bob took up a position blocking one of the roads out of the area the local authorities believed Butch and his hostage were holed up in. Mike had a borrowed walkie-talkie now, and they were on the local sheriff's department frequency to supplement the use of their cell phones.

The report of the incident at the Grossman farm, and of what had happened to that young family, had sent Mike's blood pressure soaring. Butch had to be stopped before someone else was hurt or killed. And that someone could be Erika. He didn't say that to Bob, but it was obvious the young man was having similar thoughts. Once again, Erika had shown extraordinary courage. Despite his worry, Mike was impressed by Erika. The worst in Butch was bringing out the best in her.

Mike prowled restlessly as he watched for traffic. Suddenly the radio came to life. He listened intently, then ran over to the rented Durango and reported what he had just heard to his two young companions. "A plane has spotted the Grossman truck headed north. It's several miles northwest of their farm. It's turned and is heading south again toward the interstate. A deputy is pursuing them even as we speak."

"If that creep hurts her—" Bob began through gritted teeth.

"Isn't there something we can do?" Jan interrupted, addressing herself to Mike.

"No. We'll just have to wait for now."

He held the radio up. A dispatcher's voice was calling all cars. "Be advised that the suspect vehicle, a light-brown Ford F250 four by four, has turned east. It's off the road but still moving fast. The pursuing officer's car is disabled, but the plane is still in visual contact with the suspect vehicle. I have the pilot on another frequency."

Bob jumped in the car and had the engine running when Mike signaled for Jan to get in. He pointed to the passenger side of the front seat as he moved to Bob's side. "Okay if I drive?" he asked Bob as Jan jumped in the other side. "Things could get sticky."

"Sure, I'm so stressed I'd probably crash anyway."

He started to get out, but Mike said, "Just slide over. Let's get on our way."

Bob slid over, and as he pressed gently against Jan, he couldn't, despite his worries and stress, help but feel something strange. It felt good to be close to her. And he couldn't understand why.

Jan was also feeling something, but she knew why. She tried not to think about it though. And the way Mike was driving made it a little easier for her. The older officer wanted to get this ordeal over with, and he was driving as fast as he dared in the direction Butch had last been seen.

Mike had his walkie-talkie in his lap. He handed it to Bob and said, "Give this to Jan. I don't want to drop it."

Bob handed it over just as the dispatcher's voice again came on the air. "The plane is down. The pilot was forced to land on a dirt road after taking fire from the suspect. Another plane, with this frequency, will be airborne shortly." She then gave the latest location of Butch, and Mike coaxed more speed from the Durango.

They hadn't gone five miles before the second plane's pilot came on the air. "I'm receiving fire," he said, his voice high with alarm. "I'm pulling away. My plane has been hit. I'm heading back for the airport."

Mike slammed his fist on the dash, causing the Durango to careen. As he straightened it out, he complained bitterly, "We'll lose them again, unless someone gets lucky."

It was just a few minutes before they were spotted again, but it was not lucky for a state trooper. He suddenly came on the air, reporting seeing them and making chase. "I'm eastbound," he said excitedly. A moment later he said, "The suspect vehicle is stopping." He named the location. There was a pause, then, "I'm under fire!"

Nothing more was heard from the trooper, and everyone converged on a road about ten miles west of the Grossman farm as directed by the dispatcher. Mike was one of the closest cars and was the third to arrive at the bullet-ridden cruiser of the seriously injured officer. "Butch is getting more dangerous by the minute," Mike said a short while later as the young trooper was being loaded in an ambulance.

***

Butch was angry and frustrated. He'd been boxed in and he didn't like it. Erika, despite her earlier resolve to try to get along with him, was becoming more afraid by the minute that people would begin dying. For all she knew the trooper was dead! She was almost overcome with worry—for everyone that got in Butch's path. He didn't care who he hurt.

And now they were speeding in the direction of the Grossman farm again. And she was afraid for that innocent little family. But she was also terrified for herself. Twice, as Butch slowed the truck to negotiate curves, she had thought about simply opening the door and diving out. She knew she could be seriously hurt if she did, but that wasn't the reason she didn't jump. She was convinced that Butch would stop, despite his wild flight, and kill her. So she just hung on and prayed.

She was sure they were effectively trapped. Butch was not his usual cool, conspiring self. He was running like a chased rabbit. Several times he cursed. Once he said, "They'll never take me alive." And again, later, he said, "I'll make them wish they'd left me alone."

What really frightened Erika though, was when Butch said, "It's all their fault. They'll pay for this!"

She didn't dare ask who's fault he thought it was, but it didn't take long to figure out who he meant. He said, "I don't know how they ever got loose. I tied them so tight they should have stayed there forever."

The Grossmans! The very people Butch had left tied in their house, and whose truck he was driving, were becoming the focal point of his frustration. "I don't know how they did it," he repeated, "but somehow they got hold of the cops. I'll make them wish they hadn't."

As Butch ranted on about the Grossmans, she could only think about the sweet little boy she had held and his frightened mother. She had, in the short time she was with her, grown to respect Sandy. She hadn't been sure of their names until they heard them talked about on the radio, but she felt now like she had known the little family forever. She also recalled the school bus that had been coming up the road as she and Butch left, and she wondered if there were more children. That would explain how they had managed to alert the police so quickly. And the thought that Butch might do some horrible thing to them was almost more than she could bear.

Butch slowed the truck as they neared the Grossmans' yard. It was getting dark, but he didn't turn on the lights as they drove very slowly forward, finally pulling off onto a small lane that led to a large field. He stopped a short distance up it and opened his door. "We'll walk from here," he announced as he searched in the glove compartment and pulled out a flashlight.

"No," Erika said before she could stop herself. "Please, let's just keep going."

Butch's hand moved like a rattler and caught her on the side of the face, causing her head to snap back and pain to shoot up her neck. "Get out," he ordered.

She could do nothing else, so she climbed out, her head ringing and cheek burning. The truck was not easily visible from the road, and Butch ordered her to lead the way on foot through the field. It was fully dark by the time they reached the corrals behind Bill Grossman's barn. They opened a gate and went in. A horse whinnied and moved away from them. Butch paid the animal no attention, but headed straight for the barn. Then using the flashlight only when it was absolutely necessary, he found a door, opened it, and pushed Erika in ahead of him.

Butch had become very silent as they walked, and a terrible sense of doom descended like a dark cloud over Erika. Once in the barn, when she could stand the suspense no longer, she asked, "What are you going to do, Butch? Please don't hurt the Grossmans. Anyway, shouldn't we be trying to get as far away from here as possible?"

Butch whirled on her, once again striking her face with the palm of his hand. She stumbled backward in the darkness and he was instantly upon her. He grabbed her by the throat and snarled, "Don't you tell me what to do! It's getting on my nerves, girl."

Erika cried out, but Butch backhanded her on the mouth. "Shut up!" he ordered. "I'm going in the house and you're waiting here."

"What are you—" she began, but once again Butch struck her face with his open palm, and then he drew back and threw a hard punch that caught her right in the middle of the stomach. She doubled over, gasping, and Butch grabbed her head and shoved her hard onto the concrete floor of the barn. Erika was sure she was about to die. And for a long and terrible moment, she didn't even care.

As she lay there, crying, Butch began shining the light about. He stepped away from her and she could hear him grunting. She looked up after listening to him moving farther away. Large doors had stood open in the front when they had entered the barn. They were now shut, and his light flickered on the far side of the building from where she lay. For just a moment, she thought about trying to run, but the idea had scarcely entered her mind when she heard him coming back. Now he would kill her, she thought. Erika dropped her head again onto the cool, hard concrete and tried to think a prayer.

When Butch was almost to her, she opened her eyes. He was carrying his light with his left hand, which he favored due to the nasty shoulder injury. But in his right hand he was carrying a piece of rope. He came right to her, leaned down, grabbed her by the hair and jerked her upright. So he was not going to kill her yet, she decided, but she knew then what he was about to do, and she struggled to get up and twist away from him, but he held her firmly. The rope was soon around her wrists, and they were tied securely behind her back.

She dared not think about what he might do next. Death was not the worst thing he could inflict on her. But all he did was force her to walk across the barn. He shined his light on a ladder that led to a loft. "Up there," he ordered.

She looked up. "I can't," she protested.

Once more, she felt the power of his right hand as it struck her battered face. "Climb," he said.

She climbed. He held her from behind and followed. It was terribly difficult, for she had no use of her hands and she was in pain, but she eventually reached the top. He shoved her onto the rough board surface and clambered onto the loft behind her. Then he twisted her legs until they were behind her back, and he secured them to her wrists.

"You have a lesson to learn," he said when he had finished. "If you try to move, you'll fall, and it's a long way to the floor. So you just stay put. Maybe I'll be back. Maybe I won't."

Erika was beyond crying. She was beyond resisting. She just lay in the painful position in which he'd left her and listened numbly as he descended from the loft. A few moments later she heard the big doors as they moved slightly. She imagined he was leaving the barn. She didn't hear the doors close again. She was in pain; her stomach hurt, her head hurt, her whole body ached. And yet, despite all that she was suffering, she could only think frantically of the little family in the house across the yard, and wondered what was going to happen to them.

She prayed, not for herself, but for Sandy Grossman and her family. After a while time seemed to be suspended, and she was not conscious of her pain, her anger, or her fear. She was conscious of nothing until she felt the loft move ever so slightly and opened her eyes to see a small bundle being shoved toward her. And she heard Butch's cold voice as he said, "Lie still, Erika, or you might push little Stevie over the edge." Then he was gone.

Several minutes passed. She listened to the sobbing of the child that was now beside her and her heart was heavy. She knew it was not the baby, for even in the darkness she could tell he was much bigger. She gathered her courage and her faith, what little she had, and said, "Stevie, are you hurt?"

"Who are you?" a frightened little voice asked.

"I . . . I'm your friend," she said hesitantly. "I'm Erika."

"Erika." He seemed to be testing the name on his tongue. Apparently it felt alright, for he said it again. "Erika, that man . . . will he kill me?"

"Not if I can help it," she heard herself say, and wondered how she could possibly prevent it. "Maybe he won't come back anyway."

"He will," the little fellow said. "He's going to get my dad's truck."

"He told you that?"

"Yes."

"What else did he tell you?"

"Nothing," he said, and again he began to cry.

"Stevie, where's the rest of your family?" she asked, not wanting to know, afraid of what he'd say, but feeling compelled to hear their fate.

It took a moment before he could answer. Then he told her.

And she cried for the little family.

CHAPTER 12

"I wonder where they are now," Jan said as they again manned a roadblock on an obscure dirt road.

"Well, it's hard to tell. The Grossman place is . . . No, I can't imagine them . . ."

Before Mike could finish, the walkie-talkie in his hand came on again. The now-familiar voice of the female dispatcher said rapidly, "A vehicle drove by the Kramers' place about two hours ago. Mrs. Kramer has been worrying and just now called in and said she wishes someone would check on the Grossmans who are without a phone. She didn't get a good look at the vehicle, but she thinks it might have been a truck."

There being no better leads, several officers, including Mike and Jan, raced to the Grossman farm. The officers pulled up short. The brown pickup was nowhere to be seen. Their car was where it had been before, all four tires very flat.

"The place is dark. They're probably trying to sleep in there," one of the men said glumly. "Looks like a false alarm."

"Maybe, maybe not," Mike said. "Let's check things out anyway." He told Bob to stay in the car, which he left parked as far from the house and barn as possible. Then he and Jan, along with several local officers, surrounded the yard on foot.

The big John Deere tractor was in front of the log barn. The large double doors were closed. While Jan stayed by the tractor, Mike circled to the rear, into the corrals, and up to the back door of the barn. There was a locked padlock on the hasp. He found another door on the east side where a well-worn path led from there through a picket gate and up to the back of the house. That barn door was also padlocked.

Mike rejoined Jan. "Both of the other doors are padlocked," he reported. "I suppose if Butch did come back that the truck could be in there. I don't have a good feeling about the situation here. I feel like we're being watched."

"We're getting tired, Mike," Jan suggested with a weary smile. "I'm feeling that way too, but everything looks so peaceful here. I'll bet they got clear out of the county on us."

"But the roads are blocked, Jan. They must be somewhere in the area, off the road perhaps, and holed up," Mike said thoughtfully. "The house is dark and no one has come out to see what all the fuss is about out here. Someone needs to check things out in there."

Jan agreed and Mike lifted his borrowed radio and spoke into it.

"Ten-four," came the reply, and an officer slipped from behind a tree and ran to the porch. He knocked on the door. There was no response. He knocked again. Still no response. He tried to open it. The door was locked.

Mike spoke on the radio again. "Try the back door," he suggested. "And be careful."

Mike and Jan had moved farther from the barn and were beside a giant weeping willow tree. They watched tensely as the deputy worked his way around the house. A minute later he spoke into his radio. "It's locked back here too."

Mike's skin crawled. "Something's wrong here, Jan. Mrs. Kramer said the Grossmans were staying put tonight. Their car has flat tires, and they have no phone to call anyone to pick them up. By alrights they should be here."

"Come on, Mike," Jan said, "Don't you think someone should go in and check the house?"

"That's my feeling too, but we're not in charge here. Let's see if we can figure out who is and get them moving. That other fellow is back on the front porch. Let's join him."

They did and Mike urged him to break in. "I need to call my sergeant. I think he's on his way," he protested evasively.

"Then check with him! We're wasting valuable time here," Mike said impatiently.

The sergeant gave the go ahead to check all the windows. "If there's one open, go ahead and enter. If not, then wait. It looks like I'm going to be awhile."

All the windows were secure. "What about the upstairs ones?" Jan asked, pointing.

"Can't get to them. Either those people are in there and in trouble or they left, locking the doors and windows behind them," Mike said. "Deputy, call your sergeant again. Tell him that I think we need to force our way in."

He called. The sergeant didn't answer. A booming voice Mike had not heard before did. "Do not enter the house. I repeat, do not enter the house. I'm on my way. You're to take no further action until I arrive. Do you read me?"

"Loud and clear, Lieutenant," the young deputy said tersely. Then, turning to Mike and pulling a sour face he said, "Just our luck. That was Lieutenant Red Blauser. When he says wait, you wait. He thinks he's king."

"Deputy, it'll be dark in a few minutes. We don't have time to wait," Mike said testily.

"Sorry, we have to wait."

"But there could be people in there dying."

"Sorry, but I don't cross Blauser. *Nobody* crosses Blauser."

Mike could see he was beat, so he signaled for Jan to follow and returned to his vantage point beside the weeping willow tree. Mike shined his light on the barn. He had already checked the big doors. They were locked from the inside. There were several windows, including one high up in the loft. "I'll check the barn windows," he said. "I've got to be doing something."

"I'll wait here," Jan said.

Every window was secure. They were a type not designed to be opened. When Mike returned to Jan, he said, "The only way out of that barn is through those big doors. Not that I really think anyone's in there. Let's go back to the house. This Blauser guy ought to be getting here pretty soon."

"Shouldn't someone watch the barn. The four local guys are all scattered around the house now," Jan said.

"Go get Bob. He could stand here while we check out the house. Tell him to stay out of sight beside this tree but to watch those big front doors closely. We don't want anyone slipping out of there if they are inside. But if he sees something suspicious, anything at all, tell him to get back to his car and honk. He's not to get involved in any way. Make sure he understands that, Jan."

Jan did as Mike asked, thinking about Bob as she walked toward the blue Durango. He was one of the nicest guys she'd ever met and was very smart. And very worried—about another woman. She had to do something to keep from being attracted to him. It wasn't fair to Erika. She was suffering. She didn't need Jan distracting Bob. Not that he *was* distracted, she reminded herself. "Knock it off, Jan!" she said under her breath.

With that scolding, she resolved to do everything she could to control her feelings. She knew that Mike could see that she had been attracted to Bob, so now she knew that she must do whatever she could to change that. She was tapping on the glass even as she thought of him. Bob sat up quickly and rolled the window of the Durango down.

"We need your help," she said flatly.

"Sure thing," he said, brightening quickly. "What can I do?"

She told him, cautioning him to run back to his car if anything happened that seemed in the least bit suspicious. He promised he would only watch, not do anything more. Then she led him to his post and looked around for Sergeant O'Connor. It was her theory that it was easier not to develop feelings for Bob if she simply didn't spend any more time with him than necessary. She spotted Mike just before he disappeared behind the barn. She quickly ran after him, climbing into the corral at the rear where she found him closely inspecting the lock on the door there. He never touched it, but the door was secure; they could both see that. The padlock was new. It sparkled when Mike shined his light on it. The same was true of the small side door which they checked next.

When they returned, Bob was standing beside the huge weeping willow tree, almost invisible in its shadow. They spoke with him briefly, then Mike led Jan back to the house. Mike was becoming cross. "Deputy," he said at last, "where is that lieutenant of yours? We need to be having a look in there."

"He'll be along."

"That's what you said ten minutes ago! We're wasting time here. Call him why don't you? This Butch Snyder is no Sunday school kid. While we fiddle around, heaven only knows where he is and what he's up to."

"I'll call, Sergeant," the young deputy replied reluctantly.

"Two minutes," was Blauser's answer to his inquiry, and in two minutes he rolled up in a cloud of dust and strutted over to where two of the deputies waited beneath a large yard light, not far from Mike and Jan.

"You officers cover me," he said, without waiting to be filled in on what had already been done, and he approached the house.

Mike went after him and spoke just as the burly, red-haired lieutenant knocked on the front door. "I'm Sergeant Mike O'Connor, and we've already checked the doors and windows," he said.

"I'm Lieutenant Red Blauser, and you can't be too thorough. Lights are off," he observed.

"You don't say," Mike retorted, struggling to keep his temper.

"Where else could the family be?" Blauser asked.

"In the barn, I suppose."

"Let's check it."

"Good grief, Lieutenant, what do you think we've been doing for the last forty-five minutes?" Mike snapped. "The barn is locked tighter than a drum."

"What about the sheds and garage?" Lieutenant Blauser asked, unruffled by Mike's anger.

"Checked them as well."

Red scratched his head, shined his flashlight through the window of the front door and finally said, "Looks to me like we better go inside the house and have a look."

"No kidding," Mike mumbled as Red pulled his radio from his gun belt and ordered more officers to approach the house. Jan hurried up the walk and joined Mike. "You're gonna love this guy," Mike whispered.

"I'm too young to fall in love," Jan said with a straight face.

Mike chuckled. "Let's help him out, should we? He's still trying the door knob."

As if on cue, Red lifted a big-booted foot and said, "Stand back, everyone. I'm going to have to kick it in."

Mike stepped in front of the boot. "Here, let me open it." Red's foot dropped back onto the porch floor as Mike reached beneath his jacket and pulled his service revolver. He took it by the barrel and tapped at one small square pane of glass. It broke and he reached through, turned the knob on the lock and cautioned, "We ought to be watching for an ambush. You never know, Butch could be in there."

Red grunted, "The truck's not here, so neither is he." He shouldered Mike aside, swung the door open and brazenly entered the house. He flipped on the light switch and looked around the room. "Sergeant O'Connor, you and your little gal can come in now. It's all secure in here. You too, Hal. Everyone else is to stay outside and keep an eye on things."

As soon as Mike's eyes had adjusted to the light, he studied Red, who was explaining how he wanted the search of the house conducted. His hair was a darker, richer red than Mike's own, wavy and cut fairly short. He stood well over six feet and was well built, but on the husky side. His wide-set eyes were green, overcast with heavy red eyebrows, and looked past a slightly broad nose. A flaming moustache decorated his upper lip. His jaws were square above a thick neck and broad shoulders. He was a most imposing figure with personality to match.

Jan was not at all repulsed by him, just annoyed at his arrogance. Mike clearly didn't care for the guy. She just smiled to herself, coming quickly to the conclusion that she might have to keep the two of them from kicking each other in the teeth. Mike fidgeted as Red gave his lengthy instructions. She even placed a hand on Mike's shoulder when she could see that he was about to blow. That calmed him down, and finally Red was through. Then the four officers systematically checked the main level. There was no one in any of the rooms. "Let's check upstairs now," Red said in a clear tenor voice. Mike bristled as the lieutenant took Jan by the arm and said, "Come on, Trooper, you can help an old man up the stairs."

Red couldn't be much over thirty, but he'd surely taken a shine to Jan. And she didn't seem to mind a bit. Mike stomped up the stairs behind them. They found two rooms up there, and both were empty.

"Well, so much for anybody being in here," Red said.

"I wonder if there's an attic," Jan mused, looking at the ceiling. "I remember when I was a little girl and used to play at my grandparents' house. They had an attic with a wooden floor above the upstairs bedrooms."

"Looks like a piece of false ceiling there," Mike acknowledged, following Jan's eyes. He reached up and pushed. It gave way. "A trap-door of sorts," he said, nodding at Jan.

He moved it easily out of the way, grabbed a chair, and positioned it under the hole. Suddenly, a small bat flew with a swish from the opening and careened crazily around the room. Everyone hit the floor. It darted around for several seconds before finally landing on Jan's head. She screamed, but before it did any damage Red grabbed a pillowcase, wrapped it around his hand, and pulled the ugly creature from her hair and threw it with resounding force onto the hardwood floor.

"Thanks, Lieutenant," Jan said, trembling. "I'm terrified of bats. My dad killed a rabid one when I was small. I had nightmares about it for weeks."

The big lieutenant beamed at Jan. "No problem," he said, a blush visible in the yellowish light of the naked hundred-watt bulb above his head.

Jan turned to Mike. "Anything up there?" she asked.

Shaking his head, Mike stepped onto the chair and said, "I was just going to look."

The attic was empty. He slid the trap door back in place and the four officers tromped down the stairs. Red left the house immediately. Hal and Mike followed. "Where's the trooper?" Red demanded a moment later.

"Guess she's still inside," Mike responded. "I'll go see what's keeping her."

Jan was standing very still in the center of the room. She put a finger to her lips when Mike started toward her. After a moment, she said, "Mike, I heard a thumping sound. I'd swear it came from beneath the floor."

"Hey, you two, let's go," Red thundered from the doorway.

"Shh, I think I heard it again," Jan said urgently.

"I can't hear anything. What is it?" Red asked.

She explained, and they all listened for a moment. "It must have been my imagination," she said at last and started toward the door. She stopped suddenly. "Wait, did you hear that?"

"No," Mike said.

"You're right, Trooper. You're hearing things," Red said gruffly. "We'd better leave. We're going to have to explain why we broke in here anyway."

"Not so fast," Jan said impatiently, holding her hand up. She tapped with the toe of her shoe on the large woven rug she was standing on.

Mike heard a soft thumping sound from below the floor this time. "If I didn't know better," he said, "I'd say you were being answered."

"See, I told you," Jan said quickly. "What do you think it is?"

"I don't know, but—"

"It's nothing," Red interrupted gruffly.

"Nothing, my eye! Help me move this rug," Jan demanded.

Red watched, his green eyes burning. Mike and Jan grabbed the rug and pulled it away, revealing a hidden door under it. Red moved now. He grabbed the recessed handle and lifted the door. The old hinges squeaked, but the door came up easily. Mike shined his light through the opening. A rotting wooden stairway led out of sight into the dark abyss.

"Let me take the lead," Red demanded, pushing past Mike and shining his own light into the stairwell. Red started down the stairs, Jan followed gingerly, and Mike took up the rear. The odor of musty, damp soil mixed with mold pinched Mike's nostrils. Red flashed his light about, revealing many layers of dust-laden, sagging spiderwebs, mostly uninhabited. The room, about fifteen by twenty feet, contained empty, rotting shelves along the earthen walls.

"What was that?" Jan squealed, grabbing Red's arm as they stepped off the last step.

"I didn't hear anything," he said.

"I did," Mike pitched in. "Look under the stairway."

Red circled to his left, Jan following closely. He shot the beam of light under the stairs just as Mike reached their side, shining his own light there.

"It's Erika!" Mike exclaimed as the light exposed a head of dark hair on a female lying face down on the stale dirt, tightly bound.

The light moved over two more securely bound forms—one a man and the other a baby. "They're alive!" Jan exclaimed, rushing along with Mike to their aid.

Mike gently turned the woman over and discovered it was not Erika. The dark hair belonged to a woman who could only be Sandy Grossman. The others were her husband, Bill, and their little boy. Mike could see that the thumping sound had been produced by Bill lifting his tightly bound feet and bumping the toes of his boots on the hard dirt floor.

The officers rapidly removed the gags from their mouths and cut them free. Jan carried the baby up the rickety stairs, followed by Mike and Red assisting the unsteady parents. Sandy was crying uncontrollably and brushing dirt from her face and clothing.

"You're okay now," Mike consoled her after they had reached the light of the living room.

Sandy tried to speak but couldn't. Bill, his voice cracking, said, "It's our other son, Stevie. He's gone. Butch took him when he left us there to die. You've got to help us find him."

Mike felt a cold chill descend on him. The baby started to cry. Jan, suddenly trembling terribly, had to get rid of the baby before she dropped him. She handed him to his mother who, still sobbing, sat on the couch. Sandy turned her attention to her son, comforting him. As Jan walked nervously around the room, Mike steered Bill next to his wife and little boy. "Now," he said, "if you folks would tell us what happened."

Bill composed himself and explained. "We were sitting here watching TV. I had my gun on the end table. Right here," he said, touching it like it was hot. "All of a sudden I felt something pressed against my neck. It was a gun barrel. Butch was standing right there beside the sofa! He said to do as he told us or we would all die. I couldn't believe it. I hadn't heard a thing."

"Was Erika with him?" Jan asked. She was still shaking, but had pretty much regained her composure.

"Never saw her at all. Just Butch. Anyway, he mumbled something about insurance and about cops being all over the countryside." Bill stopped for a minute, fighting to maintain control of his emotions. "He grabbed Stevie . . . he was sitting here," he finally managed to say, motioning to the space on the sofa beside him.

"He said he was going to take Stevie for 'insurance.' Stevie started to cry and said, 'Daddy, we should have hid under the floor.' Butch mumbled something like, 'What's under the floor?' I told him there was nothing there. He said, 'Kids don't lie!' Then he said, 'Quit jerking me around,' and threatened to kill us all if we didn't show him, so I pulled back the rug and showed him."

"And he tied you up, gagged you, and left you down there. Then he left with Stevie?" Red asked.

"That's right, and he laughed when he left us in the cellar, saying it would become our grave before anyone ever found us."

"How did he get in the house?" Red asked.

"I don't know. I must not have locked one of the windows. He sure did it quietly though."

"Prints will show how he got in, not that it matters though," Mike said. "How did he lock the doors behind himself? You have dead bolts, I noticed."

"He took my key to the back door," Bill said, wringing his hands. "I could tell by the sound of his footsteps on the floor up here that he took Stevie out that way."

"Let's go," Mike said decisively. "We've got to find the boy."

Sandy was crying again, and Jan was trying to comfort her. She was having very little success. "You stay here, Jan, and we'll go look for Stevie," Mike said, wondering why Butch needed a second hostage, or . . . did he? Maybe something had happened to Erika. The thought made him shiver.

Jan nodded and Mike left, joining Bob under the weeping willow tree. He quickly explained what had happened in the house, emphasizing that Erika had not been in there while also trying not to alarm him.

"Maybe she finally got away," Bob suggested hopefully. Then his face dropped and his eyes watered. "Or she is hurt or . . ." He couldn't continue.

"See anything out here, Bob?" Mike asked, attempting to steer him away from the dark, depressing thoughts of Erika and her possible fate.

Red, Hal, and a couple of other officers were strolling across the yard, their flashlights cutting jagged streaks in the darkness. "Well, there was one thing, Mike," Bob began as his eyes followed the officers. Then he hesitated.

"What is it, Bob?" Mike pressed.

"That window up there," Bob said hesitantly, pointing at the window in the loft. "I thought I saw something move up there when you first went in the house. I know this sounds crazy, but for a second I thought there was a face pressed against the glass. I'm sure I'm wrong though. I'm just going nuts, that's all."

Mike stared up at the window intently. He could see nothing but black glass, but somehow, he didn't believe that Bob had been seeing things. He may be under stress, but he was a highly intelligent young man and seemed very much in control of himself. If he thought he saw something, then he probably did. "It's dark. You can hardly see the window," he said to Bob in an effort to pry more information from him.

"I know, but a patrol car pulled into the yard just then and the lights had it lit up for a moment," Bob explained.

"Here, I'll shine this light up there," Red offered. He had just arrived and heard the last of their conversation. He directed a bright beam from his large flashlight.

There was no movement. The men looked at each other. "If Bob saw a face, it could have been Butch . . . or Erika . . . or little Stevie. Wait here, Bob," Mike said, signaling for Red to follow him and hurried back to the house.

Inside he asked Bill, "Did you lock the barn when you did your chores this evening?"

Bill looked surprised. "No," he said. "The only door that can be locked is the big double one in the front, and it has a heavy crossbar on the inside."

Mike's mouth dropped open. "Do you mean to tell me that you don't have hasps and padlocks on the rear and side doors?"

"I know I should have them. I had planned to install some. A guy should lock everything these days," Bill said, "but I haven't got around to it yet. I did buy some hasps and padlocks a few weeks ago, but they're still on the workbench in the barn. I've just been too busy—"

"Bill," Red interrupted, "did you shut the doors?"

"Oh, yeah. I always shut them. I'm sure I did that. I was in a hurry today though, and I shut the big doors without barring them and left my tractor outside. Why are you so interested in my barn?" he asked, clearly becoming upset. "I was hoping you'd be out looking for Stevie."

"Bill," Mike said firmly, "all three doors on the barn are locked. The big door can't be moved, and there are shiny new Master Lock padlocks on the small doors."

"That can't be! I tell you, it simply can't be!" He was agitated and working his way to the back door as they talked.

"Okay, Bill, settle down," Lieutenant Blauser said. "We'll try to figure out what's going on."

"I'm coming," Bill said.

"It would be better if—" Mike began.

"Don't tell me what I can or can't do on my own place!" Bill exploded. "I'm going out there with you guys!"

Mike and Red looked at each other then at Jan, who had just joined them. They shrugged their shoulders in unison and Red said, "All right, but I insist that you do what I say. You got that, Bill?"

Bill got it, or at least the look on his face said he did.

Jan cast a hopeful glance at Mike as the men left, but he shook his head and said, "Would you stay with Sandy?" Resigned, she turned back to the distraught mother and her youngest child.

When they reached the barn Mike turned to Bill who was looking intently toward the high window. "What do you have up there behind the glass?"

"Nothing. There's just an empty loft up there." He hadn't taken his eyes off the window, and Hal had a light shining on it. "Stevie likes to play up there. It's his favorite place. He may have left a few toys scattered around the loft."

"One of the men thought he saw a face up there a little while—" Mike started.

Bill burst from the group and ran to the big door, grabbed a metal handle and pulled. Red and Mike were right behind him. Red grabbed Bill by the arm and said, "Hey, slow down there. You could get someone killed. There could be a trap set in there for all we know."

Bill struggled, but Red's grip only tightened. "They're barred, Bill. Now step back."

"Let go of me, Lieutenant," Bill ordered through gritted teeth.

"Not until you agree to do it my way," Red said firmly.

"Okay, okay, but hurry. My boy might be in there."

Red released him slowly. Bill stepped away from him, nearer to Mike. "Here, come with me, Bill," Mike said. "We'll have another look at the other doors."

Bill followed quietly, but Mike heard a sharp intake of breath when he shined his light on the side door padlock. "That can't be!" he said incredulously.

Mike stooped and shined the light on the ground beneath the door. Red walked up. "What do you have there, Sergeant?" he asked.

"Wood shavings. Fresh too."

"Someone has done this since I did my chores," Bill said, a chill in his voice. Mike's skin crawled. "Let's look at the back door," Bill went on.

The four men trailed around, through a corral gate, and up to the back door. Their light reflected again off of a new lock and hasp. Fresh wood shavings were mixed with dry manure and dirt on the ground.

Back at the weeping willow a minute later, Mike asked Bob, "Are you sure no one has come out of the big doors."

"Not since I've been here. I would have honked and got out of sight, like you said, if I'd seen anyone," Bob said sharply.

"I'm sorry. I didn't mean to imply anything, but all the doors are locked," Mike said, wiping his mouth absently. "The small ones are locked from the outside. Only those big doors are locked from the inside. There is no other way anyone could have gotten out since we got here."

"Well, seems to me we need to get inside," Red said. "Hal, go relieve Jan, that Colorado trooper. She's still in the house. Have her come out here."

Mike looked at Red with surprise. "Why did you—" he began.

Red cut him off. "She's a bright gal and we need every good head we can get right now," he said, his face reddening in the glow of the flashlights.

Mike chuckled and said, as he stepped back, "And mighty pretty too."

Bob leaned close. "What's going on, Mike?"

"I think our big bully lieutenant has been struck with a case of Jan fever," he said with a grin. The serious expression on Bob's face wiped out Mike's grin. "Red's right of course. We do need Jan's help. She's really sharp, Bob. Who knows what might be going on in that barn right now."

"I wonder if Erika's in there," Bob said, shivering visibly.

"So do I, my boy. So do I."

Jan came running up. "Thanks for sending for me, Red," she said breathlessly, ignoring Mike. "What's up?"

Red filled her in, then she said, "What are we waiting for? Let's open the big doors."

"How?" Red asked. "They're barred from the inside."

"I was thinking we might hook a chain on the door handles and pull with the tractor. Something will give, and I suspect it'll be Bill's bar."

"That should work," Bill agreed. "The handles won't give first. They're fastened with large bolts."

"Good thinking, Jan," Red said with enthusiasm.

"Thanks, Red," she said, flashing him a brief smile. "And we ought to have a couple of patrol cars pulled up with their bright lights shining on the doors from both sides of the tractor. That way we'll have light in there when they pop open. And everyone needs to be under cover until we go in."

"Good idea," Red said awkwardly. "There's a chain in my car. I'll—"

"We can use the one in the tractor," Bill cut in. "I'll drive it."

"It could be dangerous," Mike warned. Bill ignored him and mounted the cab of the tractor, threw out the chain, and fired up the engine. He backed it to within about four feet of the barn. In the meantime, two patrol cars were driven over and positioned with their lights on the doors. The chain was threaded through the two stout steel handles and fastened to the tractor.

"Looks like we're ready," Mike said to Red after they had crouched behind the patrol cars. "Anytime you say. Everyone's in position."

Red gave the word and Bill eased the powerful green tractor forward. The big doors trembled, and then, with a loud crack, the two-by-four snapped and the tractor stopped. Bill backed it up, and Mike unhooked the chain, pulled it from the door handles, dropped it and flung the doors wide.

Light flooded inside. Bill's brown pickup stared at them, but nothing moved except the officers who rapidly entered the big barn, pistols drawn. Red and Jan went to the right of the truck. Mike and a deputy went to the left. Mike located the power switch where Bill had told him it would be, and the barn lit up like high noon.

Systematically, they checked the inside of the building. They found no one. Even the stables on either end were empty. Mike examined the workbench. He found the plastic and paper wrapping the hasps had been in and two empty padlock boxes. Remembering that every lock came with two keys, he rummaged around in the debris and found two spares, carelessly abandoned.

With interest, he examined a cordless electric drill and Phillips-head screwdriver that were piled on top of the debris. Upon closer examination, he discovered that the drill held a bit that was much too large for tapping holes to start screws in. He was unable to find a smaller bit on the bench. "Can't figure that out," he said to the deputy who was watching him. "We'll have to think on that some."

Jan interrupted. "Red wants to check out the loft."

Mike nodded and turned his attention to it. The loft came out about twenty feet from the wall. It rested on huge beams which in turn sat atop poles that were set in the cement of the floor on either side of the door. It was really nothing more than a giant shelf, open at the front. From his position, Mike could see nothing up there.

He and Hal held their guns steady while Red climbed the steep ladder, Jan at his heels. As soon as his head popped over the top of the loft floor, Red shined his flashlight into the dark area at the back where the barn lights from below left only deep shadows. For a moment he just stood there, then he clambered onto the high floor. After rustling around for a moment, he came into view, threw some ropes down and descended.

Together they examined the ropes. There were a half dozen pieces. They had clearly been cut in several places. "Someone was tied up there," Mike finally concluded.

"They were in here. They were all in here," Jan said thoughtfully. "And these ropes must have been used on both Stevie and Erika. There's more than you'd ever use on just one person."

"But they're gone now," Mike said angrily. "How in the world did Butch and Erika get out of here?" he asked. "I just know they were in here when we first arrived."

Jan felt faint. They might still be close. A shiver of fear went through her. But she shook it off. Butch now had two hostages, unless . . . She tried not to let her thoughts drift any further.

Red sent for Bob. When he walked into the brightly lit barn, Red asked him, "Are you absolutely sure they didn't come out of the barn while you were out front?"

"Positive. I've told you all before. No one came out of here!" Bob said angrily.

"If they did, how could they have locked it from the inside again?" Jan asked sensibly.

Red's face flushed, and anger flashed in his eyes. The bright flush moved like a brush fire down his neck. Mike thought that if it had been anyone but Jan, Red would have him stretched out on the floor. "I'm sorry, Red. I didn't mean that the way it sounded." She smiled, and Red forced a chuckle.

"Stupid of me, I guess," he admitted.

"Not really," Jan said softly, laying a hand on his arm. "I don't hear anyone else explaining how they got out of here, assuming of course that they were in here when we first came and discovered the doors locked. But then, there was the face Bob saw. It had to have been Erika."

"By golly, Jan, I think you've got it," Mike said. "She wasn't in the house with Butch when Stevie was taken. She must have been tied up here all along. And then later he must have put Stevie with her. But then what did he do? Why didn't they leave right then?" He scratched his chin. "That aside, we know one thing. They're out there somewhere on foot, because the truck is right here."

"I'll get my people alerted," Red said, his normal color returning. "We need to find them before Butch steals another car."

"That's right," Mike said. He turned and walked to the back door. He murmured and struck the door with his fist in frustration.

The door swung open!

He was shocked by what he had just done. Jan and Bob joined him, followed by Bill, who'd said nothing since they'd found that his little boy wasn't in the barn. Bill reached down and picked up a slender drill bit. "I wonder how this got here," he said.

Mike snapped his fingers. "I've got it," he said, remembering the cordless drill on the workbench. He stepped outside and shined his light on the lock. As he suspected, the padlock was still locked and firmly in place, but the hasp dangled from the door. Four oversized holes stared back at him like dark eyes from the door frame. Four screws dangled from the back of the plate. He closed the door and, guiding the screws into the waiting holes, pressed the hasp and lock back into place. It appeared secure again.

"That's it, alright," he said in amazement. "Butch rigged it to look like this door was locked when it wasn't. If I'd have tugged on the door instead of just looking at it, it would have swung open, and . . . I suppose I'd be dead now. I'm sure Butch was waiting here, knowing that if someone tried the door it would open," he concluded, "but he correctly assumed that we wouldn't."

"Why did he go to so much trouble?" Jan asked. "Why didn't they just leave before we got here?"

"Too many roadblocks and cops in the area," Mike reasoned. "My guess is that he grabbed the boy to use as another hostage. He probably thought that we'd leave when we didn't find the family and he could wait until the heat was off in this area and drive out in the truck. He had rigged the locks just to be on the safe side. With the barn locked, if we hadn't found the family, chances are we would never have looked in here. He was probably counting on us not finding them and leaving with him still in here. Man, Butch is smart. He rigged the locks just in case before we came, and then locked the big door from the inside and waited, knowing his best chance of escape—if he had to leave without the truck—was out the back door."

"Erika must be scared to death," Bob said sadly. Then he had a terrible thought.

Jan noticed the change that came over his face. "What is it, Bob?" she asked.

"He took Stevie. He must be through with Erika. He will probably . . ." He couldn't go on. The thoughts he had were too terrible to express. But Jan knew what he was thinking.

So did Mike, who said, "Well, we better help Red and his men. Butch and Erika and Stevie can't be too far away on foot. They couldn't have left more than a half hour ago."

It was time to get back to the hunt, a hunt which had taken on a new and harrowing urgency.

CHAPTER 13

The night was not as dark as it had been; a sliver of moon had risen. The flight through the fields from the Grossman barn was taking its toll. Erika, already hurting from the beating Butch had given her and from being tied up for so long, picked up additional bruises and scrapes. And she was dirty and exhausted. The refreshing shower and meal at the farmhouse seemed like days ago, and the suitcase full of clean clothes and personal items was back in the barn, still in the bed of the brown truck.

Little Stevie Grossman refused to let go of Erika's hand for so much as a second or two, and his short little legs ached as he jogged to keep up. Butch was sullen, and refused to explain to Erika what the purpose of bringing Stevie along had been. They'd left the barn when the officers began to search the house. Butch had planned to wait until they left and then escape in the truck again. But when it became apparent that they were intent on a thorough search, he panicked, and they went out the back, securing the false locks simply to keep the officers fooled longer. And it also gave Butch time to get away on foot and find a car to steal.

At one point, twenty or twenty-five minutes into their flight, Butch stopped. He had to be very tired and in a lot of pain, but he refused to admit it. Erika wondered where he got the energy to keep going.

But he blamed her for slowing them down. "You've got to keep up, Erika," he growled at her. "We won't have them fooled forever you know."

"I'm trying," she cried. "And so is Stevie." She dared not anger him again if she didn't have to, for she knew now that he wouldn't hesitate to hurt her . . . or worse.

Butch stopped at her words. "Erika, have you learned your lesson? You do as I say, only as I say?"

"Yes, I've learned," she admitted.

"Good, then I won't need the kid after all." He pulled the pistol from his pocket and pointed it at the little boy.

Erika didn't even have time to think she simply acted from instinct as she threw herself between the boy and Butch. "What are you doing!" he thundered.

"Butch, I'll do whatever you ask. I'll go wherever you say, and I won't try to get away from you—if you just won't hurt this little boy. He's done nothing to you," she cried. "Please, I promise."

For a moment, Butch hesitated, holding the gun threateningly as Stevie cowered behind Erika. Then he slowly lowered it and put it in his pocket. "Okay, for now, until you prove yourself, I'll let him come, but you better not let him slow us up."

"I will, Butch. I will if I have to carry him." Her heart surged with love for Stevie. She had never known he existed until this very night. But she knew that she would die, as afraid of that as she was, before she'd let Butch take his sweet and innocent life.

"You better, Erika. If you don't, he will—"

"I know," she broke in. She couldn't bear to hear him say what he'd intended to do. "I'll take care of him."

Without another word, Butch turned and started away. Stevie and Erika followed, driven beyond their physical capacity by fear, the desire to live, and the bond that had developed between them. And as they scurried along, she prayed and thanked God for the miracle He had just given her.

They didn't stop again until they were across the road from a dark house, lit only by a yard light a hundred yards beyond. Butch forced them to lie in the tall weeds beside the road while he studied the house. Erika held Stevie tightly against her side, thinking of Bob and remembering what she had seen from the barn. She and Stevie, together, very carefully and slowly had squirmed their way away from the edge of the loft and to the window before Butch came back with the truck. He hadn't bothered to check on them when he returned. He simply busied himself doing something else. It wasn't until later that she learned he'd been putting locks on the small doors. She and

Stevie waited painfully, fearfully in the dark near the window. Two or three times she pressed her face to the glass and looked out.

The last time, after the officers had come, she had at first seen only shadowy figures. The closest person had been standing beside a tree. She was studying him when the headlights of a car had lit up the yard. She had almost fainted. Bob Evans was standing beneath a large weeping willow tree, and he was looking right at her, or at least it seemed like it.

Her heart had surged with hope. Was his presence an answer to her prayers? Was he here to rescue her? She had resolved right then to do whatever it took to keep Butch from hurting her again and to give Bob and the officers a chance to get her safely away from Butch. But at the same time, as she felt little Stevie stir beside her, she promised herself she would protect him at all costs.

She turned her head. Butch, breathing heavily at her side, looked like death warmed over. Tears of anger, hopelessness, and frustration streamed down her face and formed tiny mud droplets on the dry soil beneath her. She wiped the tears away and looked at Butch again. Confusion overcame her. Maybe if she and Butch and Stevie could get another car and go to Canada, like Butch had earlier mentioned he planned to do, then maybe she and Stevie could slip away . . . someday soon. Maybe he would even let them go. He wouldn't need her then. That was it. He would let them go and she could return the boy to his parents, *if they were alive,* then go home, go back to Bob, and he would be so glad to see her, and everything would be alright. But maybe, before all that, Bob would save them from Butch. This is what she silently prayed for now.

The house across the road was old, but with a fairly new two-car garage attached to it. Butch stirred. "There's got to be a car in that garage. The ground looks level from there to the road. We'll roll it out, close the door, push it to the road, start it up and we're on our way, Erika," Butch explained. "What time is it?"

She pressed the light button on her watch. "Almost two o'clock."

"We better go. Those cops will figure out sooner or later that we aren't in the barn. You follow me. We're going to the side of the garage." He hesitated, then he added, "And don't you let that brat make a sound."

"Stevie," she said to the little boy who clung tightly to her arm, "you must do what Butch says, okay? Stay with me, don't make a sound, and you'll be safe."

"I'll try really hard, Erika," he responded, and she hugged him to her fondly.

They scrambled toward the house a moment later. The garage had only one wide overhead door. Butch didn't even check it, but proceeded as he had said they would to the small side door on the west that entered the garage from the yard. The door was locked. So then Butch slipped around front and tried the big door. Same condition. He was swearing under his breath as he returned and leaned the rifle up against the garage.

He slipped his knife from its sheath and carefully worked the point of the blade toward the plunger. When the tip hit metal, he pressed a little more, then twisted. The door was not a tight fit, and he was soon able to force the plunger back and pull the door open. He grabbed the rifle and they stepped through, Butch shutting the door behind them, making sure it was locked. He was glad to see it was an older car parked there. He would have it started in no time at all. He opened the driver's side door and, using the little bit of illumination created by the dome light, located a screwdriver on a clean and orderly workbench. With that he carefully broke away a large piece of the steering column in the old, dark-blue Pontiac, revealing a pair of small levers and springs. He forced one lever down until the steering wheel unlocked.

Erika silently put Stevie in the backseat, then she got in the car to steer while Butch noiselessly opened the overhead door, pushed the sedan outside, and closed the door again, making sure it was locked. Together they pushed the car to the road. To Erika, the sound of the tires on the gravel was as loud as firecrackers, but no one came out of the house to investigate. She was afraid that she wouldn't be able to convince Butch to spare their lives as she had the forest worker in Utah.

"Get in. I'll start it," Butch said after checking for distant headlights in both directions on the road. He pulled the screwdriver from his pocket, touched another lever in the exposed part of the steering column, and pressed. The engine began to purr. He dropped the screwdriver on the floor, pushed it under the seat, and drove east. Stevie, uninvited, crawled over the seat and nestled himself onto Erika's lap.

"How do you like the way I started this car?" Butch asked a few minutes later, ignoring the presence of the little boy.

Erika didn't care, but she knew she better seem interested for her sake and for her little friend's. "Where did you learn to do that?" she asked.

"I don't know if it will work on newer models, but there are other ways. I learned it in prison. A guy can learn a lot in prison if he pays attention."

"I never knew it was so easy to steal a car," she said. "Do you think your luck will hold out now?"

As he explained to her that luck came from partly being smart and partly being careful, he had no way of knowing that he was just about to get a real lucky break—one that had nothing to do with either brains or caution.

***

Frank Kramer reached for the phone on the fourth ring, mumbling, "Who would be calling at this hour?"

Millie watched his face as he listened intently. His brow creased and he said,"Oh, the poor kids. Are they alright?" There was a long pause, and then he said, "Yes, ma'am, we'll be real careful. I have a gun and I know how to use it." He listened again, then said, "They're both parked in the garage. I locked it, yes, and the keys are right here in the house with us." He listened once more, then said, "Thank you very much. We'll call if we see or hear anything. I sure hope little Stevie Grossman is okay. Good-bye, ma'am."

"Was that the police?" Millie asked.

"Yes. They want us to be real careful. She said the Grossmans had another terrible scare and that Butch took little Stevie. And then, apparently, he and the girl and Stevie got away on foot. I'm taking the car and truck keys to bed with us, and a gun. They're not taking our car or truck."

"Oh, poor Sandy. Poor, poor little Stevie. What a terrible thing. And to think that they're out there somewhere right now," Millie sobbed. "Whatever can we do?"

"There's nothing we can do," Frank said. "I just wish there was."

***

Butch entered the freeway, speeding as fast as he dared, intent on reaching the turnoff to Kemmerer as soon as possible. They encountered no roadblocks and made good time. He commented to Erika that the police obviously thought they were still back there on foot. He pulled off the freeway to gas up about four in the morning. He told Erika to pay for the gas and buy some junk food with some of the money Butch had stolen. And he made it clear that Stevie was to stay in the car and out of sight while she was doing her errand.

Stevie would have no part of it. Erika begged him to get in the backseat and lay down. "I'll only be a minute," she promised.

But he clung to her until Butch suddenly jerked him from her, clamped his hand over the terrified boy's mouth, and threatened he would do terrible things if Stevie didn't cooperate. Stevie struggled, twisting and kicking. Erika tried to console him, but he would not be consoled. In his little mind, staying for even a minute with Butch was the most dangerous thing he could do.

Erika began to plead. "Let him come with me. They won't know him. What difference does it make?"

The look she got from Butch sent shivers of terror through her. Stevie's life was in danger. Praying silently, hopefully, she left Butch, with Stevie still struggling in his arms, and rushed to make her purchases and pay for the gas.

When she returned to the car, she sighed in relief to find Stevie still alive. She took him in her arms, smothering him with kisses as Butch again pulled onto the road. After little Stevie had finally calmed down, she spoke to Butch, though it took some effort.

"You were lucky again, Butch," Erika said to him. "Your picture was hanging on the wall in there!"

"See," he argued, "luck comes from being smart. Why do you think I had you go pay?"

"I guess you're right," she agreed grudgingly. She was convinced that he was smart, but he was also very, very evil.

A few minutes later he did something that proved her right. He pulled off the road in a desolate, dark stretch of highway and stopped the car. He pushed his door open, then turned to Erika. "Give me the boy," he commanded.

She twisted in the seat, protecting Stevie the best she could with her body. "You said you wouldn't hurt him," she cried.

"Who said I was going to?" he said gruffly. "He's going to ride in the back from now on, that's all."

"Butch, you can't do that. He's only six! Please," she begged, crying hysterically.

But Butch had made up his mind. He grabbed Erika by the hair and jammed her head over the back of the seat. She began to choke and her grip on Stevie loosened. Butch, with his other hand, grabbed the boy. Then he let go of Erika, slapped her hard across the face, and leaped from the car.

She fumbled with the door, forced it open, and literally fell out the door. By the time she was able to get to her feet, Butch had bound and gagged the little boy, and was lifting him into the back.

She attacked Butch with fury. But he again struck her, causing her to fall. Before she could again get to her feet, Stevie was on the floorboard in the back, a shawl that had been on the seat thrown over him and the door slammed shut. She faced Butch, for the moment not caring what he did to her, only caring about the little boy. He laughed in her face and said, "Oh, Erika, you've got so much to learn. I thought you'd be smarter than this. I can't believe you're making things so hard for me."

She took a deep breath and said, "I'm not the one making things hard. We were doing okay until you took Stevie from his family." She pointed at the car. "You can do whatever you want with me, but I can't let you hurt him."

He laughed. "Who said anything about hurting him. It's just better if he rides back there."

Erika didn't trust Butch. She feared for Stevie's life, and told Butch so. "Well, Erika," he responded, "there's only one way to assure that he lives."

"What?" she asked hopefully.

"You do whatever I ask for as long as I ask."

"I'll do it," she promised, as she had before.

"No more trouble out of you, that's the first thing. I don't want to have to hurt you, Erika. You are so beautiful," he said, a sickeningly wistful, almost soft tone in his voice.

She shuddered. He'd already hurt her, but nothing like he could. Fear for herself returned, fear of things worse than death. Who knows what he might do? But her greatest fear was still for little Stevie Grossman. She hung her head and nodded. "I'll do what you want, just don't hurt Stevie," she agreed.

"You realize you're mine," he added, his words filling the already dark night with terror she hadn't known was possible.

Five long hours later they pulled the stolen Pontiac into a campground in the Grand Teton National Park. Erika had bought more food and gas in Jackson Hole, and Butch had decided that they needed to keep off the highway for the day and sleep in the car. They had seen several police cars during the long night's drive, but not one officer had paid any attention to them.

They ate some junk food, and Butch even allowed Erika to feed Stevie and hold him for a minute. Then he was put back on the floorboards and covered with the shawl. Butch stretched out as best he could in the car and fell asleep. Erika watched him for several minutes. He finally seemed to be sleeping deeply, and she made a difficult and dangerous decision. She would take Stevie from the back and run. Surely someone in this park would help them.

Slowly, as silently as possible, Erika opened her door, then looked over at Butch. He didn't stir. So she slipped out, leaving the door slightly ajar. Her heart was pounding fiercely, and fear almost made her abandon her plan. But she prayed for courage, and after standing silently beside the car for a full minute, she proceeded to open the back door. She flinched at the click it made, and glanced again at Butch, but he still seemed to be sleeping soundly.

Erika slowly pulled the door open, and reached down and flipped back the shawl. She touched her lips, warning the boy to be quiet. He nodded his head in understanding, and she took his hand, gently pulling him into a sitting position. Her head was beneath the back of the seat as she worked.

Something cold and hard touched her neck and Erika froze. "I ought to just kill you right now," Butch said. "You didn't really think you could just take him and carry him off did you?"

For a moment, terror clogged Erika's brain. She had been so certain that Butch was sleeping soundly. She honestly thought for a long, terrifying moment that her life and little Stevie's were over. But when Butch didn't fire his weapon, she cleared her mind and tried to think of something to say.

An idea formed, and she said, "Butch, he needs to use the bathroom. I was only going to let him stand here by the tree." She waited while he pressed the gun ever tighter against her skin, then she breathed a sigh of relief when he pulled it away. She straightened up, bringing Stevie with her and standing upright beside the car.

Butch still had the gun pointed at them, and Erika wasn't sure he still didn't intend to kill them, but she did the only thing she could and stood the boy on the ground, led him the half dozen steps to the nearest tree and whispered, "Use the bathroom, Stevie."

Fortunately, Stevie was able to cooperate, and she soon had him bedded down on the floor in the back of the car again. Without a word she climbed back in beside Butch. "Next time, you ask permission first," he hissed.

"Okay," was all she could say. She had tried and failed. She didn't know if she would ever dare try again. Butch was a much lighter sleeper than she had hoped. Several minutes passed before the wild beating of her heart subsided. In the meantime, Butch appeared to be sleeping again.

Erika stretched out the best she could, having decided that she could not get away. Another time, Butch might not give her the time to come up with an excuse. Exhausted, she finally drifted into a fitful sleep.

They were awakened by a pounding on the window. It was a ranger, and he was shouting, "Hey you! What do you two think you're doing?"

Erika almost panicked. She was damp with perspiration from the warmth of the car's interior, and her heart began to beat wildly. She glanced at Butch. He was white as a ghost, but calmly said, "Roll down your window, Erika. If he has us pegged, I'll shoot him. If you try to warn him anyway, I'll shoot you."

With shaking hands, Erika rolled the window down. "Can we help you, sir?" she asked, her voice betraying the terror that had come over her, not only for herself, but for the ranger, for all of them.

"You sure can," he said. "You can pay for this camping spot or leave. You can't just pull in, take up a spot, and snooze."

"We're sorry, sir," she said, welcome relief flooding over her. "We were so tired that we just weren't thinking, I guess. How much is it?" she asked.

He told her and she looked over at Butch. "Pay the man," he said. "We owe it."

She counted out the bills. He thanked her and left. "Wow, that was close," Butch said, sagging back in his seat and grimacing with pain. "Those pills that woman gave me aren't helping very much I guess. My shoulder and arm hurt clear to my elbow. Come around here and look at it."

She got out, circled the car, opened his door, and helped him take off the blue western shirt Sandy Grossman had helped him into. Ugly red steaks ran down his arm from his shoulder to his elbow. Close to the blood-soaked bandage, his skin was puffed and purple. With Butch's knife, she cut the tape and removed the bandage. She recoiled in horror as the stench of rotting flesh attacked her sensitive nostrils, and she stared at the ugly mounds of dark-yellow, blood-streaked pus that filled the wound.

"This is terrible, Butch," she said. Not that she cared in the least, but she couldn't imagine how he even used his left arm. The pain she still felt from his vicious blows reminded her that he could. "You really need a doctor," she told him.

"That would be smart," he mocked. "I just need a little more rest. See if you can find a first-aid kit in this car. Maybe there'll be some ointment or something that you can put on this. Then you can bandage me up again."

The glove compartment produced a small kit under the registration and a small stack of other papers which she absently dropped on the seat. Butch picked the registration card up and read as she rounded the car again to tend to his wound.

"Hey, we'll be Millie and Frank Kramer. That's who this car belongs to," he said, waving the card and dropping it beside him.

"Why?" she asked.

"It just seems like a good idea," he said curtly. "So, remember, you're Millie Kramer, and I'm Frank Kramer. Got that?"

"I'm Millie and you're Frank" she repeated dutifully as she tried to hold her head back—where the nauseating stench of Butch's wound was diluted by the light forest breeze blowing gently from the west.

She couldn't bring herself to touch the wound, so she smeared a small tube of burn ointment on a compress, applied it to the wound, and began to tape it in place. The longer she worked the sicker it made her.

"What's the matter with you, Millie?" he asked, with emphasis on the assumed name. "You look like you're going to throw up all over me."

"I think I'm going to be sick, B . . . Frank," she stammered.

"Hey, I'm the one with the stinking arm, not you!" he protested.

"Yeah, I know. That's what's making me sick," she said, gagging. "Gotta go!"

She turned away, stumbled blindly to the foot of a towering pine tree and retched. After her stomach was empty she felt good enough to finish bandaging Butch's arm.

They tried to fall asleep again, but it was impossible in the sizzling heat of the car. Erika rolled all the windows down. That cooled things off a bit, but she wondered how little Stevie was doing. If only she could do more for him. She gazed through the windshield at the swaying pine branches and bright streaks of sunlight that penetrated them.

She thought of her earlier attempt to leave. She longed to be free of Butch, away from the reign of terror through which he controlled her. But she had tried and failed. And in failing she had endangered both her life and that of Stevie Grossman. She was under Butch's power. He was controlling her life. She had no power to act on her own. It would be stupid to try to escape again. She was so depressed that she began to sob.

That made Butch angry. "What are you bawling about?" he growled at her. "Do you need something to do while I rest?"

She shook her head. "I'm okay," she said.

But he was studying her thoughtfully, his white face beaded with sweat. "I'm getting worse," he mumbled. "You've got to help me. I think I might need a doctor."

"That's what I said."

"Shut up! I need to think."

She recoiled and sat silently, trying desperately to quit crying. After a couple of minutes he said, "We've got to see a doctor, get fixed up, then get away without him causing us problems. That might mean we have to pay right then."

She wondered how that could ever happen. Surely a doctor would be suspicious if he was paid in cash. And anyway, they didn't have much stolen money left. But Butch had an idea. "Erika, you can get some money for us."

"How?" she cried in dismay.

"Just listen," he said. "There are several motor homes and large camp trailers in this campground. Some of them probably have money in them. Rich people leave things like that lying around," he reasoned. "Your job is to find the money and bring it to me."

She started to cry out in protest, then remembered her earlier resolve. He punctuated that resolve by simply saying, "I would do it myself if I could, but I can't; and if you don't, it will be the end of Stevie. Now go!"

She would do it for Stevie. And she resolved to be careful. If she got caught, it would cost the little boy his life. She had to succeed for his sake. Without a word, she got out of the car and began walking slowly along the road, her heart hammering. She began to walk faster, looking over the assorted trailers, motor homes, and tents that adorned the area. Many of them were deserted, just like Butch had reasoned they would be. The campers were out somewhere sight-seeing in their cars and trucks, she guessed.

She picked out a trailer with no vehicles around it, looked nervously about and, seeing no one, walked up to the door and knocked. When there was no answer she tried the handle with a shaking hand. To her relief it wasn't locked. She pushed it open and looked around again, half expecting to see Butch lurking nearby. When she didn't see him she stepped in, shutting the door behind her.

Her heart raced faster than ever, and her palms were moist and shaking as she searched the trailer, alert for any sound outside that might be the owner returning.

Butch was right again!

There was a gaudy purple purse on the bed.

She opened it quickly, wanting to get this terrifying excursion over with as quickly as possible. She was disappointed when she only found a few dollars. She took them, stuffed them into her pocket, closed the purse, and put it back on the bed. As she turned to leave, she noticed that a nail file had fallen from the purse. That could alert the owner of the purse that someone had been in here she realized. She picked it up and fled from the trailer.

Back on the road that wound through the campground, she sighed with relief, then once again looked for Butch. She couldn't see him, *but that didn't mean he wasn't watching.* She had to go through it all again. The few dollars she'd stolen were not nearly enough to satisfy him.

To her dismay, the next trailer was locked. She tried inserting the nail file she had in her hand like Butch had done with his knife. It didn't work, so she moved on. The next one she tried was also locked, but she was successful in sliding the flimsy catch with the nail file this time. She looked around, saw no one, and entered. There was no money.

She wanted to scream. She couldn't keep this up, but she had no choice. She tried praying again. Just a little prayer. A short prayer. A very discouraged prayer.

She opened the door of the trailer and stepped out.

"Hi there." A young man with shoulder-length hair and a bandana around his head was standing right in the middle of the road, a big grin on his face.

Erika jumped. Her mind raced, trying to think of an excuse for being in the trailer. He stepped toward her, his smile growing broader, and looked her over with bold admiration.

"My name's Freddie," he said. "I didn't mean to startle you." His hand was extended. She wiped hers on a pant leg and shook his. "Do you have a name? Why, you're the prettiest girl I've seen in days, even if you have been in an accident." He laughed lightly. "You're really banged up, but still very pretty."

Relief cooled her worried mind even as she wondered just how bad her face looked. She realized that he must have just been out for a walk and didn't belong to this trailer. "Hi, I'm E . . . Millie," she stuttered.

"Hi, E . . . Millie," he mimicked with a grin.

She had almost said her real name. She had to cover her mistake. Putting on the charm and easing away from the trailer, she said, "Just Millie. Forward guys make me . . . eh . . . nervous," she said, emphasizing the "eh" and ducking her head shyly.

"I'm sorry," he said. "I can't help it if I like beautiful girls. Going my way?"

"Which way's that?"

He pointed.

"Nope, sorry, I'm was going to go the other way," she said quickly.

"Me too," he said with his easy grin. "I was just fooling. I'm going your way."

This was not working. She had to do something to get rid of him. Inspiration struck. She said, "Sorry, Freddie, but my husband might not like me walking with a stranger."

His eyes darted to her ring finger. She quickly put her hands behind her back, then she added, "Well, he's kind of my husband. You know what I mean. He gets awful jealous since we've been together."

"Okay, I get the hint. I'm leaving," he said, gazing at her longingly before striding away.

Her successful handling of the encounter increased her confidence. She brushed an errant strand of long dark hair from her face and resolutely selected a huge motor home, made sure it was unoccupied, and entered.

It was plush and reeked of wealth. She found more money—lots of money. She stuffed several one-hundred-dollar bills in her pocket, took some smaller ones and started to leave. She stopped, looked for the bathroom, and was startled when she examined herself in the mirror. Her face was badly bruised, her lip was swollen, and her eyes were red. She turned and fled from the motor home and hurried back to the car. Butch was asleep.

She opened a back door, praying that nothing had happened to Stevie while she had been gone. He looked up at her as she removed the shawl. His little eyes were full of pain. They seemed to plead with her to help him. She patted his head, lifted him out, and held him for several minutes. She helped him go to the bathroom again, fed him, and wiped his brow. To her surprise Butch hadn't stirred. Maybe for once he really was sound asleep. Could she try getting away again? Or would it only get both of them killed? Then she had an idea.

It was dangerous for her if she succeeded, but far better for Stevie. She tried not to think what Butch would do when he found out. Checking Butch once more, she thought that this time he was truly sound asleep. Perhaps his infection was taking its toll on him. She had to try to save Stevie. She put a small pillow that was on the seat beneath the shawl and adjusted it so that, without a close inspection, Butch wouldn't realize the little boy wasn't there. Then she pushed the door shut but didn't latch it, fearing that the click might awaken Butch.

Then, holding Stevie tightly in her aching arms, she backed slowly away from the car, her eyes never leaving the back of Butch's head. She returned to the expensive motor home. She had little Stevie stand beside her as she again opened the door. She looked around, praying that Butch hadn't followed her. Seeing no sign of him, she took Stevie into the motor home. She patiently but quickly explained that he was to stay here and wait. He was to be very quiet and was not to cry or to go outside. "I love you, Stevie, but it's best this way. The people who live in this place will take you back to your family."

He hugged her, she kissed him, and she knew she better leave now. He was a very bright boy, and somehow he seemed to understand that Erika was only trying to free him from Butch. He trusted and believed her. She left him looking at a magazine, wiping her eyes, wondering if she would ever see him again.

Her emotions were very close to the surface as she left the motor home. She almost jumped out of her skin when she heard Butch's voice. "Didn't think I wouldn't watch you, did you?" He was leaning against a tree across the road, a smirk on his face.

Erika had no idea how much he'd seen. She feared the worst, but was relieved when he asked with a grimace, "So, did you do any good?"

She reached in her pocket and pulled out the wad of bills. "Wow," he said, his pained eyes lighting up "That's great. We better go though, before someone finds out they've been robbed."

Erika nodded in agreement and led the way back to the car, anxious to prevent him from checking on Stevie. If he missed him, there was no telling what he might do. He was weak and walked slowly, giving her time to pull the back door open. She checked the shawl. It appeared undisturbed. She pushed the door shut and prepared to get in the front.

"You drive," Butch told her. "I feel a lot worse."

He looked a lot worse, and it was an effort for him to even climb in the car. Erika couldn't help but wonder if, as weak as he was, she might be able to overpower him. But she took no action on the thought. She was afraid to. All she wanted now was to get away from here and hope that help would soon arrive for her little friend, one she had grown so very fond of. It struck her that she loved Stevie more than she loved herself.

Butch was silent as Erika fumbled with the screwdriver and started the engine. "Go back to Jackson Hole. Find a doctor or a hospital. I'm awful weak," he said as she backed out. His sentences were choppy and dribbled from his mouth.

"I can do that," she said.

"And Erika," he said with his eyes closed and his head leaning back on the headrest, "don't even think of trying anything stupid."

She already may have done so, but she wasn't about to tell him. She drove faster than was prudent, but she was wound so tight she couldn't help it. At the outskirts of the city she picked out a phone booth and looked up the address of the hospital.

Butch insisted that they park far back in a corner of the parking lot where the car would be less likely to be spotted. She noticed that he was removing the knife from his side as she got out and walked around the car. However, the bulge in his front pocket told her he still had his pistol. She glanced in the back as if checking on Stevie. If Butch looked, it would seem like the little boy was there. Unless he moved the shawl and exposed the pillow, he wouldn't know any different.

She was exhausted by the time she had half carried Butch through the lot, up a long walk, and into the emergency room. She was praying that officers would come, that Bob would come, that by some miracle it would all end right here at this hospital. Surely Butch was so sick now that someone, somehow, would be able to stop him and free her from his oppressive control.

She helped Butch to a chair in the small waiting area of the emergency room. He more fell than sat down. Two other patients were waiting there. Their eyes popped, and she was aware of them whispering. They both moved as the stench from his wound filled the room. A nurse entered, took one look at Butch and said, "Oh, my!" and called for assistance.

"She stays with me," Butch said as they started to help him behind a curtain. What sounded like a plea was really an order. Erika knew that only too well and wondered what would happen if they found the pistol in his pocket.

Two nurses began to work on Butch as soon as the privacy curtain was pulled shut. With professional efficiency they examined Butch, then removed his shirt. When one of them removed the bandage

Erika had applied that morning, the horrid odor of rotting flesh mushroomed, filling the room like poison gas.

"What happened to him?" a nurse asked, grabbing supplies from a cupboard above Erika's head. And then looking more closely at her, she said, "And what happened to you?"

She had worried all the way back to Jackson Hole about how she would respond when this question came up. She remembered to use the false names Butch had suggested, and she had settled on a story she hoped would satisfy them. She said as calmly as she could, "We wrecked on a four-wheeler a few days ago. You should have seen my face then." She forced a laugh then continued, "But I'm alright. Frank, he was cut on his head and something poked a hole through his shoulder."

"Why didn't you get this attended to earlier?" a nurse asked.

Butch was ready for that question. "We did," he said. "They cleaned the wound and gave us a prescription for penicillin, but it got infected anyway. Show them one of the pills, Millie."

Erika reached into the pocket of her tight-fitting, very dirty jeans and fished out one of the pills. "I had to change the bandage. I didn't do very good, did I? Here's one of the pills."

One of the nurses took the pill from Erika's outstretched hand. "This should have helped," she said. She dropped the pill on the counter next to a sparkling sink and turned her attention back to Butch.

She extracted the thermometer she had earlier stuck beneath Butch's tongue and held it up to the light. "He has a fever of 104 degrees," she said.

Erika was stunned—104 degrees! That was dangerously high. She broke out in a cold sweat and fidgeted nervously with her hands. She stuck stubbornly at their sides as they cleaned the wounds. She held her breath when the two nurses began to remove his Levis. Butch was very much awake, and he was, she was sure, prepared to forcibly take the gun and use it if they discovered it.

"Please, don't take my pants," he begged. "Just fix my shoulder."

She slowly let the breath ease out when one of them said, "Alright, for now, but when we take you to a room, you'll have to get in a hospital gown."

"That'll be okay then, but only if you let my wife help me," he said stubbornly.

Both of the nurses smiled. "I'm sure that will be fine. But for the moment, you need something to curb that infection. Rest now, and we'll be right back."

They parted the curtain, then closed it behind them, leaving Erika alone again with Butch. He turned his head toward her and said, "You stay right beside me, Millie."

She was powerless to do otherwise. His hand was actually in the pocket where he carried his pistol. "When they give me my shots or whatever, then we'll let them take me to a room. Then you make sure they leave us alone before I have to give up these pants."

She nodded. "This isn't going to work, Butch."

"Sure it is. And it won't cost us a dime of that money you stole," he whispered. "Because when they leave us in that room alone, we're going to figure out a way to get out of here."

Surely help would arrive before they left. She couldn't go on like this. A nurse walked back in just then. She held a needle with a large dose of something in it. She injected it into Butch's good shoulder, then said, "Okay, a doctor will be in shortly to take care of that wound."

They waited several minutes before a young doctor and a different nurse parted the curtains and stepped in. "This is pretty nasty," he commented as the nurse laid out an array of instruments on the bed beside Butch. For the next twenty minutes, after deadening the area around his wounds, they worked on both Butch's shoulder and his head. They disinfected, sutured, and hooked up an IV. Finally, the doctor said, "There, you'll soon be good as new. A couple days rest and plenty of medication is all you need."

Butch mumbled a quiet thanks as the two left. A moment later the first nurses they had seen bustled in. "Okay," the older one said with a smile. "Off we go to a room. And you'll need to get in a gown."

"Millie'll help me," Butch said. "And I want that shirt," he said, pointing to the blue western shirt of Bill Grossman's.

"It needs to be cleaned," he was told. "You won't need it for a little while."

"Get it, Millie," he growled.

The nurses both shook their heads as Erika did as she was told and handed it to Butch. A moment later, they opened the curtains all the way and began wheeling him out of the emergency room. They ended up on the main floor in a private room. Butch looked around. Erika followed his gaze.

It was a small room, but had a large window that opened onto a stretch of lawn hidden from the parking lot by a wing of the hospital. Once they were alone, Butch said, "I'm already feeling better. A few hours with this medicine going in me and I'll be just fine, then we'll get out of here."

"Butch, you're sick," she began to protest.

Butch just laughed. "Just think, you stole all that money and we won't even have to pay. And remember, Erika. It was you who stole it, not me. I was asleep in the car. You're a criminal now, and don't forget it."

He had just fastened one more hook in her. Oh how she hated him. But at least, by now, Stevie Grossman should be okay. The people in the motor home had lost some money, but what a shock they must have had when they found a young boy there. She just hoped they would see that he was returned to his family.

"Hey, help me get these pants off and this silly thing on," Butch said. Erika had turned away from him. When she turned back, he was holding the gun. As she pulled off his pants, he slid it beneath his pillow. "Can't be too careful, now, can we?" he said.

After Butch was in his hospital gown and lying quietly on his bed, the pistol beneath his pillow, Erika's thoughts turned to her family and Bob.

Butch interrupted those thoughts. "Don't think I'll go to sleep, Erika. We won't be here that long." He laughed and she turned toward the window, her eyes misted again. Erika wasn't sure if he said it, or if she just imagined it—either way, it didn't matter, for it might well be true. "You'll never get away from me, girl. Never!"

Chapter 14

Warm water splashed off Mike's upturned face as he held it close to the showerhead. He was still trying to wake up, and the water was slowly getting the job done. He had slept like a baby for six hours, but that just wasn't enough after the grueling hours he'd spent the past few days. The human body can endure only so much before it requires rest. His body, not getting any younger, was certainly no exception.

After a few more minutes in the shower he began to feel human again. He guessed he would be able to get going after all. His stomach made its presence known with an angry growl. Food was something else the human body couldn't go without for long before sending out distress signals. The signals were getting stronger, urging Mike to get out of the shower, shave, dress, and go in search of something to eat.

"Your turn, Bob," he said a few minutes later to his tired young roommate. "We've got to get a move on."

Bob groaned and pulled himself up and swung his legs over the edge of the bed. "Come on, kid," Mike teased in good nature, "I thought you wanted to be a doctor. You'll be getting out of bed with a lot less sleep than this once you reach that lofty goal."

"Maybe I better rethink it, then," Bob moaned.

"Oh, get moving. The shower will help. Believe me, I know."

Bob struggled to his feet, rubbing the sleep from his eyes. "I wonder where they are now," he said groggily as he stumbled across the room.

Mike shook his head sadly as the door closed behind Bob. The real world was certainly delivering the young man a wake-up call. He glanced at his watch. Ten after two. They'd searched all night in the fields and on the hills around the Grossman farm. It was as if Butch,

Stevie, and Erika had vanished into thin air. There had been no reports of a stolen car in the area. In fact, all the homeowners for several miles around had been contacted. They all accounted for their vehicles and reported seeing no one on foot in the area.

Mike picked up the phone and dialed. He wasn't surprised to learn that a stolen car had finally been reported. But what did surprise him was that it was the Grossmans' closest neighbors, the Kramers, who had made the report. When Frank had needed his truck an hour ago he'd entered the garage to find his car gone, but both garage doors locked. He'd been distraught, Red reported to Mike. When quizzed, neither the old farmer nor his wife could even make a good guess when it had been taken.

"I can guess," Mike said. "Probably before we even began our ground search. I'll bet they passed the cars called in off the roadblocks and just drove away as pretty as you please."

Mike hung up, finished dressing, then called Jan's room. Her line was busy. He waited a few minutes and tried again. She answered, her voice as fresh as a spring breeze. "Hello," she said.

"Jan, Mike here. They've stolen another car. The Kramers—"

"I know," she interrupted. "Red just called me. They've put an APB out on it. He has permission to go if anyone reports seeing it."

"I see," Mike said, less than enthusiastic. Although Red had been fine to work with all night long, he couldn't get that negative first impression out of his thick head; Red liked to call the shots, and he was too sure of himself. And he did not like the effect Red was having on Jan. Not that it was any of his business, but it bothered him just the same.

"I'll be over as soon as I finish dressing," Jan said cheerfully.

Mike grunted and put the phone down, still thinking about Lieutenant Red Blauser. He'd learned a little about him from the young deputy, Hal. Red had been married once, but had divorced a year ago. Hal offered no opinions over who might have been more at fault in the failed marriage, but he did say there hadn't been any children. He also said that Red had practically lived for his job since then, paying very little attention to women. He had simply told the few men with whom he shared any of his personal life that his marriage had been a bad scene, and he was not about to hurry into such an arrangement again.

Mike had the sinking foreboding that Red's feelings might have changed. The big lieutenant had managed to maneuver things so that Jan was working with him all night long. In fact, he thought with despair and not a little anger, Jan was probably the only reason Red wanted to pursue this case. Yes, he had been clearly taken by the attractive trooper, and Mike didn't like it. He didn't like it one bit!

Bob was dressed and looking like he'd been reborn by the time Jan tapped at the door. She was as bright and pretty as a rose. Her auburn hair shone and her face lit up as she smiled. Mike guessed that she made up for what he lacked in energy this afternoon.

Bob couldn't help but notice how nice Jan looked. If it wasn't for Erika, he might like to take her out. But of course, that was out of the question. He shouldn't even be thinking such things. But he couldn't deny the attraction that was there. And it was not just a physical thing. There was something about her, the way she talked and the way she laughed. And then there was that other thing, the sudden fear that came and then vanished almost before he was sure he'd seen it. It was strange, but it also drew an air of mystery around her that was, well, intriguing.

He bristled as he thought of her this morning. What business was it of his if she seemed so taken by this Lieutenant Red Blauser? None, except that he wasn't good enough for her, and he thought she was smart enough to know it!

Jan couldn't help but stare at Bob for a moment. He looked really good this morning, and she couldn't deny the fluttering he stimulated in her heart. But she pulled her eyes away from his face, attempting to resist the attraction. She'd made up her mind to stick close to Red for the duration of the investigation. He'd invited himself to follow it to the end, and it seemed to her like a good way to avoid too much contact with Bob. Oh, she knew it would send false impressions to both Bob and Mike, but that was what she wanted. After all, Bob was spoken for.

Bob noticed the difference in Jan, and it bothered him. It was that Blauser guy. What could she possibly see in the man? Surely arrogance wasn't attractive.

But that wasn't his problem. Erika was attractive, and he cared about her. And she seemed to have vanished. He was as puzzled as the officers about where Butch had taken her and the poor little boy the night before. He'd prayed earnestly in the privacy of the bathroom just moments ago. There was little he could do now but leave her in the hands of the Lord. He felt so helpless.

The phone rang. Mike snatched it on the first ring. "Mike, this is Red. I just tried to call Jan, but she wasn't in and she's not answering her cell phone."

Mike didn't volunteer her location and kept a straight face for Jan's sake. Red could talk to him instead of her, whether he liked it or not. He knew he'd ask to talk to Jan if he thought she was there. "What can I do for you?" Mike offered.

"We just got a hot lead. Real hot. A park ranger at Teton thinks he saw Butch and Erika about ten this morning. They were sleeping in the Kramers' car at a campground. He got them to pay for the camping spot, but when he went back just an hour or so ago, they were gone. And get this," he said excitedly, "some rich couple from back east came back to their motor home a few minutes ago and discovered that someone had been in it and lifted several hundred dollars in cash. And it gets even more amazing. Stevie Grossman was asleep on their sofa!"

Mike was stunned. He hadn't expected this. "I'll be right over, Mike," Red went on. "Tell Jan when she shows up that I'll be heading up there in an unmarked car. She'd be welcome to come with me if she'd like."

Mike had a feeling Jan would go with him. "Jan has the number of my cell phone. Bob and I would like to keep in touch with you and Jan," Mike said, his voice full of ice, and he hung up.

"Was that Red?" Jan asked brightly.

"Yes." He made no attempt to disguise his contempt.

"What did he want? Something's happened, hasn't it?"

"He wants you to go with him."

Bob's sea-blue eyes were miniature glaciers. "Go where, Sergeant?"

"To see and talk to Stevie Grossman," he said, enjoying the look on Jan's pretty face. He explained about the money and the motor home, and then finished by saying, "So off to the north we go. They're probably in Yellowstone by now."

A few minutes later, his hunger unappeased, Mike, accompanied by a strangely sullen Bob, was driving the Durango north, following Jan and Red. Mike had called ahead before they left and discovered that the police at Jackson Hole were already searching for leads. He hoped there would be something solid to go on by the time they got there. He looked at his watch. Three-thirty. There wouldn't be a lot of daylight left when they reached Jackson Hole.

Mike, unable to quiet the grumbling in his stomach, reached for his phone and called Jan. He suggested they stop somewhere and eat. They made a short stop. He felt better after that, and Bob seemed less gloomy. Mike tried to get him to talk. "You seem pretty down this morning, Bob. Anything I can help with?"

Bob looked over and smiled. He liked this officer. He was down to earth. He realized he had been rather bad company. "I'm sorry, Sergeant," he said. "It's just that, well, I'm so grateful Stevie Grossman is okay. But what about Erika?"

"Well, look at it this way, Bob," Mike said, trying to sound positive. "If Butch dumped Stevie, then Erika is almost certainly still okay. He seems to be intent on keeping a hostage, so my guess is that he decided Erika was the one to keep. I know that's not a great thought, but it's better than some of the things we considered last night."

"Thanks, Sergeant. That is a good thought. Mine have been more gloomy. I know I need to stay positive." He added, "I'll try not to be so negative."

Mike grinned. "Not that anyone can blame you, kid. You must be going through a lot, the girl you love in such a terrible situation and all."

"Sergeant, I like Erika a lot. That's why I'm here. And I guess we have been girlfriend, boyfriend. But love? I'm not sure we're at that stage in our relationship. At least I'm not. Maybe it'll come to that, but, well, I guess I'm confusing you, aren't I?"

Mike was not as surprised as Bob might have thought he'd be by this revelation of his feelings. He chuckled, trying to lighten things up. Then he said, "No, I don't think I'm getting confused, just enlightened. But I think you may be just a little confused, and I don't blame you. There's a lot about Jan Hallinan that could confuse any young man."

"Jan!" Bob exclaimed, feigning surprise.

"Yes, Jan," Mike said firmly. "There is a certain something, I guess you could call it an attraction, or maybe just good chemistry between you two."

For a moment Bob just stared at Mike, then he grinned. "That obvious, huh?" he admitted.

"Yes, that obvious. Want to talk about it?"

"Sergeant O'Connor, I came out here because I care about Erika. I care a lot. But you're right. There's something about Jan that just hits me right here." He touched his chest directly over his heart. "She's so mature and intelligent. And there's this air of mystery about her. Yes, you're right, I'm attracted to her, intrigued by her—but don't get me wrong. I do have feelings for Erika, and my whole focus has got to be on her."

"Speaking of maturity, I suspect that when we get Erika back, you'll find she's grown up a ton," Mike observed.

"So do I," Bob agreed.

"And you might find more of what you like in her. She might be more attractive to you in the ways that really count."

"I've thought a lot about that. It's like we might need to get acquainted all over again," Bob observed.

"That's right, Bob. And now, could I give you just one little piece of advice, from a man who's been there? I chose the right girl, and we've had a great marriage. But it wasn't the easiest thing for me either. You know, I was dating two other gals. I liked them both a lot. I kept thinking I needed to decide who I liked the most. Then I met another girl. I fell in love, and I married her. My advice is this, Bob. Don't force matters of the heart. Just let them happen. Make any sense?"

"Yes, it does, and thanks." Bob was silent and thoughtful for a minute or two, then he looked over at Mike and said, "Surely Jan can't see anything in that Blauser guy, can she?"

Mike frowned. "I hope not. But who knows? Maybe she's just afraid of some feelings she's experiencing for a young man she doesn't think she has a chance to ever get close to. Maybe she's just protecting herself."

"I'm causing trouble, aren't I?" Bob said.

"No, I wouldn't say that at all. Just remember. Follow your heart. It won't lead you astray."

When they finally reached Jackson, the sun was hanging low in the west. Mike immediately made contact with the sheriff's office and met Jan and Red there. He was disappointed to hear that no one had reported seeing the old blue Pontiac since it had disappeared from the Teton campground.

"Others are looking for the car," Mike said to Red and Jan. "Why don't we go see what we can learn from the little Grossman boy."

They met Stevie at the sheriff's office. He was really a charming little guy, and seemed none the worse for wear after the ordeal he'd been through. He grinned when they introduced themselves. "Where's Erika?" he asked innocently, as if he expected to see her with them.

"We don't know, Stevie. We're hoping you can help us find her by telling us everything that happened," Jan said.

Stevie was a sharp kid. He gave them details of his experience that surprised them all. When he'd finished his story, Jan's eyes were sore from wiping away tears. Bob broke down and alternately cried and paced the floor, mentioning things he could do to Butch if he ever got his hands on him. Mike was more worried than ever about Erika. If and when Butch found out what had happened to Stevie, one could only guess what Butch might do to Erika. It was not pleasant to think about.

After a while, Bob calmed down and said, "Erika saved his life. She risked her own for Stevie. She's something else, isn't she?"

No one could argue with that. What they had learned from little Stevie Grossman about what Erika had done was truly selfless and loving. They were all impressed that Erika was changing—from what they'd heard of her and the changes were good. Butch, on the other hand, would not be impressed.

After leaving the little boy, whose parents were expected to arrive shortly, Mike asked for and received directions on locating the park ranger who it appeared had spoken to Butch and Erika that morning. Outside the office he said, "Let's go talk to the ranger and have a look around the campground."

"Why?" Jan asked. "What do you hope to find there?"

"Anything. At this point we're just going to look around and talk to people. There may be nothing come of it, but then again we might get a clue of some kind. I learned long ago that the cops that get lucky are the ones who keep digging, even when they don't know what they expect to find."

"That's right, Jan," Red agreed importantly. "I was just going to say that very thing."

Bob gave him a dark look while Jan smiled at him. But he didn't think the smile was genuine. It looked a little forced. Mike only grunted and said, "So let's move, folks."

Darkness had set in and there was a slight chill in the air by the time they had located the ranger. "I realize you're off duty," Mike told him, "but we'd sure appreciate it if you would show us the campground, where they were parked, and where the little boy was found, if you know that."

"I do, just follow me," the ranger said.

A few minutes later they stopped inside the campground. "This is the spot, Sergeant. You're in luck; it's still empty," the ranger remarked.

"Excellent. Well, start looking," Mike said, flashing his light around at the graveled ground, cement table, and large fire pit. "Better yet, I'll look around here. Red, don't you think it would be a good idea to start interviewing a few of the campers right away?"

"I was just going to suggest that," Red said. "Jan and I'll see if we can find anyone who might have seen them."

The ranger protested, saying, "We don't like to disturb our campers if it's not absolutely necessary. You know, an emergency or something."

"This is an emergency!" Mike said, turning on the ranger. "A young woman's life is in jeopardy. Butch Snyder has killed before, and he could do it again. Several people, including my sheriff, have had close calls. He's shot more people than I care to think about. We're just lucky nobody else has died these past few days, but we want to keep it that way. Is that emergency enough for you?"

"Oh, yes, sir. But I'm confused about that girl with him. She did most of the talking. She sure didn't act like a hostage," he said uncertainly. "And she said nothing to me about the little boy who you say was in the back and who turned up later in that motor home."

"She was terrorized and protecting the boy," Mike responded. "Remember, he did kidnap her, and her life is very much in danger—especially since she helped the little boy get away."

"I'm sorry, but—" the ranger began.

"Would you help interview some of the campers?" Mike asked. "I'll come along as soon as I've had a chance to look things over here. Bob, you wait with me."

"Whatever you say, Sergeant," the ranger said, and trooped off after Red and Jan.

"I wish we had some daylight left," Mike said to Bob as he began to shine his flashlight on the ground. "It's hard not to miss things using a flashlight, but we've got to look."

Bob grunted and leaned against the Durango. Mike could see that his thoughts were somewhere else, so without another word, he went to work. Slowly and methodically, he scanned the area, oblivious to the bracing scent of the cool forest air and the soothing silence of the night. For thirty minutes he searched, and was about to give it up when his light reflected off something white at the base of a large pine several feet away.

He walked over and stooped down. His heart quickened when he recognized the object as a badly soiled bandage. He remembered Sandy Grossman telling him about Butch's wounds and the dressings she had applied. He poked at the bandage with a stick. It had been a neat, professional job—something that would probably have been done by someone . . . well . . . like Sandy. She was a nurse.

Upon closer examination, Mike could see that it had been chewed on. Probably a squirrel, he thought. That would account for it being so far from where the car had been parked. Of most interest was the vile odor and dried-up, nasty-looking stuff on the dressing. It looked like pus, and that could mean only one thing: Butch had a bad infection.

Thorough cop that he was, Mike laid the bandage on the table and began to search the entire area again. He discovered some scraps of paper which, upon close examination, appeared to be from a first-aid kit. "They must have put a clean dressing on Butch's wound," he said to Bob, who had finally joined him.

Bob had a flashlight and began doing a little looking of his own. He mumbled some response to Mike then said, "Hey, what's this? Looks like . . ." He stopped.

Mike hurried over and stooped down. "Looks like barf," Mike said. "Someone's been sick." He stood up and scratched his head. "Well, I guess that's about all we can do here. Should we see what the others have turned up?"

Red had talked to another couple whose trailer had been entered. Jan talked to the young man who had tried to get a girl to walk with him. "He said her face looked pretty rough. He thought she'd been in a wreck or something," Jan reported.

"She was," Bob reminded them. "But I'll bet most of it came from Butch."

Other than that, no one was of much help.

Mike was certain that Butch was sick. Stevie had told them that he was asleep when Erika got him out of the car. And for some reason that none of them could explain, she had done the stealing while he was in the car. "I think he threatened Stevie," Jan suggested. "Maybe he told Erika that if she didn't do what he asked, that he would take it out on Stevie."

"That makes sense," Mike agreed. "And it also makes sense that Butch was too sick to help her do the burglarizing." He turned to the ranger. "Did he appear sick to you when you were talking to them?"

"Now that you mention it, yes. I thought maybe it was because he'd been asleep, but he never did sit up straight while I spoke to them. He hardly said anything and never moved his head much. Yes, he could've been sick," the ranger concluded.

Mike explained about the bandage then said, "Well, thanks for your help, Ranger. I think we'll be getting back to Jackson Hole."

"Then what?" Jan asked.

"Start checking with doctors there. We should check the hospital too, although I would think that Butch would feel it was too risky to go there," Mike answered.

"Right," Red said quickly. "We'll see if he's finally sought medical attention."

"Actually, I suppose we'll have to wait until morning, the—"

"The doctors' offices and clinics would be closed now," Red butted in. "So we'll just have to be content with checking with the emergency room at the hospital tonight."

Mike shook his head and climbed wearily into the Durango with Bob. Back in Jackson they left Bob in the hospital parking lot and entered the emergency room, but there had been two serious car wrecks and no one had time to speak with them at length. But there had definitely been no one treated for a gunshot wound. They also learned that it was a different shift that had worked earlier that day, so descriptions didn't help. At the main desk they asked if there was a Butch Snyder in the hospital. When they were told there was no one by that name, Red said, "Then let's call it a night. We can start again in the morning. There'll be plenty of doctors to check with then."

When they got back to the cars, Bob was disappointed. He had really hoped Butch and Erika would be in there and this nightmare would end. "Isn't there something we can do?" he asked as Red began to open his car door for Jan.

"Yes, we can wait until morning," Red said gruffly. "And I'm not sure why you're here anyway. Seems to me that you ought to be waiting somewhere while we cops get our work done."

Jan bristled, but even though she didn't like the way he said it, she realized that Red might be right. Bob probably shouldn't be here. And it would be easier for her if he wasn't. But she couldn't bring herself to say so. Instead she suggested, "Let's go find some rooms."

Mike said nothing, and when Bob glanced at him, he was staring back toward the hospital and seemed deep in thought. He wasn't sure he'd heard any of the conversation. If he had, he would surely have mentioned that he was without a car and needed Bob to chauffeur him around.

Or did he?

Mike could always ride with Red and Jan. Somebody needed to. Red was such a jerk, and he was far too possessive of Jan. Red closed Jan's door and walked around to his side of the car and got in. After Red had started the engine, Jan rolled her window down and said, "Follow us." But Mike didn't hear, and Bob didn't feel like saying anything. It was so difficult not to be angry at Red Blauser. He watched them drive off and turned back to his own car.

He climbed in and started the engine. Mike joined him, still strangely silent. Bob began backing out, but suddenly Mike said, "Stop!"

Bob slammed on the brakes, wondering what Mike had seen. Before he could ask, the sergeant said, "Pull back in and park it, Bob. I'm going back in there. But I think it would be best if you stay in the car while I do."

"Oh no you don't, Sergeant! If you're going back in, then so am I. You aren't convinced he isn't in there, are you?"

"In all honesty, I'm not, but Bob, if they happen to be, it'll be dangerous. This is a police matter. I must insist that you stay out here because I won't be leaving that building again until I know. I can't let you get yourself hurt or put Erika in more danger." Mike was firm and Bob made no move to get out of the Durango, although his face was a study in anguish. Mike looked toward the hospital and back at Bob. Then he added, "Would you move the car to the back of the lot Bob? I don't want you to be too close to the hospital."

"Sure," Bob said glumly. "If you say so."

Something was nagging at Mike. An idea was in the corner of his mind, but he couldn't quite reach it. Bob started the engine as Mike got out. Deep in thought, he started toward the hospital.

Suddenly, Bob had a thought, and he rolled down the window and called to Mike. "Sergeant, what if Butch is using a different name?"

Mike stopped and turned back. That was it! That was the thought that had been eluding him. "You're right, Bob," he said. "Of course they would use a different name. But what name?"

Bob had no idea, but Mike did. It was a long shot, but it was worth a try. If that didn't work he would go back to the emergency room and dig until he learned something. He'd find out if anyone matching Butch's description had been treated for any kind of injuries. And if so, he'd learn if he might've been in the company of someone who matched Erika's description.

Mike approached the clerk at the front desk. It was a different woman than had been there just minutes ago, so he identified himself and asked, "Do you have a Frank Kramer in the hospital?"

After a quick check of the records, the receptionist brushed her graying hair back and looked up. "Yes we do."

Mike's heart quickened. His hunch was right. Butch was using the name of the man who owned the car he'd stolen. "He's an escaped prisoner and is wanted for murder, ma'am," he said as calmly as he could. He was satisfied with the expression his comment created on the face of the otherwise disinterested lady. "Can you tell me what room he's in?"

Her slightly wrinkled face lost the look of alarm almost as fast as it had come. "I'm sorry," she said stiffly, seeming unsure of herself. "I don't usually work here, but I think you'll need to have someone from the local police here before we can allow you to go to the room."

"Would you get them on the line, please?" he said with guarded control. He needed backup anyway.

She dialed, but with a frown on her face. "Yes, this is the hospital. There's an officer here who wants to talk to you," she said into the phone and handed it to Mike.

As she shuffled the papers in front of her, Mike spoke quickly. "This is Sergeant Mike O'Connor. Put me through to whoever is in charge tonight."

"I'm sorry, he's out of the office. Would you like to leave a message?" an efficient feminine voice said.

"No, this is urgent. I'm at the hospital. I just learned that Butch Snyder has been admitted here."

"Officer," the hospital receptionist interrupted huffily, "you're quite mistaken."

Mike impatiently waved her off and continued speaking into the phone. "He's in the hospital here right now. Would you please have some officers come over as quickly as possible?"

"I'll do that, and Sergeant, there's a man here from the FBI, a Special Agent Harry Reed. He's trying to take the phone away from me," she said with a pleasant giggle.

"Well, let him," Mike responded.

"Mike, this is Harry. I just drove into town. Sorry I've been so little help so far, but what can I do now?" came the welcome voice of the bulbous-nosed agent.

"Am I glad to hear from you, Harry. Would you make sure some city boys get headed this way, then come yourself? I'm at the hospital. Butch is here, and I hope Erika is as well. They would prefer I don't do a thing until someone local gets here," he said, ignoring the repeated signals from the graying and angry receptionist.

"I'll be right there with the troops," Harry said, and the phone clicked.

"Sergeant," the receptionist scolded, "we don't have the man you're looking for here!"

"What! But you just read it! Kramer. Frank Kramer. Please look again," Mike said urgently.

"We do have a Mr. Kramer, Officer. You seem to be quite confused. You told the police department that we have a Butch—"

Mike cut her off with relief. "I'm sorry. I'm really not confused, but I'm sure confusing you. His real name is Butch Snyder. He's going under an alias, Frank Kramer. Does that help, ma'am?"

She threw Mike a look that told him she had no idea what was going on, smiled, and said, "I guess you can go to the room, if you like."

But Mike said, "No, I'll wait for backup. They won't be long, I'm sure, but you can give me the room number."

While he waited, he pulled his cell phone from his belt and rang Jan's number. She answered almost immediately. "Where are you, Mike?"

"I'm at the hospital, Jan. And so is Butch Snyder."

CHAPTER 15

"Wake up, Erika! I hear a siren. It's time to get out of here," Butch hissed.

She'd been dozing in the big chair beside Butch's bed. She jumped as he spoke. The pistol was in his hand. She wanted to cry out in anger and frustration. She'd waited for hours, praying that he'd fall asleep so she could make a break for it. Then she'd dozed off herself and didn't have a clue how long she'd slept. But what frustrated her the most was that, for all she knew, he too might have been sleeping. Her chance to get away had passed and it was almost more than she could bear.

"Get my clothes," he ordered, waving at the closet where she'd put them earlier.

Butch was amazingly strong for as sick as he'd been when they came in. Hopelessly, she got up and moved to the closet as he yanked the IV needle from his arm. Blood oozed and she dropped his pants and shirt beside him and began to dab at the blood with a Kleenex. "Leave it be," he growled. "Just help me with these clothes and my boots."

As soon as he was dressed, he said, "See if anyone in the hallway is headed this way."

Erika opened the door. "I don't see anyone," she reported.

"Then let's get out of here," Butch said, sliding off the bed and standing shakily on his feet.

"I'm a little dizzy still, but I'll make it. Let's get going."

She was confused. There was no way they could just walk out, gun or not. But Butch had other ideas. Angrily he said, "Open that window. We're going out that way. And hurry."

She opened it, but it would be difficult if not impossible to get through. It was hinged and opened down, leaving a gap less than a foot wide, and to go through it would require climbing over the open glass first. Again, Butch had a solution. He'd obviously thought it out earlier. He grabbed the window and jerked down hard. The hinges gave and the window sagged down, creating plenty of room to climb out.

"You first," he said, waving the pistol at her.

She scrambled through, dropping to the grass outside. He followed, grunting as he stumbled and fell, but he was on his feet in an instant and, to Erika's dismay, didn't even drop his pistol! "Okay, move now. We'll go around the building here and head for the car. And if we see cops, don't try anything stupid. We'll stay away from the lights as much as possible so we won't be noticed."

It was late enough at night that they didn't meet anyone as they moved through the nearly empty parking lot. It was quite well lit, and it turned out that they had parked almost directly beneath a light pole. When they reached the car, Erika opened the passenger door for Butch as he ordered. After he was in, she shut the door, turned and nearly fainted.

Bob was getting out of a dark-blue Durango just a few spaces away. He looked her way, and their eyes locked.

"Erika!" he called out to her.

The sound of his voice catapulted her back to happier times. Her heart surged with joy and caused her to move toward him even as Bob started eagerly in her direction. His eyes were shining, and shock blanketed his face.

"Stop, Erika!" she heard someone call out, but it did not register that Butch had given an order. Her nightmare had vanished at the sight of Bob coming for her.

Butch called again, louder, more harshly. She did not look back, but confused, she stopped at the sound of that feared voice. Her mind was pirouetting. It was no longer up to Butch what she did. Not now. *Bob was here, and he was coming for her!* It was all okay now.

She took another step toward Bob, and for the third time Butch called out, "Come back here, Erika." Butch's voice was so cold it nearly froze the blood in her veins. She stopped again, her knees trembling but her mind confused. "I don't know who that guy is, but you're with me now, and don't you ever forget it!" Butch added.

Bob didn't dare move. He wanted to scream, to run to Erika, to sweep her up in his arms and carry her away from here . . . from *him*. But the killer had a small pistol pointed at Erika's back.

If Erika kept coming toward him, she would die.

And most likely, Bob would die with her. Tears swamped his cheeks. He had to do what he could to save her life, and there was only one way. She was still a hostage. She could die. The very thought tore at his heart, but now was not the time for hysterical heroics.

She again took a step toward him and Bob called out in a voice that cracked, one filled with frustration, anger, even hatred for the man who controlled her. *"Go back, Erika!"*

Erika, whose fear had been whisked away by the sight of the man she loved and then hurled back at her by the voice of one she hated, wanted only to be with Bob. He was mere steps away. *So why was Bob telling her to go with Butch?* Why would he do such a terrible thing? She stood frozen, unable to act.

"Now, Erika," Butch said. "Get in the car and drive."

"Go with him," Bob agreed, his voice going weak with emotion. "Go now! He'll shoot you if you don't!"

Erika's world collapsed, but sanity returned. She turned to face Butch with his angry face and steady pistol. Sick at heart, Erika walked around the car and slid beneath the steering wheel. She did not look at Butch as she fumbled with the screwdriver. Such hatred welled up inside of her that she wanted to plunge that screwdriver into him, but she couldn't; the .38 was pointed at her head. The engine started, and Erika sped out of the lot, crying and angry and afraid.

***

As soon as Erica was safely on her way, Bob, tears streaming down his face, raced for the hospital. She had been so glad to see him that she'd nearly made a fatal blunder. There was no question what Butch was going to do. And once she realized Butch was pointing the gun at her, she knew too. The terror and pain on her battered face was almost more than he could bear.

He was stopped at the doors by an officer. "You can't go in there," he was told. "There's an emergency."

"Not anymore," he cried urgently. "They're gone."

"Who's gone?" the officer asked.

"The ones you're looking for. I need to find to Sergeant O'Conner."

"How do you know who we're looking for?" the young officer asked.

"I know! Believe me, I know," Bob shouted.

The officer keyed the radio that hung from his belt and spoke into the little mic that was clipped to his collar. "I think the suspect is gone," he said.

Bob sank slowly to his knees on the concrete sidewalk. He did not look up until a gentle hand touched his shoulder and a soft, sweet voice said, "Bob, are you sure they left?"

He looked up and into the pretty hazel eyes of Trooper Jan Hallinan. He nodded and she asked, "How?"

"They left in an old blue car."

She reached for his hand and helped him to his feet. A moment later she held him as he cried, trying to comfort him—trying to make sense of what had happened. Then Red and Mike appeared in the hospital doors, and Red led her briskly away as Mike began to speak to the young man from San Diego, a young man whose heart was breaking.

***

Erika raced on for several blocks, then Butch ordered, "Slow down! There's a light on in that garage over there. Pull in there!"

Too numb to care, she did as she was told and turned into a small garage. She stopped in front of an open bay door. "Pull inside!" Butch ordered.

She did and Butch got out. A greasy man in his late twenties came through a door to their right, a bottle of whiskey in his hand. "Hey, it's nearly midnight. I'm closed."

"Get out of the car," Butch hissed at Erika.

She did as she was told, and the fellow looked admiringly at her. "I guess I could help for a minute if it's an emergency," he said. "I just got in from a wrecker call a little while ago." He waved the bottle of liquor and grinned. "I was just relaxing for a minute and then I was going to pull the wrecker in here for the night," he said, explaining why the door they had driven through had been open. "So is there something I can do for you?"

"Yes," Butch answered as he produced his pistol. "We need to borrow that wrecker of yours."

The mechanic opened his mouth, then snapped it shut again, his eyes on the business end of the little gun. Finally finding his voice, he said, "Take the wrecker and go then. The keys are in it."

"You're coming too," Butch informed him coldly. He waved the pistol at Erika. "Erika, get our stuff from the car, all but the kid. We're leaving him here." He had no idea, even yet, that Stevie was long gone. At least now he would never know what she'd done, not that it mattered anymore. It seemed that her nightmare was never going to end.

"You, mister, close the garage doors and lock them," Butch ordered, waving the gun threateningly.

As soon as their meager supply of food, the rifle, and ammunition were in the wrecker, Butch ordered the mechanic to drive. "I don't think I better. I've had a little too much of this," he said, taking another swig from the bottle.

"Give me that," Butch said. "You drive and I'll drink this for you."

The mechanic, seeing that to defy Butch could be very dangerous, handed him the bottle and climbed into his wrecker. Butch told Erika to get in beside the driver, then he took a long drink from the bottle, put the lid on, and joined them.

They left Jackson Hole, traveling north. Several police cars passed. When they saw them, Butch ducked out of sight, forcing Erika to do the same. They encountered no roadblocks and were soon well on their way back to the Grand Teton National Park.

As they rode, Butch continued to drink. Erika, afraid and nervous, absently pulled a ring from her finger. It was a CTR ring that Bob had given her the day before she left California with her family. She turned it over in her hand several times. She could hardly bear to think of Bob. She'd been so close to him, almost into his arms, and then Butch had done his thing again. She felt like she was going to explode. She had to do something. Finally, she turned to the wrecker driver at her side. "What's your name?" she asked as she continued to finger the little ring.

"Mac Smith," he said sullenly, the smell of alcohol from his breath almost overpowering her. "So you left a kid in your car? That seems stupid. You better hope someone finds him."

"He'll be alright," she said honestly.

"Where are we going?" he then asked. "What are you going to do with me? May I call my wife? She'll be worried about me. And she could look after your kid." He stopped for air.

"Hey, slow down, man," Butch growled.

Mac eased his foot from the gas pedal to the brake and slowed the wrecker.

"Don't be an idiot!" Butch shouted, angered by him. "Don't slow the truck down, just your mouth, you fool. I'll tell you what you need to know when I'm good and ready. So shut up and let me think. I want—"

Butch and Erika shot forward, slamming into the dash. Mac, his foot still on the brake, had jammed down hard. The bottle of whisky broke on the dash, spilling the smelly liquid. Before Butch or Erika realized what was happening, Mac opened the door and leaped out. The wrecker, although it was going slowly now, careened wildly. Clinging tightly to the pistol, Butch reached across Erika, grabbing for the steering wheel, Erika screaming all the while. The truck bounced off the road.

They were passing through dense forest, and the wrecker only went a short distance before hitting a tree, sending both passengers into the dash again. Fortunately for both of them, the slow speed lessened the impact. Erika was dazed but unhurt. The smell of whiskey filled the cab of the truck.

Butch shook his head and cursed. Then he glared at Erika, pointing his gun at her head. "You had to go shooting your mouth off to that guy." He slapped her face. "Let's get out of here, but you go first, and don't try to get away." She started to slide beneath the wheel so she could go out the driver's door. "Not that way, you little fool!" Butch screamed at her.

She numbly climbed over him, doing her best not to touch him, then climbed down from the wrecker. Butch followed and ordered Erika to move ahead of him into the trees. "You go get the food from the wrecker," he ordered as he slowly sank to the ground behind a large pine. After she returned with it, he ordered, "Get the rifle now and the bullets, and don't even think about trying to load it."

She again did as she was told. After she had given the rifle to him, Butch said, "If I ever catch up with Mac, he'll regret what he just did."

Erika heard a car stopping on the highway. Butch waved the pistol at her. "Get going," he ordered. "We've got to get away from here."

He had struggled to his feet and, with the rifle slung over his shoulder, followed Erika deeper into the forest. They walked for a half hour through the trees, stumbling frequently in the darkness and stopping often to rest.

After an hour or more, Erika could hear the occasional whine of traffic on the highway, although she couldn't see it. They must have been walking in circles, for she thought they'd been going deeper into the forest at every step. Butch, who had been a few steps behind her caught up with her, took her arm, and directed her to the edge of the forest. "You're going to help now, Erika," he said gruffly. "We need a car and you are going to help me get it. So do exactly as I say and I won't have to hurt you again."

She listened without a word as Butch gave her some instructions, then she nodded her head and stepped out of the trees, knowing the pistol was aimed at her back, but also knowing he would be hard to see from the road. She waited at the edge of the pavement, as he had instructed her, and when lights appeared going north, she stuck out her thumb. The car didn't even slow down. Three more passed over the next ten minutes before one finally stopped, and a young man in his early twenties stuck his head out the driver's window and said cheerfully, "Kind of late at night to be hitchhiking, pretty lady, but if you need a ride, we can make room. Hop in."

She eyed the car closely. A southbound car passed by, and she could see that the car she was being offered a ride in was a bright blue Nissan. She could also see that there was another fellow in the front seat and one in back.

"I have some bags over there," she said, pointing to where Butch and his guns were waiting a few feet away, hidden by the shadows.

"We'll get them," the driver said, and all three young men piled out. The driver had a flashlight, and he shined it in the direction Erika had pointed.

But he didn't light up any bags, only Butch who was standing a few feet away, his rifle pointing right at the flashlight.

"Hey, what's going on here?" the young man demanded.

"Just keep moving!" Butch ordered brusquely.

In unison, the three turned and looked at Erika. "Just do as he says," she told them. "He'll use that thing. Believe me, I know."

"I can't believe this!" one of the young men exclaimed.

"Believe it and keep walking," Butch ordered. "And don't look back or you'll regret it."

They walked, cursing helplessly, into the dark forest. Butch and Erika approached the Nissan. Butch said, "You drive," as he climbed in. A minute later, she pulled into the traffic lane and headed north.

CHAPTER 16

"I can't believe how that Pontiac vanished. Someone should have seen it somewhere by now. I'm betting it's still in town someplace," Sergeant Mike O'Connor was saying.

"Maybe," Lieutenant Red Blauser said thoughtfully.

The officers were meeting in Jackson, discussing the escape that Butch and Erika had made from the hospital and the incredible way in which they had vanished so quickly. A large number of officers had responded when the call went out, but no one had seen the elusive pair or the stolen car since Bob had watched them drive away.

"Let's go over it all again," Special Agent Harry Reed suggested, rubbing his bulbous nose thoughtfully. "There has to be a clue somewhere."

Jan was standing near the back wall beside Bob. Her heart was aching for him. She couldn't imagine how hard it must have been for him to tell Erika to go with Butch after being so close to her. And her heart went out to Erika. What a terrible thing she was suffering. She wondered how much longer she could handle things so bravely. And she feared what would happen when she couldn't do so any longer.

She shuddered, at the same time trying to think. An idea came to her and she said, "Hey, Sergeant O'Connor, the wrecker wreck they told us about . . ."

"What about it?" Mike asked, eyeing her curiously.

"They said the driver wasn't there," she noted thoughtfully. "Maybe Butch and Erika were in it."

"But the owner's wife was contacted," the local chief said with confidence. "She said he regularly goes that way after stranded motorists. In fact, he had left the house to take a call earlier and may have actually been on that call when he ran off the road. She also said he may have been drinking before he left the shop and that, if so, he'd come home after he sobered up. So there's no need to connect that wreck with your killer."

"Where's the wrecker now?" Red asked.

"Mrs. Smith said to just drop it off by the garage. That's where it is, I'm sure," the chief said.

"We'll check it out," Jan stated, grabbing Bob by the arm and heading for the door.

Red jumped to his feet. "I'll take you," he said.

"She can handle it, Lieutenant," Mike interjected. "Let's go over the rest of this and see if there's anything else we need to follow up on."

Red sat down, frowning at Mike. "I'll have one of my officers meet them there," the chief said, picking up a phone and dialing. "I'm certain there's nothing there, but as long as they're going, they may want to talk to Smith's wife and he can locate her for them."

Jan and Bob reentered the room breathlessly thirty minutes later. "They were in the wrecker," Jan panted. "We'd better go out to where they wrecked. I'm sure—"

"Slow down, Trooper," Mike said. "Why do you say they were in the wrecker?"

"We found this," she said, pointing to Bob who opened his fist, revealing a small ring. "It's called a CTR ring. Bob gave it to her just before she left on vacation. It was on the floor of the wrecker. We talked to Mrs. Smith. She's scared now—really scared. There was a broken whiskey bottle in the wrecker too. Someone had been drinking. "

"Sounds like—" Mike broke in.

"And here's the big one," Jan said, ignoring Mike. "There's a blue Pontiac in his shop! It's locked, and Mrs. Smith doesn't have a key, but we could see the car when we shined a flashlight through the window. We couldn't see the plates because it was too close to the door, but it's got to be the Kramers' car."

"Thanks Jan," Mike said, rising to his feet. "You've done a great job. We need to get up there and see what we can learn at the scene of the wreck."

It didn't take long to figure out that Erika and Butch had gone on foot into the woods, but Mike was puzzled. Where was the wrecker driver? Was he tied up somewhere? Maybe in the shop he thought.

A radio call sent officers scurrying, a locksmith in tow, to the garage. In a few minutes Mike was told that Mac was not there, but confirmed that the Pontiac did belong to Frank and Millie Kramer.

A couple of dog teams were on their way. Mike and Harry figured the best and fastest way to track the pair down was by using canine, especially since daybreak was still a few hours off. Red wanted to start trying to track them with flashlights, but Harry said it was foolhardy and they would wait. And that's what they did, despite Red's angry protests.

When the dogs arrived they were allowed to sniff the seat where Erika and Butch had been seated. The two big German shepherds picked up the trail immediately and led their handlers into the dark forest at a trot. They never faltered and moved rapidly through the heavy timber.

Jan and Bob waited with the vehicles while Red, Mike, Harry, and several local officers followed the dog teams. Bob paced beside the road, shaking his head. "What if Erika doesn't come out of this alive? I should have done something. I just let him take her."

Jan trembled. "You didn't let Butch do anything. You saved her life, Bob. She knows that and so do you. She'll come out of this thing alright yet," Jan said, afraid that she might be wrong, but praying that she would be proven right.

"I hope," he said.

"You really love her don't you?" Jan observed quietly. "And I can see why. She's a good girl. She does the right thing when the chips are down."

"She's good, that's for sure. But, Jan, there's something you don't understand."

"Oh, what's that?" she asked, turning as he did and walking back in the direction they had just come.

"I'm not in love with Erika."

Jan's heart nearly quit beating. "But I thought . . ." she began.

He stopped and turned toward her. The early, predawn light was breaking the darkness, and she could clearly see the outline of his face. "I'm worried sick about her. She's a great friend. I'm very fond of her, and would do anything I could to help her out of this mess she's in. But love? No, we are not at that point yet. At least, I'm not. It could happen, though, if we ever get the chance to resume our relationship."

"Then it will," Jan said, her eyes glistening. She was glad it was still too dark for him to notice. "She'll be alright."

She had said it again, knowing that it might not be true. Erika's situation was getting more desperate and dangerous by the hour. She was sure of that. But Bob needed a boost, not a kick.

"I sure hope so," he agreed. Bob wanted to tell her that he wasn't sure he wanted things to develop further between Erika and him. He wanted to tell Jan that he also liked her a lot. But now was not the time. Maybe there would never be a time. He turned and started walking again.

Jan kept pace with him. She wanted to reach out and take his hand. She wanted to tell him that he was the greatest guy she'd ever met. But she didn't. She couldn't. It just wouldn't be right.

When they reached the cars, they leaned up against the Durango, side by side. It felt so good to both of them just to be near each other. And yet neither could say what was really in their hearts. But finally Jan, compelled to speak, to let some of the feeling she had out without giving herself away, said, "You're really a great guy, Bob. I feel lucky to have gotten to know you."

Bob felt especially awkward then. Jan was one of the best people he'd ever known. A guy would be lucky to have her. Some guy . . .

And Red Blauser wanted to be that guy.

That grated on Bob. Jan was too good for Red. And he was not her type at all. Bob wanted to tell her so, but wisely, he did not bring Red's name up. Instead, he said simply, but with a somewhat playful tone in his voice, "Thanks, Jan. You're okay yourself."

"Hey," she said, her voice solemn, "how about if we just have a prayer right now for her. I've prayed for her, and so have you, but maybe it wouldn't hurt if we did it together."

Bob was touched. "Sure. Will you offer it?" he asked.

"I'd be glad to," she responded. "But let's step into the trees where we won't be seen by passing motorists."

He nodded, instinctively reached for her hand, and led her into the trees. There they knelt and Jan began to pray. Bob was impressed by the sincerity of her prayer. She prayed with such feeling and love. His eyes began to water. She prayed for Erika: for her safety, for her faith, for her strength to endure, and for her deliverance from the evil man who had taken her. And she prayed that Butch wouldn't harm her. Her voice trembled as she mentioned Butch's name, and Bob couldn't help but open his eyes and glance at her in the growing light.

There was unmistakable fear on her face again, and one hand was slowly rubbing the small red spot on her face. He closed his eyes again, wondering. Bob was touched as she prayed for him. His whole body tingled as she asked the Lord to give him strength, to help him to understand Erika, and to bring the two of them together again. When she neared the end of her prayer, she said, "These blessings we pray for, dear Heavenly Father, but we recognize Thy wisdom and will in all things. So may Thy will be done and may we be willing to accept Thy will." She closed her prayer and looked over at him and smiled.

He touched her hand. "Thank you," he said. Their eyes lingered, each looking deeply into the other's. Then he asked, "Are you afraid of Butch?"

A visible change came over her. The smile left her face. Terror entered those soft hazel eyes. She didn't answer. She didn't need to.

***

Mike worried most about an ambush. He said to Harry, "The shape Butch was in, I can't see him going too far before giving out. We need to be on our toes. He could be watching us as we talk. I wouldn't put anything beyond him."

"But we're being led right back toward the highway, Mike," Harry observed. "I'm thinking they've simply got a ride and are on the road somewhere now."

By the time the tracking dogs had led them back to the road it was light enough to see. A careful examination of the area revealed three sets of footprints besides those of Butch and Erika. They led into the forest for a short distance, then back to the highway. Butch's and Erika's also led to the pavement.

"Now I'm really stumped," Mike said, rubbing his chin. "Butch must have stolen a car and let the owners, or rather forced them, to go into the forest. Question is, since we know the three they stole the car from came back to the road, why haven't we got a report of a stolen car? Where did they go from here? They must have caught a ride or we would have seen them."

"Or did they report it and someone forget to mention it to us?" Red asked, frowning at the closest local officer.

"Sorry, Lieutenant. We didn't screw up," the deputy said sarcastically. "No stolen car reports have come to us overnight."

"But it's still early," Mike said. "People are just now beginning to get up. Maybe someone will discover they're missing a car, and then we'll get a report."

"Meaning maybe Butch stole a car from thieves?" Jan asked shrewdly.

"Could be," Mike agreed. He yawned. "I don't know about the rest of you, but I need sleep."

***

They had scarcely arrived back in Jackson when a young man called the police department and reported that someone had stolen his blue Nissan Sentra. "It was right there in our driveway just before my wife and I went to bed," the distraught fellow told Mike and the others a few minutes later.

The description of the car was broadcast, and Bob, Mike, Jan, and Red found motel rooms and prepared to get a few hours' sleep.

"I'm going to call my wife," Mike announced to Jan as the two of them sat in Mike's room discussing the case early that evening after getting some much-needed rest. "I think she might get used to my being away and start to like it. I better just remind her that I still love her."

"You miss her, don't you Mike?" Jan said. "I guess it would be hard for a married guy to be away from home for several days."

"Yes, I miss my family, but they've learned to understand and put up with the occasional absences. It's just part of having a cop for a husband and father. What do you plan to do tonight? Until we get another lead, we don't even know which way to go. There's no need for everyone to just sit and wait. I can do that for all of us."

"Red asked me out tonight," Jan said with a smile. "I guess if we're going to be stuck here for a while, I might just as well take him up on it. He wants to take me to dinner and a movie."

"Well, I'm just glad it's you and not me," Mike said with a chuckle. "I wonder what Bob's plans are. I feel sorry for the kid. Maybe I ought to try to talk him into returning to California."

"He's such a nice guy. I really feel sorry for him, but he won't go home, Mike," Jan said confidently. "Anyway, he's been a big help. I think our chances of catching Butch would be better if he stayed."

Mike studied Jan's pretty face thoughtfully. "You're probably right, but I'll see what Bob wants to do as soon as he comes back from the store. Now, you better go get ready for your hot date with Lieutenant Blauser. He won't want to be kept waiting."

Jan smiled at Mike and went to her room. Mike stood outside, leaning against the second story railing, thinking about the bizarre case. He had to stop Butch. The man had already caused so much hurt to so many people that it made Mike boil. And then there was Erika. She was such a good girl. He remembered how sweet and innocent she'd been that morning in the café in Pineview. What was happening to her was so unfair. He kicked the railing in frustration and returned to his room.

There was a light knock on the door thirty minutes later. Mike had just hung up from talking to his family. He thought about how much he missed them as he stepped to the door. It was Bob that Mike found standing there. Bob had insisted on his own room this time so he could think. Mike invited him in.

"What's going on now, Mike?" he asked. "Where is everyone?"

"Just relaxing. There's not much we can do right now but wait. Why don't you and I go get something to eat, Bob?" Mike asked, hoping that he might find an easy way to suggest he return to California like Erika's family had done, a fact he had just learned from his wife.

"Thanks, Mike, but I was thinking about seeing if Jan would go to dinner with me. I've been thinking about your advice. And anyway, I think I owe her one. She's been really good to me, you know."

Mike cleared an imaginary frog from his throat. "I believe she's gone already," he said evasively.

"Gone where?" Bob pressed.

"To eat."

"Who's she eating with?" he asked, then his face dropped. "Oh, of course. She's with Lieutenant Blauser, isn't she?"

"Yeah, I think so."

"I don't much care for him, Sergeant," Bob said with feeling. "The rest of you cops have been really good, but he's so . . . so . . . stuck on himself."

"That may be, but Jan's a big girl, Bob. She can go to dinner with anyone she chooses. And I'm sure she'd go with you if you asked her. Next time the opportunity comes up, you just beat him to the punch," Mike suggested, wondering why he'd said that. This was no way to lead up to suggesting the young man return to California. "Anyway, why don't we go get something to eat now," Mike said. "I'm not much to look at, but I'm company."

"Sure, that'll be fine."

A few minutes later Mike and Bob were seated in a steak house waiting for their salads to come. "The Leightons have returned to San Diego," Mike ventured. "They decided it would be easier to wait there. Anyway, I understand Erika's dad had to get back to his business."

"I guess that's best. There's nothing they could do in Pineview," Bob said without looking at Mike.

"What about you, Bob? This thing could drag on for a long time yet. Don't you have to start school fairly soon?"

"Are you trying to get rid of me?" Bob asked, frowning as he glanced up.

"No, I just thought it might be easier for you."

"Sergeant O'Connor, I have the car, remember?" Bob said. "I can't leave you and Jan on foot."

"Red has a car, and so does Harry."

"That's another thing. Somebody's got to protect Jan from that creep, and you don't seem to be doing very good at it, so I better try." Bob was grinning now, but his tone was serious.

"Bob, what about school?"

"That can wait if it needs to. There are much more important things to take care of here. Erika's life and safety matter more by far than one semester at school. I really want to stay. If I get in the way, just say so and I'll back off. But please don't make me leave," Bob begged.

Mike relented. "Okay, Bob, but I hope we can get Butch under wraps soon. I sure hate to see a promising young fellow like yourself not taking advantage of schooling opportunities right now. It takes a lot of years to become a doctor."

Their salads arrived and they began to eat with enthusiasm. When they returned to the motel, Bob said, "I can't see Red's car. They must be having a long dinner."

"I think they were going to a movie too," Mike said uncomfortably.

"Oh, that's great," Bob said with a frown and headed for his room.

Mike was up early the next morning. He called the local police and learned that there were still no leads except that Mac had been found. He'd broken a leg in his jump from the wrecker, but had draggged himself as far from the wreck as possible, fearing that Butch would come after him. Between the injuries and the alcohol he'd consumed, he'd fallen asleep in a thicket of trees. He'd slept for hours before waking up and dragging himself back to the highway. Mike was told that he could visit Mac in a couple of hours. He wasn't sure it would do much good, but then again, something Butch had said after stealing the wrecker might give them a clue where he was headed.

So, with time to kill, Mike pulled on a pair of sweats and his running shoes. He'd neglected his fitness since the incident in Pineview. This morning it took him a little while to shake out the stiffness, but then he got into his running, enjoying the cool Jackson Hole air. He ran about two miles, finishing by running uphill toward the motel. He decided to walk around the block a few times to cool down. On the second time around he found himself in the company of a beautiful lady.

"Come on, Mike," Jan said with a grin as she jogged up beside him, "I could use some company. You can at least go another mile or two, can't you?" she coaxed.

"I suppose, but it's been a few days, and I'm a little out of condition. Let's walk another time around the block, then I'll jog with you."

Bob came out as they finished the lap. He was also dressed to run. Jan brightened at the sight of him and yelled, "Hey, Bob, why don't you join us? We were just going ourselves."

They jogged down the sloping street. Mike stayed with them for several blocks, then he said, "You two go on. I couldn't keep up with you if I were fresh, and I'm not. Buzz me when you're through and we'll have breakfast, then go see what Mac has to say."

Mike had showered, shaved, and dressed, and he was just pulling on his tall black boots when the phone rang. It was Red. "Where is everyone?" he inquired.

"I'm right here in my room, as you can tell," Mike chided.

"Where's Jan?" he asked brusquely. "She's not in her room."

"I don't know for sure. When I last saw her she was with Bob several blocks west of here. They were running too fast for me, so I came back."

"Oh, I see," Red answered sullenly. "When are we eating?"

"When they get back and have a chance to shower. I'll call you when we're ready," Mike said and then explained that Mac had turned up and that they would be able to see him later.

At breakfast Red was still sullen. "What's with the sudden fitness kick?" His question was directed at Jan.

"There's nothing sudden about it," she answered sweetly. "Don't you try to keep in shape, Red?"

"I'm in shape. I don't need to go running around in silly looking garb to stay that way!"

"What do you do to stay in shape, aerobics?" Jan asked with a twinkle in her eye.

Red turned *red*.

Mike chuckled and Bob sat back, watching the exchange with interest.

"I don't have to do anything special," Red blurted angrily. "I just stay in shape."

"Oh, I see," Jan said seriously. "You're a man without a plan. You really should have a fitness program, Red. Everybody should keep themselves in good condition, even old men like Mike." She ignored Mike's mock stern look and went on. "Police officers especially need to stay in shape. We never know when we're going to have to exert ourselves to the limit. I think we owe it to ourselves and to the public we serve and protect." She leaned toward him, put her hand over one of his and smiled at him.

"Thanks for the lecture, Jan. I'll think about it. You may be right," Red said, recovering his composure.

"I am right," Jan said with a smile. "I'd be glad to help you set up a routine when you're ready."

Bob didn't like the sound of that, but he kept his feelings to himself. Mike, however, could see the reaction on his face, so he quickly changed the focus of their conversation. "I think it's about time we go over to the hospital. I want to talk to Mac as soon as possible. Maybe he can shed some light on Butch and Erika."

Nobody disagreed, and in a few minutes they were outside of the intensive care unit. "Only one of you may go in, and please don't take more than five minutes. He's a very sick man," the grandmotherly nurse said sweetly.

"I thought he just had a broken leg," Mike said. He hadn't expected him to be in ICU.

"So did we at first, but he's also busted up inside. And a cold night in the forest didn't help him any. So, who's going in?"

"I'll be the one going in," Mike said quickly. "I won't be long." Harry, who had just joined them there, nodded in agreement.

Mike pushed the door and entered the sterile, busy intensive care unit as Red began to object. Mike had always felt uncomfortable in rooms like this, with critically ill and dying people all around. It made him feel guilty, in a way, for being so whole and healthy while the suffering lay in long, neat rows, connected to an assortment of complex instruments. He guessed that beyond the sympathy he felt was a fear that someday he would find himself in here, resenting those who walked in all whole and healthy.

"He's right over there, Officer," the gentle nurse said. Then, as if she had perceived his thoughts, she went on, saying, "It bothers me too, Officer, but we'll save most of them with all the new wonders we've learned, and with God's help of course."

Mike nodded and smiled, feeling a little better. He stepped beside the bed and looked down at the injured mechanic. "Hi, Mac. I'm Sergeant Mike O'Connor. I need to ask you a few questions."

"Sure," Mac said in a whisper.

Mike leaned down and said, "We're looking for the guy who stole your wrecker, and for the girl he took hostage."

"Butch. At least that's what the girl with him called him," Mac said weakly. "He's bad news, that guy. That girl don't stand a chance. He beats her. I could tell that. She's scared to death of him."

"That's why we've got to find them. Where were they going? Did they give you any idea?"

"North. I remember Butch saying something about Canada."

"That helps," Mike said. Then he asked what kind of shape Butch was in, and Mac told him he looked pretty rough.

"Can you think of anything else he said that we should know?"

"No, well, there's the kid. They left some kid in the car in my shop. I can't imagine how anybody could do that, but—"

Mike interrupted. "The boy's okay," he said, "thanks to Erika."

Mac couldn't tell him anything else that might help, so he rejoined the others.

"Butch is getting more violent and will continue to," he told them as they walked down the long hallway after the interview was over. Red grumbled something about how they should have given them more time, that there were a few questions he would like to have asked.

Mike didn't improve Red's attitude when he said, "I think I learned about all there was to learn from him."

"Did he say how Butch looked?" Jan asked, her voice just a little shaky.

Bob glanced at her. She had that *look* in her eyes again. What was it about the very mention of Butch that gave her such a reaction?

"Yes," Mike said in answer to Jan's question. "He said Butch looked pretty bad, but he could still move okay. But Butch will need more medical attention, I would guess. At the least, he'll need lots of rest. I don't think they'll travel too far at a time now. But since it appears that they're heading for Canada, let's head north ourselves."

In less than an hour they were on the road. Jan had climbed in with the still-sullen Red Blauser, taking the edge off his attitude. Mike drove the rented Durango and led the way through the Grand Teton National Park. Special Agent Reed, who was really the man in charge now, the only one with jurisdiction, followed.

Mike was tense and worried, and mentioned the reason to Bob. "Someone else is going to get hurt, I'm afraid, and I don't know if we can stop it. I'm afraid Butch may begin, despite his illness, to be more careful and leave fewer clues for us to follow."

"Where are we going now?" Bob asked, glancing over at Mike.

"I don't know, Bob," he said. "Just north, I guess. It's the best we can do."

Chapter 17

Erika had slept on and off for sixteen hours. Tied with her hands behind her back and her feet bound together, it was a wonder she'd slept at all. But exhaustion had overcome her, as it had Butch. He hadn't apologized for binding her so tightly, because, he told her, it was the only way to keep her from running off. And that he would never allow.

She was in mortal fear of him and what he could do to her. Why he continued to drag her along was a mystery. For some reason he wanted her, and that alone was probably the only reason she was still alive. He was quite sick again, which was to her benefit, and she found herself praying constantly that he would never get better.

The stolen Nissan was parked out front, but it had different plates on it. She had driven until Butch ordered her to stop the night before. Then he'd made her find a similar car, exchange the plates, and then check them into this motel in West Yellowstone, Montana.

She glanced over at Butch who was still sleeping soundly in the bed next to hers. She knew that when he awoke he would be hungry, as was she. She hoped that he wouldn't sleep much longer, because she wasn't sure how much longer she could stand the pain she was in from the ropes that were rubbing her skin raw. An hour later he awoke and said it was time to get some food and head for Canada. It took several minutes after he removed the ropes before she could move her limbs well enough to walk. When she was finally up to it, he made her stuff her hair down her collar and put on a green baseball cap. Then they again hit the road in the stolen Nissan. The first stop they made was for food, but Butch also spent some of the money Erika had stolen on two western hats. He ordered Erika to replace the baseball cap with one of the hats, keeping her hair out of sight. He wore the other one. A quick stop for gas followed. Then they headed north.

Butch didn't mention to Erika the shiny blue Durango and the large brown Ford Crown Victoria he spotted next to a set of gas pumps as they passed another service station on the outskirts of town. Nor did he mention the tall blonde man that walked into the station as he went by. It was almost certainly the man Erika had seen and started toward in the hospital parking lot in Jackson, because that man had been standing beside a blue Durango.

Butch didn't recognize the tall, redheaded man who was standing beside the Ford, looking at them as they drove by. But he was a cop. Of that Butch was certain. And that cop had seen them. In the mirror, he saw him writing something on his hand.

***

What Red was writing on his hand was a license number, but he also saw the cowboy hats and concluded that it was not the stolen car. Just to be sure though, he checked the plate number from his hand against the number he'd written down earlier in the car. It didn't match, and he promptly put it out of his mind. It wasn't until nearly thirty minutes later that he noticed another blue Nissan, pointed it out to Jan, looked closely at the old lady driving it, and then said, "That's the second one today."

"Second one!" Jan exclaimed. "You didn't mention seeing another Nissan. Was it blue?"

"Yeah, but like this one, it didn't have Butch and Erika in it, and the plates didn't match," he said.

"Did you get a good look at its occupants?" she demanded.

"Of course. Couple of cowboys."

"Cowboys?"

"Sure. Big hats, brims hanging down front and rear. You know, typical of the area."

Jan had a terrible sinking feeling in the pit of her stomach. "What was the plate number?" she asked, "or did you even write it down?"

Red bristled. "Of course I wrote it down, Jan. And I checked it against this one," he said, pointing at the number written on a notebook that was clipped to his visor.

"So, what was it?" she pressed.

"Hey, I checked it, Trooper! And it was the wrong number. Different car. Different people. Now forget it."

But Jan didn't give up easily. The feeling she had was too strong. So she pressed him. "What was the number, Lieutenant?"

"Oh, good grief, it's right here," he said, showing her the palm of his left hand.

She wrote it down and grabbed her cell phone. "What are you doing?" Red demanded.

"I'm doing what you should have done when you couldn't be absolutely sure you didn't see the stolen car."

"I didn't see it."

"Maybe you did," Jan said angrily. "Butch isn't dumb. He could easily have obtained a couple of western hats. Now be quiet while I make a call."

Harry Reed had the frequencies to several of the dispatch stations in the area. She called him and held her phone open while he checked on the plate number. Her heart almost stopped when he came back on the phone and said, "That plate was reported stolen less than an hour ago from a car in West Yellowstone."

"It was them," Jan said angrily to Red while Harry waited. "Where did you see it and when?"

"Don't be silly, Trooper," he said with a forced laugh. "I tell you it wasn't them."

"And I tell you it was!" she shouted. "Where did you see them?"

"I saw *the car,*" he said through gritted teeth, "while we were getting gas. I never did see *them.*"

"Pull over," she demanded.

"What?"

"Stop this car. Mike and Bob are right behind us and I need to talk to them."

As Red reluctantly slowed down, Jan gave Harry the information she had just obtained from Red. He promised to get it out to all the surrounding areas, particularly to the north. As soon as the Ford had stopped, Jan leaped out, and began waving her arms. Mike was driving the Durango, and he pulled over, stopped, and jumped out.

"Jan, what in the world is—" he began.

"They're probably just ahead of us," she said breathlessly. And as quickly as she could, she explained. Mike used a couple of words he ordinarily avoided when he was around Jan. Then he stomped up to Red's car. "Why didn't you—" he began.

Red threw his car in gear and peeled out, spraying Mike with gravel from the side of the road.

"I'm sorry," Mike said, turning to Jan, "but I don't share your admiration for that poor excuse of a cop." Mike was embarrassed at his outburst as quickly as he'd made it.

"Tolerance, not *admiration,"* Jan corrected. Mike could not possibly know why she had allowed herself to get involved with Red and how pushy and intolerable he'd become. "Did he say where he was going?"

"Not a word. And he left you high and dry," Mike said, and then despite himself, he chuckled.

Jan hit him on the shoulder. "Then I guess I'll have to bum a ride," she answered. Turning to Bob, who was just now getting out of the Durango, she said, "I just lost my ride. Would you give a lady a lift?"

"Sure, but what's going on? What made Red spin out like that?"

"Jump in. I'll drive, and Jan can explain as we go," Mike said.

Once they were on the road, the engine whining, Jan quickly told Bob what had transpired. "They're not far ahead of us, Bob. They can't be, and we can't fail Erika this time."

Mike was driving fast, but he was also thinking. "Jan, we passed an intersection ten or fifteen miles back. Highway 287, if I remember right. They could have gone that way."

Jan used her cell phone again. Harry Reed was several miles ahead of them. "We're getting roadblocks set up," he told her. "You guys better turn back and take 287. I'll keep going north on 191. Oh, and by the way, what happened to Red? I thought you were with him?"

"Not anymore," Jan said. "He's alone and behind you somewhere."

***

Lieutenant Red Blauser was alone, but he was not behind Harry Reed. Embarrassed and angry, he'd pulled off the road just moments after showering Sergeant O'Connor with gravel. He'd waited until they went by, then pulled onto the highway and headed south. His motivation for being involved in the search had been Trooper Jan Hallinan. But like all the other women in Red's life, she had proven to be a waste of his time. He was going home. He'd have a story when he got there that would fit the outstanding cop he felt that he was.

In the meantime, he was hungry. He stopped at a little convenience store in West Yellowstone and left his car idling while he ran in for some chips and a drink. When he came out just moments later, he howled in anger.

His patrol car had vanished.

***

Butch laughed so hard his side hurt as he raced out of West Yellowstone in a stolen cop car. "This'll outrun anybody," he bragged to his tearful hostage. "Not that we're likely to need to, because they all think we're going north."

"How do you know that?" Erika asked.

"I'm not stupid, girl," was the only answer he gave her.

No, indeed it appeared that he wasn't stupid. For reasons he never told her, he'd pulled off the highway and into the trees just a few miles north of West Yellowstone. After waiting for over a half hour, he had pulled back onto the road and headed south. As they drove into the town, he'd said it was time to get another car. They had then deserted the Nissan in a grocery store parking lot, and the two of them walked back to the main route. It was there that they watched the tall red-haired man—that Butch somehow knew was a cop—leave his car idling while he strolled into the convenience store.

Now they had his car and everyone thought they were going north. Erika slumped down in the seat. Everything always turned against her she felt. Was she doomed to end her life with Butch Snyder? she wondered as she closed her eyes and willed sleep to come.

***

Bob Evans's mind was working hard. Riding in the backseat, alone, he'd been going over what had happened the past little while. After they'd turned north on Highway 287, he was worried. Everyone was convinced that Butch was taking Erika north, except him. Finally, he couldn't stand it anymore and spoke up. "Sergeant," he said, "if Red saw Butch and Erika in the Nissan in West Yellowstone, how do we know Butch didn't also see us?"

"Well, I suppose it's possible," Mike admitted.

"And if he did, what was there to stop him from turning back to the south?"

Mike slammed on the brakes, pulled to the side of the road and whipped around. "Why didn't I think of that?" he moaned.

"I didn't either," Jan admitted, turning and smiling at Bob. "Thanks," she said. "I don't know what we'd do without you."

"I could be wrong," he said modestly.

"But we're betting you aren't," she countered. "Why do you think we let you hang around anyway?"

Mike was revving the Durango. "Jan, call Harry. We better get roadblocks set up that way too."

***

When Mike pulled into West Yellowstone, he was surprised to see a cop car with its lights flashing parked beside a convenience store. "Something's happened here," he said to the others. "We better stop and find out what's going on. It might have something to do with Butch."

He whipped into the parking area and got out of the car. "Jan, let's find out what's going on here. Bob, you better stay put until we figure things out."

As they approached the police cruiser, Jan stooped down and peered inside the open passenger window. "Red!" she blurted, recognizing the back of his head instantly.

He turned, and seeing her, opened the door and stepped out. "Jan, Mike, is it ever good to see you two," he said, his voice coated with honey.

"What's going on here?" Jan demanded. Her voice had no honey on it. She was still angry with Red for the delay he'd caused. "Where's your car?"

The West Yellowstone officer had exited his cruiser and spoke before Red did. "It seems it's been stolen."

"Stolen?" Mike said. "How in the world did you let it get stolen?"

"He left the keys in it," the officer said.

"I only ran into the store for a moment," Red said angrily.

"A moment too long," the young officer emphasized, not at all intimidated by Red Blauser.

"I'll ride with you guys now, I guess," Red said. "Where are you headed anyway? I thought Butch was going north."

"We think he doubled back. We don't have time to—" Mike began.

"Sergeant," Bob interrupted.

Mike turned. Bob was pacing impatiently beside the Durango. "Could it have been Butch?"

Jan knew immediately what Bob was thinking. "Oh my word!" she exclaimed. "I wonder where he left the Nissan. Mike, we better find it. It's got to be close by."

"What's the matter with you people?" Red stormed. "You can't possibly think that Butch took my car? Trust Bob Evans to come up with something like that. I can't believe you're still letting that *boy* tag along. Butch is on his way to Canada and you're all wasting your time down here. *Butch stole my car,* " he sneered. "That's the stupidest thing I've ever heard of."

Jan turned on him angrily. She'd had all she could take of Lieutenant Red Blauser. "Well, you are the stupidest thing I've ever heard of," she retorted.

Mike chuckled at her outburst, but once again, he was sure that Bob was on the right track. "Let's get moving here. There's one way to be sure, and that's to find the Nissan."

The three of them climbed back in and left Red fuming and cursing as they pulled out and began to cruise around town. The young city officer also left Red without a ride as he joined in the search. It only took them ten minutes to locate the Nissan, parked among a bunch of other cars in the parking lot of a grocery store. Mike called Special Agent Harry Reed to report what they'd discovered while Jan checked the inside of the car.

"Butch left the rifle," she said. "So all he has is his pistol now . . ." Her face paled and she amended her conclusion with, "And whatever weapons Red Blauser had in his car."

***

"Erika, wake up," Butch said, shaking her arm.

"What! Where are we?" she asked as her mind began to clear itself of sleep.

"I think there's a roadblock ahead," Butch said. "We're going to make a run for it."

She glanced at Butch. His face was hard as stone and his mouth clamped shut like a vise. She was repulsed and frightened.

"Erika, are you awake yet?" Butch demanded harshly. "You better pay attention, girl. I'm not stopping for those cops up there."

Erika looked ahead and saw two cop cars parked in the road, their lights flashing a stern warning. Butch drove steadily toward them. "They don't know much about setting roadblocks," he said grimly. "Duck. Get out of sight. Those cops might shoot." No sooner had she ducked out of sight than he rammed the gas feed to the floor and the big Ford responded with a powerful surge.

Erika's heart pounded and her hands grew clammy. She felt the car swerve and was thrown from the seat to the floor as it fishtailed and bounced wildly through the grass beside the road. Glass flew in concert with a loud bang. A second shot rang out, then they were back on the pavement, fishtailing violently, but still gaining speed.

Butch let out with a whoop. "I did it! They'll never catch us." He laughed and pounded his fist on the steering wheel. Erika scrambled back onto the seat. It was covered with glass. She brushed it onto the floor before she realized where it had come from. The back window and the side window next to her had disintegrated.

She glanced over at the speedometer. It read just over 100 mph. "Can't we slow down now, Butch?" she shouted above the wind that was whipping through the broken windows with the force of a tornado.

"They'll be coming. We've got to get away now and find another car. I hate to give this one up, it's so fast, but with the windows out, it makes us too easy to spot," he shouted.

Erika wiped her hand across her forehead. The sweat was from fear, not heat since it wasn't a hot day, and the wind blowing in was cool. Her hand felt sticky and she looked at it and gasped. Blood was oozing from a nasty gash in her palm. She must have cut it sweeping the glass from the seat.

"I cut my hand," she cried, fighting back the tears. Her head and her hand both throbbed. She dug through Red's jockey box and found a napkin he'd stuffed there. She wadded it up and clutched it tightly in her hand in an attempt to stop the bleeding.

"Where are we, Butch?" she asked a few minutes later. Butch was driving slower now but still too fast for the mountainous terrain they were going through.

"We're getting close to Jackson Hole," he said, glancing in the rearview mirror. "Can't see anyone behind us yet."

"They must not be coming, Butch. Can't you slow down?" she asked, terrorized at the speed they were driving. She had survived two accidents with Butch already, but they were at much slower speeds. He would kill them both if he kept driving like this.

"Oh, they're coming alright, but I'm going to take a side road. We'll give them the slip."

Butch eased up on the speed and turned onto a paved road that led upward, into the mountains. Butch's face was screwed into a tight ball as he concentrated on his driving. He veered dangerously on the curves but kept the big car going as fast as possible. "Put your seat belt on," Butch ordered suddenly. "I don't want you bouncing around on the floor again—it makes it hard to drive."

She slid near the door where the cool mountain air was streaming through the broken window and grabbed the seat belt as her long hair whipped about her face. The blood-soaked napkin fell from her hand as she snapped the belt in place, then twisted and looked back. No cops were in sight.

"They aren't coming, Butch. Please slow down," Erika pleaded.

Butch slowed up again and fastened his own belt. He hadn't done that before and her fear intensified. He sped up again and the trees flew by in a blur of green and brown, making her dizzy and slightly nauseated.

They'd gone two or three more miles when they came to a long, sweeping curve. They were almost through it, the tires screaming on the pavement, when a deer bounded into the road. Erika screamed and Butch swerved. The deer flew onto the hood, breaking the windshield into thousands of glittering pieces. Then it was gone.

The big car spun sideways and slid out of control. Erika's scream was louder as the edge of the road rushed toward her. There was nothing but sky out her window when the car left the road and the air bags exploded, pinning her against the seat's back. As they plunged down the steep mountainside she was vaguely aware of a blur of rocks and trees and clear blue sky as the car first rolled, then flipped end over end into the deep ravine.

Chapter 18

When it finally came to rest and the dust had settled, the car was resting against a huge pine tree, right side up. Erika tried to sit up, but the air bag held her tight, and her head bumped the roof. It took her a minute to orient herself and realize the roof was caved in almost level with the back of the seat. She felt for the seat belt release, forcing the air bag around, but excruciating pain shot up her arm and shoulder. She struggled and twisted until she finally got her arm in front of her face. She could hear as well as feel the bones grating in her forearm. With horror, she realized her arm was broken just above the wrist.

She heard a moan and saw Butch's head near hers. She had visions of the car exploding in a ball of flames. Her fear-racked mind told her she had to get out. She could feel Butch struggling. "I got my belt undone," he moaned. "I'm getting out of here."

He would escape and let the car burn her alive! she thought. Terrorized, she worked her left hand until she finally found the catch and succeeded in releasing her seat belt. She kicked at the door, bruising her foot. It didn't budge. She began screaming.

"Shut up!" Butch ordered. "You'll bring the cops right to us. I've got to think."

Erika continued to scream and kick, bumping her head on the roof until blood seeped down her face, partially blinding her. She wanted the cops to find them. Butch somehow got hold of her right arm and shook it. The bones grated, again shooting intense pain from her shoulder to her finger tips, and she screamed even louder. "It's broken, Butch!" she yelled. "Don't touch me!"

He let go of her, and she gradually calmed down, thinking mostly of the pain. She finally quit thrashing and lay still, sobbing while Butch squirmed and twisted beside her. He was finally able to get his head through the window on his side of the car. It was tight, but he succeeded in crawling through and within minutes Erika had followed. Using a stick, Butch retrieved their coats. Then he found a stick and popped the trunk open. "Ah, this will help," he said as he pulled a large handgun from the mess in the trunk and stuffed it in his waist band. He rummaged around some more, locating some bullets which went in his pocket with the gun.

"That ought to do. And it seems we're not badly hurt," he said, glancing up toward the road. "The cops must have gone on by," he said, "so we better get going."

"Butch, I can't. I'm cut all over and my arm's broken," she cried hysterically.

Butch whirled and with his palm open delivered a resounding blow to her face. She whimpered, but quit crying. "That's better," he said harshly. "Now come on. You're with me. I'm not leaving you here for the cops to rescue. We'll splint your arm as soon as we get far enough away from the car to be safe. You'll just have to deal with it for now."

Erika stumbled and fell frequently as they descended the steep hillside. She ripped a long hole in her pants above the right knee and more blood spilled from an ugly gash on her thigh. Still, Butch forced her to go on. They finally reached the bottom where a gushing mountain stream blew cold white foam on them.

Erika glanced back toward the car, but it was hidden from view by the trees. "Help me with my arm, Butch," she pleaded. "I can't see the car anymore."

"Are you crazy?" he muttered. "We can't stop yet. The cops won't have any trouble following us the way we're tearing up the hillside. Get moving! We'll wade up the stream a ways and then climb out on the other side. That'll slow them down."

Butch started up the stream in the white-capped, knee-deep water. Erika stood at the edge, in more pain than she'd ever experienced in her life. She wanted desperately to turn back, and actually thought that if she just stood there he might leave her. But she was wrong. Butch pulled Red's pistol from his waistband and pointed it at her. "Now, Erika," he said, his voice so angry that she knew she would die if she didn't follow him.

In desperation, she plunged into the ice-cold water and struggled up the bitter cold stream. They fought the swift current for several hundred feet before Butch finally climbed out on the far side where the bank was not so steep, but was heavily wooded. She struggled along behind him, and he led the way at an angle up the hillside. He kept them in thick timber, invisible from the road above as they moved slowly along in a westerly direction.

"No cops yet," he observed after they'd walked for another ten or fifteen minutes. "Maybe we can get lead enough on them to get away before they find the car."

"Butch," she whined, "my arm's killing me."

"And mine's not?" he said, reminding her of his wounded and infected shoulder.

She didn't care about his problem. She was hurting so badly that she could think of nothing but her own pain. "I can't go on," she cried.

"Knock it off, Erika. Just a little farther and I'll help you with your arm," he said roughly. "You're such a crybaby."

Despite the slow going, Butch told Erika they were at least a mile from the car when he stopped at last and helped her take off her coat. She sat on a rock and looked around, doing her best to ignore the intense pain. They had entered a little green side canyon, thick with pine trees. The sun bore down through a break in the branches and warmed her chilled and trembling body.

Butch, grimacing in pain from his old wounds and a host of bruises from the accident, knelt beside her and examined her arm. He finally took out his knife and cut some green branches from the nearest tree and whittled three of them until they were quite smooth. Then he cut the right sleeve from her coat. "You won't be needing this, so we'll use it on your arm," he said.

She gritted her teeth while he padded her arm with part of the coat sleeve and cut the rest into strips which he used to tie the splints into place. That done, he fashioned a crude sling from his bandanna and part of his shirt. He helped her put her coat back on and zipped it up, the broken arm held securely inside.

"There, you can quit whining now," he said gruffly.

"It doesn't hurt as much," she admitted. "It mostly just throbs now, but my head hurts and my leg too," she said, fingering the caked blood on her thigh.

"The bleeding's stopped and you're not hurt. Let's get going again," he said, rising to his feet and reaching for her left hand and pulling her up. "You better keep up now," he said.

She was weak and cold and wet, but she forced herself to follow him up the ravine. They progressed slowly but steadily, working their way to a high pass barely visible through the trees above them.

***

Sergeant Mike O'Connor was awakened by the buzzing of his car phone. "That was Harry," he told the others after a short conversation with the FBI agent. "They almost got Butch in a roadblock, but he took to the borrow pit and got around them. However, the officers didn't see Erika at all so they fired, shooting some windows out. But they said she sat up as they were fleeing the roadblock."

"They could have killed her, and Butch got away again," Jan moaned.

"Yes. They chased them south but lost them. They must have taken a side road and driven into the mountains."

"Great. He'll probably find a campground, steal some unsuspecting camper's car and slip out of there unseen," Bob moaned. "I wish we were closer."

***

"What do you mean, they shot the windows out? What kind of stupid officers do you have around here anyway? Don't they know that's a police car they were driving? I'll have somebody's job for this!"

"I'm sorry, Lieutenant Blauser. I'm just the dispatcher. I can only tell you what I've been told. Whose police car was it anyway?" the sweet female voice questioned in the telephone.

"It was mine, you fool! Whose did you think it was?" Red blared. He was standing at a pay phone in Jackson Hole, and he was livid. He'd been forced to spend his own money to rent a car to drive home in.

He'd been told to return at once, but after hearing what had happened to his car, he decided to go after Butch despite the sheriff's orders.

And now this—an airheaded dispatcher! He growled at her again and she came right back at him this time. "I didn't know whose it was, but I would think a cop would know better than to let someone steal his car right from under his nose!"

"You're a real smart one," he said angrily. "Which way did they go?"

"Which way did who go?" she asked.

"Geronimo and his band!" Red shouted.

Click.

Red swore and slammed the pay phone so hard that he rattled the change in it. He started toward his rental car, then whirled around and charged back. He dialed the dispatch office again. The same sweet voice answered.

Red needed information. He took a deep breath and said, "I'm sorry I got upset, ma'am. This is Lieutenant Blauser again. I really need to know which way they went."

"We don't know," she said curtly.

"Don't know? How could you not know? Where was the roadblock?"

She told him. "But they must have gone into the mountains somewhere north of there," she explained.

"Lost them!" Red thundered. "The crazy, incompetent fools. Can't they even handle a simple little—"

Click.

He cursed, rattled the change in the phone again, stomped to his car, climbed in, and sped away, oblivious to the pickup that ran clear over the curb to avoid a collision with him.

Red was determined to catch Butch. The notoriety he got would be enough to keep the sheriff from disciplining him. A horn blared, Red swerved recklessly, straightened his car out, and sped back to the north, the way he'd come from just minutes before.

***

With darkness came a biting chill in the high mountain air. Erika's jeans had dried, but her shoes were still damp and her body trembled with the cold. The pain in her arm was intense and her leg hurt too, as did a hundred other bumps and bruises. Added to all that trauma was a pampered stomach that was being deprived and unbearably aching muscles.

"Butch, I can't go on," she whined. "We've got to stop and rest. They won't keep coming in the dark, will they?"

"I'm tired too, babe, but they will keep coming." He paused, then said, "All right, we'll stop, but first let's get where we can build a fire without it being seen."

He chose a thick stand of timber deep in a ravine. He cleared a spot of ground and soon had a small, but warm, fire glowing. Erika sat on the ground leaning against the rough bark of a pine tree, her bare feet roasting near the flames. Her shoes and socks were spread on a rock where steam rose from them as they dried.

Butch sat near Erika. "Wish we had more food," he complained.

"Me too," Erika agreed. "I don't know if I can go on without something to eat."

"Maybe I can shoot a deer in the morning. I hate to make a noise, but we'll have to shoot something if we hope to get out of these hills alive."

"But, Butch, we've walked a long ways. Nobody could hear a shot, could they?" she asked naively.

"That all depends on how far behind us the cops are. If we're really lucky, they may not have found the car yet. Anyway, we'll have to take a chance. For now though, let's try to get some rest." He closed his eyes and leaned back.

Erika sobbed quietly. She had never been so afraid in her life. She watched Butch in the firelight. She hated him! But she was afraid to leave him now. She had no idea which way to go to find a road. And she wasn't sure how far she could go without food.

"Hey, Erika, quit bawling. It's getting on my nerves," Butch said curtly.

That upset her more and she couldn't control her emotions. He was glaring at her. The fire cast a red reflection in his eyes, a symbol of evil to her terrorized mind. Her fear intensified so dramatically that it choked off her sobs and she sat with her knees pulled up against her body—as tightly as she could with the broken arm in the way.

Several minutes passed. A moan in the trees overhead revealed a rising wind. Erika shivered and stared into the flames. "Go to sleep!" Butch ordered. "You won't hurt so bad when you're asleep."

"I'll try," she said.

She stretched out, her feet near enough to the fire to be warm. For an hour or so she tossed on her bed of old pine needles. No matter how she lay, the broken arm throbbed and the other pains gnawed at her. But at last she fell asleep from sheer exhaustion.

***

It was late, and Mike felt like they were chasing ghosts as he and his companions climbed out of the Durango and met Harry outside a café in Jackson. Inside the café they met the local sheriff and several other officers. "So we missed the road he turned off on somewhere."

No one disagreed. Roadblocks had been set up in every direction for miles around and the pair hadn't appeared at any of them. "Does that mean they've holed up somewhere in the area?" Jan asked.

"It's a big area that we have blocked off. But yes, I believe they're still in it and the sheriff to the south does too." The man speaking was the sheriff, a large man with a high voice and chubby face. "Officers are checking every road and we've put out a warning on the local radio and TV stations to the people in the area. No one has called to report any sightings."

"Would someone direct me to the area where the roadblock they ran was set up?" Mike asked.

"Sure," the sheriff responded, and in a few minutes Mike and his party were northbound.

No one noticed the car that followed at a discreet distance as they left town. If Mike had been aware that Lieutenant Red Blauser was nearby he would have stopped right then and checked every car that came along until he found him, but he wasn't even thinking about Red anymore.

Later, at the scene of the failed roadblock, Mike spoke to one of the Wyoming troopers who had manned it. "After he got by, we jumped in our cars and took off, but that guy had that Ford wrapped up so tight it was humming. I just couldn't stay with him on the curves."

"That's understandable," Mike said. "I'd hate to be in a high-speed chase with Butch Snyder. He has no regard for life or property. Now, how far did you go before you figured you'd lost him?"

"Nearly back to Jackson. There was a roadblock there that he never reached," the trooper answered.

"Any side roads ahead?" Harry asked.

"Several, but most of them are pretty rough. We've checked them all. One is paved and goes east. It takes you way up into the forest and eventually comes out on the other side of the mountain. It's twisty and steep and would be really dangerous at high speeds. We've been clear through and have a roadblock at the other end. They never went that way. What I think they did is hid when we went by and then doubled back."

"Show me the road that goes through the mountains," Mike said, ignoring the trooper's opinion.

"Sure thing, Sergeant, but I really don't think they went that way."

"Never hurts to double-check things. We've got to be doing something, and I want to have a look," Mike said politely.

Harry and Mike rode together and led the way up the canyon. Jan and Bob followed in the Durango. They had driven several miles up the twisting mountain road when Harry said, " I better stop. Bob's flashing his lights at us."

Jan and Bob approached them at a trot after they had pulled over. "I tried to call you, but I can't get a signal on the cell phone. I thought you should know that someone's following us, Mike," Jan reported.

"Why would they be doing that?" Mike asked skeptically.

"I don't know, but Bob noticed the lights behind us. When we slowed, they slowed, and when we sped up so did they. Bob even stopped once and so did the other car, and the lights went out. When Bob started up again nothing happened. We went around a curve and slowed way down and there came the lights again. Then the other car slowed down once more. I don't like it," she said, looking over her shoulder. "See, there it comes now. It should be stopping pretty soon."

But this time it didn't. It sped up and passed at a dangerously high speed. Mike spun around as it went by. "Rental car," he observed, noting the sticker on the bumper. "Anybody get a good look at the driver?"

"Only the back of his head after he passed and was in Harry's headlights. It reminded me of somebody," Bob replied thoughtfully.

"Red Blauser!" Jan shouted. "I'll bet it was Red! He might be in a rental car."

"That's it, Jan," Bob said. "He looked like Red from the back. Of course I can't be sure."

"Who else could it be?" Mike interrupted. "He's probably been tailing us for hours, and here I thought he'd gone home."

"He'll probably pull off ahead somewhere and let us pass again," Harry suggested.

"Probably. We'll keep a lookout for him, but let's look for skid marks or anything else that could give us a clue to Butch's and Erika's whereabouts," Mike cautioned. "I wouldn't be surprised if Butch's car is over the edge."

"Oh . . ." Bob said gasping. "Is that why we're up here?"

"Not just that. They could be camped somewhere, but we can't leave out any possibilities. We'll check the campgrounds on top too. They may have left Red's car and stolen another one, though I don't think there'll be many campers up here. It's getting too late in the summer and too chilly," he said, zipping up his coat.

They traveled slowly, stopping frequently to shine their lights over the edge. On a long, sweeping curve, Mike asked, "What was that beside the road, Harry?"

"Looked like a dead deer," Harry responded.

"Let's have a look. Maybe our friend Red hit it."

They stopped and got out. Mike was bent over the deer when Jan walked up. "It's been dead quite a while. It's cold," he said, straightening up.

They all started walking up the road. "Hey, skid marks," Jan said, shining her light up the road's surface. "It's a critical speed scuff."

"A what?" Bob asked.

"A critical speed scuff," Jan replied as she followed the curved black marks. "That's the kind of mark that car tires leave on the road when they're turning in too tight of a curve. They're usually followed by a rollover."

They had reached the edge of the road. Bob and Jan shined their lights into the black ravine. "There it is!" Jan shouted. "There's a car down there!"

Bob let out a gasp of distress and began to clamber recklessly down the mountainside. "Hey, slow down there!" Mike ordered.

But the young man could only think of Erika and he kept going. "I mean it, Bob. Stop right now!" Mike shouted at the top of his lungs.

This time Bob heard and he ceased his suicidal trek. Mike caught up with him and said, "You could run right into an ambush, Bob. Get behind me and stay there. Jan," he called back to where she was gingerly making her way down, "keep him back. Harry and I'll check things out down there first."

They descended slowly. Rocks, brush, and clumps of grass dotted the side of the ravine. "It's Red's," Mike said when they were almost to the wreck. "It looks bad."

He and the FBI agent, weapons drawn, moved toward it slowly, crouching low to the ground. Mike reached it first. "It's empty," he shouted back up the hill as he holstered his pistol.

Bob sighed with relief and slowly worked his way down the hill and then sat down on a rock several yards above the wreck. He had been filled with horrible visions of finding Erika's body in the bent and twisted wreckage.

"They've had a rough time getting out, I'll bet. Look at the way it's crushed," Jan said after leaving Bob and shining her light across the wreckage.

Harry reached in with a stick and pulled out a blood-soaked napkin. "Someone's been bleeding," he observed. "There's blood on the seat too."

"Most of the blood is on the passenger side," Mike said softly to Harry. "It must be Erika who's hurt."

After more examination, Mike said, "I don't see any guns in the trunk. I know Red admitted that there was a pistol there. Butch must have taken it."

"They've gone downhill," Jan called a moment later. She'd been scouting around the car, searching for their tracks.

The other officers joined her and they followed the tracks down the hill to the stream bed. "They crossed I guess. Let's get some help before we go on," Mike said. "They're almost certainly back in the mountains somewhere. I'd like to go after them, but I don't believe we want to catch up with Butch in the dark. This is a daylight job."

They trudged the short distance back to Red's wrecked cruiser. Bob still sat on the rock, his head between his knees. Jan's heart pained her as she glanced toward his shadowy form. She knew what he was doing. He was praying. In her heart she did the same.

None of them saw the form of a man peering from the edge of the road above them. But then he wasn't there long. A rental car pulled up the road with its lights off long before they reached the road's edge after a hard climb up the steep mountainside.

CHAPTER 19

A shot rang out, waking Erika from a deep and troubled sleep. She sat up with a jerk, her body in a cold sweat. She looked about her. Tall pines swayed softly, lit by the soft, golden glow of the newly risen sun. The fire was but a bed of crimson coals, and her bare feet were numb with cold. Her broken arm throbbed sharply and Butch was nowhere in sight. She climbed stiffly to her feet and threw some sticks on the fire from a small pile Butch must have made while she was sleeping. Soon the flames leaped high and cast welcome warmth her way.

Erika pulled on her socks and shoes, struggling with her left arm. It took her a long time, but they were warm and took the chill from her feet. Then she huddled over the fire savoring the welcome heat.

Erika's stomach growled. She couldn't remember a time when she'd ever been so hungry. Without something to eat she didn't think she could walk very far, and she knew Butch would be insisting that they move on as soon as he returned to the fire.

Her thoughts turned to Bob. She missed him desperately. "Help me, oh please, somebody help me," she sobbed.

She looked around again for Butch and when there was still no sight of him, Erika stiffly dropped to her knees and began to pray. At first she could do nothing but plead, "Help me, please help me." Then her thoughts cleared and she slowly began to tell her Heavenly Father what a terrible ordeal she was going through. She recounted what had happened to her the past few days and prayed fervently for deliverance from the evil clutches of Butch Snyder.

Then she prayed for Bob and for her family. Finally she prayed for the officers who had so faithfully pursued Butch. "Please help them to find us," she pled.

Suddenly, a shot rang out, interrupting her prayer. Butch must be near. Were there others? she wondered. Had he killed someone? She shivered uncontrollably, her terror of Butch worse than it had ever been. She closed her eyes once more, prayed again for the officers and for Bob and asked God to make her strong enough to endure and to help her control her fear. Finally, Erika did something she'd never done before. She promised the Lord that if He would deliver her, she would do all she could to serve others for the rest of her life. Then she closed her prayer, but for a long time she knelt there, her eyes closed, wondering at the calmness that descended upon her and at the warmth she felt in her heart.

The Lord had not forgotten her.

And she vowed that she would never again forget Him, for at times, she realized, she hadn't been as faithful as she could have been. She certainly hadn't measured up to the standards Bob had set for himself.

As she rose from her knees, Butch appeared, carrying a large chunk of raw, red meat. "Breakfast," he announced. "Venison. I just shot a deer."

So that was the shot that had awakened her, she thought with some relief. At least he hadn't hurt anyone. Erika struggled to retain the feelings of peace she felt as she watched Butch carve out a couple of small pieces of meat and roast them on sharpened sticks over the fire. The meat cooked fast, and Erika found that it tasted surprisingly good. As soon as it was gone, Butch kicked some dirt on the fire and said, "Let's get moving."

She followed Butch through the trees, feeling surprisingly strong. And the sweet memory of the peace that she'd felt for those few minutes lingered pleasantly and gave her hope. The pain she was suffering was as intense as ever, but her strength to endure had miraculously increased. The Lord really hadn't forgotten her, as she had wondered so many times these past few days. She could endure to the end, whatever that end might be.

It occurred to Erika that suffering didn't always end in recovery. It sometimes ended in death. Even that thought didn't frighten her now. She could and would accept whatever her Heavenly Father had in mind for her. Deliverance from the clutches of the evil man who'd held her and hurt her and terrorized her was all she wanted. She'd finally been given the strength to accept the will of the Lord, and she promised herself that she would let Him decide what was best for her.

***

"They stopped here," a wiry young sheriff's deputy said, pointing out to Mike a tiny fragment of cloth on the ground.

Mike nodded and looked up the side of the hill. "Let's keep going. They can't be too far ahead of us."

The big German shepherd lunged against the leash, and they surged up the hill at a hammering pace. Mike had warned the dog handlers to use caution and be constantly alert, for Butch would not hesitate to kill in an ambush. For that reason, the tracking dogs were kept on leash as they followed the scent.

Harry and four local officers were in the group spread out below Mike and the dog handlers. Jan and Bob brought up the rear. The local men had protested the presence of a civilian and a female. But Jan had insisted that she was coming. Somehow, she felt that the end of her own personal nightmare, the one she had never spoken of to a soul, would end on this mountain. Mike had taken her side, assuring the other officers that Jan could keep up with the best of them. And Jan simply insisted that Bob be allowed to come along, promising that he would not create any problems or be in the officers' way.

Mike was angered over the presence of a third set of tracks that had appeared over those of Butch and Erika that they'd been following. "Red Blauser is going to cause tragic problems I'm afraid," he commented to Harry as they stared at the large boot prints.

***

Red Blauser was exhausted. He'd spent much of the night following the tracks Butch and Erika had left. Progress had been slow as he'd picked his way along the steep hillsides and heavy timber with the aid of a flashlight. Once daylight came, the tracks were easier to follow, and by noon he'd found their campfire.

He smiled grimly as he forged through the thick trees, the sweet smell of pine filling his nose pleasantly. The glory of single-handedly bringing in the dangerous quarry he pursued drove him relentlessly on despite his protesting, poorly conditioned body. He would also get revenge, for he had been unfairly treated by Jan Hallinan, and even now he seethed with anger at the way she'd left him with a simple, "We don't need your help," as she and the others drove south from West Yellowstone.

The trail led for a short distance around a steep side hill beneath looming sandstone ledges. The trees were scarce between the ledges, but were thick just beyond them. He was anxious to reach cover again, for he was uncomfortable as he hiked across the open space, exposed and vulnerable. He tried to go faster but slipped and nearly fell. He slowed down, but kept going, carefully watching the ground at his feet.

When he looked up again, he was almost there. Breathing heavily, he trudged on with his head bent, sweating profusely at the effort. His head popped up at the sharp sound of a snapping branch. For the briefest moment his eyes grew wide with the realization of his error.

Red spun and leaped to the uphill side of the slope as he grabbed desperately for the pistol at his side. He scarcely heard the shot that stole from him both revenge and glory. The pain that tore through his leg surprised him as did the steeply sloping ground that rushed up at him. And he wondered at how he'd so blindly walked into such a simple, but deadly trap. He rolled over and over down the slope until his body struck a large pine. He struggled to sit up, staring at the blood that was oozing from his leg. Then he tried to stand, but broken bones and loss of strength prevented it. Red Blauser wondered if he would ingloriously die in this lonesome place. He cursed the day he'd met Jan Hallinan. Somehow this was all her fault.

***

"Who was it, Butch?" Erika asked, trembling and not wanting to know, but frightened over who it might have been.

"Just a big redheaded cop. The fool was alone," Butch said with a laugh.

"Alone?" she whispered. "Is he dead?"

"What do you think?" Butch asked, his eyes blazing as he grabbed her by the arm and pulled her up the slope.

***

"We're closing in on them," Harry observed as the afternoon wore into evening.

"So is Red," Mike muttered bitterly. "That fool fully intends to take Butch alone."

Towering sandstone ledges loomed just ahead. The tracks led out of the thick trees and across a steeply sloping clearing. "I don't like this. Perfect place for an ambush," one of the dog handlers said.

"What choice do we have? Anyway, Red's ahead of us," he observed, pointing at the size-twelve boot track. "If you like, I'll take the lead until we reach the trees over there."

"No, it's okay, Sergeant. It's just a spooky place for some reason," the deputy said. He watched his dog for a moment. "My dog's even spooked," he said seriously. "It's like he smells fear scent."

"Here, I'll lead out," Mike volunteered again.

"No, we'll go," the deputy said, and he urged his cowering dog onto the steeply sloping clearing. The second dog acted just like the first, but after some urging, it too began to cross.

The others followed in single file, Bob bringing up the rear. The dogs and their handlers had disappeared into the trees on the other side and Mike was just stepping into them when he heard Bob yell from behind him. "Hey, Sergeant, Red's tracks are gone."

Mike turned back to see Jan and Bob studying the ground intently. He looked down and sorted out the tracks beneath him and then slowly worked his way back. "You're right," he said. "I don't see them either. Of course we've all tromped through here now. When did you first notice they were gone?"

"Just now. Right here," Bob said.

A sick feeling stirred Mike's stomach and he directed his gaze down the steep hillside. Jan gasped and Bob went pale when they saw a still form lying at the base of a large pine. "It's Red, isn't it?" Bob asked, almost choking on his words.

Mike nodded and rapidly descended the slope. Jan, Harry, and Bob were right behind him. He shouted up the hill at the last local deputies, who were just disappearing into the trees. "Hey, men, we need help here. Stop the men with the dogs."

Jan spoke to Red, who was barely conscious and softly moaning. "We'll get you out of here, Red." She was examining the bullet wound. It was not too deep, luckily for Red, or he might have bled to death. But he did have a number of broken bones. "Just lie still while we see what we can do to help you," she said as tenderly as she could, feeling both pity and anger, for he was suffering, and yet he was once again delaying the search.

An hour was lost helping Lieutenant Blauser. But once he was loaded onto a helicopter and safely en route to a hospital, Harry and Mike decided they had better push on. "But we must use more caution than ever," Mike warned. "Butch clearly won't hesitate to shoot."

***

A stiff wind cut like ice through Erika's thin coat as she stumbled across a high, barren ridge. The sun was sinking low behind them, hid by a thick bank of clouds, but it was still light enough to see clearly. "Get down," Butch ordered suddenly and dropped to the ground.

Erika obeyed and followed Butch's eyes back down the ridge. Far in the distance were several tiny dots. They moved slowly across a clearing on a lower, distant ridge.

"They have dogs," Butch hissed, cursing softly. "They're tracking us with dogs."

He was silent, watching intently for a full minute before he finally said, "They're into the trees again. We can go now. I'll outsmart those dogs," he said, smirking. "Get up, Erika. We've got to hurry."

Her body screamed its protest, but Butch's hard, dangerous look forced her to ignore the pain, and once more she trudged along behind him. Tears filled her dark eyes, but she didn't complain.

Butch soon slowed down, and Erika realized with some relief that his body was weakening fast and that he too was in pain. She wondered how long he could go on and hoped fervently that he would soon simply drop from exhaustion. She began to believe that she could outlast him. She just might come out of this alive yet, for the officer Butch had shot was not the only one in pursuit. More help was on the way.

Dusk overtook them before they reached a moderate mountain stream that flowed down a gently sloping canyon. Butch stopped at the bank and tested the depth of the water with a stick. Satisfied, he turned to Erika. "We can't stop until we throw the dogs off our trail. We'll wade downstream. The water will wash away our scent and we'll leave no tracks. They'll get confused and think we've gone upstream. That will give us an even greater advantage, and we'll be able to stop for the night."

Erika was resigned to doing whatever he suggested. She was filled with hope now, not that the pain and aching of her body wasn't almost unbearable. But somehow she felt the end was drawing closer, and that God really was watching out for her. It was her newfound faith that kept her moving steadily along behind her captor.

The water was ice cold and about a foot deep. Occasionally it was shallower where it flowed more rapidly and other times it was clear to her thighs, numbing the long, angry cut there. They both stumbled frequently, soaking themselves thoroughly, and they were soon numbed by the bitter cold. Erika's chest ached and she coughed occasionally. Ahead of her Butch was coughing too—violently at times.

After what seemed like an eternity, and in full darkness, Butch climbed out of the stream on the far bank. Erika followed blindly. "I'll build a fire. I've got to get dry." His words came slowly and with great effort. Erika didn't answer. She just dropped and lay still until Butch had a roaring fire going, then she crawled toward it, soaking the blessed heat through her drenched clothing.

Nearly an hour had passed before Butch, with short, slow movements, pulled the meat that was left over from their breakfast out of a coat pocket. He sharpened a single stick and began to roast a piece of it. It was still more than half raw when he offered Erika some. She took it and began to chew.

***

"We'd better knock off until daylight. We don't want to walk into an ambush the way Lieutenant Blauser did. And we better take turns standing guard. There are eight of us now. We'll take ninety-minute shifts, two at a time. Mike and I'll be first." Harry gave his orders in the chill of the mountain night air.

One of the deputies shook Jan's arm in the middle of the night. "Your turn to keep watch," he said. "O'Connor said that Bob will help you."

She rubbed her eyes and got to her feet as the deputy woke Bob up. It was her turn to watch for Butch, and the thought frightened her terribly. She should never have come on this final attempt to apprehend Butch. She'd faced her nightmares long enough. She should have let the men handle it.

Bob joined her and said, "I guess we've got the watch now."

"Yes, I guess so," she said in a voice filled with fear.

"What's the matter, Jan?" he asked. "Are you alright?"

"I'm okay," she said, knowing that she was not. She led the way from the fire into the terrifying darkness of the night, a darkness where Butch might be waiting for *her*.

CHAPTER 20

Mike hadn't been able to sleep since he and Harry had completed their watch. He had sat, hunching miserably near the little fire, for the past thirty minutes. He was aware of Jan and Bob as they stirred, and wondered if he should volunteer to take one of their places. But before he stood to do so, he heard something that sent chills up his spine.

What he heard was Jan's voice as she spoke to Bob. It didn't sound quite right, although he knew it was her. What it sounded like was a voice from the past, a terrified voice he had heard only once but had never forgotten. Suddenly, Mike came to understand some things about Jan Hallinan that he'd never even suspected, and it brought bitter tears to his eyes. And he now knew why she had that red spot on her face—the one she subconsciously rubbed whenever she was upset or nervous. And he wondered how she'd ever endured these past few days. He rose to his feet. He couldn't let her stand out there in the darkness where her nightmares and Butch Snyder lurked, awaiting her, seeking to destroy her.

***

Bob was alarmed. Something was terribly wrong with Jan. She was sobbing as they walked together in a circle surrounding the camp. When they stopped to listen to the stillness of the night, there was just enough light from a sliver of moon that poked between thick clouds to enable him to see her face. Her hand was touching her cheek, fingering the small red spot below her cheekbone. What a strange habit that was.

He stepped close to her and whispered. "Jan, someone else can help me. You go lie down."

"No, I can do it," she insisted. "I'm the cop here."

This was not the Jan he had come to know and admire, and . . . more. "Hey, something's wrong. Please, won't you talk about it? I'm a good listener."

For a long time, Jan stood very still, listening in pure terror to the sounds of the night that filled the darkness surrounding her. Her heart hammered in her chest and beads of sweat covered her face. For five years she'd faced the nightmare and controlled it, but tonight, in this darkness with *him* out there, it was unbearable. Silently, as she had so many times, she prayed for strength and courage.

A gentle hand touched her shoulder and she turned. "Please, what is it?" Bob asked softly. "I'm your friend. You can talk to me about anything, can't you?"

Mike had approached silently but stopped a few steps from them when he heard Bob speak. Jan began to talk softly. "I've never told anyone this, Bob. I swore I never would."

"Please, tell me," he urged, wanting so badly to ease whatever hurt it was that had caused this change in her.

She was silent again for a good minute or more, then she said very softly, and with a voice that trembled, "It's *him,* Bob. It's *Butch.* He wants me dead!"

Stunned, Bob stepped closer to her. "What are you talking about?" he asked.

Her eyes gazed into the dark forest. She didn't see the shadows there. She saw only a scene that had haunted her for five long years. She continued, speaking as much to the darkness as to the young man who had now taken both her hands in his. "I was there, Bob. Five years ago I was there. I saw *him,* and *he* saw me. He said he would find me someday and kill me."

"Who? Saw what, Jan?" Bob demanded.

Mike, standing silently just beyond them knew *who* and *what.*

"Butch. I saw him murder . . ." She could not go on. She didn't need to. Now Bob understood. Mike had told him of a witness, a teenage girl who had phoned him and reported the murder but had refused to identity herself. She had been shot, not seriously, but shot nonetheless. Could that explain that mysterious red spot? Was it the scar from a shotgun pellet?

"Is that why you became a cop?" Bob asked as understanding dawned.

"Yes," she whispered. "I had to face my fears. I left Utah. It had to be in Colorado. I asked to be stationed in Pineview. I thought I'd be okay after I'd been there for a while. And I guess I was, until *he escaped.*"

Bob pulled Jan close to him, let her rest her head against his chest, encircled her with his arms. "I'm so sorry," he whispered. "I had no idea."

"You're the only person I've ever told," she said.

"I'm glad you told me," he said, wondering at the strange but wonderful beating in his heart. "I'm so afraid of him," Jan cried. "I've pretended, but I've always been afraid."

Bob's arms closed tighter around her. She sobbed for a moment more, then said in a simple but strained voice, "Poor Erika. Poor, poor Erika."

Mike had heard enough, but he couldn't interrupt these two young people. He moved silently away from them, determined to keep watch with them and for them. Erika was not the only hostage Butch had taken. For five long years Jan had also been his hostage, and it made his anger at Butch more fierce than ever, as it did his determination. He gritted his teeth. This day, this nightmare for two haunted young women must end. They must be freed from the evil man who had done so much to scar their lives.

***

Morning finally came, gray and dismal. The fresh smell of impending storm filled the air. Butch, despite a racking cough, seemed to have a little more energy. He roasted the last of the venison. They ate it as they walked through the somber forest. Erika wondered at the queer flavor it had developed during the night, but forced herself to eat, knowing she needed the strength it would provide.

Erika had lost all sense of direction and followed Butch blindly. She struggled to renew her faith, to recover her hope as she silently prayed. Feeling better after a few minutes, she found it easier to keep up with him, not to provoke his angry outbursts and foul language. They hadn't gone more than a couple of miles, most of that downhill, before it began raining. It was light at first, but increased with intensity after a few minutes. They were soon soaked to the skin, but Butch didn't stop. An hour later he stumbled and fell. He coughed for several minutes before finally struggling to his feet. All the color was gone from his face, and he said weakly, "We can't stay here." He coughed violently and spit a bloody mouthful of phlegm onto the ground at his feet. "So get moving, Erika."

She held her stomach tightly, trying to keep from throwing up. For some reason she'd become terribly nauseous, and Butch's gross and bloody phlegm didn't help. "This way," he ordered, and she forced her feet to shuffle up the slope ahead of them.

A few minutes, but not a long distance later, Butch stopped. "This is perfect," he said weakly.

Erika wiped her eyes with the back of her good arm and peered ahead. They had reached a dead end. There was no way to go farther. "This is just perfect," Butch repeated.

He found shelter beneath a low overhang behind several large rocks. Erika surveyed the area with increasing despair. They were in a box canyon, out of sight of anyone entering the canyon. With the rain washing away their tracks, the search party might go right on by. Despair crushed her and hope fled. She and Butch might die right here.

For a little while they sat and let their weary bodies rest, then Butch ventured out into the storm and gathered some wood. He used his knife to whittle through the dampness and produce some dry kindling. He was able, after several attempts with the last of his matches, to get a fire going. Before long Erika was warm and her clothing was steaming, but her stomach was in terrible pain and her coughing was almost a match for Butch's.

***

"They've entered right here," one of the dog handlers announced as he peered across the stream. "I don't suppose I can get much wetter," he moaned sarcastically. "I'll wade across and see if I can find their trail on the other side."

Mike and the others waited in a huddle while he crossed. The rain was pouring, and he shivered from the cold. When the officer returned, he said, "They either went upstream or down. They didn't get out on the other side. From the way my dog's acting, I'd say they went downstream."

"Will that foul the dogs up?" Bob asked.

"Not entirely. Scent stays on damp surfaces very well. If they went down the stream, staying in the water, their scent will be clinging to the banks. It'll be tougher, but with a dog on each side, we should be okay."

"All right, we'll split up. Jan, Bob, and one of you fellows," Mike said, nodding to the deputies, "come with me and one of the handlers. We'll go across. The rest of you stay on this side with Harry."

The dogs picked up the scent, and for a mile or so they made their way down the edges of the stream, fighting branches, fallen trees and steep hillsides. Mike and his group stumbled right onto the abandoned campfire. The ashes still smoldered despite the rain.

"Looks like they spent the night here," Mike said.

"Do you think they went back in the stream this morning?" Jan asked.

"Anything is possible," he answered. "Let's see what the dog does. Unfortunately this rain will have washed away their tracks."

The big German shepherd worked rapidly back and forth at its handler's commands. Within a minute he'd found the scent and lunged eagerly against the leash. Harry and his group crossed the stream and the other dog also found the scent, beginning to strain and whine eagerly.

They stopped a short time later during a lull in the storm. The dogs needed rest and food. So did the officers. While they rested, they discussed the task ahead.

"I think we're real close," Mike said, leaning against the rough bark of a tall pine.

"So what do we do?" Jan asked, her face creased with worry, her eyes still reflecting the fear she had admitted to Bob during the night.

"Good question," Mike said, watching the tender look Bob gave her and the way he took her hand in his and squeezed it reassuringly.

He turned to the dog handlers for advice. They discussed their options at length. "Looks like we don't have much choice but to let you men continue as you are," he finally said to the handlers. "The rest of us will hang back and spread out to either side."

Warily, they proceeded, and an hour later the dogs turned up a narrow box canyon. The officers regrouped and Mike said, "Funny, but this is not the kind of place a man in his right mind would have gone."

"He must be losing his grip," Special Agent Reed agreed soberly.

"Hey, look. There's smoke coming from under the ledges," one of the officers said excitedly.

Mike shook his head in disbelief. The smoke dissipated rapidly in the light rain, but it was still visible. He tugged at his chin as he sized up the situation. It could be a trap or a decoy of some kind, or Butch could have simply run out of steam. At any rate, Mike was not taking any chances.

He sent one of the local officers up one side of the canyon and one up the other, with instructions to stay well back in the trees. "Crawl if you have to, but don't get in a hurry. The rest of us will wait here."

A slow half hour dragged by before the voice of one of the officers broke the silence of the portable radios. "There are some boulders blocking my view," he whispered, "but the smoke is coming from directly behind them."

"How far can the rest of us make it up the bottom of the canyon before we run out of cover?" Mike asked.

"You can get to within a couple hundred feet. I'm closer than that myself, but I can't go any farther."

The other officer called next and reported that he couldn't go any farther either. "Okay, stay put and cover us," Mike ordered. "We'll move up."

In twenty minutes they were spread across the narrow canyon, Jan and Bob behind the others. Mike carefully looked over the area in front of him. The canyon floor rose steeply and was strewn with rocks of varying sizes and an occasional tree. If Butch and Erika were beside the fire that was producing the smoke, they were trapped.

Bob crawled up behind Mike. His face was strained. "What is it?" Mike whispered.

"What if Butch threatens to kill Erika again? What will you do?"

"I don't know. We can only wait and see. Now you and Jan stay back. We'll handle it from here."

The young man nodded unhappily and crawled away.

"Okay," Mike whispered into his radio. "You two climb up the hill a ways and see if you can get to where you can see behind the rocks, even if you aren't as close as you are now. We've got to know if they're there or not."

He waited ten tense minutes. Finally one of the officers called. "I can see them. The girl is right beside Butch, and she's hurt. One arm appears to be in a makeshift sling. They're both coughing."

"Are they awake and alert?" Mike asked.

"Yes, it appears so."

"All right," Mike said. "Everyone hold tight. We'll just wait. Maybe Butch'll fall asleep, or he may even try to come out. As long as he doesn't know we're here we have the advantage."

The rain stopped, and the sun broke out. As it filtered through the trees, steam began to rise from the ground in little wisps. Mike's whole body ached, but he waited patiently, hoping the end was near.

***

Butch stirred. "I'm hungry," he said. "We better have a few bites. I have a little meat left."

"I'm too sick to eat," Erika replied with effort. "I think that meat we ate this morning was spoiled."

"It's just in your head," Butch scoffed. "Thanks to the rain and the stream it'll be a long time before they come along. By then we'll be long gone. We'll head down later and find a road."

Erika had no idea what made him think that would happen, but she said nothing. Somehow, she didn't think he could possibly go on, and she knew she couldn't. They were both desperately sick, and she knew they could easily die before anyone found them. She closed her eyes again and dozed, her back against the rocks.

Butch shook her arm a few minutes later. "Erika, did you hear that dog bark?" It was Butch's voice penetrating her tired brain. "Erika, do you hear me? A dog barked," he hissed as he shook her again.

Erika awoke with a start and threw up foul, bitter chunks of meat and bile all over her ragged, muddy pants and on the dirt between her legs. Butch swore vehemently, both at her for throwing up and at the cops.

"They're out there somewhere!" he insisted. "One of their dogs barked. Quit that, Erika!" he screamed. "You're making me sick."

She couldn't stop heaving, even after her stomach was empty. "The cops found us," he repeated and cursed again.

Erika finally quit retching and swung her head toward Butch. She lifted her long dark hair out of the way with her left hand and looked at him. What she saw threw panic into her heart. His face was contorted with rage and his pale eyes were glazed. He held both pistols in his hands. He was like a crazy animal; he was insane.

"I'll kill them! I'll kill them all!" he screamed after a fit of coughing. "Come and get me, pigs!" He shouted his challenge at the top of his lungs and swayed like a tree in a stiff wind. "No one can take me!" he screamed after still another round of coughing. He then let out a stream of vile oaths and staggered back and forth beside the dying fire.

Erika cowered against the wall. He turned on her. "Come on!" he ordered, murder in his glazed eyes. "We're going to fight them, and kill them, and leave!"

Terrified, she tried to move, but when she couldn't he threatened her, pointing both guns at her face. Fear sent the adrenalin flowing through her sick and wounded body, and she struggled to her feet. "Butch," she wailed, "I can't."

Butch's right arm moved like a striking rattler. The blue steel of the small .38 smashed against the tight copper skin of her face. She flew backward and he struck again. The gun discharged with a resounding explosion and Erika sank to her knees, then tumbled slowly forward, her face in the dirt. Willing herself to remain conscious despite terrible injury and pain, she offered a short, desperate prayer. "Heavenly Father, please don't let me die," she cried.

A moment later she heard Butch emit a bloodcurdling scream. She turned her head and looked up through a mist of tears, blood, and wet, soiled hair. She saw him move with power fed by a frenzied mind. He leaped a rock and disappeared.

***

Jan, her pistol drawn, lay on the wet ground. Battling her terror, she'd left Bob and pulled into line with the other officers. Then she'd heard the gunshot and the terrible scream and suppressed her own. Butch was coming. Somehow, she knew it. She tried desperately to still her shaking hand. Her weapon was useless if she couldn't quit shaking.

She heard another scream and looked up the canyon. She saw Butch at the same time she heard him running down the canyon toward her. He was cursing, waving two guns around. She lifted her weapon. She couldn't hold it still, so she forced herself onto one knee. She attempted to steady her gun hand on that knee, but her whole body shook.

He was coming straight at her. He was so close she could see the insanity in his eyes. And yet, somehow she knew he'd recognized her. At that instant, he began firing both weapons. Something hot and searing scorched her cheek and she felt herself falling backward as a thunderous barrage of gunfire erupted around her—Jan thought her head would explode from the deafening noise. Echoes pounded off the ledges and steep canyon walls. Jan hadn't pulled the trigger of her own weapon, but she saw Butch jerk in midair and watched as his body hit the ground, rolled over, then lay still. Jan collapsed and grabbed her cheek. It was warm, sticky, and painful. She pulled her hand away and looked at it. It was covered with blood! Her blood. Blood drawn by another bullet from another gun, but fired by the hand of the *same killer*.

Butch Snyder.

Butch had shot her again. He'd attempted to do what he'd threatened five long years ago. But, she thought as the echoes died away, she had won. She was still alive! As she lay there, a lonely and haunting moan started up and grew in intensity as a sudden wind roared over the ledges and through the trees. Somehow, she knew the source of her terror would haunt her no more and she forced herself to her feet.

***

Erika also heard the haunting moan of the wind, and she too somehow knew that it was over. Butch could threaten her no more. He could hurt her no more. With that thought, her face again turned into the dirt and she lapsed into peaceful blackness.

***

Mike was running up the ravine, aware of Bob at his heels and Harry to his right. The local officers were off to the left. He paused only momentarily to look at Butch, who had died as he had lived, full of hate and violence. Mike ran on and reached Erika only a few steps after Bob. They'd both heard the gunshot before Butch began his demented assault, and they feared the worst.

With Bob's help, Mike turned Erika gently onto her back. Her chest rose and fell softly. A cursory glance brought relief when he saw there were no gaping bullet wounds in her battered and filthy body. Her right eye had swollen shut, an ugly gash had bared her cheekbone, and blood oozed from another cut on her forehead.

Bob was on his knees, bending over Erika, great sobs racking his hunched body. A deputy was calling for help on his radio, requesting a life-flight helicopter for Erika and another one to airlift the rest of them out of the mountains. Erika moaned, and Bob's name slipped from her swollen lips as Mike began tending to her injuries.

"I'm right here," Bob said gently, "It's okay now, I'm here." A faint smile creased her battered face.

Jan was just approaching but was still several feet away. Blood still poured from the bullet wound that had reopened that old scar. She stopped several feet away, watching the scene before her through tear-filled eyes.

Mike glanced up and was shocked to see blood running down Jan's cheek. But that was not all, her face was stricken as she watched Bob tend to Erika. Mike stood and started toward her, but she waved him away. "Help her," she said in a voice choked with emotion. Then she turned and trudged down the muddy canyon, a dejected and broken figure—a figure no one would ever have recognized as the stalwart Officer Hallinan.

Bob looked up and saw Mike's sad gaze directed down the canyon. He turned his head, wondering what Mike was looking at and saw Jan, plodding slowly down the hill, her shoulders hunched. For the briefest moment she glanced back, and Bob saw the blood that covered her cheek. He started to rise, ready to go after her, but just then Erika moaned and he looked down at her bruised face.

A wave of tenderness washed over him. He couldn't leave Erika. [illegible] needed him. Once more he peered at Jan's retreating figure and [illegible]ears burned his eyes. She was hurt, she was suffering, but she was [illegible] Her nightmare was over and her secret was safe with him.

Erika needed him the most. With a painful twist in his heart, he drew his eyes from the lonely girl walking away from him, walking out of his life, and began to tenderly care for Erika—the one he'd come all these miles to save from Butch Snyder's relentless control.

CHAPTER 21

Jan felt awkward and out of place in the hospital. "Just relax, Jan," Mike urged as Erika's family reentered the waiting room. Bob was not with them, meaning he'd stayed behind with Erika. He had every right, and it made perfect sense. After all, he'd unselfishly given of both his time and money to help in the search for her these past few days. And she'd suffered unspeakable horrors and was seriously in need of comfort, the kind of comfort that only Bob could give.

But that didn't change what had happened to Jan over those same few days. Butch's death had rid her of the terror and the nightmares that had affected her periodically since that first time she saw him five years before. But meeting Bob Evans had caused a new kind of pain to enter her heart. She really hadn't intended to fall for him the way she had. She'd even tried to avoid it as she felt the attraction growing. But her heart had failed to cooperate from the very first day, and now she had to say good-bye and walk away. And she simply had to get over him.

Mike understood perfectly what Jan was feeling. And his heart ached for her. "Hey, go on in there," he encouraged her. "Erika has the right to meet you before we head home for Pineview. After all, you two have a lot in common."

"Don't we though?" she said. "We both fell for the same guy."

"That's not what I meant," Mike scolded with a grin. "I hate to admit this, but I overheard your conversation with Bob on the mountain—I know what happened with you and Butch five years ago. You're the girl that called me." He smiled sympathetically at Jan's surprise. "So get in there," he continued, "and tell her about your own experience with Butch. A kindred spirit might do her good. She's been through a lot, and a little comfort from someone else who's felt the same kinds of things wouldn't hurt her at all."

Jan wasn't at all sure she could face Bob and Erika. She hadn't planned on coming here at all, thinking it would be best if she simply returned to Pineview immediately. But Mike had insisted, and she'd come. She still wasn't sure it was fair to them, but before she could say so to Mike, Erika's father interrupted them. "I don't know how I can ever thank you two enough," he began. "I know I wasn't easy on you back in Pineview. I'm sorry, but I realize now how much you both risked for my daughter."

"It was something we had to do for ourselves too," Mike said honestly. "We both had our personal reasons to see Butch stopped."

"So I understand," Jim Leighton said. "Bob was telling us about what you went through not an hour ago, Miss Hallinan, while we were waiting to see Erika. He certainly admires your courage."

Jan winced. She didn't want to be admired, just loved.

"Don't you think she'd like to meet Jan?" Mike asked Jim slyly. He wanted her to see Bob again. For some reason it just didn't seem right for the two of them to part without so much as a good-bye.

"Of course. Please, go on in. Bob's with her now, but I'm certain she'd love to meet you and thank you," he urged. "And I mean both of you."

Simple things often take more than their share of courage to accomplish. This was one of those things. Jan felt so uncomfortable, but it would be rude to decline Mr. Leighton's invitation. She was grateful for his request that Mike go with her. That would make it a little easier.

Bob looked up from his chair beside Erika's bed as Jan pushed the door open and stepped through. His face lit up, and Jan's heart began to race. "Erika," he said even as his eyes searched Jan's face, "You remember Sergeant O'Connor."

Erika turned a badly bruised face on the pillow. "Sergeant O'Connor," she said in a weak voice. "Thank you for all you did for me."

"Wasn't much," he said modestly.

"And this is Trooper Jan Hallinan," Bob said. "She stuck with us all the way."

"You're the one *he* shot," Erika said sadly. "I'm sorry."

Jan stepped beside the bed. She noticed how tenderly Bob was holding Erika's left hand. She tried to repress her feelings as she forced a smile and said stiffly, "They say you're going to be alright. I'm go glad."

"Thank you," Erika said with what was undoubtedly an attempt at a smile, her battered face making any facial expression almost impossible.

They visited for the next few minutes, but Erika was tiring fast, and Jan said, "We need to let you get your rest. Anyway, Sergeant O'Connor and I have to get back to Pineview."

Bob's eyes lingered on Jan as she turned and walked quickly to the door. Then he turned to Erika. "I'll be right back," he said. "There's something I need to do." For a moment, her grip on his hand tightened, and he didn't have the heart to pull his hand away.

But finally, her fingers relaxed, and he said, "I won't be long. You try to rest."

By the time he stepped into the hall, Mike and Jan had already vanished. He walked rapidly to the waiting area. But they weren't there. He passed Erika's family at a trot, pushed open the front doors and jogged toward the parking lot. Mike and Jan were already getting into a rental car halfway across the lot. He ran toward them as Mike began to pull away. He waved frantically, and just when he thought they hadn't seen him, Mike hit the brakes.

Jan was out of the car by the time Bob reached them. "What's the matter, Bob?" she asked urgently. "Is something wrong?"

"Yes," he said breathlessly, glancing toward Mike who was sitting quietly in the car. "You didn't say good-bye."

Her eyes glistened. "I'm sorry, but I was never good at good-byes."

Bob reached out, took her by the hand, and pulled her close, glancing again toward Mike, who was staring stonily in the other direction. "Jan, maybe I'll see you again sometime. I'd like to."

"Bob, don't," she said, as tears began to flow. "You have a life to live. And Erika needs you."

"Jan, there's something special about you. I have to give things with Erika a chance, but I told you once before, we're really just good friends."

"And you also said it could become more," she reminded him, wiping at her eyes. "She's a changed person now."

"Yes, a more mature one, that's for sure, but . . . well, I don't know, Jan. I'm sorry. I'm really confused right now."

Jan spread a brave smile across her face. "You're a great guy. I'm glad I had the chance to get to know you. Now, you go take care of Erika. She's been through more than anyone should ever have to endure." Impulsively, she stretched upward and kissed him lightly on the cheek. "Good-bye, Bob," she whispered.

Bob's arms folded her tightly against him in a big hug. He released her and said, "Now that was a decent good-bye, Jan. Thanks."

Jan's heart was racing out of control, and all she could say was, "Take care." And she turned to the car, climbing in beside a grinning Mike O'Connor.

"Let's go, and you can quit grinning," she said sternly.

"So that was good-bye," he mused.

"That was good-bye," she agreed firmly.

"I'll bet," he said under his breath.

"What was that?" she asked.

"Oh, nothing."

***

It was hard to find time to get away from school, but Bob made the effort. Erika was a different girl than he'd known that summer. She was mature beyond her years, very serious, and not the happy-go-lucky girl whose company he'd so enjoyed. She was always glad to see him, and they still had a lot of fun when they were together, but somehow it wasn't the same. She seemed distracted and less sure of herself, and their relationship felt a little awkward.

Bob felt like Erika needed something he couldn't give. She carried scars and fears that he was unable to rid her of no matter what he said to her. Whatever he did or said, it was never quite the right thing, or at least it seemed that way to him. He wondered if she needed counseling to deal with the horrors she'd experienced. She needed something.

At the Thanksgiving break, after sharing a movie and dinner, they sat in the swing in Erika's backyard. The evening had been strained. Bob was afraid it was him. She simply needed and deserved more than he could give right now.

She was holding his hand, her head back, pushing the swing with one foot when she suddenly said, "You mean a lot to me, Bob."

"I do?" he asked before he could stop himself.

"Yes. Thoughts of you helped me when things were the toughest with . . . *him,*" she said.

Erika never spoke Butch's name. The memories were still too terrifying. It was rare that she even referred to him. Bob had understood and never brought the subject of her abduction up. But she wanted to talk about it tonight. "After I saw you, after I knew it was you and that you'd somehow convinced Sergeant O'Connor to let you help them, it lifted me just to think of you."

Bob smiled uncomfortably. "I'm glad I helped."

"You more than helped, Bob, and I'll never be able to thank you enough." She slipped an arm around his waist and leaned against his shoulder. She nestled there for a moment, then she said, "I don't know how to say this, Bob. You're the last person in the world I'd ever want to hurt."

Bob wasn't sure what was coming, and his stomach rolled uncomfortably. He liked Erika more than any girl he'd ever known . . .well, almost. But he'd moved no closer to loving her in a romantic sense over these past few weeks than he'd been when he first went rushing off to Colorado at the first news of her troubles there. He didn't know what to say now, so he said nothing.

"Bob, something happened on the mountain one morning. I've never mentioned it to anyone, but it was the thing that helped me make it through that last day or so."

"Really, what was it?" Bob asked, wondering if it had to do with him again.

But it didn't. It had to do with God. She explained about her prayer and about the promise she'd made to the Lord to do all she could to serve Him. "I wasn't strong like you,"she admitted. "I always sort of took the Church for granted. Not anymore. The feeling that came over me when I offered that prayer was like nothing I'd ever experienced before. That feeling carried me when I thought I couldn't go another step. That feeling saved my life Bob, and . . ." she stopped and pulled herself away from him and stood up.

"And?" he pressed as he too got to his feet.

She said nothing for a long time. He waited until she finally turned toward him. "And I've wondered what things I could do to keep my end of the bargain I made with Heavenly Father. He certainly kept His."

"There are lots of things," Bob began.

"Yes, there are," she cut in quickly. "But one particular thing has been on my mind ever since I got home."

"Oh, and what's that?" he asked.

"I want to go on a mission."

"A mission," he said, stunned.

"Yes, a mission," she said. "Is that a bad idea?"

"Oh, no, you'd be a great missionary. It's just that, well, you're not quite nineteen yet, and you have to be twenty-one and—"

She cut him off with a smile and a finger to his lips. "I know all that," she said. "And that's why it's been so hard for me to tell you. But I need this for a lot of reasons. I think it'll help me get to know myself again, help me work out some problems—and help me get to really know my Heavenly Father."

"Uhh . . . That sounds great to me. He'll certainly help you, Erika," he said awkwardly.

"Bob," she said as though she hadn't heard him. "I thought I was in love with you, but . . ."

He cut in. "Was?"

"Yes, but, well, I've changed so much, and . . . I don't know what I think about us anymore. I'm sorry, Bob. You're the greatest guy I've ever known, but I really want to do this, and I can't ask you to wait simply *because* I'm not sure of what I want—with a lot of things. I think this is how I can find out."

Bob didn't know what to say. He really hadn't expected this at all. He was both happy for her, relieved for himself, and yet crushed in a way. But why? Maybe it was just an ego thing he admitted to himself.

"Bob, I'm sorry," she cried, misunderstanding his silence.

Bob smiled at her reassuringly. "It's okay, Erika. I'll be fine. You do what you feel is right. You've always got to go with your feelings, especially when they involve prayer."

"Thank you," she said, and stepped close. "May I have a kiss?" she asked. "Just one more?"

EPILOGUE

The sleek green Grand Am rounded the last curve into town, and Bob eased up on the gas. He was on his Christmas break from school, and a welcome break it was. He'd spent Christmas day with his family and hit the road the next morning.

Pineview looked strange but beautiful beneath its blanket of white. He felt a little foolish, driving into town this way. No one knew he was coming. But as the weeks had passed since Thanksgiving, Bob had come to know that a part of his heart was in this town. He'd decided to make the trip to see if he could reclaim it.

He drove the full length of the main street, passing the school, the grocery store, the café, and finally driving between the insurance office and the Quick Stop. The little store had been completely remodeled and looked inviting and clean. He drove on until he'd passed the cemetery at the far edge of town. The headstones shined beneath their veils of white snow, but he didn't linger there. He flipped a U-turn and drove slowly back up the street.

It was early afternoon and he hadn't eaten for hours, so he turned into the little gravel parking area in front of the café and parked. A moment later he stepped inside. There was not another customer in the place. "Howdy, stranger," Penny greeted him as she came from the back, wiping her hands on her apron. "The counter or a table?"

"Table, please," he said.

After sitting down, Penny eyed him closely and asked, "Do I know you?"

"Bob Evans," he said. "I've eaten here before."

Her eyes popped wide with surprise. "You're the guy . . . You're *that girl's* boyfriend!" she exclaimed. "How's she doing? We all feel so bad about what happened to her. Is she going to be okay?"

Bob smiled pleasantly at her. "She's fine."

"Oh, that's so good to hear. She was such a perty thing." Penny leaned toward him. "Isn't she with you?"

"No," he said. "She has her life now, and I have mine."

"Oh, my! I'm so sorry," Penny said.

"It's okay."

"What would you like to eat?" she asked awkwardly, and he remembered that they didn't use a menu in here.

"Cheeseburger and fries would be great," he said. "And bring me a large glass of buttermilk."

"But no coffee," she said with a wink.

"That's right."

The bell above the door tinkled as Penny placed Bob's greasy meal in front of him a few minutes later. Bob's back was to the door and he couldn't see who'd just entered. From the look on Penny's face, he thought it must be someone special. "Will you look who's here?" she cried in delight.

Bob thought she meant for him to look, but as he started to turn his head, her plump finger pointed at *him*. He continued to turn anyway, and his heart leaped!

"Bob!"

"Jan!"

He slid from his seat and waited while the most beautiful girl to ever adorn a state trooper's uniform glided hesitantly toward him. "What are you doing here?" she asked as she stopped midway between his table and the door.

"Looking for you," he said boldly. "I've missed you."

Penny was grinning from ear to ear.

Jan's eyes misted. She looked like she might be in shock. He stepped toward her. She stood frozen. He reached for her, and she recovered miraculously. "And I've missed you," she cried as she fell into his arms.

"Still want to be a cop the rest of your life?" he asked mischievously, his voice low.

"Depends on whether I get a better offer," she laughed.

"Well, we'll have to just see then, won't we? Could I buy you dinner?"

Not just this time, but forever, he was thinking.

As many times as you like for the rest of my life, she was thinking.

"Yes, Bob," she answered with a smile.

About the Author

Clair M. Poulson spent many years in his native Duchesne County as a highway patrolman and deputy sheriff. He completed his law enforcement career with eight years as Duchesne County Sheriff. During that time he served on numerous boards and committees, including serving as president of the Utah Sheriff's Association, and a member of a national advisory board to the FBI.

For the past ten years Clair has served as a Justice Court Judge in Duchesne County, and currently represents the Justice Court judges of the state as a member of Utah's Judicial Council.

Clair also does a little farming, his main interest being horses. Both Clair and his wife currently help their oldest son run the grocery store in Duchesne.

Clair has always been an avid reader, but his interest in creating fiction began many years ago when he would tell bedtime stories to his small children. They would beg for just one more "make-up story" before going to sleep. *Relentless* is Clair's seventh published novel.

Service in the Church has always been a priority for Clair. He has served in a variety of stake and ward callings. He and his wife, Ruth, an accomplished piano teacher, are the parents of five children, and they have six grandchildren.

EXCERPT FROM A NEW NOVEL BY SIÂN ANN BESSEY:

Cover of DARKNESS

Instinctively, Megan went to scream, but just as instinctively, the person behind her clapped a hand over her mouth, muffling the sound before it had time to truly form, and leaving Megan an immobile, mute, and terrified captive.

"A girl!"

Megan heard the surprise in her captor's voice, and with it the American accent. Memories of the conversation overheard at Plas Newydd came flooding back, and without warning, she felt herself starting to tremble. The man behind her must have felt it too, because without removing his hand from her mouth, he swung her around slightly so that he could see her face.

"Megan!" The shock in Joe Marks's voice was unmistakable, and he immediately dropped the hand that had been covering her mouth, although he continued to keep his other hand on her—more to keep her upright that to restrain her, Megan thought. "What are you doing here?"

Megan tried to speak, but found the words didn't come easily. "T. . .t . . . trying to s . . . s . . . save a d . . . d . . . dog," she sputtered.

"What?"

"Trying to save a dog!" Megan repeated more firmly, her initial terror beginning to subside. "What are you doing here? Or do you usually spend the evening accosting people?"

She knew she was playing with fire, but she also knew that Joe Marks had no idea that she had overheard a clandestine conversation earlier in the day, or that she had any suspicions about him. Furthermore, Megan Harmer didn't have red hair for nothing—her indignation was on the rise.

"No, I . . . I . . . " Joe was still coming to terms with finding Megan in his arms. "What did you say you're doing?"

"Trying to save a dog!" Megan repeated one more time, with impatience. "And you've wasted so much of my time that I'm not going to make it," she added bitterly. Then, as the realization dawned that she may have actually found aid sooner than she could have hoped, she added quickly, "Joe, d'you have a knife?"

"A knife?" he asked warily.

"Yes," Megan said, her agitation mounting. "You know, a pocket knife, or something—anything that could cut through fishing line?"

Joe let go of Megan and put his hand into his pocket. He drew out a Swiss Army knife—the kind that had every type of implement imaginable—and showed it to her.

"Oh, that's perfect!" she cried. "Will you come and help me?" This time Megan grabbed his arm and pulled him toward the retaining wall.

"Come with you where?" Joe asked.

"Onto the beach, of course," Megan replied as if it were the most obvious thing in the world. "To get the dog," she added as an afterthought before she scrambled onto the wall once more and jumped down to the other side.

She heard Joe land heavily near her, but didn't stop to talk to him again. She started running in the general direction of the stranded dog, listening for any sound and straining to see his form in the deepening darkness. As she did so, she realized that she had put fear for her own safety aside automatically. Perhaps she was just too innocent and gullible, but she couldn't think of Joe Marks in the same evil terms as she did those faceless men whom she'd overheard. She didn't understand it. She only knew that when she'd realized who was restraining her on the pathway, her initial terror subsided rather than intensified. It made no sense at all, but she didn't have time to analyze it.

* * * * *

Joe set off quickly toward the retaining wall, and it was a scramble for Megan to keep up with him. She was so intent on pursuit, that she didn't realize he'd stopped until she plowed right into him.

"Oh, sorr—" Her apology was muffled almost immediately by Joe's hand. He removed it almost as fast, but kept his index finger over her lips, signaling her to silence. She didn't move, and above the rush of the coastal waves she heard the unmistakable sound of footsteps along the promenade. They were drawing closer.

Joe swung around, placing his body between Megan and the wall. The dog continued to hover nearby, barking occasionally and weaving circles around their legs.

"Megan," he whispered, "I've no time to explain. If you could just trust me one more time, I promise I'll explain this to you. Play along with me okay?"

"What d'you mean 'play along with . . .' " her question was stifled in one swift movement as Joe put his arms around her, pulled her close and lowered his lips to hers. Megan pushed against his chest, desperately trying to free herself, but his arms only tightened around her, pinning her even closer. And then she felt the gun, hard and cold under his shirt. She knew what it was at once, and felt the fear she'd suppressed since he'd first grabbed her on the promenade well up again.

She must have trembled in his arms, because she sensed Joe's iron muscles ease their grip slightly, only to have them retighten as the rhythmic footsteps faltered and stopped immediately above them. The dog's giddy movement ceased and he faced the wall and barked a few times. Suddenly a bright light hit them—a small, narrow beam, but blinding in its intensity, coming as it did out of the darkness. She felt Joe flinch, but he kept his head bent over hers. The light flickered over them once more, the dog barked, and after what seemed like an interminable silence, the footsteps began again, walking on toward the bridge.

Only when the footsteps had faded into the night did Joe release her. Megan pushed away from him, stumbling backwards. He put out a hand to steady her, but she brushed it aside.

"And what," she spat at him, "was all that in aid of?" Her fear level was rising at an alarming rate, but she refused to give in to it, and so she lashed out.

Joe didn't answer her. Instead he looked down the beach following the direction the footsteps had taken.